Unknown Predator

A. Dru Kristenev

To Silvia,
With prayers for
our nation.
God Bless You,
my sister!
Dru
A-Dru Kristenev
7/13/18

UNKNOWN PREDATOR

"Unknown Predator"
By A. Dru Kristenev
First Edition 2018

Cover Design:
A. Dru Kristenev

ISBN-13:
978-0692063996

ISBN-10:
0692063994

This book is dedicated to my two inspired Bible teachers, both of whom have gone on to meet The Lord -
John Anderson and Norman Warner.

They encouraged me to make the "leap of faith" to undertake the journey that has emboldened me to write this book and much more.

May I never forget the other half of the teaching duos, their learned wives. My deepest thanks to Ann Marie and Jeanie, my dear friends and faith partners.

UNKNOWN PREDATOR

[FOR MOST JOURNALISTS]
IT'S ALWAYS THAT MAN IS A PERPETRATOR OF EVIL AGAINST NATURE.
THEY FORGET THAT THEY, LIKE US, AS MEMBERS OF MANKIND,
ARE PART OF NATURE, NOT ITS ADVERSARY.

J. LAKEN

Author's Note

The divide between the People and government has become a chasm so deep and wide that American citizens have despaired, wondering if the gap can ever be closed. It's a legitimate concern.

Government bureaucracies have been whittling away private property rights for decades and they haven't been picky about their methods. Regulatory agencies have used cunningly innovative, unscrupulous and fraudulent means to achieve their objective. Which is? The disenfranchisement of the American Dream. Of course, the average student has little concept of what that entails, having been steeped in socialistic propaganda from the first day they entered public school.

The American Dream has been twisted to mean the forced sharing among the less fortunate of what other people have accumulated. It's called redistribution, or, in the case of this book, land conservation. No longer is our youth imbued with the desire to build empire. That's considered selfish, cruel and inhumane when it is the opposite that is true.

Consider the falsehoods propagated in the educational system (I should know, I taught college alongside professors imparting these misconceptions for 20-plus years.): that wealth is finite; caring for yourself and your family is egotistic; identifying as a member of an individual nation is racist, and I could go on.

Interestingly, just these three random statements counter what is biblical truth. 1) God's riches are infinite. He created the universe, after all. 2) Taking responsibility for your own welfare is good stewardship of God's abundance, allowing individuals to gain wealth and provide for the needy. 3) The one kingdom where citizenship is open to "whosoever" is God's Kingdom. It's an identity that is singular yet available to everyone and hardly racist.

The point is that this nation was founded on these and other biblical truths such as "All Men are created equal," which is not to say that all people will achieve equally. God gave us free will and our choices determine how we use the equality with which we start off in life. And it is the drive to achieve our desires that is requisite to seek the American Dream.

That dream, unfortunately, has been hijacked and equality has been redefined to mean equally denuded of rights by government decree, otherwise known as regulation. Toddy Littman defines regulation as making everything 'regular' or the same. Sound about right? It is the imposition of regulation that strips individuals of their individuality and makes everyone equally miserable under tyrannical rules. Is not this why the American colonies separated from England? Because of oppressive taxation and regulation? If you're unsure, read the whole of the Declaration of Independence to understand precisely what kind of evils were perpetrated on a subjugated people. And yet, today's educated elite is attempting to reinstitute the same kind of oligarchy that we escaped 242 years ago.

This tale is one of realizing how regulatory overstepping of government agencies in cahoots (don't you love that word?) with quasi-governmental and nonprofit entities have worked to reconfigure our nation after the pattern of feudalism, er, socialism, uh, communism... Get the picture? Different 'isms,' the same outcome: a noble class (bureaucracy, i.e. the Swamp) dominating the working class, better known as serfs, proletariat or just plain equally submissive poor - the bourgeoisie or middle class no longer exists in their perfect administrative world.

However, we have recourse.

Our Founders were much smarter than the modern mundane D.C.

denizen. They established a system that actually works IF we're clever enough to use the tools they provided, and that is what this book is about.

Six years of delving into the consequences of introducing Canadian Gray Wolves into the Northwest has led to the completion of Unknown Predator. The name of this fact-based novel originates from a column I wrote that ran in the regional paper, La Grande Observer, in 2011. Don't worry, it's been scrubbed from their archives. It can be found in my book Pay Attention!!

When doing local research on the massive parcel of land owned and operated by a multi-national land trust as a 52 square mile conservation project in Northeast Oregon, the original opinion column I was writing in 2012 turned into four - and growing - pages. It didn't take much to realize that this needed to be a book. There were too many individuals that had contact with the trust's efforts and had experienced egregious depredation from wolves to leave the issue to lie fallow.

Over the ensuing years, where I have been posted in Oregon and other places across the United States as a missionary, I continued to dig into the situation facing rural Oregon regarding land consumption by real estate corporations masquerading as land conservation organizations. The rest of the nation, or the world for that matter, has not been immune to the devouring of privately owned productive land by reserves, preserves, conservancies, refuges, national monuments and other so-called public benefit repositories.

We've watched federal agents brandishing firearms confront landowners, making dubious claims on their private property. Some have been railroaded through criminal proceedings and are serving time for disputable charges. In one instance, where the jurisdiction of federal agencies, such as the Bureau of Land Management, was nonviolently challenged, a literal ambush was engineered by federal agents and a man was shot dead for his temerity to travel a public road on his way to visit the county sheriff. (My article on LaVoy Finicum's shocking assassination can be found at CanadaFreePress.com.)

It is time that citizens realize there is remedy other than armed conflict. Court challenges require patience and forethought. That is what this book offers gift-wrapped in a suspense novel.

Outside of actual news mentioned within the narration, events in the book are fictional and timelines are condensed for the sake of the story.

Let me emphasize that none of the characters are based on real people although I have interviewed dozens of individuals with personal knowledge of the critical issues covered in this story, many of whom were uneasy about allowing me to divulge their identities because of possible retribution. Yes, it does happen and I am unwilling to place anyone in harm's way that spoke in confidence. The Baron Series books may appear to be over-the-top when detailing the danger posed by zealous environmentalists, civilian or government employed, but too many eco-terror incidents and individual menacings have proven otherwise.

Allow me to thank those who have assisted my research along the way: Judy Bothum for sharing her extensive experience and knowledge of ranching and the ranch community in Northeast Oregon; Wanda Sorweide for reminiscing on her years of ranching the Hells Canyon benchlands in the mid-20th century. Kerry Tienhaara, rancher, Oregon Wolf Education charter member and wolf reporter, who also helped proof this work; Wayne Bronson, former Range Rider; Fred Steen, former Wallowa County Sheriff and current wolf depredation investigator for the Sheriff's Department; Todd Nash, Oregon Cattlemen's Association Wolf Task Force; Jill McLaren, President of Wallowa County Stockgrowers Association; Sheriff's

Deputy Sharan Newell; members of local law enforcement and many ranchers and land owners who have experienced wolf depredation and/or have had dealings with local land trust agents on a variety of levels.

I would also like to extend my sincere thanks to my friends, Lili Christensen and Karen Daniel who were willing to read this story as it developed. Those who have undertaken this task for an author can appreciate the hard work it entails.

Although I rarely name characters after real people, it seemed appropriate for **Unknown Predator**. The lead character's young daughter, who discovers faith to help her navigate life's challenges, carries the name of Lili's dear friend, Patricia, who lost her life to ALS and whose faith in Christ gave her strength.

Most of all, I must thank ChangingWind Ministries' phenomenal legal researcher Toddy Littman, whose decades spent studying administrative procedure has given me the means and reason to write this book in the first place. There are thousands of books in the marketplace complaining about what has occurred to destroy the freedoms in this nation, but there are few that supply workable solutions, though no one said they were easy to follow. As ever, all mistakes are mine.

And I must give special thanks to Judi McLeod, publisher of CanadaFreePress.com who has been willing to publish my columns for the last three and a half years and had these kind words to say, giving me more credit than I deserve:

"Unknown Predator" author, Dru Kristenev, was an on-scene missionary during many of the heart-wrenching land battles, there to console landowners left bereft up to the present day. Only a God-loving missionary would include a recourse that is as inspirational as it is hopeful."

Plainly, it has taken more than a century to allow our nation to reach the deplorable (yup, intentional word choice) state that we are now suffering. It is not going to be a cakewalk (another intentional pun) to extricate us from the morass. Answers are available and I pray that this novel will help each of us to arm ourselves with facts about legal recourse, many that can be found between these pages, put them into practice and win back this nation.

God bless,

A. Dru Kristenev
February 1, 2018

changingwind@earthlink.net
Twitter: @GoldBaron08
Facebook: A. Dru Kristenev
Columnist at CanadaFreePress.com
ChangingWind.Org

A DRU KRISTENEV

FOR I KNOW THIS, THAT AFTER MY DEPARTING SHALL GRIEVOUS
WOLVES ENTER IN AMONG YOU, NOT SPARING THE FLOCK.

ACTS 20:29

PROLOGUE

Bushed after a long day, half of it in the saddle, he was within yards of the corral and minutes from sitting down to a well-deserved dinner once he'd hung up his tack.

Before riding in he checked on the steer calves penned in the feedlot, readying them for auction in the fall. Fat and sassy, seeing their heads buried in deep piles of hay triggered his stomach to growling. He was famished after spending the afternoon repairing fence that had been knocked down by the errant elk plowing through it to get to his water supply.

Water was becoming a bitter point of contention now that the management at the neighboring Gaston Buttes Preserve had back-filled better than half of the watering holes that used to dot the prairie.

In his parents' day, that miles-wide flat was the best summer grazing in the region. High-protein bunchgrass in abundance fed local beef for decades. It was his wife's grandfather who'd dug out close to twenty catch basins that kept the ranchers' herds hydrated through the hot season. Now that they'd been eliminated, along with most of the fencing on the preserve - though he still couldn't figure out why the conservation trust that now owned the property would take such measures - the game animals flocked to private water sources, competing with cattle and sheep of beleaguered ranchers already fighting to stay afloat financially.

The thing of it was, he *could* imagine why Terra Ferus, to an experienced cattleman, was making ruinous decisions, ignoring his and every other ranchers' opinions. Obviously, they had another agenda. One that was nonsensical as the bunchgrass withered to a few caged fields that the trust was now in the predicament of needing to "save."

Tired of scratching his head at the myopic vision of a trust that created the opposite effect of its stated purpose to preserve the land, he was left with tackling the surge of problems Terra Ferus' mismanagement thrust on his and others' stock operations.

Lifting his hip to throw his leg over his horse's back, he felt his cell phone vibrate in his breast pocket, signaling a text message. Resettling in the saddle for a moment, he pulled it out and saw a notification from the range rider. A telemetry signal from a radio-collared wolf had been identified roaming the northeast sector.

Hardly taking the time to type in "OK," he turned his horse back the way he had just come and rode out to check on his cows, having moved the main herd to that pasture the day before.

His horse didn't need the motivation of spurs in his side to sense his rider's urgency. They flew across the lower pasture to the creek bed and, ascending the incline, the horse dodged through the brush to reach the fields on the upper bench that overlooked the wider river canyon.

Climbing out of the gully, about a half-mile out he could see cows bolting right and left. In the sunset's gold glow, he could make out at least three dark shadows darting through the herd, scaring the hell out of them. Riding up on the scene, he spotted a downed cow, a wolf straddling the bawling animal, still alive as jagged fangs ripped open its belly.

Stretching behind him, he drew his rifle from the scabbard, planted the stock against his shoulder, aimed and fired at the stationary predator. One shot and it crumpled into a lifeless heap but the other wolves, rather than fleeing at the blast of the gun, rushed straight at his horse.

Cows were bellowing and scrambling every which way to put distance between them and the wolves that circled his mount snapping and biting at his fetlocks. Just as he was targeting one of the beasts with his rifle, the horse suddenly reared up to kick the attackers. Even as he lost his seat he expertly drilled a bullet into the head of one of the wolves.

The last two marauders sped off over the ridge and, in his fright the horse lost his footing and fell back, crushing his rider underneath him.

The horse wasn't injured and quickly came to his feet but the cowboy wasn't so lucky. He lay practically on top of the dead wolf, broken ribs puncturing both lungs. Standing guard to keep the frantic cows from trampling his immobile master, the horse nudged the rancher with his muzzle.

Regaining consciousness, he was able to extract the cell phone from his pocket and call his wife to tell her where he was. He hadn't enough breath to explain the circumstances, though his gasping for air was alarming enough. If the rancher knew it, he didn't let on that he was drowning in his own blood.

Hearing the distress in his voice, she dashed out of the house. Jumping behind the wheel of the Jeep, she chose the shortest route to his location, dialing 911 as she drove. Dry-eyed and determined to get to him as fast as humanly possible, she rattled her bones hurtling over the rough ground at breakneck speed, tires crunching over the gravel, the deep treads spitting rocks into the tall grass that edged the track.

Alternately cursing and praying all the way to the distant pasture, by the time she got to the site there was a hollow sense that she hadn't made it in time. She skidded to a halt, leapt from the rig with adrenaline-amped agility, and ran to where the horse patrolled vigilantly to protect his crippled rider from scavengers and wild-eyed cows. Sinking to the ground next to his broken body, her legs collapsed under her. He was already gone.

Unable to control her emotions any longer, tears spilled down her face as she lifted his head to cradle him in her lap. No concept of the passing of time, she sat rocking him. Jumbled thoughts flitted uncontrolled through her mind of cows, wolves, children and the incomprehensible idea that her beloved husband wasn't coming home for the dinner that was turning cold in the kitchen.

Staring into space, she was barely aware of the ambulance's arrival and the EMTs rushing forward to help. Immediately, they assessed the situation and realizing that no lifesaving technique could revive the patient, they stood aside until she was ready to relinquish her embrace.

When she finally ceded her place so the medics could tend to the victim, they informed her that the sheriff was en route, not that it mattered. He was dead and the wolves were long gone.

Standing off to the side and blocking out the carnage around her, she was thankful that her little girl had wanted to go to her grandmother's after school. Too young to stay alone at the house, had her daughter been home she would have had no choice but to come along. This way, she was spared a ghastly specter that would have haunted her for the rest of her life.

Stinging deeper still was that tonight she had planned to tell her husband how their dream of having another child was finally coming true.

Instead, the nightmare had just begun.

CHAPTER 1

"Streamers of coral, vermillion and crimson clouds swathed the sky, the stark outline of buttes dipping deeper into blackness as the sun descended behind them.

"Quiet prevailed during the brilliant display, the audience absorbing the view with feet propped on the balustrade fronting their preferred balcony seating in the outdoor theatre of the wild."

"A bit overdone even with your penchant for flowery turns of phrase, don't you think?" Gary tipped his coffee mug to take a drink before Anthea caught the mocking twist of his mouth, hoping he could swallow before he laughed.

She saw it all out of the corner of her eye and, ignoring his cheeky remark, leaning out of her chair, she snatched her iPad out of his hand and deleted the file.

"Fine. The peanut gallery has let me know that I'm more suited to write news than prose," she attempted to retain her dignity, which was a challenge dressed in shorts and an old "Killer Koala" t-shirt from a decades' past trip Down Under. "Seeing a sunset like that and being able to kick back and enjoy it…" She sighed. "There just aren't words to describe God's handiwork without sounding trite." She set down the notepad in her lap and took a swallow from her own cup.

He clamped his mouth shut before digging himself in deeper. For a talented writer, his wife could sometimes work a phrase to death until it sounded like, well, *that*. Though he did agree with her that watching something as soul-stirring as one of these canyon sunsets would inspire an attempt to describe it, even when it's indescribable. "Let's just say that words will always fall short in an instance like this."

"Which is why we have cameras in our iPads," Anthea said as she held it up to catch the sky-engulfing light show before it faded.

"Except even this photo can't capture all the wonder of the colors and even if it could, that doesn't help someone who has lost their sight."

"Like your cousin in Philly." He took another sip. "Oh. So that's why you were trying your hand to convey the glory of the view with words."

"I like that. 'Glory.' That says it perfectly." Anthea started typing again.

"But she can't read the text on a computer, either, can she?"

"No, but they have apps that read the script aloud for the blind. Pretty cool stuff. Between the Braille keyboard and voice activated programs, she's well set technologically."

"'Will wonders never cease,' as my ol' Da used to say."

"Your 'ol' Da' never said any such thing. You've been watching too many old movies," scoffed Anthea.

"What else are you gonna do on vacation besides relaxing on the deck, enjoying an aromatic beverage and watching and discussing sunsets?" he grinned.

"Just drink your coffee." Having said that, she followed her own command and sipped from her mug.

Kicking back in the Adirondack chairs arranged on the private deck of their accommodations at the Nacqus Rocks Bed and Breakfast, Gary and Anthea gazed out over the narrow valley as evening settled in.

The semester had ended at both colleges where Gary was currently teaching and as soon as he finished submitting grades for his classes, they skipped town to a place they'd heard about but had never taken the time to visit. It was close enough, about four hours from their house in the tri-state region where Washington, Idaho and Oregon converged. With books literally closed for the term, they grabbed the opportunity to reserve a week at this end-of-the-road inn situated twenty-plus miles outside of the little burg of Rory.

The Mathers' were thoroughly enjoying their jaunt into the canyonlands that divided the rolling prairies and craggy peaks rising far south of their home base on the Snake River.

The lodge reflected the agrarian and Native traditions of

remote Koyama County. Upon entering the inn, the massive wooden door swung open to reveal historical and cultural artifacts that dressed the walls, immersing guests in the rugged West's rich past. Bighorn sheep, mule deer and elk antlers, a massive moose head, and coyote and cougar skins hung mounted around the cavernous great-room. Indian relics and beaded regalia were displayed alongside old branding irons and chaps that had belonged to local pioneers. Ornamental tack fashioned from silver inset with old turquoise stones, the like that were nearly impossible to find anymore, hung from a rack by the door.

The upstairs room they occupied retained the ranch house flavor while offering all the accoutrements of modern life, including satellite television and fairly reliable internet service. Everything a media professional needed, even on holiday.

Gary might be finished with the term and relatively free for the summer, but Anthea's work demanded she keep abreast of current reports in order to best represent her clients. These days everything was political, including press relations. No matter how abhorrent the idea, if you wanted publicity there was no such thing as just relaying good news. If it didn't tie-in with what was trending, media wouldn't pick it up. Because of the degradation of modern press, Anthea was grateful for social media that bypassed their unilateral thinking... if you could slip it past the claws of politically correct censorship. This posed a challenge for her since many of her clients were Christian business people, entertainers and writers. The Big SM (which she didn't separate too far from the old sexually perverted definition) were overtly opposed to disseminating scriptural "good news."

For the moment, Anthea and Gary had their feet propped up and had erased the world's folly from their minds. They were there to unwind and simply absorb nature's spectacle.

Stars began appearing in the dusk as they leaned back to see the Milky Way emerging in an arc across the darkening sky. The night deepened and then they heard an unusual howling floating on the slight breeze.

It wasn't anything like the baying dogs in the neighborhood at home or the yipping of coyotes near the house Gary had built on the Marcasite River. This was hollow and ghostly, making them postulate about the sound's origins. Bawling cattle? Probably not.

Getting nowhere with their guesses, they leaned over the banister and, seeing the proprietors on the porch downstairs were also listening, Gary bluntly asked, "What is that?"

Doug and Eleanor Darby had stilled their matching rocking chairs to better hear the howling. They were both graying, Doug whiter up top than his wife and neither of them as trim as they'd been in their youth when they'd ranched the family homestead further downriver.

Gary's interruption of the otherwise silent evening with his query startled the rapt Ellie but not the unperturbable Doug. Looking up at the pair peering over the rail, he answered matter-of-factly, "Wolves."

"Really. I was aware they were out here but I assumed they'd be more in the wilderness, off in the trees or up in the mountains," Anthea said.

"We've had quite a time with them lately," replied Doug. There was just enough light from the porch lamp to see he was not a happy camper about having wolves lurking in his neighborhood.

"Is that so," Gary asked without asking, hoping to initiate a conversation.

"If you want to hear more, come on down and bring your cups with you." Doug had noticed each clasped a mug in one of their hands resting on the banister. "I'll refill your coffee."

"Good deal," said Anthea, her journalist's juices starting to pump. "We'll be right there."

Chapter 2

While the first hay crop was being cut and baled in the valley, the benchlands were still green with long, ripening grass waving in the breeze that sliced across the landings stretching the length of the river as it flowed to Hell's Canyon. One, two, seven levels of basalt steps climbed the steep walls of the Nacqus chasm to reach alternating rounded and rugged summits. Every mile the water cascaded eastward, the earth's gouge grew deeper until, at its confluence with the Snake, five thousand feet separated the riverbed and the canyon rim.

Only a dirt track had ever been cut into the mountainside along the last ten miles of the river's downhill route, limiting access to horses, ATVs and hardy four-wheel drives. Prime rangeland, cattle could be seen grazing on each bit of level ground, heads down, chewing placidly in the late spring afternoon.

Near the end of the one-lane gravel road, before it turned into the washboard Jeep trail, an empty horse trailer was hitched to a mud-spattered Ford F-250 parked in the only turn-around within a mile going back upriver.

Three riders topped the last yards of the rocky stair after climbing the mile from the road in single-file, two working dogs jogging along in their wake. Sauntering up the cow track, this was a routine check on the herd, having moved it to the summer pasture less than a week ago.

Cresting the rise, a distant din intermittently caught their ear over the jingling of the bridles. The lead rider held up his hand signaling them to stop for a moment and listen. Filtering through the slight gusts of wind that stirred the grass was an abnormal caterwauling. Immediately recognizing it to be distressed cattle, he spurred his mount toward the racket, the other two right behind with the dogs fanning out to the side.

This ten thousand-acre parcel accounted for one of the few

tracts left of privately held land abutting the nature preserve that lay to the north. A fence ran along the property line but enough of it was in disrepair because the not-so-neighborly neighbors made it their business to ignore its upkeep, considering it an inconvenient obstacle to their free-roaming ruminants. That left it to Quint Edwards, who leased this range, to keep it serviceable, replacing wire and posts trampled by either six hundred-pound elk or their overzealous bipedal protectors.

As the cowhands raced across the field and over a low ridge, they found dozens of cows and calves huddled into a corner of the fence that was still standing on this sector of Edwards' lease. Rolling eyes, scuffling hooves and high-pitched cries greeted the riders as they approached, reining in the horses to avoid further alarming the already panicked cows.

At first glance, Quint and his two teenagers couldn't discern the cause of the cows' fright but as they scanned the pasture, they discovered a couple of forms half-hidden in the tall grass a few hundred feet away. Telling the kids to stay put and try to calm the cows, Quint rode over to take a closer look, having a pretty good notion of what he would find.

Dismounting, he wasn't surprised to see three of his animals sprawled on the ground. One of this year's calves was dead, its hindquarters torn open and half-eaten. A yearling bull had also been gutted by a predator. It was dead, too. But the cow lying another fifty feet away, intestines spilling out of its ripped belly, was still breathing, too exhausted by pain and shock to voice a whimper.

Without hesitating, Quint unholstered his gun and shot her in the head to halt her suffering. He didn't have to look too closely to identify oversized canine paw prints crisscrossing the ground that had been softened by a recent downpour. He'd seen wolf kill enough times to distinguish the signs without any trouble, and this met all the criteria.

No doubt in his mind. Examining the differences in the tracks covering the place where the cows were jumped, he could see that there were at least four wolves, maybe more in the pack.

Anger boiling through him that his herd had suffered yet another loss from wolf predation, he took his time walking his horse back to the kids, afraid his tongue would get away from him and he'd say something he'd later regret.

Last night, they'd camped a few miles away near the cows he had pastured west of here. Even though they'd been up on the prairie and he'd had a cell signal, he hadn't received any notice that there were wolves in the area. Either the radio collars weren't working, which happened often enough with the batteries only lasting a few years at most, or these wolves weren't tagged, which was highly possible. Wolves in Oregon were breeding at a much faster rate than Fish and Wildlife would publicly admit and they hadn't nabbed and collared a fraction of the wolves roving this region's forests and range.

Between three occasions over this last year, Quint had witnessed two separate packs fleeing across the fields. Between them, he'd counted fifteen grown wolves, the alphas significantly dissimilar in coloring enough to know he was watching different packs. Officially, there was only one pack operating in the area, which made him think that these kills were perpetrated by a sub-pack where none of the adults had been collared yet.

Reliable witnesses reported numerous sightings and encounters, but too many of the incidents were sloughed off by Oregon Department of Fish and Wildlife as unverified or attributed to coyotes or cougars. Oregon was the only remaining state where the feds refused to delist the wolf as an endangered species despite the state having finally done so. For some reason incomprehensible to area ranchers, the legislature was resolute in championing the "re-introduction" of Canadian Gray wolves to Oregon. Problem was, the species had never inhabited the region. Quint's grandmother had been one of the last people to sight a native timber wolf on the Nacqus bench sixty years prior to the government establishing a presence of the larger, ultra-predatory Canadian extracts.

They'd just heard about the re-emergence of a male wolf that had been thought dead for over a year. It had shown up on their 'radar' along the eastern border with Idaho, in the company of a new mate.

What it proved was that the radio-collar strategy was less than efficient. No shock there. US Fish and Wildlife Service and other nations' attempts to track protected species have admitted the problems of telemetry for years, and the techniques and equipment haven't made significant improvement.

His daughter and son watched their father's tall, sturdy form tread methodically back toward them, leading his horse. They couldn't see his eyes, shaded by the rim of his hat, but the stiffness in his stride was a signal that he'd discovered something that really ticked him off. Had they been the ones about to suffer his displeasure, they'd have been worried. Their dad wasn't the most amiable guy when he was annoyed, but he also knew how to control his temper. While they waited, the dogs tromped agitatedly around their feet, the palpable fright of the traumatized cows influencing their unease.

The probability that this was an unacknowledged sub-pack that killed three head of cattle was lodging in Quint's thoughts. Mulling over how he was going to handle things this time out, the prospect of waiting around for the sheriff and then ODFW plus entourage to haul their useless butts up here wasn't gaining traction.

The trail of wolf tracks leading away from his slaughtered beef couldn't have been any clearer if they had painted a huge sign pointing the way of their escape. It went straight east toward an isolated stand of pines. Considering that the recent rain left the ground malleable enough that four or five wolves averaging more than a hundred pounds would leave plenty of prints, Quint finished weighing the options.

This was between him and a pack of killers.

CHAPTER 3

A pitted, lonely strand of gravel road stretched across miles of grassy expanse. Two forlorn buttes rose above the plain, scraggly conifers sprouting from furrows in their rocky flanks, summits bare from eons of harsh wind whipping over their crowns.

Only the first few miles leading to a partially renovated barn were well maintained. Beyond that the road deteriorated into an iffy track, wide enough for two semis to pass but long-since abandoned to the ravaging elements. Each year's melting snow puddled the surface until washboard and potholes had created an obstacle course deter - ring traffic. Whether that was the intention of the landowner was up to speculation.

This morning, a weather beaten pickup that could have passed for a typical farm truck, a common sight in this rural county, was dodging depressions in the road capable of busting an axle. The driver's destination was a good five miles past the end of the graded surface. Grumbling at the poor road condition, it took both hands on the wheel to avoid getting stuck in the mud. If it weren't for the money being offered, he'd never have bothered with this meeting. All he could think as he bounced around the edge of a particularly nasty sinkhole was, "This had better be worth it."

Fifteen minutes later he sighted a single structure. Wondering what could possibly be housed in a dilapidated sheep shed, he parked next to a late model Hummer. The building was small enough that a top-of-the-line generator situated next to a 500-gallon fuel tank was visible despite masking them under an attached leanto. Another incongruity was a satellite dish extending from the building's south face.

"Strange place for a ranch office, but, oh well," he said aloud as he swung open the creaking cab door.

The soil around the building had mostly dried from the recent rain leaving a clear path to the front door where he stopped to knock, although he knew very well that the occupant had heard him drive up.

"Come in."

Turning the knob he entered the one room shack, immediate - ly noticing the comfortable furnishings that belied its rough exterior. The latest in electronic and computer equipment was situated on and around two desks with a wide-screen TV on one wall facing a leather couch. The furniture just fit inside the building that also housed a three-quarter bath for convenience. Outside, the old outhouse had been left in disrepair to lend authenticity to the decrepit appearance of the site.

Pushing the plank door all the way aside to accommodate his passage, the visitor instinctively wiped his feet on the sisal mat that wasn't printed with the usual, "Welcome." Nor did the occupant make him feel so.

Rising from his seat behind one of the desks, a trim man pre - sented an open hand toward an empty chair in front of his own place. "Have a seat."

No offer of refreshment, the administrator delved straight into business. "Thanks for coming all the way out here. It's a drive but it was the best place to have this conversation."

The visitor didn't respond in kind. "Makes me wonder why you'd have an office way out in the middle of nowhere. Hardly a handy location, which leaves the need for privacy."

Ignoring the observation, the man at the desk asked, "Are you interested in my proposition or did you have another reason for tak - ing up my time?"

Squirming slightly in the captain's chair, the guest realized that this was a one-shot deal. He needed the income and decided whatever motivated this guy to set-up shop in the sticks wasn't really his business. He came here to find out what the job was and how much it was worth. Nor was he going to work cheap. Not after check - ing out the luxury ride parked out front.

"I'm here to discuss a contract," he said leaning forward to show he wasn't in the habit of being admonished or cowed by uppity *lawyers, which this guy reeked of Oregon's Westside privilege. The visitor may look like a scruffy yahoo but he'd been around the block enough times with the administrator's type that it didn't take much to figure him out. He was about profit, power, and possibly, some high-minded agenda. If the price was right, the visitor would assist the man's quest.*

"Good." He placed an envelope on the table but left his hand in place, flat across the thick packet. "This is what I need."

Dropping onto a rough-hewn settee with bear track upholstery that fit the backwoodsy décor, Anthea and Gary Mathers held out their mugs as Ellie poured the promised coffee. Gary sat back, his usual nonchalance taking the form of long legs stretched out, crossed at the ankles. Anthea, on the other hand, although she'd run a PR firm for years, as soon as she got the whiff of a story her newshound past would kick in.

Attempting to look as casually interested as her husband actually was, she refastened the clip in her generally unruly hair. Both of them had gray in their caps now, Gary much more than Anthea's few strands but she declined to color her mop as being too much trouble to keep up. He didn't mind and neither did she so they were content to go natural while keeping otherwise fit and active. The fifties, which decade she joined this year, were serving them well.

"You said that you've had some problems with wolves around here. What kind of trouble?" Anthea jump-started the question and answer session.

"Not as much at this place on the river as we had where we used to live," said Eleanor as she placed the carafe on the warmer. They kept a coffee maker out on the porch during the high season for guests' and their own convenience.

"Where did you live before?"

"Downriver about fifteen miles. Doug's family had a ranch

out there they'd established in the 1930s."

"Still do," said Doug. "Though it's a fraction the size of the old spread. Too much pressure from environmentalists, government and now *reintroduced* wildlife." His inflection wasn't exactly respect-ful. More like exasperated. "My brother has been hanging on to the land by his teeth, having to fight the authorities over just about every-thing, making it near impossible to make a living anymore."

"We've heard that from a lot farmers and ranchers up in Idaho, too," said Gary. "It seems to be getting harder and harder no matter who you talk to."

"It is. The last straw for me was having to sit out with the herd practically all night, night after night, to protect them from the increasing wolf presence. You know, you're not allowed to shoot one of them unless you catch them with their teeth dug into your animal's haunch. Instead they want you to put out little colored flags that whip in the wind..."

"I've heard of that. Don't they call it 'fladry?'" cut in Anthea.

"Yeah, the most moronic concept created by college educated wildlife experts. Wolves are smart enough to know what's a threat and what isn't. And flipping bits of plastic don't deter anything, whether it's elk or wolves. It's the modern scarecrow, most of which don't work either. I could go through the list of deterrents Fish and Wildlife have come up with, none of which do any good, that ranchers are sup-posed to institute before they're even allowed to shoot in the air to scare them off. At some point, that doesn't work either because wolves figure out that it's not aimed at them. Especially the one's that've been around for a while, harassing and killing stock without any punishment. And when you finally *do* get a kill permit, it's only good for so many weeks during which, if you can't shoot the sucker, it's free to come back and kill some more."

Gary and Anthea were appalled at the description of how wolves seem to have a free pass to wander from ranch to ranch and take an animal with virtually no repercussions.

"I'd read somewhere that ranchers were compensated for any stock that's killed or injured," said Anthea.

"Hardly," said Ellie. "If, and it's a big *if*, you can prove to ODFW's satisfaction that it was a wolf that killed your cow, the fund for compensation is too paltry to cover the cost of the animal, let alone its progeny and replacement value." She shook her head, obviously recalling the frustration they'd had dealing with government officials. "A single cow's value isn't just that of the cow itself. If it's breeding stock, then its worth involves the many generations of offspring it would produce, whether a cow or a prize bull. The value of some animals can run to a hundred thousand dollars depending on its age and how many generations worth of calves it will produce. When you're in the beef business, not all animals are steers. That's a concept the environmentalists don't understand, unless they're talking about some game animal or protected species. *That* they get."

"Logic goes by the wayside if someone is forced to apply the same equation to a situation they disagree with, as in looking at elk populations and cattle. They refuse to make the connection by saying there's no comparison," said Gary. "And, they believe it."

"Like bigots who can't recognize their own bigotry," added Anthea. "You know a person of color saying it's impossible for them to be racist, that only whites are racist. No logic." She shook her head, "No common sense." She looked at the others, "Sorry, I see so much crossover in this kind of thinking that I tend to tie it all together."

"You're right though," agreed Ellie. "It's the same thinking when it comes to the idea of compensation. Shoot a wolf and you're fined more than six thousand dollars, and up to a hundred K on the westside of the state where they're still listed as endangered, but they don't see any value in beef... or sheep, horses or a working dog."

"But the fact is, none of these are even native wolves. Those were smaller and disappeared fifty years ago. Instead, they brought in foreign wolves to re-populate the state. Only it's not, because, like I said, these wolves were never here to begin with," said Doug.

"So, what happened at your ranch?" Anthea wanted the whole story.

"Really, it wasn't any different for us than it has been for a dozen other small cattle operations around here," replied Doug.

"We'd been finding wolf tracks out by the north quadrant and, more than once, had come to check on the cattle only to find them acting abnormally, like they'd been messed with. When calving season came up around February, we kept the pregnant cows closer to home in case there were any problem births. I moved a camper out near the pasture. It was easier to do that than try to stay at the house, but it was also cold as all get-out even in the lower valley.

"Three nights in a row, I'd had to chase off a pair of wolves skulking around the herd. By the fourth night, I'd had little to no sleep. There'd been a breech birth one night and a stillborn another, so I was plumb exhausted. I'm guessing those wolves knew it. They're clever and they stalk their prey, getting a good lay of the land and any danger they might come against, which, in this case, was me.

"That night, I'd been hard asleep and it took quite a commotion to wake me up, but when I did, I pulled on my boots… kept 'em close, just in case… and grabbed the rifle. This wasn't a cow travailing, this was just plain ear-piercing bawling. You could feel the cows' fright.

"When I got to the cows, one of 'em was on the ground, belly ripped open and the uterus pulled out. The unborn calf was still half in the sac but already partially consumed by one of the wolves and the other two - there were three this time - had their fangs deep into the haunch of another cow, actually taking chunks of flesh out and eating it while she was still on her feet. As I came up, she stumbled, but I focused on the one eating the calf and shot it. The other two wolves lit out of there faster than I could fire off a couple more shots."

Anthea's eyes were wide and she shook her head in disbelief. "The wolves were eating the cows while they were still alive?"

Doug tilted his head. "Most people don't realize how vicious wolves really are. They've got this romantic idea of their beauty and, I don't know whatchacallit…"

"Nobility?" offered Gary.

"Yeah. Folks think they're these noble creatures of the wild when they're really killing machines. They feed on live prey and they kill for the sake of killing, leaving it there uneaten because they never intended to eat their kill." Doug sat back in his rocker. "They can be the picture of pure evil, doesn't matter what folks want to believe."

"What happened then?" Anthea was stunned at the waste but needed to hear the rest.

"I shot the cow that was down. The calf was dead, for sure. Then checking out the one the other two had mauled, she had no chance so I had to shoot her, too.

"Then, I did the right thing and reported the whole incident. Two days later, after the evidence was so deteriorated that they couldn't get good samples of anything because of the weather, the snow had melted some and the tracks were gone, the old sheriff and ODFW wolf coordinator showed up. Even though I had photos of the damage that I'd taken as soon as it was light, after Fish and Wildlife went over the remains of the dead cows and the dead wolf, this is what the state guys said... the one cow was obviously a wolf attack. How could they deny it? The dead wolf was right there. But the other cow they said could have been anything, maybe a bunch of coyotes even though I told them I *saw* the other two wolves latched onto her haunches.

"And do you know what? I was *still* fined for the wolf's killing because they couldn't see any fladry up on this particular pasture and I hadn't immediately reported the sightings the other nights just before the incident. And because of that, they refused to compensate us for the two breeding cows and the two dead calves. The injured cow was also pregnant. I was out thousands of dollars in stock, let alone their future offspring, and on top of that, the $6,250 fine.

"That's why we finally sold out to my little brother and came here. We were tired of the runaround and we weren't getting any younger. Fact is, dealing with government officials will age you quicker than a heart attack."

"And Doug's had one of those, too," added Ellie. "Pretty much as a result of Oregon Fish and Wildlife shenanigans."

"That's quite the story," sympathized Anthea.

"And it's nowhere near as bad as what some of our friends and neighbors have been through." Ellie rocked back in her chair, fingers draped over the knobs carved at the ends of the armrests. Years of hard labor had left her knuckles gnarled with advancing arthritis that she obviously hadn't allowed to impede her needlework. A project of intricate design sat on the end table, untouched for the last hour.

"Do you think any of them would be willing to talk to us about their experiences?" Anthea was getting the inklings of a story though she hadn't considered if she'd be able to peddle it anywhere. Press releases were one thing but getting a news article picked up was completely different. It all depended on the spin to catch an editor's interest.

"Maybe. Most of them have already had their words twisted by some reporter to make them sound like some rube who can hardly read when most ranchers and farmers have college degrees. You practically need one to wade through government red tape to stay in operation," replied Doug. "They're a little skittish when it comes to folks who call themselves journalists."

"I don't blame them."

"Yeah, if I were them, I'd probably keep my distance, too," Gary threw in his opinion.

"Tell you what, though," Doug got up and was headed into the proprietor's quarters. "I've got one article that'll give you some background about the wolves and how they got here."

"Thanks. That'd be a starting point," Anthea tried to keep her enthusiasm in check. Watching his wife, Gary had a tough time restraining a chuckle. Curiosity may have killed the cat, and nearly put the two of them in pine boxes a few years back, but that wasn't about to deter her from following up on a potential story. He closed his eyes, shut his mouth and shook his head.

Chapter 4

Loping through a stunted forest of white pine that had been devastated by fire years before were a rangy band of wolves, seven in total. The alpha male was a big mottled black and gray specimen weighing in at over 130 pounds. Not far behind trotted the female that had delivered the two pups peddling hard to keep up with their sire. Two yearlings from the previous litter followed the leaders and some ways back trailed a grown male that had recently attached itself to the pack.

The new addition's standing among the little clan wasn't yet solidified and he kept some distance between himself and the parent pair until, and if, he gained acceptance. His size was something of an obstacle to that end, carrying some 120 pounds on his wooly frame. He was large enough to be considered a threat to the alpha that had no intention of relinquishing his position to some upstart that had magically appeared from out of the woods.

The alpha nor his mate had ever been caught and collared. In fact, none of the family grouping had ever officially been sighted by any ODFW employees or rangers that periodically scouted the region. Truth be known, this small pack had gone unnoticed and unnamed by the resident wolf coordinator since it had formed a cou - ple years back.

The tagalong was sporting a radio collar that was half-chewed and ready to come apart. More fluke than anything else had led to the outsider's capture and fitting with a monitor in another state just about the same time this sub-pack had formed. Forced to move on, as many males are after attaining adulthood, the loner had covered some real mileage, crossing the Snake River at Brownlee Dam when it shrank during a drought. Arriving in Eastern Oregon, he eventually linked up with this group.

The association between the newbie and the alpha male wasn't *progressing well. After the last hunt, the loner hadn't submitted to the pecking order according to pack etiquette. Attempting to snag some meat before the alpha had finished gorging had met with a severe rebuke that relegated him to bringing up the rear and keeping a wary eye open for further retribution. Still hungry and on the outs with the pack wasn't a good place to be.*

The two-month-old pups were just about weaned and ready to travel with the clan now that it was time to abandon the den. This kill was the first where they'd been given meat of their own but they tired out easily having to pump their little legs to keep up with the longer strides of the older wolves.

They'd traveled a couple of miles from the kill site that wasn't far from the Gaston Buttes' southern perimeter when they left one scruffy forest, crossed a marshy stream and headed toward another taller stand of pines. This is where the alpha male decided to draw the line.

Turning back, he allowed the entourage of bitch, pups and youths to pass him before he crouched down to confront the less hefty interloper. There was no room in the pack for a social climber that didn't abide by the rules and the piebald alpha was prepared to send the party-crasher on his way.

Lunging at the recruit, black and gray fur from both the ani - mals flew in the sultry afternoon air, most of which was tawny gray scratched from the hide of the newcomer. Scuffling for a couple of brief rounds, the altercation was rapidly concluded with the younger wolf turning tail. He headed back through the cattails edging the stream the pack had crossed only minutes before.

Truly a loner now, the foreign wolf followed the winding creek that tripped over rocks and rills on its way to the Nacqus coursing toward the Snake River and Hell's Canyon.

Chapter 5

Quint Edwards' measured steps brought him to where he'd left his two teens who were in a quandary on how to soothe the cows and mewling calves clustered together, backed against the fence that was straining under the pressure of thousands of pounds of scared beef.

Eying him with curiosity, Shaley and Cam wondered what their father's plan was going to be. They'd seen wolf sign before and knew very well that what lay out in the field was probably the result of an attack, the shot confirming the losses. The dogs had finally plunked themselves down in the grass, panting, having nothing to occupy them since the cows were too frightened to move.

The Edwards' ranch had taken quite a few hits from wolf depredation over the last couple years. As many as eighteen head had been either killed outright or suffered such injury that they had to be put down. The losses went far beyond the pittance that was authorized in compensation. He'd laughed when he heard that the fund, sponsored by conservationists that called themselves allies of the ranchers who were being financially drained by wild animal attacks, was a paltry hundred thousand dollars. That didn't cover the cost of one prize bull killed by wolves looking for an easy meal.

His decision was going to be tough because what he was contemplating could cost him more than a few thousand dollars, it could mean jail time and that'd be hard on the kids. Shaley was graduating from high school this year, expecting to go on to college in the fall. Cam, rough and tumble boy that he was, was already going through a trial, having reached that age where hormones could run a youth into all kinds of trouble. Shaley had a good head on her shoulders, having learned to be pragmatic in the wake of her mother's leaving but Cam still needed a father's guidance.

Not an easy choice but, within minutes, he knew what it would be.

They were just a couple miles from where the truck and trailer were parked and the afternoon was advancing. It was obvious that the herd couldn't be left unattended tonight because of the possibility that the wolves hadn't left the area. Although they were more apt to kill, whether for food or random inclination, eat and move on, it wasn't unheard of for a pack to hang around if there was easy prey and young ones that might need nourishing. Wolves didn't range far from a den if there were pups still occupying it. But, as far as Quint knew, there wasn't a den in the region, at least, not one that had been reported.

After standing aside with his hands on his hips for a number of minutes, Quint looked over at the kids. They were good shots and used to camping rough, with or without him.

"Okay, I want you to set up camp for the night to protect the herd in case the wolves come back. I'm going to call Del and have him stay with you tonight just to be safe."

From that, Shaley easily deduced that her father had other plans in mind. "What are you going to do, Dad?"

"I'll tell you what I'm not going to do. I'm not going to wait around until Turlow decides to show up in a couple days to hem and haw over my dead stock, then tell me that he can't confirm whether it was wolves, cougar, a pack of coyotes or a wild kangaroo that killed our cattle." He removed his hat and ran fingers through his thatch of short blond hair, trying to get comfortable with his decision. At least the kids were underage and not liable for whatever he did. "I want you to wait until Del gets here and then you three discreetly bury the dead cows and don't tell anyone what we found."

He thought further on the discrepancy of numbers of head. "As far as you know, we had three cows that disappeared. They could've wandered off and fallen down an arroyo and we just couldn't locate them." He searched their faces to see if they were on board.

"Sure, dad. We've got it," agreed Shaley. Both of them were well aware of the hassles and frustration every rancher, including their dad, had been forced to deal with regarding wolf predation.

Nonetheless, Cam still had questions. "But why not tell the

wolf reps what happened? Shouldn't they know about the wolves?"

"Cam, you know how much time we've wasted with government workers over the past couple of years. They take their notes and lots of pictures then make you clear miles of red tape before they finally deny you compensation because they've concluded that wolves weren't responsible for the loss. Am I right?"

"Yeah."

"We all know ODFW isn't going to authorize reimbursement for the kills let alone even admit what kind of predator we're dealing with, evidence or not. They haven't acknowledged that there's even a pack operating in this area."

"So, what are you going to do?"

"It's not like I haven't thought of this before but, I think now's the time to act." Quint checked the level of the sun. It was June and the longest days of the year were here. He still had plenty of daylight.

"Since there doesn't appear to be any recognition of what I assume is a sub-pack, we're burying the dead cows. The ground's soft enough after that rain to get through it with the shovels. Del can pack in another one when he comes.

"I'm going to track 'em down and take 'em out. There's been enough damage caused by wolves, and whatever ODFW says, they don't really know how many there are. Even if they did, they couldn't admit the truth because then they'd be allowing that the population had grown enough that they don't need protecting anymore. Right now, Fish and Wildlife keep trying to pin everything on the Nacqus Pack that ranges thirty miles from here, calling what we're experiencing "isolated incidents." More than just us have been victims to this nonexistent rogue pack and it's time they were cleared out."

He pulled his phone out to check for a signal. "I'm calling Del now and see if he's on his way. When he gets here, tell him I had to go down the draw to check something out and to keep everything to himself. I don't want to be too explicit on the phone." He gave the kids another serious look. "Are we all together in this? If not, tell me now."

Both answered that they had no problem with what their dad

had decided to do.

"Okay. Wait until Del gets here to take care of the carcasses. Be careful." He pierced them with a determined but softening gaze. "I love you."

"We know, Dad," replied Shaley. Cam just nodded, like average teenage boys who aren't sure about expressing affection.

Walking toward the lip of the canyon, Quint scrolled through his contacts to land on Del's number and touched the phone's screen. Placing the call, he hoped Del wasn't in some deadzone ditch.

It rang a few times and he picked up, "Yowp. What's up Quint?"

He'd caught Del at an opportune location. Signals were as schitzy as the weather. "Are you on your way out to the south range?"

"Uh-huh. Just about to pull up next to your truck."

"Good. Look, I left the kids with the cows to calm them down. They're waiting for you to get there."

"Calm the cows? You got trouble?"

"Yep. And I'm not going to bother calling Tandy or ODFW. I'm tired of mucking with those Fish and Wildlife lupus loafers so I'm not going to waste my time or theirs. Which, if they knew, they'd thank me for," Quint scanned the direction the wolves had gone while he talked to his cowhand.

"Look, I need to go check things at the bunkhouse and I'd like you to help the kids, make sure everything is tidy and safe. Camp for the night to watch the herd and keep an eye out that the cows don't get too anxious. Tomorrow you'd better assess whether we should move them back to the lower pasture so we can keep a closer eye on them."

"What are you gonna do?" asked Del.

"I'm gonna go for a trail ride and do some thinking. Maybe get rid of a couple of bothersome burrs under my saddle. I may be gone for a couple-three days. The kids are waiting for you to take care of the cows and move 'em tomorrow, if need be."

"Anything special you want me tell Audrey?"

"Just tell Mom I've gone down Ramshead Creek and will be back before long. I'll call if I get to a place where there's a signal. Losing this one. Keep an eye on my family. I'm counting on you, Del."

"No problem, Quint."

Quint checked his rifle, made sure he had plenty of cartridges, cinched up the saddle, hugged his daughter and grabbed his son's shoulder in a strong grip.

"Del will be here before long. He was just pulling up next to the truck when I called. Like I told him, let Grandmom know that I'll be back tomorrow or the day after. I'm going to stop by the old bunkhouse on Ramshead Creek, probably stay there the night. Got that?"

"Yep, Pop. We've got it," Cam said as he pulled a fold-up shovel out of his pack. "We'll see you when you get home."

"Thanks, kids. I'll call when I'm somewhere there's cell coverage." He turned his horse and walked back to where he'd left the dead cows. That's where he'd pick up the marauders' trail.

Scanning the mess of tracks around the cow that had still been alive, it looked like that was the last spot where the wolves were before leaving the scene. Paw prints pressed into muddy depressions made the trail easy enough to follow. As much as they hadn't really enjoyed camping in the rain the night before, it turned out to be a godsend for him.

Mounting his paint, Quint thought, *Thank goodness these pirates have no concept of covering their tracks like their human counterparts. I sure appreciate them helping me to hunt down their rotten skins.*

The pattern of wolf tracks went over hard ground and through soft dirt toward a stand of pines. Leaning over his horse's neck, Edwards was able to detect signs of their passage. Disturbed pine needles indicated where more than one predator had padded through the piled up detritus left by years of deadfall. He could see that there were at least four grown wolves. *No way were these coyote tracks.* The prints visible in the wet ground were twice the size of the smaller canines. Training his eyes on the trail of spoor, he continued down the draw.

After another mile, Quint noticed some new prints added to the merry band of cattle raiders. Slipping out of the saddle, he hunkered down to take a closer look at the muddle of tracks. It looked like there was a convergence of two groups of animals. Leaving his horse to graze a little, he followed the trail to where it split, a family tribe apparently had come from a hidden glen and joined the larger wolves. Here he backtracked a set of adult prints and two smaller sets, obviously a litter. He didn't get too far into the brush before he found the place of origin... a den, and one that hadn't been found by the range rider. He knew Crenshaw well, and if he'd located this place, he'd have informed ODFW and the ranchers running stock in the area.

This was an unidentified den, which meant that the wolves he was chasing were what he thought they were, an unknown pack.

Noting that the band's tracks were moving away from the den, he surmised that the litter was old enough now to travel and they were abandoning the den for greener pastures. Keeping a close eye on the prints, he retraced his own back to the horse and remounted. He wanted to make sure he didn't lose them before darkness closed in on the hollows.

Wolves could move fast and cover a lot of ground but the fact that they had two pups running to keep up with the big dogs, they were bound to be traveling at a much slower pace. The adults would have to let the little ones rest at intervals, impeding their progress. Nor did they know that they were being pursued. That was good news for the hunter. It meant that he had a better chance of catching up to them before the sun hit the canyon rim.

CHAPTER 6

Cohesion of a group of wolves was dependent on sticking to the rules. No member of a pack could set boundaries except the leader. Attempting to change the way things were done was considered a challenge to authority and immediately met with rectifying force. The offender was castigated and either submitted to the alpha's domination or separated from the pack. There was no in-between. Unlike civilized society, there was no room for individualism. Members had to go along to get along or get gone. Having crossed the line one too many times, the only choice given to the draftee was to be cut loose.

The black and gray alpha turned to rejoin the family clan under his charge, now diminished in numbers by one. There was no hurry in their trek. As far as the lead male knew, there was nothing behind them to encourage a faster pace. This particular group hadn't encountered much to hamper their hunting practices since their formation.

Because elk and deer had been plentiful, spreading unhindered on the Gaston Buttes preserve, this pack hadn't been in the habit of taking domestic stock for food. Not until the lead female had suffered an injury. That changed the leader's methods for feeding the previous litter when they weren't yet old enough to assist in the hunt.

By then, the alpha had discovered the ease of taking down a defenseless cow. The territory he appropriated was sparsely populated by humans and he'd avoided contact with them even after preying on the wide-flung herds. Suffering no reprisal after taking a calf or two, his experience had taught him that cattle were preferred targets. The problem was that the young wolves attached to the pack were now trained to hunt cattle, not wild game.

Instinct compelled the pack to forsake the den but without any natural enemies in the region, they weren't about to leave behind the

43

bountiful food supply. They trekked toward another stand of trees that sprouted from a deep crevice in the canyon wall with the little ones bounding after their mother, setting a staccato pace. At the edge of the wood of mixed fir, ponderosa pine and a few volunteer apple trees, the band stopped for the pups to rest and play in the tall grass. Danger wasn't a concern.

CHAPTER 7

Carefully picking his way through a flush of spring runoff, Quint's horse forged a stony brook where the wolves' tracks had disappeared into the shallow water. On the other side of the stream he studied the gravel bank for indentations they had made exiting the water. The pack hadn't made a direct line in crossing, they had turned upstream and climbed the bank where there was less of an incline, taking a winding route up the hill. Muddy spots in the deer track they had followed revealed distinct paw prints, making Quint's search practically effortless.

The tracks were relatively fresh and the rancher knew that he wasn't too far behind the band of cattle thieves.

Because the wolves had chosen the least challenging path out of the gully, his horse didn't have to strain to reach the top. Keeping the trail in view, he found himself looking across a flat plain. Knee-high grass lay trampled where the pack's passage was still visible in the bent blades that hadn't yet sprung back up. Peering across the fields, he couldn't discern any movement, so he continued to follow the path they'd cut in the meadow that led to a distant stand of trees.

Feeling that he was closing in on his quarry, Quint put his heels to his horse's sides and galloped toward the thicket of pines. A couple hundred yards from the edge of the wood, he spotted a place where the grass had been flattened and torn. Reining in, he dropped to the ground and took a closer look at the site.

Impressed in the earth was a jumble of spoor and tufts of hair were strewn over the crushed grass. It was evident there'd been a scuffle between two of the animals by the appearance of the prints. Scanning the fight zone, Quint's eyes landed on something that reflected the sun. Metal, for sure, and obviously manmade. Bending over, he picked up a tattered radio collar that had been chewed and ripped apart.

He'd read about certain packs, particularly one in the Yellowstone area, that had a predilection for gnawing through their collars. Examining it, Quint noticed that what had caught his eye was the buckle, not much else in the collar was metal, unlike the newer designs that were constructed to deter chewing. Upon closer inspection, he could see that this collar was at least a few years old, discolored by weather and wear. The battery appeared to be damaged and, as best as he could tell, hadn't worked for some time. It may even have been defective from the getgo.

He pondered the implications of his find. *Probably why we hadn't gotten any info from ODFW about the wolf's proximity to my lease, 'cause it looks like this pack had never officially been on their map. Considering that there are dozens more wolves than they want to admit, that'd make sense.* He turned the frayed collar over in his hands. *Bet this guy wasn't even from this state but a wanderer that latched onto a local sub-pack, and if this boxing ring is anything to go by, he was seriously reprimanded. Oh well...*

Stashing the item in his saddlebag, Quint loosened his rifle in the scabbard for easy extraction. The wolves weren't far ahead and he wanted to be ready to act. He mounted his horse and followed the clear trail that veered off toward the pines.

Adrenaline beginning to pump, he was prepared for the confrontation.

CHAPTER 8

After hearing their hosts' wolf tales, whetting her appetite for more information about Koyama County, Anthea shanghaied Gary into exploring the environs with more purpose than idle tourism.

Gary often wondered if his wife was capable of turning off the spinning of her brain, entertaining suspicions of the political machinations behind events. One thing she said, with which Gary was inclined to agree - *everything* was political. And what a sad commentary on modern life it was. His own time spent in uniform, military and law enforcement, taught him the inescapable truth of it. Transitioning to teaching college, surrounded by militant PC shysters and revolutionaries, proved the theory.

The bed and breakfast where they were lodging hugged the edges of the river's shifting channel a few miles downstream from the village of Nacqus where Anthea had hopes of chatting up the locals.

Calling it a village was probably something of a stretch. The main street of Nacqus was also the only street. Downtown consisted of a café-laundromat, an all-purpose mercantile, a peculiar antique store whose proprietor hung the open sign according to whim, and a part-time post office. The majority of Nacqus' population of forty-seven was strung along the river, mostly occupying a few houses on the highway, some small farms, retirement retreats and ranch houses. Children were bussed twenty miles into Rory to attend school. There being so few students in the Nacqus Valley and with the road improvements made in the seventies, last century's one-room schoolhouse had closed up shop nearly fifty years before.

Driving the five or six miles of twisting river road was a scenic jaunt. Carved into the canyon walls that rose more than two thousand feet in steps cut by ancient flood plains, the blacktop ended (or began, depending on your perspective) two miles past the Nacqus Rocks Bed and Breakfast.

Gary maneuvered the truck around the curves, slowing down just to gaze at the water tumbling over the flats and through the ravines on its way to the deepest canyon in North America. Steering around the last corner onto Nacqus' main and single drag, he parked in one of the total ten oblique spots 'downtown' in front of the Wild River Mercantile. The shingle swaying in the breeze said, "Purveyors of all things necessary and… everything else."

"I like that," commented Anthea as she climbed down from the Dodge. "I haven't got a clue what's necessary to make life cruise along in these parts, but I'm ready to find out."

"A boat might be at the top of that list. How much you want to bet they don't sell them."

"Is there anything you don't put a literal spin on?"

Gary shrugged. "I learned from the best spin artist I know. Isn't that what marketing's all about?"

"I give up."

"Good, for once I win an argument," he grinned as he held the door open for her.

Walking inside was a step back in time. Selections of modern kitchen appliances like food processors and one-touch coffee grinder/brewers lined shelves next to antique washboards and flat irons.

Anthea's hands skimmed the items representing a wide range of timesaving devices. "I guess you can choose which era you prefer, electric or muscle power," she said as she picked up a brand new hand-cranked beater. "I must be in the middle, still using my mother's forty-year-old plug-in portable mixer."

"Always wondered about that ancient thing and why you don't buy a new one," said Gary.

"Sentiment. And the fact that I don't bake that much."

"I noticed."

"Is that a hint?"

"No, I've grown fond of salads, smoothies and raw meat."

"Funny," Anthea couldn't help chuckling. "It's a good thing you know how to fire up a barbecue or you'd get no meat at all."

"Tell me about it."

At the end of the aisle of kitchen gadgets was a bookcase with new and vintage cookbooks that drew Anthea's attention. Picking up an original edition of "Joy of Cooking," she noticed a very old volume next to it.

"Don't tell me that you've decided you really are interested in becoming a kitchen maven," said Gary, looking over her shoulder at her find.

"No. It's just that I haven't seen one of these for decades. It's just like my grandmother's favorite cookbook. It had the best Potage St. Germain recipe ever."

"What's that? Sounds familiar."

"Soup made with fresh green peas. I used to love it."

"What happened to the book? You have a few well-thumbed cookbooks that look like someone was an avid chef, but I don't recall seeing this one."

"You wouldn't because my ex decided to sell anything he laid his hand on, including some items of real value. Someone snagged it at a garage sale before I could rescue what was left of my library or they'd all be gone."

Deciding to leave the comment alone rather than dredge up sore memories, Gary asked if Anthea was going to purchase the book.

"I think so. I've missed this one."

"Does that mean I will experience delectably authentic French cooking?"

"If it comes out of my kitchen it'll be debatable as to how authentic it'll be, let alone edible."

"Let me get this," said Gary, taking the book of yellowing pages from her hand. "I'm willing to take the chance if you are."

"You're on." She relinquished her clutch with a wink that could have meant anything from, "this'll be fun" to "you have no idea what you're asking for."

He hadn't gotten halfway down the aisle when a woman came around the corner, dark auburn hair loosely pulled back in a short ponytail. "Are you finding everything?"

"Is that of the 'necessary' variety or the 'everything else' department?" queried Gary, swinging back around and answering her before Anthea could respond.

Cressy Dillat, whose establishment this was, was caught off-guard by the question. Then she shook her head and smiled. "Right, you're referring to my sign. You had me there for a minute. I get plenty of folks with smart comebacks, but that's the first time anyone quoted the shop motto back at me."

"Does that make him clever or a *smart* ass?" quipped Anthea. Before Gary protested, she laughed, "Never mind. The answer is probably self-evident."

His eyes widened in feigned injury. "Hmm, who should be more offended - me, Ms. Shop Owner or my wife for my misguided attempt to amuse? Could it be, we just dove into the snowflake culture of micro-aggressions?"

Anthea rolled her eyes. "I believe you're the only one who's all wet, my love. May as well come up for air." She turned to face the proprietor. "I'm Anthea and this is my husband, Gary. I take it he's correct and you're the owner here?"

"Yes. Cressy." She held out her hand to shake theirs. "And in answer to your original question... 'yes.'"

"Well, that takes care of that," said Gary with finality. "This is a terrific place you have. An eclectic assortment of goods."

"Thanks, we try to appeal to everybody's tastes."

"I'd say you've succeeded," approved Anthea. "I found something I didn't even know I'd been missing all these years. I wonder what else you have hidden away here that I can't live without."

"Uh-oh. Trigger words that every husband fears," said Cressy.

"But, I'm lucky," said Gary. "This particular wife isn't especially fond of collections unless you include Lladró, Beanie Babies and giraffes..."

"None of which I have," cut in Anthea with a smirk. "Books are all that I have a passion to accumulate, as you see," she said pointing to the old hardbound cookbook in Gary's grasp.

"I'm glad we had something that caught your fancy," said Cressy.

"There is something else that I collect, though," Anthea said, opening a new direction in the conversation.

"And, what's that?" Cressy was being drawn in unknowingly.

Here it comes, thought Gary.

"Information."

That was just about the last thing Cressy expected to hear. "Information about what?"

"All kinds of things, actually. Right now, I'm interested in learning more about wolves."

Cressy's demeanor instantly changed, not that she was aware of how it showed on her face. Her brows furrowed and her lips pinched, diminishing her beauty with the obvious adverse reaction.

Anthea would have to be completely obtuse not to notice. Immediately, she backtracked before losing her first informant, who promised to have a whopper of a story if Anthea was any judge of emotional responses. "I didn't mean to hit a sour note, Cressy. After talking to our hosts at the bed and breakfast down the river, we seemed to stumble across more acrimony about the wolves than expected. I mean, we've heard all kinds of tales from people we've met in Idaho, but had no idea how egregious the problem had become down here."

"Frankly, we were surprised that they were such trouble here. Originally from the Westside, I never visited this area before," said Gary trying to smooth over the negativity Cressy's countenance revealed, "even since relocating to the Clearwater Valley about ten years ago."

"Well, you wouldn't know. We only started having real trouble around 2009 when the first wave, that we know of, got established in our mountains," Cressy offered, allowing her hackles to retract.

Anthea carefully re-entered the conversation. "It's evident that you've had run-ins with wolves. I'm sorry if I raised an old phantom. It certainly wasn't my intention to upset you."

"I should be the one to apologize," sighed Cressy. "You didn't mean any harm and you couldn't have used a better word to describe it than 'phantom.' No matter how well we think we've dealt with things or buried the past, it's not until an unexpected comment blind-sides me that I realize I'm still haunted." Cressy didn't notice how she slipped from the all-inclusive 'we' to the very personal 'I' but Anthea and Gary did.

Hit a hurdle bolting right out of the gate, thought Anthea, hoping that she hadn't stepped in it so deep that a great story was lost before it was ever told.

"Truthfully, you probably can't talk to anyone who lives out here in the sticks that hasn't had some kind of problem with wolves. They're pretty much everywhere, ranging within a few miles of Rory itself."

"That doesn't sound like a great selling point for real estate brokers," observed Anthea. "'Spacious home, four bedrooms, three baths with a mountain view, English country garden, all in coveted wolf territory. Shotgun optional.'"

Cressy laughed in spite of her memories. "You know, that would probably attract more inquiries by fascinated suburbanites than you think. They have no idea that even pets need bodyguards in wolf country."

"Are people so ignorant?" Gary asked rhetorically.

"You know they are," Anthea reminded him. "You share faculty offices with bigger fools than that."

"Luckily, I rarely show my face there. Teaching online has its benefits."

"Where do you teach?" Cressy was interested in going anywhere other than wolf talk.

"A couple of colleges. One out of Portland and the other in Idaho where we live."

Looking at Anthea, she asked, "Do you teach also?"

"Not if I can help it. Love the students, can't handle most of the educator mindset. I run a small PR firm and stick my nose into political controversy where it's least appreciated."

"It's a holdover from her newspaper days," added Gary. "And why she's on a tear to find out what's the beef about wolves and, uh, beef, if you'll pardon the expression."

"Do I have a choice?" Cressy was more relaxed and Anthea saw an opening to pry some facts out of the shop owner.

"So wolves are becoming ubiquitous where they were pretty much eradicated, is that the case?"

"Yes and no. Wolves *were* eradicated years ago but they have been re-introduced by college-trained wildlife experts who think they understand land management better than farmers and ranchers who've been doing it for generations." Cressy leaned against a bookshelf and crossed her arms. "It's the whole academia versus experience argument. I, of course, side with experience because I come from a ranch family and, even though most of us have ag degrees these days - you can't keep up with regulations without one anymore - results from trial and error trumps theory every time. Not that you could get many university professors to agree with that."

"Don't I know it," agreed Gary.

"I'm kind of reticent to ask now, but, if you're willing, would you share what happened that prompted your reaction when I brought up wolves?" Cressy's face started to close down, so Anthea jumped back in adding, "It's fine with us if you'd prefer not to talk about it. Some things are too personal or too intense to confide in strangers, which, face it, we are."

"What I will tell you is that it's because of wolves that my daughter will not have the same opportunities growing up that I had. The state-sponsored repatriation, as they're calling it, of wolves has raised hell among cattlemen trying to protect their livestock from non-native predators." The bitterness was palpable, but the source of it was an enigma to Cressy's questioners. "We were caught in the middle of a regulatory fiasco that is ongoing because the feds refuse to delist wolves in parts of Oregon as an endangered species. In the meantime, Idaho, Montana, Wyoming and Washington have all delisted them and even instituted some hunting opportunities to get the populations under control. Oregon, on the other hand, has wolf proponents that want over a thousand wolves roaming rangeland."

"That makes no sense," said Anthea.

"It does if you believe that ranchers are misusing the land and should be put out of business."

"I'm with Anthea. That makes no sense. Are all these folks vegans or something?"

"The "or something" is probably as close as you're going to get. A lot of these wolf advocates live on the Westside and do eat meat but I guess they don't know how it gets to the supermarket. Or, if they do, they're prepared to buy foreign produced meat that we can't be sure is even safe for consumption."

"Why is that," asked Anthea.

"Because the other countries that import beef aren't required to pass inspection that American beef does. You don't really know what you're eating in some cases, because trade agreements like NAFTA protect foreign producers but penalize American growers, making our product more expensive."

"That's hardly sensible," said Gary. "You'd think we'd want to give our industry the advantage, especially when producers are subject to meeting all kinds of quality standards."

"Yeah, you'd think, but that's not the way it is. It makes you wonder how much influence certain lobbies have over legislation and regulation. Certain products have a magic wand waved over them if their processing has to do with meeting religious standards," said Cressy.

"You mean, like halal products?" Anthea pre-supposed.

"Yes, and I won't go into my take on that, it'll ruin your lunch."

"That's okay, I've looked into that for articles I've written. At home, we buy local produce when we can."

"Smart. As you can see, I'm not a real fan of a lot of government interference. It's created far more problems than it's ever helped," concluded Cressy.

"From what you said earlier, I take it that you had a major issue involving wolves."

Cressy only nodded.

"I'd really be interested in visiting one of the cattle growers around here, assuming that most of them are modest operations. Do you know anyone who'd be willing to show us around, explain some of the challenges, especially relating to protected predators?"

Cressy mulled over the request. "I might. How long are you going to be in the area?"

"We're supposed to be on vacation for a week," said Gary with a sardonic twist. "But I don't think we're going to be doing the typical touristy thang." He gave Anthea a sidelong look. "We rarely do." He smiled. "Then again, I'd probably find that boring in comparison. So, fact-finding it is."

Lifting an eyebrow in speculation, Cressy observed, "You two are quite the pair."

"Thank you for not adding 'of what' to that. It might hurt our feelings," remarked Anthea.

"You've piqued my interest, so, I'll tell you what. Let me see if I can get May to cover for me tomorrow and I'll take you out to a place myself. That is, if you're game."

Anthea tried not to jump in too hastily exclaiming *yes!* A little decorum was called for, "Thank you so much, Cressy. We'd be delighted to take you up on your generous offer."

"I'll second that," grinned Gary, knowing his wife was ecstatic and struggling to stay composed. Anthea would see this as a terrific opportunity to get "the rest of the story" as Paul Harvey used to phrase it. She'll let the rebel yell loose in the truck.

And true to form, that's exactly what Anthea did when they'd driven out of sight. "All right!" Slapping her hand on the dashboard, she said, "You know she's got a powerful tale. I just hope that she'll let us in on it and let me write it."

"I don't know, Anthea. It seemed way too fresh for her to be spilling her guts to a journalist," he was reticent about encouraging her excitement. "And one she just met, on top of it."

"Then it's up to me to prove I'm trustworthy enough to gain her confidence."

"That's asking for a miracle in this era of fake journalism." Gary understood his wife's enthusiasm for finding and revealing truth in a world hostile to it. All because facts have a strange tendency to blow away people's wishful thinking about how things ought to be. He dealt with what he referred to as the *blinders theory of reality* every day he taught.

"The stigma is well-earned by the mainstream media outlets who lost their objectivity years ago," agreed Anthea. "That's a massive obstacle to clear and I'd lay money she's already been scorched by the press, scarring her in ways I don't want to imagine. But that's what makes her story so compelling, and I don't even know what it is yet."

"Let's hope she sees fit to tell you."

Chapter 9

Clambering over rough ground, Edwards' paint was sure-footed and still able to keep up a good clip without skidding or tripping. Sensing the presence of fieldstones concealed among the clumped grass, the horse had an uncanny ability to avoid pitfalls while moving at speed.

Quint reckoned he was about five miles from the old bunkhouse on Ramshead Creek. Ranch hands would use this stopover when roundup was too far out to return before nightfall.

He crossed another shallow cut in the hillside, elderberries and willows lining the trickle of water that splashed through the center. Coming out on the other side, the pack's trail was clearly defined in the soft patches of earth that opened up between the tall hay and scattered rocks. Winding its way up onto the bench, it pointed toward a far off dense stand of conifers fringed by broad-leafed trees shooting out branches from under the taller boughs. The tracks were fresh, not more than an hour old.

He was closing in.

Some time after climbing out of the ravine, he halted for a moment. Pulling his rifle out of the scabbard, he rechecked the scope for accuracy. No way was he going to miss. If he was going to shoot, he was determined to do it right and kill the brutes before they did any more damage to his or neighbors' herds. Bleeding hearts viewed wolves as some kind of aristocratic creatures when they were really little more than land sharks, slashing and gnawing live prey, leaving them, bowels flayed, dying in agony.

Directing his horse with his knees, Quint picked up speed as he cantered over the hill toward the grove. A crisp wind rose as the afternoon waned, covering the sound of his approach.

Before the pack took any notice of the rider converging on its temporary shelter at the edge of the wood, Quint saw the two pups tumbling around in the grass, their dam coming out from the shade to nudge them back into line. To one side were two teen wolves taking a breather in the fading sun and just as he slowed his horse to raise the gun, the alpha male appeared out of the shadow. It was a clear shot and he didn't hesitate for a second. Just as the mottled black and grey wolf leveled his yellow eyes on the hunter, Quint pulled the trigger.

CHAPTER 10

Free of the irritating collar that he and other pack members had scratched and gnawed at since he'd been tranquilized and tagged three winters ago and hundreds of miles away, the solitary wolf tried to shake out the matted fur around his neck.

He was on his own again traipsing over grassy knolls that looked much like the golden country from which he'd originally come. Features of the deep canyons in the volcanic east didn't seem much different to him than the towering, black-pillared cliffs of the Snake's sweeping route west. Nor did it matter where he was as long as his needs were met - a place to sleep in relative safety and game when he was hungry.

As many twists that his journey had taken, he'd learned a few important things. How to stay out of sight of the two-legged creatures that posed the only real danger, having seen one send a projectile in his direction that clawed the earth next to him. He'd also learned to avoid shaggy bears that were much larger and stronger than he was, that he couldn't down an elk without assistance and it was smarter to leave moose to themselves. One of the most valuable lessons he was taught was during this last sojourn with the pack that had just kicked him loose. And that was how to hunt the easy way, especially if you were working alone.

Now that he was no longer attached to a group, there was less to restrain him but more to accomplish to stay alive. Either way, it didn't give him any pause. Today was just another day putting dis - tance between the territory claimed by the alpha that had done one thing to help him: he'd freed him from that troublesome choker. He stopped again to scratch at the place where it used to chafe his neck.

After being chased off, he located another path down the canyon. Skirting the open range of the benchland above the Nacqus, he kept to depressions that cut across the fields, often with skiffs of water flitting over stones down the middle of the crevices. He passed from side to side wherever the ground was less rough.

Weaving in and out of the trees, he felt more secure keeping to the shadows. During the past few years, he'd covered miles by him - self, experience teaching him that the less he was seen the less he'd have to flee any threat. Unlike traveling with a pack where there was safety in numbers, to be on his own meant being more cautious.

Every so often, he'd approach some deer that would dash off in a fluster. Or he'd disturb a batch of quail that swooped off in a panic. Coming across some cattle, they reacted to his presence with high-pitched mooing. Uninterested, he loped on his way. For the time being he'd lost his appetite nor had any inclination to hunt.

Traveling at a swift pace, he seemed to be driven to find new territory where he could establish his own boundaries. Where that would be, he didn't know... yet. Until then, he continued to swing west along the winding waterway that emptied into the Snake River basin that lay in the opposite direction. He'd already been that way and there was no call to go back.

CHAPTER 11

Shots echoed off the canyon walls where no one heard the blasts except Edwards and the wolves as he dispatched them one after another. His aim was true and not a single shot went awry. One, two, three, four. Every bullet hit its mark and the marauders were taken out in quick succession.

The pack hadn't confronted any human threats since forming, lulling them into a false sense of safety. For wild creatures whose instincts should have kept them wary, they were unsuspecting and sluggish to respond, spelling their destruction.

Riding into the dell where the pack had been indolently catching the lengthening afternoon's rays, Quint was frankly astonished that he'd been able to ambush the wolves; that they'd hardly moved after he fired the first round. He unholstered his revolver as he approached, assuming that he'd probably have to finish off any of the animals that weren't dead even though he'd seen each one hit and collapse.

The closer he drew to the scene, his mount slowed until coming to a full stop, four crumpled canine forms laid in a half circle around horse and rider. Walking through what the wildlife advocates would call a crime scene, it didn't take long to determine that all the grown wolves were indeed dead. Extra shots were unnecessary.

Thanking his stars that he didn't need to use the handgun, Quint went back to his horse and extracted a folding shovel from his gear, but he wouldn't be able to just bury the carcasses. First, he'd have to dig out the bullets just in case someone ever stumbled across what was soon to become the pack's graveyard. He wasn't about to make it easy for anyone to nail him with destroying this bunch of cattle raiders by leaving traceable evidence, and that also meant collecting the spent casings.

Immediately, he got to work before the shadows got any longer.

Using his knife, it didn't take long to pull the rounds out of the dead animals. Quint poked around the edge of the wood until he found a spot where the earth was still moist from the rains, making it a choice place to dig a pit deep enough to bury four hefty wolves.

An hour later, he was soaked from his toil, standing over a deep trench just under the eaves of the copse. Hauling the corpses to the hole, he pushed them over the edge into the grave then backfilled it, one shovelful at a time. The whole operation had taken him just under two hours with an extra fifteen minutes to try to clean up the area enough that it didn't look obviously disturbed. Strewing old leaves and pine needles from under the trees, Quint had the grave well camouflaged. Within a few days it would look much like it had before the wolves had stopped here and unknowingly made it their final resting place.

Before burying them, Edwards had checked and none of the wolves had worn tracking devices, either collars or surgical implants that he could find. After examining the chewed collar he'd stowed, reassuring himself that it had been inoperative for months if not years, he felt comfortable that there wouldn't be any repercussion by wolf agents. This pack had been doing its dirty work under the radar for a long while, its deeds being attributed to another more distant group. Not that any real investigation had ever been done to establish that the main Nacqus Pack was responsible for the reported preda-tions on Quint's and neighboring land.

Preoccupied with getting the carcasses buried as rapidly and efficiently as possible. It wasn't until he was collecting dead leaves to spread over the fresh fill that he noticed the two pups watching his every move. They'd taken cover under the boughs of a wild plum that scraped the ground, keeping them obscured from view. In his rush to beat the sunset, he'd completely forgotten about the cubs that he'd ini-tially seen cavorting in the grass. His full attention had to be centered on the alpha, his mate and then the two younger wolves completing the hunting quartet, making sure they were all dead.

Now he had a couple of pups not more than eight weeks old, staring at him from the edge of the wood. Inquisitive, their little noses twitched in the breeze. They hadn't yet been taught to fear anything having probably never ventured far from the den until today. Looking at them, Quint wasn't certain that they'd been fully weaned, the parents likely still feeding them with regurgitated meat until their digestive systems could handle it on their own. He'd barely noticed that the female's teats weren't completely dried up when he buried her. He'd been more concerned with hauling the wolves' bulk into the trench without leaving a trail of blood that would entice carrion eaters to dig them up. *These are the kinds of mistakes that could cost you jail time, bubba,* he castigated himself as he watched the pups.

It was growing late and he had to get to the bunkhouse before full dark. The question he now had to deal with was what to do with a couple of wolf tots?

This was their first day away from the protection of the den. They probably hadn't even cut their sharp little teeth on fresh meat, the inborn predator still waiting to be released.

Quint looked at them and scratched his chin, two-day old beard sprouting gold with a dash of gray that could hardly be seen as the afternoon was drawing down. Looking up at the sky as if plying it for an answer, he thought, *If I were smart, I'd shoot them before they die of starvation or are killed by other predators that might smell blood residue and find this grove.*

He considered the pups studying him, eyes beginning to transform to their natural yellow, they were too young to be afraid of him or any other denizen of the range.

Shaking his head in disgust at his lack of resolve, he wasn't sure he could do it. They weren't the ones that had been killing his cattle, though they were part of the reason the other wolves had done so. Given half a chance, they'd grow up to be dangerous prowlers, born in the image of their sire and following his slaughtering instincts.

Without really deciding, Quint walked over to the observant twins, watching him advance with trepidation but frozen in place.

They had no clue who or what was moving toward them, had no mother to protect them and simply had no idea what to do but cower under the brush. Reaching down, the more brazen of the two clamped onto his gloved hand, sinking his pointed little teeth into the hardy leather. Grabbing it by the scruff with his other hand, the pup released its jaws and hung there immobile.

The other one had rolled onto its back in submission and lay there until Quint clutched the flaccid skin around his neck and lifted it as well. Holding them high, he could see their sex: one male and one female.

Relaxed and motionless in his grip, just as if a parent's jaws were clamped on their scruffs, the pups' wide eyes were glued to him.

"Now what do I do with you?"

Chapter 12

Quint was dog-tired.

The spot where he'd cornered the sub-pack wasn't but a couple miles from the old bunkhouse on Ramshead Creek and it was rolling on toward dark. After expending all his energy burying the proof of his crime against the State, he wasn't about to ride more than ten miles back to join the kids and Del. Having already left instructions for dealing with the dead cows that he was confident they'd carry out, he'd also told them he'd probably be gone for the night, maybe two.

Circumstances made the decision for him. Having no other way of carrying them, he opened one of the saddlebags and placed the pups inside with their fluffy heads poking out, sniffing the air. It wasn't but a quick trot over the hill and through one more spring-fed creek to reach the weather beaten cabin that had served five generations of buckaroos working the Nacqus bench.

Bathed in the last rays of the tilting sun, the rough-hewn planks of the bunkhouse were tinted gold. By the time Quint dismounted, dropping the reins across the paint's neck, there was only a blush of daylight left to see to the needs of the three animals in his care.

No one else was at the cabin that was always left unlocked. Close to a hundred years old, ranchers and their hands had used the shelter to ride out a storm, get a good night's sleep or brew up a welcome cup of coffee on a cold workday. A common use cabin, everyone who took advantage of it was considerate of those who would come later, leaving it in good condition for the next cowboy who needed a roof for the night.

First things first, Quint went inside and fashioned a makeshift enclosure for the pups using firewood from the pile left stacked along the wall. It hadn't been that long since someone had stayed there.

They'd cleared the place of packrats and varmints that had a tendency to take up residence during the winter months when the cabin was empty for weeks at a time.

Going back outside, he took the pups from the saddlebag and carried them in to their accommodation for the night, softly plunking them inside the pen he'd constructed. He lit an oil lamp and left to take care of his horse.

A while later, as Quint came through the door, saddle over his shoulder, the young wolves perked up and stretched their front paws up on the wood to see what the commotion was about. Placing the saddle on a rail built for the purpose, he finally opened the woodstove and saw that the previous occupant had prepared the wood and kindling for the next person. He found the matchbox, removed one and struck a flame. Setting the match to the chipped wood and crumpled paper, fire immediately leapt up and he watched it catch before closing the door.

On top of the stove, an enameled coffee pot was all ready for brewing, waiting for a hot blaze to boil the water in the well-used percolator. When he readied to leave in the morning, Quint would perform the same courtesy for the next cowpoke, making sure there was cut wood stacked in the corner, a fire set in the stove ready for lighting, and the coffee pot perched to perk.

While the water heated in the pot, he dug through the canned goods in the open-shelved cupboard to see what was there. Among the usual staples he found a few cans of dog food and, pulling one out, tossed it up and down in his hand. Not knowing if they'd begun eating solid food, Quint opened the tin, set the contents onto a plate, and placed it in their improvised pen.

Well, if they're going to be raised with their domestic cousins, they're going to have to eat like them.

Smelling the chopped and mashed up meat, and whatever other ingredients an average can of dog food consisted, the little guys recognized it as edible and plunged in without reserve. Turned out the pups were hungry enough that they weren't real picky.

Satisfied that the squirts were fine for now and having tended to his horse, Quint heard the coffee bubbling and popping on the stove. Choosing an old fifties style ceramic mug, the color of a rusty nail, he poured himself a cup and set the pot to the side to keep warm. Pushing open the door, he wandered outside to watch the last of the sunset slip into a bruised dusk. Clear turquoise sky outlined the rich scarlet of a few drifting clouds that were rapidly losing their color as night encroached. While he gazed, stars escaped the vanishing daylight to shed a faint light of their own.

Unfolding his collar against the chill of a late spring evening, Quint enjoyed the quiet that was only disturbed by the horse's munching, whirring insects and a few night birds' chattering.

Deciding it was time to check in on the crew he had left in a distant pasture, Quint took his phone from his shirt pocket. The bunkhouse was on the lip of the bench high above the canyon depths. Recalling that he'd been able to pick up a cell signal here in the past, he was gratified to see a couple of bars show up so he could make a call.

Going to his list of recent calls, he touched the number for Del so he could talk with all of them.

"Where are you?" asked his top hand and friend.

"Settled in at the bunkhouse for the night," Quint replied. "How did things go for you this afternoon? Did you get your chores accomplished?" He wasn't interested in using direct language to discuss the loss of the cows to wolf predation. Although he wasn't and had never been at cross purposes with the law, he had no intention of letting an incautious word land him, Del or the kids in a compromising position opposite Fish and Wildlife.

Del was familiar with the adage regarding the growing wolf problem and how some ranchers were taking care of the situation their own way - shoot, shovel and shut-up. Cell calls weren't secure and he was ready to be cagey with his words. "Got 'er done without a problem. Everything's neat and tidy over here. How about you? Any trouble?"

"Nope. Found what I was looking for and I'm tucked in for the night at the cabin. How are the kids?"

"Fine. They are good workers getting the fence fixed and the cows checked."

"Good. Let me talk to Shaley will you?"

Del handed the phone to Quint's oldest. "Hey, Dad. Was it a good ride?" She was no slouch when it came to understanding that her father had made a perilous decision to take care of the offending wolves rather than putter around waiting for the authorities. As much trouble as the wolf population was causing ranchers in the area, the legal system could bollix up your life in a heartbeat.

"Yep. I just have one thing to take care of tomorrow so I'll be home tomorrow night or the next day. How's your camp for the night?"

"A little stingy when it comes to wood for a fire. This range didn't have a whole lot to offer but luckily it's not all that cold tonight."

"Good, can't have my girl freezing. Your grandmother would have my hide," he grinned as he thought of his mother ragging his tail for making her sweet baby suffer.

"It's a nice night out and the cows are calm."

"Great. I don't want to run down the phone batteries, so let me speak to your brother real quick. Love you."

"Sure, Dad. Love you, too."

"Hi, Pop." Cam wasn't one for conversing on the phone, even with his friends from school. He liked to keep his talk clipped with no fuss.

"Hey, Cam. Everything okay with you?"

"Sure. We're set."

"Glad to hear it. I'll catch up with you after we all get back to the house. Thanks for being a rock for your sister… and me."

"Oh, okay."

"Have a good night, Cam. Love you."

"Uh, you too, Dad."

Quint closed the call happy enough to get that much response from his son. Fourteen was an age he'd never want to relive, especially with a split family. He felt for Cam who loved his mom but had found out that he couldn't trust her. It hurt Quint deeply to see a budding young man think that he had to compartmentalize his feelings. He prayed that it wouldn't scar him so much that, when he was ready to settle down, he'd shy away from the right girl. You never knew how the actions of parents would influence a child's choices later in life and Quint hoped that Cam would be stronger for it instead of wounded by it.

After getting briefed that all was quiet and under control with his kids and the cattle had settled down, Quint called his mother, Audrey. He knew he'd had to give an accounting on the kids, Del, the cows and himself.

Luckily, she didn't give him any guff and didn't question him on why he left Shaley and Cam with Del up on the bench. Audrey knew her son to be responsible and concerned about his children, especially now that he was overseeing their upbringing without the benefit of a mother. She hadn't really understood why Kim left, but that wasn't for her to figure out. Her son was handling the situation the best he could and she trusted his judgment, even if she didn't agree with him all the time.

They covered the bases, Quint letting her know he'd probably return late the next day. Saying goodnight, he hung up and headed back inside the bunkhouse.

Turning on another battery-powered lamp to give him more light, he poured himself another cup of coffee then he checked through the supplies to see what sounded like an appetizing and easy meal. Although he was hungry, he was more tired and just wanted to fix something simple for dinner. Locating a can of chili, it didn't take him long to get it opened and heated up. Quint filled a plate and, adding some biscuits left over from last night's campout, he laid the fare on the table's worn cedar surface. Sitting on the handcrafted bench that matched the trestle table, he took his time before digging in. Elbows on the table, he sipped his coffee. He cracked a smile knowing that if his mom were there she'd slap his arms, reminding him of his manners.

Thinking of that, his attention was drawn to the wolf pups.

They'd devoured their dinner and were curled up in a tight knot of gray and tan fuzz, fast asleep without a care in the world.

You're just the tip of trouble, aren't you, thought Quint as he took a bite.

Chapter 13

Her window rolled down, Anthea took a deep breath of fresh air. Again traveling the narrow river road, they were enjoying the dramatic vistas of east Koyama County and the mountains that shared the moniker. The promontories rimming the Nacqus River canyon skirted the southern perimeter of the high prairies that had supplied generations of prime grazing for local cattlemen.

She and Gary were driving back into Nacqus village to catch up with Cressy Dillat who had arranged to guide them around a substantial spread where the owners had suffered multiple wolf attacks.

Koyama County had been built on ranching and farming and, for the most part, the region still reflected that agricultural heritage. Like so many idyllic communities across the nation, the understated beauty and quiet lifestyle attracted artists, writers and retirees to take advantage of the wide, open spaces and set up housekeeping. After selling off overpriced suburban properties for a handsome profit, transplants were flocking over the Cascades to settle in the remote eastside of the state. Slurping up traditionally productive agricultural acreage, they constructed estates, mountain chalets and modest homesteads, the majority becoming snowbird retreats.

Not that locals didn't appreciate and welcome the arrival of additional neighbors, but it perplexed oldtimers when, before long, newcomers vocalized dissatisfaction with the community. Increasingly, established agriculture operations were being pressured to buckle under to recent arrivals who complained about the very attributes of the bucolic countryside that had beckoned them. It turned out they weren't happy being wakened by crowing roosters and bawling calves or the noise of farm equipment. Nor were they thrilled with the fecund odor of manure, or being stuck behind a combine trundling down the two-lane highway, hindering their hurry.

On the other hand, they fed the deer, encouraging them to

hover in their yards where they'd become a nuisance blocking traffic and, during the rut, by bucks occasionally charging walkers on their daily constitutional.

More than one rural community had been transformed into a holiday, weekend and tourist destination by an influx of urbanites looking to escape the city. Except they brought the city with them, changing a region's complexion into what they'd fled in the first place.

The absurdity of it continually struck the Mathers' who were transplants themselves. They couldn't find sense in relocating to a pastoral setting for the view and serenity, then insist on having all the amenities of a large population center.

Anthea and Gary had moved to rural Idaho individually for a slower paced life and that was where they met. Loving the outlying communities where they settled, they preferred that the rustic flavor wasn't lost to the rising flood of Westsiders, or flatlanders as some locals called them.

The Mathers' hoped the farm communities would stay farm communities, which fired-up Anthea's ire when it came to newcomers' and Westside influence promoting wildlife preservation at the high cost of driving ranchers and farmers out of business. It was an irrational love affair with anything that was anti-capitalist even if it took food out of families' refrigerators. But then, she supposed some of the wildlife advocates would do away with refrigerators too, unless, of course, it was theirs. It had come to the point that common sense was something she rarely expected to encounter and, unfortunately, most people lived up to those expectations.

Seeing how much of this corner of Koyama County had gone unchanged for decades, it brought to mind the incongruity of city dwellers trying to conform the country to their impractical ideal of what it should be.

Musing aloud, Anthea spoke out the window more than to Gary. "You know, the reason people hold wolves in such adoration is they swathe them in this unrealistic dream of what it must be like to wander freely, taking what they want when they want. No bars or restraints on desire. Think about it," she said, turning toward him. "If you believe that ultimate happiness is doing whatever you want when you get the primal urge to do it, then a wolf's existence is perfection. Just go ahead and appropriate someone's property to satisfy your own animal craving."

Gary mulled over what she'd said. "It's a pretty basic illustration of the selfishness that we've allowed and actually encouraged in the world these days. Take what you think you need, want or deserve, without considering the value to the owner or whether they should be paid for it, especially after the property has been consumed or destroyed. Makes me think of the Occupy movement a few years ago that morphed into the Antifa riots. Overindulged trust fund babies and undisciplined youth setting up camp in public parks and trashing neighborhoods. Stealing, vagrancy, attacking the homeless, vandalizing and demolishing businesses and neighborhoods. Some of those so-called occupiers raped, looted and plundered without conscience. It's mind-blowing.

"Now the anti-anything-civilized pillagers come out, calling themselves protesters but are there purely for the conflict and, in some cases, bloodshed. Like you said, it's the typical life of a predator. What's worse are the mercenaries paid to attack anyone expressing the *wrong* opinion. I'm kind of adding to the base predator instinct with that last bit but it could be said that these anarchists, taught to believe that nothing is as important as their own emotions, fulfill the selfish role that wolves epitomize."

"Talk about a mouthful. And I thought I was growing morbidly philosophical in my spiel," laughed Anthea. "So, what would you have done if you were still on the force?"

"Truthfully? I don't know if I would have been able to hold my tongue if confronted with such blatant disrespect from obvious jerks and black-masked cowards throwing rocks, feces and urine or pepper spraying innocent bystanders. Luckily, I wouldn't have had to deal with them in the streets, being on the anti-terror task force."

"If you ask me, Occupiers and this Antifa are little more than shipped-in terrorists doing their damnedest to destroy local commerce for a few bucks or jollies," observed Anthea.

"That's a point, but the municipality would never name these guys as terrorists so I likely wouldn't have been deployed. On another level, how the activists figure they can survive without the products and services business provides is beyond me. You can only plunder until everything is gone, then you'd better be prepared to work or starve," added Gary.

"No way are they willing to do either, just move on to assault the next victims." Anthea sighed, exasperated with the whole concept. "Wolves at heart, all right."

Suspended above the entrance, and as old as the building, a 'welcome' bell tinkled when Anthea pushed open the heavy wood-framed door of the Wild River Mercantile. From somewhere within the store's depths Cressy called out the standard greeting of every busy proprietor, "Be with you in a minute!" She was explaining to her on-call assistant, who was going to keep an eye on the shop, a request involving the church group that was due to arrive while she escorted Anthea and Gary around the county.

In the rear of the building was a meeting room that Cressy made available to community groups for parties, banquets and, like tonight, fellowship groups. Nacqus was so small there was no longer a venue for neighborhood assemblies. Once the schoolhouse had been sold off and refurbished as a residence, it dispensed with the only local gathering place.

Sunday nights, two church congregations joined together for a prayer meeting in the mercantile's back room. Since she had arranged to take the Mathers' out to visit one of the ranches, May, an older widow who lived a block away in one of the few houses in town proper, was delighted to watch the store and stay to usher in the church group as they arrived. Even after fifty years of living in this remote corner of Koyama County, it took a trained ear to understand

May's English, the Chinese lilts and lisps reminiscent of her coming to America as a young war bride.

May's husband, an army corps pilot who had grown up in the valley, had died not six months before. When he'd come back from overseas with his petite Taiwanese wife, he resettled into farm life, only this time as a crop duster and hotshot firefighter. His passing had devastated his wife and children but also left a huge hole in Nacqus' society. A raconteur par excellence, he often regaled friends and visitors with blood-curdling tales involving skin-of-the-teeth redemption from unimaginable perils, not all of which were completely factual. But that hardly mattered when listening to such a gifted storyteller.

Cressy's calls needing help at the shop were May's rescue from bouts of despondence and loneliness. At 75, her children were grown and mostly relocated to the other side of the mountains, prompting her to respond immediately, thankful for the opportunity to be busy. Bantering with tourists and neighbors was a pleasant perk.

This was one of her favorite times to be asked to fill the gap at the mercantile. May usually stayed for prayer, finding it helped her deal with bereavement. And on days when Cressy's daughter was at the shop, May encouraged her to attend the study and prayer, knowing how much the young girl was also coping with loss. There may have been a wide gulf between their ages, but it was something they could both understand.

"I ought to return before the Sunday group gets here," Cressy was giving May the rundown of her plans, "but you never know what could crop up, so, if you don't mind letting them into the back to get arranged, that'd be terrific."

"Of course," May was always enthusiastic about greeting the group. She enjoyed playing hostess. When she was given a heads-up, like she had for today, she would arrive with some confection or special appetizer, usually derived from a homeland recipe. The church always appreciated the touch of Asian culture, reminding them of the larger world for which they prayed.

"And, May, would you please keep an eye on Tricia, too? I'll be leaving her here and she'll need to do her homework. That is, if she has any. The school year's ending this week, so she probably won't. Which means she's apt to be looking for something to do and that could spell trouble if she doesn't have any guidance. Maybe she can help you restock the candy in the apothecary jars. She's good at that. Just don't let her eat too much of it."

"I know. It will spoil her dinner," smiled May, not really pronouncing the 'l's.

"Not so much tonight. You know she likes to attend the church meeting, not that I understand why since there aren't many kids here, but there will be enough to eat at the potluck afterward." Cressy looked over May's shoulder at a table already set-up in the back that had one platter with aluminum foil molded over a tall mound of munchables. "What did you bring for tonight?"

"Special dim sum. My grandmother's favorite *shu mai* made with barbecued pork."

"I think that's Tricia's favorite too." She acknowledged May's shrewdness. "But you knew that."

May just smiled wider and patted Cressy's arm as she walked to the back to set-up some chairs. "You must take care of your customers. Tricia will be fine," she added with a wink.

Cressy went to meet the Mathers' who'd been occupying themselves combing through convincing faux antique dust-gatherers that, standing beside the real thing, were difficult to distinguish from the authentic. Honestly displaying the shop's wares, items were clearly marked as originals or replicas.

Admiring a turquoise-colored, blown glass insulator hailing from the early days of creosote-covered telephone poles that lined miles of dirt roads in the middle of nowhere, Anthea remarked that it would be a great addition to a friend's collection. "Toddy has a penchant for historical communication and electrical equipment. This would be useful in the classes he teaches for the home school network." She held it up to catch the light. "He has a few others but the diversity of style and color make them objects of art as well as utility." She showed it to Gary. "Don't you think?"

"Hm-hmm. He's already working with home schoolers? But

his son is only, what, three?"

"You know Toddy. He's preparing for the next generation and I don't blame him. Public schools aren't what they used to be."

"Can't argue that. I'm glad that he and Sol will be handling his son's education. Between the two of them and a well-rounded network, all the kids should benefit. He is one proud papa."

"And soon to be again, if what I hear from Lainie is correct, which I'm sure it is. Talk about communication. There are no secrets in that family."

"Really? That's terrific." Gary was truly happy for their friends in New Mexico. Anthea had been the one who introduced the couple some years back and she and Gary were tickled that they'd hit it off so well. It was an unexpected pairing but gratifying to see their friends content.

Still extending the insulator toward the light, Anthea lowered it as Cressy joined them. "They are something to look at, especially now when anyone my age or younger knows so little about the old versus new technology. All we know how to do is use a keyboard or a touch screen."

"I'd think kids growing up out here would have a closer connection to history and not be as inundated by the digital world," said Anthea.

"Nope, computers have taken over everything. You can hardly run a farm these days without a smart phone and apps. Well, you can, but it's becoming harder and harder to be 'old school.' Everything's computerized, from milking machines to pest control. Though changing pipe is still pretty much mechanical around here."

"And good work for high school kids," added Gary.

"If they'll do it," said Cressy. "What we used to do for summer jobs has become passé. Muscling water lines around hayfields? You're lucky if you can find teenagers willing to do physical labor unless they're ranch kids. Far as I'm concerned, work is work and it's good to be productive. That's why most of us still have our kids in 4H and FFA. Work habits don't grow on trees any more than money."

Anthea was intrigued and appreciative that a woman in her

mid-thirties would extol the virtues of labor. "That's refreshing to hear."

"Well, that was something my dad used to say and my daughter's heard it more than once." Changing the subject, Cressy opened her palm toward the door, "So, are we ready to go?"

"Yes, we are," Gary replied, hooking his wife's elbow with his own. "Where's the chariot?"

"We don't have to be that archaic," said Anthea. "It's the country not ancient Rome. A carriage is more like it."

"As long as you don't expect it to be horse-drawn," put in Cressy. "We want to get to the ranch before sunset."

The carriage turned out to be Cressy's weather beaten, mud-spattered, 15-year-old Jeep. Serviceable and well suited to the task of navigating gravel roads and switchbacks, she piloted the vehicle back downriver toward the ranch where she'd received permission to bring visitors.

Following the Nacqus east for approximately five miles, they came to a fork in the road, leaving the macadam behind and turning on to the high road on the north side of the canyon. Anthea watched as the road steepened and the drop-off toward the river grew more precipitous. Where they'd been passing the tree boles on the riverside, as they gained elevation the leafy green boughs coated the hillside. Before long, she was gazing down on the tops of lofty cottonwoods.

Cressy navigated the curves with the ease of familiarity, rising a few hundred feet in just a half-mile. The angle of the road's rise became less acute as they continued to ascend.

"You don't realize how rugged this country is until you get off the beaten path, do you." Gary, who was riding shotgun, looked over at Cressy as she negotiated a particularly tight turn. "How long ago was this road built?" The yawning void that was getting deeper and more treacherous was an attention getter.

"My grandfather and another rancher widened the track into a road in the mid-fifties. Before then it was a real hassle to get down-river to the homesteads. Because of that, most would only come into town about once a month for supplies, sometimes in wagons. Before this gravel one-and-a-half-lane road was engineered, it took a few days to make the trip. We've been spoiled by the combustion engine and four-wheel drive."

"That is what I'd call a rustic lifestyle," said Anthea. "Took real fortitude and determination to make a go of it out here."

"My great-grands were living proof of that but they loved it. Nana always reminisces about the cattle drives, fishing, hunting and picking the wild fruit for preserving. Though they had cultivated orchards too."

"Do you still can, Cressy?" Anthea was interested because she'd never gotten the knack of it and, in all truth, found she wasn't cut out to be a gardener or learn to put-up the harvest. She was better off letting someone else handle that end of domestic skill. Running a vacuum cleaner was more her style.

"Sometimes, but not like I did when I was first married and I never was the canning queen that Nana and even Mom were. Running a ranch encompasses all kinds of work, including canning just about everything. At least until the advent of freezers and generators to keep them going when the power goes down."

"All that's getting to be a lost art," said Anthea. "Now you can order whatever you want over the internet."

"Yes, but that won't feed you if you're way out here and can't get through six feet of snow or UPS can't reach you."

"That's when drones come in handy," cut in Gary.

"Even those can't make it through blizzard conditions," countered Cressy.

"Ya got me there."

"Lack was never a problem for us, though. The ranch house where I grew up wasn't built until 1969 and had all the amenities, including electricity and indoor plumbing, for which I am eternally grateful." She shot them a grin as she pulled out of a hairpin turn doing 15 miles an hour. "Teenage girls definitely prefer private, heated baths to braving a chilly bath house with a star-filled sky for a roof, or a plain tub in a curtained-off corner of a cabin. I was pampered with a real shower and vanity, unlike my grandmother. I got the best of both worlds."

Continuing up the grade, tires shooting rocks and pebbles to the road shoulder when there was one, they drove another four miles until Cressy turned off along a creek flowing swiftly with spring runoff. This road was basically an improved jeep trail that followed the creek bank for another mile before departing the watercourse. There, it turned to climb to the top of the slope where, looking back, the rushing stream was in sight some fifty feet below where the flat opened out of the arroyo.

Not far up the road they came to a time worn post and lintel gate constructed of three massive logs. Beyond it stretched a sizeable spread encompassing acres of grassy knolls where a spacious split-level ranch house sat back on a circular driveway. Driving through the entrance, on the left side were corrals that butted up to a horse barn. An enormous hay shed stood behind the barn, the stacked bales diminished from winter feeding to fill a fraction of the covered interior.

Next to the house was a half-acre garden where a portion was tilled and prepared for vegetable starts to be transplanted. Freezes were still a possibility into June but some of the hardier plant varieties were already in the ground, crowned by tender shoots.

Four horses capered in a paddock near the outbuilding that housed the farm equipment - among which they could see two different sized tractors, a hay baler, two four-wheelers and a repair shop.

"Welcome to the 3C Ranch," announced Cressy as they passed under the gate with the name spelled out on a stylized metal sign riveted onto the beam spanning the entry: Cripple Calf Creek Ranch. "This used to be my home."

CHAPTER 14

Taken aback, neither Gary nor Anthea had anticipated Cressy's throwaway comment as they drove through the gate. They did hear the wistfulness, tinged with regret, buried in her voice. Anthea was cued from the first that the owner of Wild River Mercantile had a profound story, and absorbing the breadth of the ranch they'd just entered, she was thrown for a loop. An adage of Anthea's was that 'everyone has a story,' and often a good one. This tale, however, promised to be a knockout. She was about to learn why.

Unwilling to press their guide for details too soon, Anthea let Cressy open the conversation. She'd say more if the listeners allowed her to recount her saga at her own pace, encouraging her to be comfortable letting them in on what was obviously personal and, Anthea surmised, tragic.

"I grew up here. What you see is just a fraction of what the family owned and operated at one time. The ranch was split among four brothers and a sister back in the sixties and this parcel of six thousand acres was my mother's inheritance. She was an only child and got this from her mom who was the one girl of the five siblings that divided the ranch." She released a deep sigh.

"Mom and Dad retired to town because of his health issues, so my husband and I took over the operation which included leasing my uncles' adjoining acreage. Everything was going fairly smoothly - if you understand the amount of hard work it takes to make ends meet. Ranching is a 24-7 enterprise, hardly a get rich scheme or an unscrupulous plan to destroy the land. Seriously, I don't get how some people come to such ridiculous conclusions.

"We were getting by okay until there was an accident and he died suddenly." Cressy swallowed before finishing her thought. "I was faced with a legal dilemma and resulting financial situation that, for a number of reasons, I couldn't handle on my own. Long story short - I was forced to sell my family legacy."

She pulled to a stop in front of the house. "Fortunately, I found a buyer who was willing to keep this a producing cattle ranch. What was left after settling up some issues, I used to buy the mercantile and a small house near town. Tricia and I have been able to manage all right." She opened the Jeep's door and invited her passengers to step out. "Today, you get to meet the new owners of the Cripple Calf Creek and see what wolves are really capable of destroying."

Anthea's arched eyebrow, forming a question without asking prompted Cressy to add, "You'll hear it all, I promise. It's time the public was fully informed how devastating government wolf policy really is to ranching, and I have a gut feeling you're the one to do it."

Anthea's grip tightened on the door as she swung down from the car. "Whoa, I hope I can live up to that."

"I looked you up online."

"Uh-oh. I hope the press photos were flattering."

"No photos but plenty of articles. What you've written is good. Maybe this time something'll get stirred up." She paused for a moment then added in a lowered voice and with a palpable determination, "I think I'm ready for the fight."

As they walked up the flagstone footpath the front door opened abruptly, framing a small woman in her fifties, dark hair cut in a no-nonsense pageboy that curled around her jaw line. Dusting off her jeans and pink oxford workshirt, the lady of the house then lifted one hand to shield her eyes from the sun and waved them onto the porch with the other.

Cressy made the introductions before the three of them had reached the steps. "Anthea Keller and Gary Mathers, this is Joan Laken. She and her husband Chris own the 3C." They exchanged handshakes and congenial nods.

"Thank you for giving us the opportunity to tour your property," said Gary. "My wife and I are particularly interested in learning more about how wolves have affected cattle operations out here."

"So I hear from Cressy," replied Joan. "I don't know if you

planned it, but you couldn't get a better witness to the failure wolf policy has been than this woman. She's lived it all."

"I haven't told them the whole story yet," said Cressy. "It's taken a long time to get my head straight about what, if anything, could be done at this late date. And I probably would have just shelved it forever if these two hadn't just appeared at the shop."

"Fate?'

"More like serendipity."

"Well, you've come to the right place to get the mother of all wolf stories but I'm not the one to tell it," said Joan. "I can tell you what problems we've had since taking over the ranch. And we're not the only ones. Chris is out on the north range now checking out possible wolf sign reported by the range rider."

"That's a good place to start," said Anthea. "Tell me what a range rider does. We may have an idea on some of this stuff but talk to us as if we know nothing."

"Which isn't so far from the truth," grinned Gary. "We're just a couple of misplaced city folk."

"Flatlanders," laughed Joan. "I know, that's what they called us even though we'd been ranching all our lives. Just not this far out. Chris and I are originally from Central California, up around Red Bluff."

"That's nice country," said Anthea who grew up in the Los Angeles Basin. "Why'd you leave?"

"What you'll hear from most farmers and ranchers down there - government policy shutting off water access and grazing rights. It's a true shame that some of the richest agricultural land in the United States is being cordoned off, making it impractical to work." Joan made a sweeping gesture with her right hand, palm out, as if she were literally pushing the thought away. "That's for another day, come in and sit. Cressy and I will do our best to be informative."

Closing the screen door behind them, the cool, dark interior came into better focus as their eyes adjusted from the bright midday sun to take in the cedar paneled foyer. Swiveling around, Anthea tried to note what would have remained unchanged from Cressy's residency to get a better feel for her past and how it would color the story she had to tell.

"Sit down," invited Joan. "I've already set out some iced tea. Help yourself and sit where you like."

While Cressy and Gary poured glasses for themselves and Anthea, she opened her little satchel and extracted a digital recorder. "I hope you don't mind but I'd like to record this so I don't make a mistake or forget something important when and if it comes to writing." She accepted an iced tea from Gary who sat next to her on the cowhide sofa. "But if you'd rather I didn't, just say so. But I'll warn you, I don't know if my shorthand is reliable anymore. I've lost the habit since the advent of iPads, iPods and iPhones."

"I didn't think anyone knew how to take shorthand anymore," said Joan. "That's a lost art."

"More like a dead language," quipped Gary. "But if Hebrew could be resurrected to become the state language of Israel, I suppose somebody's bound to find a purpose for the long lost secretarial code. Start a secret society, maybe."

Anthea rolled her eyes and held out the recorder. "Do I get to spare myself carpal tunnel?"

"Oh, go right ahead. This is for posterity after all, right Cressy?"

"Hm-hmm," she bobbed her head in assent after taking a sip of tea.

"Right then… range riders," said Anthea, clicking on the recorder.

"Essentially, they cover a vast area of Koyama County looking for evidence of wolf activity, tracking them and fending them off from bothering stock," said Joan. "It's really too great an area to travel and like taking a swat at a bear. It doesn't do a whole lot of good when even the range rider is restrained from shooting wolves unless they practically trip over them in the act of tearing into a stock animal."

"They're paid by Fish and Wildlife but not very much. Last I heard, $6500 was allotted for the position which is seasonal," said Cressy. "One guy quit because he couldn't sustain his family on the pittance. Usually, they trailer either a horse or four-wheeler into a sector. Each day they check a download of a satellite feed from the radio collars on some of the wolves, though only a fraction of wolves have been caught and collared. Then there's the fact that the collars last only so many years, so they can't be certain about locating that many of the wolves, or even how many there are. It's a guessing game to some degree."

"Talking to the guys who've worked this area, telemetry feeds don't always come through for whatever reason, so it can be hit or miss whether they're checking an area where wolves have been or might be located," Joan explained. "They look for signs of depredation, like a concentration of scavenger birds.

"If a range rider does happen upon a downed cow or other animal that shows signs of predation, they first contact the rancher with cattle in the area. Often enough, the attacks have been on private land. After that, they call the game commission and the sheriff's department. Depending on where the officials are at the time of the call or the press of work, it could take them anywhere from a couple hours, in some cases, to a couple days to get out to the scene. The last sort of situation can be due to a veterinarian being called in for examination or necropsy, and the ones that work with Fish and Wildlife are connected to the universities so they're not local even within a hundred miles."

"Is there anything the range riders are allowed to do in the way of prevention?"

"Not a lot. Wolf protocol is for anything non-lethal to haze wolves away from cattle if the rider comes across some threatening stock. The rancher is required to have fladry and use some other techniques that are virtually worthless in scaring off wolves," said Joan.

"That's an understatement," interrupted Cressy. "Wolves are smart enough to know the difference between waving bits of plastic and a real menace to their lives. And it's just not possible to fence off hundreds of acres and string flipping flags on all of it, let alone a portion of the pastures."

"You can't possibly comply with all the techniques to be

considered fully compliant. Here's one - what they call RAGs. A radio activated guard, which is a box that emits noises and light show when a radio-collared wolf is in the vicinity. First of all, like I said, very few of the wolves have collars; secondly, the sounds and light don't do much to frighten them and third, who can afford to put as many RAGs out as would be needed to protect, if you want to call it that, hundreds or thousands of acres. Now that's on private land. If you're grazing on leased forest service land, forget the whole thing. USFS rarely repairs fencing which is constantly being broken down by elk herds."

"What I've been able to learn from you and others makes me wonder who devises these techniques thinking they're functional," interjected Gary. "Unfortunately, I can guess they come from wildlife management types who get their expertise from textbooks and a few limited research projects. It's the same in law enforcement that's tied the hands of officers. Every bit of it is political correctness that hurts far more than it helps. Not that they'd hear our two-cents, but a dose of reality is sorely needed to educate the think tanks."

"Personally, I agree. The reality we're forced to deal with is the one created by people trying to develop a solution for the outside world from inside a bunker," Joan said.

"Well put," added Gary. "That perfectly describes a think *tank*."

Redirecting the conversation, Anthea asked if they could tell her about a specific incident.

Joan gave Cressy a look as if to ask is she wanted to handle this one. Cressy shook her head and offered an opener, "You had to call in the authorities a couple months ago. What about that?"

"Right. We had a pack raid our herd back in March where we lost two pregnant cows, ready to deliver, and their fetuses, of course. What wolves do to animals can be repugnant, feeding off of them while they're still alive, and these cows were torn open, the calves pulled out and eaten."

"I just heard about that - that wolves don't kill their prey before eating them." Anthea was appalled. "Isn't that unusual?"

"Not for wolves. They don't always kill for food, either.

Sometimes it's just to kill. And don't let a wolf advocate tell you differently. It's a well-established fact of certain predators that attacking and killing is almost sport, sort of like keeping their skills honed. Hawks do the same," said Cressy.

"The rest of the cows were terrorized," Joan went on with the narrative. "Five more miscarried which raised our losses dramatically, upwards of eighty-thousand dollars for starters. We're talking papered progeny sired from a prize bull. And that doesn't take into account the value of later generations that could have come from the offspring."

Joan described the depositions taken by the sheriff's deputies and then the further two days of ODFW combing over the area trying to prove, though she used the word 'disprove,' that wolves were the perpetrators. After the carcasses were sent to the lab to test the wounds for evidence of wolf bite marks and DNA, which took more than a month, Fish and Wildlife begrudgingly conceded the damage might have been inflicted by wolves. But they still wouldn't attest to that as fact in their paperwork and, in the end, officials denied confirmation that it was wolf depredation.

"It was a circus that wasted everybody's time, put Chris behind in his work and we got nothing but a determination that an unknown predator killed our cows and traumatized the herd, depleting it. And, after a couple of months of mucking around with this, no compensation for the loss was forthcoming. Not that it would cover much anyway. The amount is meager because the groups that put together the reimbursement program have no clue the value of cattle, it's replacement or progeny value." Joan huffed. "They think a cow is a cow is a cow is a steer and can't see beyond their own vegan nose.

"I may be overstating the malice toward beef producers to a degree, but the fact is, out here the groups that call themselves friends of the ranchers are actually working in opposition to them. They're more interested in championing the wildlife in hopes of making this whole region a national park." Joan leaned forward in her fervor, "We saw it happening in California. Every time you turned around, good grazing land, the best rangeland was being gobbled up by land trusts and national monument designations." She paused to take a drink. "And no, I'm not exaggerating. The last one I heard about was Berryessa Snow Mountain where 360,000 acres are being locked away from grazing and other public use. Think about the size. That's ten times the size of neighboring Gaston Buttes.

"There's a battle right here in 'River City,' and if ranchers and farmers don't pull together to meet the opposition, we're going to lose. We've already virtually lost our rights to work our land as we see fit according to time-honored, successful stewardship." She sighed. "If that's not a problem, I don't know what is."

"Gotcha. So, tell me how these organizations that call themselves friends of the ranchers aren't what they say they are," directed Anthea.

"Rangeland Defense, they call themselves. Why they have any role in the wolf issue is a mystery to me but they're the ones who say that they support ranchers and volunteer compensation for stock losses. Problem is, they don't know or ignore the market value of stock. Compensation for a cow is determined by an unrealistic formula devised by Fish and Wildlife that also contributes a pittance to the compensation fund. In Idaho they came up with a number like $268 per head lost to depredation. That doesn't pay for the animal's feed in a year. They try to make it look like they have a sense of fairness when Rangeland Defense is rabidly anti-ranching. Groups like Terra Ferus, that owns the Gaston Buttes just over yonder," Joan waved her hand off to the north of their property, "believe that grazing is and has destroyed the prairies here. The truth is, the bunchgrass that they claim to be preserving is actually dwindling because, get this, in order for the seeds to germinate properly, they *need* to go through the digestive tracts of a ruminant."

"I don't mean to sound ignorant, but I am," said Gary. "Explain a ruminant. Is that just cattle or other animals, too?"

"Since it's not a term we use often, if you'll go ahead I'll have your definition on tape," Anthea lightly touched the digital recorder.

"Sure. A ruminant is a cud-chewing animal that has four stomachs like cattle, buffalo, antelope, deer, etc."

"Or, giraffes," threw in Cressy with a grin, recalling Gary's jibe about Anthea's non-collecting habit. "If you happen to be growing bunchgrass in Africa."

Joan wondered at the remark that she figured must relate to some previous conversation, shrugged her shoulders and went on. "All these organizations and government agencies must know the cost of raising and breeding cattle despite their undervaluation. I don't think it's any revelation that the environmental movement is couched in the cloak of caring about the land and preserving it when groups like Terra Ferus are basically real estate brokers.

"I'm not sure if it's common knowledge that it's a subsidiary of Nature's Wilds, an international real estate conglomerate operating as a conservancy. All these groups, and many more, have weaseled their way into the land protection racket, making it look like they're ranch and farm advocates, all the while undercutting private land ownership and production. They're major lobbyists and money movers promoting massive regulation that deliver deathblows to ranchers, resulting in foreclosure or running people out of business and off their property. Nature's Wilds, in particular, has been caught with their hand in the cookie jar so many times that even the Washington Post ran a whole series of exposés about them in 2003 or 2004, I think. Not that it matters, they scrubbed it from their website."

"I ran across that when I was researching them on another issue in Idaho," said Anthea. "Read the articles before they were deleted in, let's see, 2012, maybe? Always wondered who got to them. Not that it matters now that Jeff Bezos owns the paper and uses it to promote his own agenda." She shook her head, "Sorry for the digression. Go on."

"Then you know how, after the landowner is beaten down to the point of having to get out from under, they swoop in and purchase the property at firesale prices. Then they resell it to the USFS, which adds to the so-called public lands while merrily pocketing the profits. What really should get taxpayers' goat is that Nature's Wilds and other conservancies manage to wheedle money out of state and federal government coffers to bankroll the initial purchases, like they did with the Oregon state lottery allocating funds to buy thousands of acres for Gaston Buttes."

"Yes, we do know what you're alluding to." agreed Anthea. "We ran into a similar scam in Idaho about eight years ago. Nature's Wilds was running it and it looks like they're still in the business of using ancillary organizations to keep the deals going."

"Like I said, it's a racket," said Joan. "And wolves are just a shill used to facilitate the conversion from private property to government-owned lands."

"I was really lucky to find Joan and Chris to purchase this property and keep it a working ranch when I was forced to sell. No way on earth was I going to allow Terra Ferus to buy me out even though they were breathing down my neck, just like they'd already pressured some of my relatives into selling," Cressy said.

"This is a problem that's occurring all across the States. The huge mess BLM forced with the rancher in Nevada, undermining grandfathered grazing rights," Gary brought up a legal battle that was being dragged out in federal court. "Turned out the it involved a land swap engineered by Senate leader at the time, Harry Reid, to turn a profit for a Chinese solar company and his son, who appeared to be the middleman. They rearranged acreage that supposedly harbored tortoises, I believe it was, by designating it as protection for an endangered species. That way they could renege on the grazing rights for the Bundy family. What most all media overlooked in their zeal to paint Bundy as a deadbeat for not paying grazing fees, was that the Nevada Constitution supported his argument. One columnist got the story right but, as usual, was ignored."

"And until recently it was bogged down in federal court, keeping the father and sons in jail and traumatizing them. I've read credible reports of atrocious mistreatment," added Anthea. "Looks like, finally, deception for withholding discovery by the feds prosecuting the Bundy's was brought to light and the judge called a mistrial, freeing the defendants. About time."

Leaning back into the couch, Joan tied up her part of the interview with, "There is something seriously wrong with what individuals are facing just for trying to bring product to market that every person in this nation needs to survive - food.

"Cressy told me she'll take you out on the property to show you around, view the workings of the ranch, some of the herds and the sites where the wolf incidents occurred." She brushed the thighs of her jeans and started to get up. Wish I could go with you but I've got appointments I can't shirk and Cressy knows the details, having lived the worst part of the wolf situation. She also knows this land better than anyone else."

Reaching out to shake hands with Gary and then Anthea, Joan iterated her appreciation. "It's a relief to have a journalist without an environmentalist agenda take a look at our wolf dilemma. We've been visited by other writers but they always slant their articles against us. No matter what we showed them as evidence, they could never think of wildlife as being a problem. It's always that man is a perpetrator of evil against nature. They forget that they, like us, as members of Mankind, are part of nature not its adversary."

Walking out to the Jeep, Anthea asked Cressy if there's much changed about the house since she sold it.

"The Lakens have made it theirs in a lot of ways, which is good. Makes it easier to visit without having to see furnishings that bring back memories." At the end of the path, she turned around and studied the home where she'd grown up and started her married life. "Sometimes, heartache is best left behind with all the things that went with it. At first I didn't want to leave, but walking those hallways and rooms feeling the emptiness close in… Now I see it's all for the better. A new start made moving on more palatable."

Pivoting to open the driver's door, Cressy adjusted her tone to be upbeat. "All aboard, folks. Time to see what's changing the face of ranching and it's not automation."

CHAPTER 15

Cressy put the Jeep in gear and turned north out of the circular drive to bump along the ranch road toward Pine Creek. Well-maintained, new gravel had been laid and graded, filling in the worst of the gouged roadbed that rivulets of melting snow had left behind. It was an annual process and another cost of doing business. Like other larger outfits, the 3C had its own gravel pit to supplement ranch income by providing area residents with crushed rock. Being self-sustaining included more than having a fruitful garden, acres of hayfields and a few milk cows.

Interested in knowing more about Cressy's life makeover, Anthea was burning to ply her with questions but held off until they were well away from the house. Bit by bit, she figured their guide would spill her story how everything had turned upside-down, plunging a prosperous cattle business into ruin. Having survived her own reincarnation, Anthea's sympathies were deeply stirred to convey what she was sure would be a compelling tale.

Patches of wild lupines and carpet blocks of buttercups painted the verdant hillsides purple and bright yellow on their way to the Pine Creek sector. Avoiding granite outcroppings, the road made more frequent bends as it rose in elevation until they reached a turnoff onto a ranch track that required Cressy to engage four-wheel drive. This seemed as good a time as any to open up the conversation.

"You said that you moved closer to town after selling to the Lakens. What kind of a place is it?"

"Modest and very different from all this," she waved her left arm out of the open window, as if to gather in the whole horizon. "It's a humble, kind of ramshackle two-story about a hundred years old, not far upriver from Nacqus on forty acres of good pasture. Kept some cows so my daughter wouldn't lose the essence of her roots and our family connection to the land. It's a legacy that I've watched too many kids throw away in their zeal to get away from the country and onto something new or exciting, like many of my friends did." Reflectively, Cressy went on, "They forget where they came from and lose touch with what's important. I'm hoping that won't be Tricia but we can't make that decision for our children, I guess."

"No, but you can instill principles that will guide them well in the future. And, more than that, you can stand up for the right things so they have a future."

"That's part of the reason why I didn't move all the way to town. Tricia may be just ten but she's learning about ranching and how agriculture is really the backbone of our nation."

"It is. But it's also a culture that those of us who grew up in the city don't fathom very easily," agreed Anthea.

"Our schools don't teach it like they should, either," added Gary. "Leaves us without a full understanding of how America came about or what it is now. While we were researching the land trusts in Idaho, it was interesting to speak with ranchers, farmers and loggers about being good stewards of the land. Even Joan used that word earlier. I hadn't really thought about stewardship in that respect but many of them said they were guided by their faith."

"Can't say that I ever looked at it from that angle. Mostly, it was tradition to be passed on to new generations." She briefly looked across at Gary ensconced in the front passenger seat. "Did they explain what they meant by faith?'

"They were Christians mostly," continued Gary. "A few of them gave scripture to back up their thinking that using the land properly was both a gift and a responsibility. Definitely a different perspective than the guilt-based environmental ideas being taught in public schools."

Cressy shrugged as she downshifted. "My folks were church-goers, taking us when we could get to town, but I never made that kind of connection. Possibly because I wasn't that interested. I just accepted the idea that you honored and took care of the land so that it can take care of you. Common sense, you know? It's more or less what the Indians believe."

"It is simple at its core and sensible," agreed Anthea. "Unlike the strange mindset that man should have zero impact or influence on the earth due to his, or our, evil intent to use everything for personal gain. Like Joan said, for some reason they think man isn't a part of nature, which we are, whether or not you believe we are God's creation or a random occurrence. Either way, we're part of the whole picture, not an outside influence."

"Nah. If you believe man is different and something other than part of the natural world then you have to believe that we're literally from another planet," concurred Cressy.

Gary couldn't resist. "Maybe that's where the 'men are from Mars, women are from Venus' idea comes from," eliciting a *you did - n't really say that* look from his wife and a verbal groan from the driver. Putting on an innocent grin, he just said, "Well?"

"Okay, if you're gonna crack that window, let's go whole hog with the alien routine," said Anthea. "You know that super-genius Stephen Hawking, in his vehemence to deny the existence of God, has come out in defense of the theory that life on earth was the planting of interstellar spores. Guess even he can't quite accept the improbability of random chemicals combining to create life forms, that they had to come from someplace. His and Francis Crick's idea of intelligent design is limited to alien transplants on earth." She rolled her eyes. "For being touted as the most brilliant men alive, it boggles my mind how they could swallow something so densely preposterous as the theory of Panspermia."

"I haven't come across that. Hawking believes what?" Cressy was incredulous.

"We may have really gotten off the beaten path here, but thinking there's a greater possibility that alien seeds were deliberately deposited or accidentally arrived by meteorite than believing in a creator is outlandish."

"I assume you meant to add, 'No pun intended,'" laughed Gary.

Jolting down the dirt track brought them into a wide field where the cows placidly moved out of the way as the Jeep slowly bounced through the herd. Some of them stopped to stare at the vehicle while others ignored the interlopers, heads down, better occupied with pulling and chewing the tall grass.

A rocky promontory formed a stunning backdrop of towering basalt columns, bristling pines singularly and in pairs sprouting from the crags. Over that crest lay thousands of acres of choice prairie, only a scrap of it remaining in the hands of independent cattlemen. The rest had been swallowed up by a land preserve.

As they moved further into the field, Cressy pointed out a draw over to the right and began recounting a story from rote, her voice taking on a detached quality that was both eerie and heartrending at the same time. It was evident to her passengers that the only way she could keep an even keel was to put distance between her emotions and the facts. This was the wall of protection she'd erected after having to give evidence in public more than once. Cressy knew it painted her as indifferent and calculating, but it was her only defense from capitulating to a flood of tears.

Not willing to allow any details to get lost because her personal sentiments could interfere with her notation, Anthea pulled out her recorder to capture the whole tale. Relying on her or Gary's memory wasn't a responsible alternative. The witness' words on tape were the best corroboration for anything she would write.

"My husband had just come back from repairing fence not far from here. He'd left the area maybe a half-hour before he got a notice from Miles, the range rider, that a telemetry signal had just come in. The first thing they do, like Joanie told you, is contact the rancher who might be affected by the wolf whose collar was detected. So Miles, the range rider, texted Terry and he immediately took off for Pine Creek without thinking to tell me where he was going." Cressy stopped the deliberate narrative for a moment.

"I'd known where he'd been all afternoon. He'd kept me updated. It was a habit with us since we didn't have a lot of help on the ranch. But this one time when it might have made all the difference, he neglected to call me because he was in too much of a rush to get to the scene." Cressy swallowed to regain her voice.

"He rode out here with only one thing on his mind, I guess. To catch the wolf, and probably wolves since they rarely hunt alone, in the act." She turned around to look at her listeners. "You've heard enough to know that if you don't arrive when they're attacking, you're SOL as far as ODFW is concerned. And even then, if you show up with video and obvious wolf prints and teeth marks, they won't believe it could possibly be that one of their precious species would molest a defenseless cow, sheep or horse." She bit back the vitriol. "Well, that kind of talk will get me nowhere. Not that being polite and withholding judgment with the wolf coordinators has made any difference in the long run."

Shrugging off the anger that was creeping up her gullet, Cressy opened the Jeep door and said, "Let's get out here."

She walked through the midst of the munching cows, trampling the grass and brush in a long stride to reach a spot that had no distinguishing features except a fieldstone marker.

"This is where it happened. Where I sat with Terry, holding his body, and right next to him was a dead wolf that he'd shot before he was crushed under the weight of his own horse." She looked at Anthea. "That's all we could figure had happened after going over the scene. When I got here he was already dead from internal bleeding, his ribs broken. His horse stood over him, haunches scratched up and his own legs bleeding from claw and bite marks. Don't get me wrong, it wasn't the horse's fault, I'm sure. That is the best horse Terry ever owned. He called him Minuteman and I still have him with me at the new place."

She turned back to the stacked stone monument. "There were wolf tracks everywhere around where Terry lay. And just over there," she pointed about twenty yards away, "Was a half-dead cow, entrails ripped out and the wolf that had been feeding on her was shot through the head right beside her. Terry had killed two of them before he died, but it looked like two more had gotten away."

Anthea and Gary said nothing to interrupt Cressy. Visiting the site was all the prompting she needed to talk about the incident and no words from them could alleviate the evident pain she was experiencing.

Pulling herself together, Cressy went on. "There were four wolves and only one was collared, the one that killed the cow. The spoor was everywhere, clear markings but a lot of it indistinguishable because so many prints were on top of each other.

"One dead cow, a herd of sixty head that were traumatized and many would be too damaged to be of value. My husband was killed in the skirmish. The authorities, after the investigation was complete, refused compensation for any of the destroyed cattle. The reasoning, in all their combined wisdom," she looked skyward shaking her head, "was that Terry had unlawfully taken two wolves. The topper? They charged my dead husband fines for killing them." Cressy ground her teeth as she delivered the last sentence.

Gary's jaw clenched when he heard her tale and Anthea's literally dropped open in disbelief. If Anthea thought there were no words to contribute before, now she was absolutely speechless.

"That wasn't the end of it. The nightmare began with Terry's death. It wasn't enough that we were denied compensation for the cattle but, because this occurred before wolves were delisted as endangered species by the state, which just happened - and you know that although the state finally removed them, the feds still haven't in part of Oregon - there were other fines and charges levied against Terry. A couple of environmental groups brought lawsuits against me as the surviving owner of the ranch for destroying endangered species. Hard to believe, but they won in court. All the court costs and time had emptied the accounts and kept me from working the ranch, so liens were placed against all the property. We, I mean 'I' since Terry was gone, was left to pay compensation to organizations that had no stake in this except calling themselves wildlife advocates."

She took a breath. "They stole everything without risking or investing a dollar or a dime's worth of sweat. Thieves hiding behind thieves; that's the government and environmentalists using wolves to cover their theft."

There were a few large rocks in the pasture and Cressy flumped down onto one, reliving the event was taking its toll. Crossing one booted foot over her knee, she worked the leather at her ankle with the fingers of both hands as if the action would calm her.

"I don't know that anything's going to change soon when it comes to the feds. Fish and Wildlife play hardball and ODFW's one of their star players. Mikey Stromberg, the gal from US Wildlife Services, hasn't got a compassionate or courteous bone in her body. She sees things from the invented viewpoint of animals, as if anyone really knew how a wolf's, cougar's or moose' mind works. She seems to think they're vulnerable babes in the woods that need human protection from human predators, which she believes are ranchers, loggers and miners." She looked at Gary and Anthea, flopping her hands open in exasperation, quirking a corner of her mouth to mock the eye-rolling condescension that nature defenders give to free enterprise advocates. "We're the ones destroying wolf habitat on whim and, though she had the good sense not to verbalize it, she implied that Terry got his just desserts. The sentiment fueled the feds, ODFW and the tagalong land conservancies to embark on a "Get Dillat" campaign."

Dropping her hands into her lap, she continued, "You wouldn't believe how many people piled onto the PR gravy train. Terra Ferus hauled in all kinds of contributions to buy up even more land in the county by throwing me, my dead husband and my daughter, there's no other way to say it, to the wolves. We were convicted in the press, most of it coming from the Westside. There were even people who came out and protested against me and Terry as wolf-killers in front of the ODFW office when I went in for a meeting with the coroner's report in hand.

"The authorities blamed Terry for his own death and, as I said, charged him with the unlawful taking of wolves without a permit. The fines were outrageous because they were a so-called endangered species. That has changed since then for this side of the state. The fine is now a fraction of that because they've compromised with ranchers that wolves are posing a problem out here. Then there were the legal fees, the judgment against us favoring wolf advocates and the fact that they had me at meeting after meeting so the work of the ranch wasn't getting done."

Cressy got up and walked over to the stacked stones that memorialized the place where Terry died. "Mom and Dad couldn't help because of Dad's health, though they tried. Some neighbors came in for roundup but they had their ranches to run. The result was that I couldn't keep the property. They almost got what they wanted." Her voice trailed off as she ran her fingers over the stone that crowned the stack.

Not being able to restrain herself anymore, Anthea finally asked, "What was that?"

"The land. Terra Ferus was nipping at my heels to sell them my ranch. I refused and had a friend hunting high and low for a buyer who would keep it to raise beef, not llamas or a deer park. He finally found the Lakens, bless their hearts. They saved me from bankruptcy and the land trusts from getting their grubby hands on my family's legacy. I just couldn't let that happen." She turned around to face the couple that had heard some bizarre and poignant stories in recent years, but this was one for the books.

After a spell of quiet, listening to the cows moving through the hay and the quail hooting at one another, Anthea broke the silence. "I don't know if it will make much difference now, but, if you're willing, I'd like to work on getting the whole story out. It's a crime that it's so far after the fact. That doesn't mean that it can't have an impact, especially since there's such pressure on the current administration to dial back the overreach of federal regulation. Your experience is the perfect vehicle to show how government uses any means, or animals and plants, to constrict the free market that is America's lifeblood. Grandiose as that sounds, it's true."

"What saddens me," said Gary, "is the inability or unwilling-ness of the sheriff to thwart what appears to be a miscarriage of jus-tice."

"I don't know what the sheriff could have done," said Cressy. "They were there to document the scene, more than anything else. If the sheriff had any jurisdiction over the situation, he didn't do anything about it. He capitulated to ODFW and Wildlife Services' control over the investigation."

"I worked for a municipal police agency but I'm familiar with the powers of a sheriff and, if anyone bothered to find out and implement it, they'd realize that a sheriff's authority is actually greater than that of the federal government."

Cressy turned her head to see the tall man, sharp gray eyes peering at her sympathetically. She hadn't really taken in his military bearing, disguised under a façade of laid-back cool. Anthea, on the other hand, was a little firebrand of righteous energy, topped by dark, barely controlled tresses highlighted with strands of varicolored grays. They were quite a mismatched pair, but trustworthy. Already, she felt better for having begun the process of depositing her story with someone who could generate an audience and, hopefully make a difference.

"So, why is it that sheriffs allow themselves to be buffaloed by the state and feds?"

"Now that's a question that would take days to answer, and then we still wouldn't have the whole picture," said Gary. Changing direction, he asked, "The incident that Joan talked about with her husband Chris, where did that occur? Anywhere around here?"

"Actually, it wasn't far from here. My guess is that the wolves have figured out that game is plentiful here, and that includes the ungulates that roam through our pasture, knocking down the fences. You see, that was what Terry and Chris had been doing, fixing fences that had been plowed over by the elk herds that are also getting out of control." She paused. "No thanks to Terra Ferus and how they manage Gaston Buttes.

"I'll take you to where Chris found his dead cattle."

Before they walked back to the Jeep, Cressy concluded the saga of the lost 3C ranch. As she placed her hand atop the stone capping the crude shrine, Anthea saw a cross carved into its face.

"While Terry's dad was here from Colorado for the services, he brought Tricia up here, he rode Minutemen and she was on her pony. She was pretty good on a horse at seven," added Cressy proudly. "They built this together on the spot where Terry passed away. Brian Dillat's a preacher who travels holding cowboy church the other side of the Rockies so we don't see him much. He helped Tricia through some of the roughest time when I was basically a basket case. It didn't help her any when I was trying to stay cool and collected so I didn't come apart at the seams." Under her breath, she said, "Except I did."

She picked up a different stone. This one was polished but still large enough not to roll from its place next to the top stone. It also had a cross engraved on it.

Replacing it, she finished her train of thought, "I don't know how we'd have managed if he hadn't been here for the first couple months."

"Much as I fought government pressure forcing me to sell the family ranch, I guess you can see why I had to pull up stakes. Every waking moment was reliving the horror of finding Terry in the field with his horse standing guard over him." She took a deep breath and exhaled slowly. "Thank God Tricia didn't see any of it - she was at my mother's - and I wasn't about to put her through any more anguish than necessary. She'd already lost her father and watched me struggle with the consequences.

"It galls me day and night that, although I was able to keep them from getting title to the land... they won this round."

CHAPTER 16

Quint woke up with the dawn, the sun's rays penetrating the sagging waves of the ancient glass windowpanes in the old Ramshead Creek bunkhouse. Collapsing onto a cot after eating, he'd slept so hard that he found himself frozen in the same position where he'd landed.

Petrified in place might be more like it. His body was cramped from the physical labor of riding, hauling carcasses and shoveling dirt. The one thing he was thankful for was that he'd fallen asleep on his back and not in some twisted pose that would have made it near impossible to unbend. He slowly pushed himself to stretch and breathe life into his cemented muscles.

After a few moments, Quint rolled onto his side and sat up on the edge of the cot, elbows on his knees and scrubbing his scalp with his fingers to stimulate brain activity.

"Coffee," was all he said as he pushed off the bed and made his way over to stoke the embers in the stove back to life.

While he was reloading the enamel coffee pot, he looked over at the makeshift pen he'd constructed for the wolf pups. He'd nearly forgotten their presence until he saw them draped over one another, still conked out. He wondered if they'd been stuck in the same position all night too. *But it won't bother them. They don't have the years of being beat up by work, weather and miles.*

He stretched his arms overhead and groaned aloud which woke the little guys, their eyes popping open. Raising their heads, they sniffed the air and stretched themselves, taking no notice how their paws stuck in each other's eyes and snouts. Standing up and shaking their coats, they started walking around the enclosure and snuffling the ground.

"Looks like you need to go outside," said Quint. Opening the door first, he went back and reached over the barrier, picking them up by their scruffs and carrying them outside to take care of business, which, to his surprise, they did as if on command. He watched them for a few minutes to see what they'd do being in a completely new environment and not having an adult to nudge them, keeping his gun to hand in case one of them ran off. He'd shoot it before taking a chance that it would escape, becoming lunch for a raptor, or growing up in the wild and harassing stock as a predator itself.

The male was a bit more intrepid than the female but neither one had the temerity to travel more than a few feet in any direction, continually smelling the air and investigating the grass and plants around the bunkhouse.

Hearing the coffee bubbling on the stove, Quint recaptured the duo and put them back into their pen. He needed coffee and to think through his plan for the day because, until now, he didn't really have one.

Filling his mug with fresh brew, he left the pups to themselves and went outside to check on his horse. It was decision time. Before he'd finished feeding his mount, the day was laid out in his mind. What he'd determined to do would tick off his neighbors and fellow ranchers - at least he assumed it would if they ever found out, which he planned to never happen - but he couldn't think how else to take care of the situation. He knew what he *should* do but, frankly, just couldn't bring himself to take that step.

Man, you are losing your edge or getting old. I don't know which, thought Quint.

No matter. He needed to get himself back to the ranch, which meant getting a move on before the sun rose above the trees. He had someone he needed to see in another state.

While he drank his coffee and chomped another leftover biscuit, he checked the battery life on his phone. The icon indicated it was half-charged. Glad he hadn't drained the power, he called Del for an update, and to give one.

"We got things squared away without trouble," relayed Del. "Didn't take but an hour or so to plant those hides and posts, ya know? Cows calmed down fine after an uneventful night. How 'bout you? Got everything handled okay?"

"Yep. All finished and I'm heading back in a few. Where are you and the kids right now?"

"We're just about to move the cows and head back to the trucks now. All saddled up and ready to go. You don't want us to wait for you, do you?"

"No, Del. It'll be a couple hours to get back to the staging area. You go ahead, load up the big trailer and leave me the single." He thought for a few seconds. "I'm not coming straight back home. Need to make a side trip, so once you get in, take care of whatever needs immediate attention and I'll talk with you tomorrow. Tell Shaley and Cam thanks, that I appreciate their good sense and hard work and I'll talk with them later."

"Will do, Quint. Watch for snakes."

Quint chuckled as he hung up. That'd been their signal to keep an eye out for the authorities in their wilder days before reality got a grip on them.

It took another twenty minutes to clean up after himself, lay the fire in the stove and wash out and prepare the coffee pot for the next occupant. By the time someone rides in after a long day working cattle or riding the fence lines, they're too bushed to cut and haul wood.

He knew it because that was him last night. Beat as he'd been walking across the wood planks that had been worn to a sheen by age and boot heels, having to do nothing more than strike a match was plenty. His duty was to provide the same comfort for the next cowpunch.

Finished packing up his gear, he shouldered the saddle and cleared the door. The paint was ready, being able to read Quint's mood as he approached. They'd been partners for several years, ridden hundreds of miles and roped thousands of cows during that time. Today was no different. They had miles to travel and the day usually started early for both of them.

The only fly in this morning's ointment was the addition of a couple of hitchhikers, the smell of which made the paint wrinkle his nose and lay back his ears. The pups didn't have quite the same odor as their sire and running mates, but the telltale wolf smell made him uneasy. He'd suffered it on the way to the bunkhouse but was glad to be relieved of it when Quint took them and the tainted saddlebag inside. Watching Quint go back in the cabin and return with the two varmints hanging helpless in his grip, the horse pranced sideways to signal his displeasure.

Tucking the pups back into the saddlebags, they appeared to recognize the travel arrangements from the day before and made no effort to climb out.

Quint patted the paint's rump, "These are just little squirts, Hodey. Not the full-grown beasts we've dealt with before. Hang with me, boy. They'll be gone by the end of the day and you'll never have to see or smell them again."

Hodey nickered at the reassuring tenor of Quint's voice and stamped his right front hoof in the ground, then stood still for the cowboy to swing one leg over his back and settle in the saddle.

"Let's go, boy." Trotting off toward the creek, the furry heads of two pups sticking out of the leather pouch, Quint picked up the shorter trail back to where he'd left Del, Shaley and Cam to deal with a nervous herd.

Taking the more direct route cut off a good hour of travel time to reach the pasture where he and the kids had come upon the cows after the no-name pack had terrorized them. Quint examined the fields to see how much evidence remained of the attack. Because the cows had been there for a while, the grass was well trampled, but the blood had been covered over with dirt and hay that Del had probably told his son and daughter to scatter.

It took him a while to locate the spot where they'd buried the carcasses and after hiking around a quarter mile square, he realized the only reason he found it was because he knew what to look for.

Satisfied that if any horseman or four-wheeler came through, they probably wouldn't notice the minor disturbances in the trodden fields loaded with piles of manure. That is, unless they had prior knowledge, and since only he, Del, his kids and his mom would know what happened, there was nothing to worry about. Every one of them understood the gravity of messing with the government's pets.

The next rain would take care of what's left, anyway.

Sauntering down the mountain, he arrived at the parking area where his truck had already been hitched to the single stall horse trailer. Silently thanking Del for saving him time, he checked his watch and saw that it was more than an hour before noon. He had an errand to run that would take the rest of the day and much of the night to accomplish.

Hands on his hips, he looked at the heap of odds and ends he kept in the truck bed. Every kind of tool, fastener, rope, rolls of fence, wooden post and plank laid in a haphazard jumble that wasn't as disorganized as it appeared. It didn't take him long to pinpoint the materials he needed. Reaching over the sides of the truck bed, he grabbed a catchall box and emptied the cords and ropes into another old, half-filled dairy carton.

Opening the back door of the crew cab, Quint snugged the box on the seat, securing it so it wouldn't slide around through the sharp turns on the river road. Nodding his head that it would stay put, he went to retrieve the wolf pups.

More patient than any other horse he'd owned, Hodey waited to be freed from the animal scent that, even as small as these wolves were, made him tense. Quint took the saddlebags off his mount and carried them to the cab, still secure in the side-pouch. Without much adieu, he deposited the pups in the box and checked that they couldn't scrabble over the sides. Both he and the wolves seemed content with the accommodations, so he loaded up Hodey, secured the back of the trailer and trundled down the Nacqus River Road to put to rest the last of this bad business.

CHAPTER 17

Rounding out the tour of Cripple Calf Creek Ranch, Cressy followed the perimeter road, divulging morsels of family history along the way. The fruit orchard planted by great-grandparents, the half-rotting remains of a windmill used to power its primitive irrigation system and an old collapsing bull pen among utilitarian structures erected at the turn of the 20th century.

Sheltered under the eaves of a granite outcropping, Native rock carvings had withstood centuries of winter blizzards and blistering summers. As long as ranchers had held the land, they had protected the petroglyphs from vandalism. For forty years, the 3C had invited regional schools to conduct field trips to the site as part of their study of local history. Occasionally, universities brought students to examine the aboriginal pictographs of hunters, their habitat and their prey. Stylistic renderings of deer and elk identified by their branched antlers, bighorn sheep, mountain goats, sun spirals and other natural features of Hells Canyon showed starkly in white against the dark rock face.

High on the prairie stood the original log home built by the pioneer Corler family, Cressy's paternal ancestors. The cabin was still intact after weathering a hundred and thirty years of harsh seasons. Regularly rechinked, it sheltered hunters each year and the rare hiker, botanist or geologist who sought consent to visit the homestead.

The 3C had a policy of strict vigilance when it came to trespassers. That included government representatives who, like everyone else, were required to receive permission before traversing any part of the ranch. Recently, it had become an increasing battle to restrain state and federal workers from intruding on private land. Acting more belligerently with each encounter, they seemed to believe they had free reign over any property.

A sore spot with Cressy, she related how ODFW and USFWS

have been progressively hiding behind protected species to gain access and regulate land use. They'd arrive with every excuse to wander and inspect the property from claiming the need to count fish to look for evidence of eagles' nests or wolf dens. There'd been USFWS agents up there claiming that cow dung was contaminating feeder brooks to the creek, and that cattle had trampled through salmon redds - except for the fact that salmon hadn't spawned up that particular creek at any time since her family had homesteaded the sector.

Returning from the daylong excursion that was meant to provide Anthea background for her story, Cressy registered both relief and regret at relinquishing ownership of what was left of the original land grant. It closed a door that a few years earlier she never considered could be so tragically opened.

Thanking Cressy for the guided tour, the writer had more questions begging for answers than when they started. Their hostess' emotional strain was evident, so she tucked away the queries for another time since further information wouldn't be supplied tonight.

Sunset was approaching and the Sunday prayer meeting was dispersing when they parked at the mercantile. Cressy was obligated to close up shop and whisk her daughter back to the house to take care of animals before dark closed in. With the height of summer solstice approaching, the days were long, making it even harder to prod Tricia off to bed at a suitable hour.

Bidding the Mathers' good night, the shopkeeper greeted the last of the church members as she went in the front door and they exited. May was standing by the counter shaking hands with the pastor, Bob Swifter and his wife, Tandy, who happened to be the newly elected sheriff of Koyama County. Under normal circumstances Cressy would have enjoyed shooting the breeze with the Swifters but after a day recounting the dread-filled memory of Terry's death and the ensuing maelstrom of legal hell she'd endured, she was exhausted mentally and physically. Sending them off with a few pleasantries was all the effort she could muster.

Finding May had already tidied up and closed out the register, Cressy received an unexpected respite. Gratefully thanking her bailout buddy, May, she walked with her and Tricia, who finally emerged from the rear of the store, out the front entrance, locking up behind them. Carrying her empty platter, May moved at remarkable speed with quick mincing steps, reaching her home in no time at all.

"Okay, time to go," Cressy said to Tricia as she watched May slip through her front door a block away. Grasping the door handle of the Jeep and swinging it wide to get in, Cressy assured herself that Tricia was buckled in before turning over the engine and heading for home.

"How did your day go, Tricia?"

Slight enough to blow away with the evening breeze, the passenger seat almost swallowed Tricia's rail-thin figure. Dressed in jeans and swimming in a sleeveless, blue plaid smock, she pumped sticklike arms with enthusiasm. "Great! This is the last week of school!"

Cressy couldn't help cracking a wide smile, watching her daughter's strawberry blonde ponytail flip around as she waggled her head with glee. "I expected you to be happy about being out for summer, but not this much. Was school so bad that being out for a couple months looks like heaven?"

"Oh no," said Tricia, calming down. "School's fine. I'm just looking forward to sleeping in, laying around. You know, doing zilch for a while." She cocked an eye at her mother to see if she'd get a rise out of her.

Mom was wise to her daughter's ways and gave her a noncommittal, "Hm-hmm. Sounds like a plan." After a pause she added, "Not!" and laughed.

"You got me, though I thought maybe Friday I *could* sleep in for an extra hour. Just to kick off summer vacation right…"

Cressy tugged lightly on Tricia's hair. "Oh, I don't see why not. We don't have anything too pressing except feeding the animals and the rest of the chores around the house before I go to work."

Feigning a pout, Tricia said, "Mo-om. Just one day to celebrate not having to get up for school."

"Okay. One day. You and I both know it's going to be a busy summer. Franma's already got big plans for you."

Tricia tipped her head back and rolled her eyes in the best drama queen sigh, "I know." Head still cocked back, she slung her eyes toward her mother. "Can't I get out of it?"

"She's been looking forward all year to working on some of these projects with you." Looking into her daughter's round pleading eyes she said, "I'll see what we can do. I'm sure I have plenty to keep you busy at the house for part of the time, but you'll enjoy being with your grands for a few days."

"Okay. But I was hoping to get to spend a week with Gretchen. Does that mean it isn't gonna happen?" Tricia whined in the most pathetic voice she could conjure for effect.

"Good grief, girl. I'm not going to chain you to the kitchen sink. Sure you'll get to spend time with your cousins. Do I look like an ogre?"

Turning her head to scrutinize her mother with one eye closed, Tricia said, "Kinda, yeah."

They both laughed.

Five minutes later, Cressy pulled into the driveway, parking in the garage that had been built onto the house by the last owners. They'd done a passable job of matching the style to the century-old structure, refinishing the shell with new siding, which was needed in any case.

Tricia popped out of the car door and was immediately met by their blue heeler, Artie. He had raced to the Jeep's passenger side before Cressy had turned off the engine, tail wagging wildly, engaging his whole backside. Smart enough to know the rules, he kept his feet on the ground and grumbled until Tricia scratched his head with her fingers. Seconds later, they were off to feed the lamb she was raising for this year's 4-H project.

Tramping around the side of the house to the pen that she and her mother had built in the back, Artie bounded in front of her darting side-to-side, excited to have his owner at home. While Tricia opened the gate to check on the lamb, the dog went about his usual routine circling the fenced area. He'd stop to sniff every rock and dirt clod now that he was free from being cooped-up.

As close as they were to the highway, Artie wasn't left to his own devices all day. He generally stuck close to home but once in a while he'd get a snoot full of squirrel, cat or other critter's scent and take off in pursuit. Vehicles constantly shot past the house traveling well over the speed limit and Cressy wasn't about to let him get run over. Tricia had suffered enough changes in the last few years. Losing her dog? Unh-uh. Cressy wasn't going to chance it.

While Tricia tended to the lamb, Artie did what came naturally, dashing around and sniffing everything with the eager curiosity explicit to dogs. He wandered over to the lonely cottonwood shading the brook that marked the property line. Pacing around the trunk, he stopped to investigate some animal droppings between the exposed roots. Blasting over to the sheep pen, Artie ran back and forth barking and hopping. Tricia raised her voice to be heard over his, telling him to be quiet over and over until she realized that he wouldn't get upset without good reason. It was unusual for the heeler to make a commotion unless he was serious about a sound or an officious odor, that excepted what he decided was perfume and would best be worn by rolling in it. In those instances, Artie and his owners did not agree on what constituted fragrance.

"Okay, okay! What's the problem, Artie? If it's a skunk, you'd better not bother him or you'll be banished from the house for at least a week and I'm not gonna wash that stink off you."

She finished filling the water trough, turned off the hose and wiped her wet hands on her jeans. She let herself out of the gate, latching it behind her. Tricia followed the dog alternating between bouncing up and down and zigzagging in front of her until he came to the tree bole standing a good fifty feet from the pen.

"What's with you, Artie? You're making enough noise to wake the neighbors, and they're old enough they just might be asleep."

As she approached the cottonwood, her mother came out of the house, hands on her hips. "What's the matter with Artie? Did the lamb get out of the pen?"

"No," Tricia shouted. "He's fine. I think Artie found something over here by the tree."

Reaching the base of the thick trunk, Tricia started hunting around for the cause of Artie's distress. Cressy left the kitchen door open in her rush to catch up with her daughter and the dog that was still barking but had dropped into a crouch by the tree.

From halfway across the lawn, Cressy called "What's down there?"

Tricia stooped over to get a look at what Artie was yapping about. "Just some dog poop. I don't know why Artie would get all worked up over some dog poop."

"To point out the obvious, it isn't his and he isn't thrilled about some other dog coming around and trolling his territory," said Cressy as she came alongside her daughter to examine the pile on the ground. She called Artie to her, bent down and patted his head, commending him for being a good dog.

"So, what's the big deal, Mom?"

Cressy weighed her answer while studying the scat.

"Must be a pretty big dog," said Tricia absently while her mother pulled out her cell phone and took a couple of photos. "But I don't see why Artie would be in such a huff."

Looking at her mother, Tricia asked, "What are you doing that for?"

Before replying, Cressy wrapped her arm around Tricia's shoulder and turned the two of them back to the house, calling Artie to 'come.'

"We're going to need to be really careful and I don't want you going out of the house by yourself for awhile, okay?"

"Sure, Mom, but why? What's wrong?"

"Well, I'm pretty sure that's from a wolf, honey, and that's why Artie was so upset. He could smell it. If I'm right then we're going to have to be extra vigilant."

Tricia's eyes instantly widened. "What about the lamb? A wolf would eat my little guy for lunch."

"We're going to set up another pen for him in the garage for now, just to be safe. I can park the car outside for a while. That way, you can keep him safe at night. And we'll have to make an exception and keep Artie inside at night too, much as I'm not big on dogs in the house."

"Yeah, I know." She looked up at her mom. "He won't like it."

"That makes two of us but I'm not going to allow him to tangle with a wolf. They're too big, and talk about being on the lunch menu, we're not going to let Artie be a wolf snack. Besides, he'll be a good warning bell while we're at home."

Going over to the sheep pen, Cressy directed Tricia to put a lead on the lamb and bring it into the garage. "We'll set up a proper pen after I take care of a few things before it gets dark."

She watched Tricia get the lamb and take it through the side door on the garage. Turning aside, she climbed the step to the back door and walking through the mudroom that led to the kitchen, Cressy's eyes fell on the shotgun she kept loaded and ready in the corner.

She had started training Tricia to shoot when she was eight and her daughter was catching up to her teacher in proficiency. Cressy was no slouch, having been an award-winning competitor during her teen years and she assumed it wouldn't be long before Tricia surpassed her skill and began taking home medals of her own.

Living isolated in the country and by themselves, Cressy had retained the habit of keeping a loaded weapon close to hand. You never knew when you might need easy access to a firearm to fend off marauders, both the two and four-legged kind. When it came to wolves, she gave no quarter, especially after what had happened to Terry. They were unpredictable.

What the uninitiated city dwellers saw as majestic denizens of the frontier, she knew to be killers, plain and simple. They had no compassion for other animals and were more vicious than most predators, preferring to eat their victim while it was breathing.

Walking over to the gun cabinet, Cressy heard Tricia come inside. "I've got the lamb tied up in the garage with water and some hay on the floor in the corner."

"That's fine for now." She opened the glass door and took out one of the rifles, checked and began loading it."

"Tricia, I'm taking Artie and going to round up the cows and bring them back to pasture by the house so I can keep an eye on them. You stay inside. Hear me?"

"Yes, Mom."

"I'll be back soon." Cressy shouldered the rifle and stepped out the kitchen door, Artie dashing ahead of her.

CHAPTER 18

Instead of going into town for dinner, Anthea and Gary had decided they'd settle for leftovers sitting in their room's refrigerator. After hearing Cressy's horror story they weren't much interested in listening to tourists bleat about saving the wilderness, having no concern for the locals who worked the land that was rapidly being cordoned off for sightseers. Not all visitors to Koyama County, being off the beaten path until it was 'discovered' by eco-tourists a few years back, bought into the exclusivity of land preservation, but there were enough that the Mathers' preferred to avoid idle yap.

Entering the portal of Nacqus Rocks B & B, they were reminded of the hard-scrabble farmers and ranchers who opened the territory that tourists now made a backwoods playground.

Eleanor met them in the foyer. "Have you had dinner yet?"

"No, we weren't feeling genial enough to play tourist tonight," said Gary. "Information overload."

"Is that right?" remarked their hostess. "Do you feel sociable enough to join us for dinner? Doug is grilling some fresh fish right now. Straight out of the river…"

The two guests exchanged looks and grinned. "Sure. That sounds definitely doable," answered Anthea with new enthusiasm. "Literate conversation is always welcome."

"Great! Meet us on the side porch in fifteen minutes. Your timing couldn't have been better planned. Dinner's almost ready."

"Thank you!" they replied in tandem. "We'll just go wash up," said Gary.

Fifteen minutes later the four were settled around a table, the sun shooting its last rays past the cliff tops, coloring the straggling clouds in rose and coral tones that was steadily shifting to dusky lavender.

Doug passed around glasses of Pinot Grigio that soothed

Anthea's palate, diluting the taste of dust and heartbreak.

The whole way back to their retreat on the river, she'd been mulling over how she might record Cressy's saga to best benefit the storyteller and the reader. Relating the facts to generate a righteous, lawful response among land use stakeholders, which exed-out fakers (aka wildlife advocates), was her objective. It had long been a sore spot with her that anyone who brandished a wildlife conservation 'cause' was elevated to 'stakeholder' when they owned no stake in land use, not even as taxpayers by benefit of nonprofit status. They were carpetbaggers in the original sense; opportunists of the worst sort. Basically, politicians.

Eleanor blandly initiated the conversation, "What was on your schedule for today?"

Pandora's box was opened.

"I'm sure you know Cressy Dillat." said Gary.

"Of course. The Corlers homesteaded here among the first families to run cattle on the prairie and in this valley," replied Doug. "Known 'em forever. Talk about a sad situation."

"Exactly," said Anthea. "I've heard all kinds of stories and, believe me, fact beats fiction every time." She sipped her wine. "She took us around the 3C and showed us the place where her husband was killed in that conflict with the wolves."

"She ended up losing the ranch because there were no witnesses other than his horse, and he couldn't give evidence in court," observed Doug.

"Interesting you saying that, because I was just thinking how wildlife advocates always say they can speak for the victims, meaning some animal species," Anthea considered aloud. "And yet, when a horse was the only living witness to a real crime perpetrated by other animals, the authorities weren't concerned with the evidence advocating for him. It's always a foregone conclusion that if a human is involved, then they must be the bad actor, not the animal. You know, instinct is as much a cause for evil as premeditated action."

Gary wrinkled his brows, "If that isn't going toward the esoteric…"

"She's right, though," agreed Eleanor. "Animal activists always want to speak for victims, as if they understood how animals think, if it suits their purpose. But if the result might go against them? Then the stupid animal should be ignored, doesn't matter what the circumstantial evidence says. Because animals can't speak for themselves, it's about circumstantial evidence, isn't it?"

"In a nutshell," said Gary.

"The injustice of Cressy's situation is that her husband was held liable for something he wasn't alive to refute," Anthea said. "I'd like to see the documentary evidence that placed him at fault. From what I've heard, thus far, the posthumous fines and judgments that dismantled a family's livelihood were levied according to tenuous testimony." She looked at Gary. "What do you think?"

"As much as we've heard to this point, I'd be apt to agree. Right now, however, we're operating on hearsay, even if it is from a reliable source."

"Figures. Ask an ex-cop and he'll always hedge to 'show me the proof,'" Anthea quirked the corner of her mouth.

"Trained response."

"All I know," said Doug, "is that more often than not, judgment comes down against the stock owner. Aside from myself, I know plenty of folks who have been denied adequate or any compensation at all for losses. And it puts added financial pressure on the rancher. All of it has contributed to the increasing number of beef growers selling their land and getting out of the business."

"All right, enough of that for now. It's time to eat." Eleanor started serving dinner and the conversation changed to admiring the flavors and the evening. At least, for a little while.

Darkness had finally settled over the river valley. The two couples reclined in the deck chairs, savoring aromatic coffee and digesting Ellie's delectable dessert. Tonight, all they could hear were coyotes yipping in the distance and the ripples of the river cascading past the rocks below.

Eleanor, who had put the kibosh on the previous conversation, re-opened it, curiosity getting the best of her. "Anthea, what are you going to do with the information? You're a reporter, after all."

"Not exactly. I worked the news industry for much of my life but I'm a PR consultant these days, though I do stir things up with opinion pieces now and again."

"She does more than that," said Gary. "If an injustice occurs where she thinks all the pertinent information hasn't been released, she goes into her investigative mode to uncover the facts."

"Not really," corrected Anthea. "To be fair, the only time I really got roped into *investigating* something shady was because of him," and she waggled her thumb at Gary. "He got a whiff of unsavory doings in Idaho and dragged me into the mêlée."

"And you don't regret it one bit, right?" He appealed to her forgiving side.

"I should since it's caused us nothing but trouble ever since. And we never made a dent in the Nature's Wilds underhanded activities."

"Nature's Wilds? You were investigating them?"

"For all the good it did. When a writer talks about 'murder and mayhem' in their story and it really happens but nothing, and I mean nothing, is done about it, it's enough to give you a lifetime of heartburn." Anthea couldn't help allowing a crumb of acrimony to slip out.

"You know that they're connected to Terra Ferus that's bought up all that grazing land to preserve it from greedy ranchers. Gaston Buttes, they've dubbed it," said Doug.

"No, I wasn't aware that there was a direct connection until today, though I assumed that all these land trusts are working in tandem."

"Yep. These guys at TF are the ones pressuring Oregon and US Fish and Wildlife to go after any violation involving protected species. They say they're supporting ranchers by putting up a few bucks for compensation of stock losses that don't pay for hardly anything. But they stab anyone in the back who even looks sideways at an elk herd that's destroying their hay crop or muscling out cattle at private watering holes."

"I don't think I've heard that," said Anthea.

"Yeah, it's part of the problem my brother's been having. Turns out the manager of Gaston Buttes…"

"Who's that?"

"A fella named Ken Demetre. Anyway, he's authorized the filling in of most of the watering stations that had been built by a rancher way back when to service cattle during the summer grazing. All the beef growers benefitted from his work for years. Then this guy comes along and takes them out while removing the land from grazing except for the elk herds, which they had done almost zero to control. The elk is overrunning the buttes and now there's not enough water for them so they compete with ranchers on their private property for the cattle's water. And, like you'd expect, ranchers aren't allowed to touch the invaders." Doug sat back and sipped his coffee to assuage his irritation.

"Maybe I need to interview this Demetre fellow," Anthea mused aloud.

"I sincerely doubt he'd talk to you," said Doug. "He's all about his political ambitions, and chatting with someone sympathetic to ranchers isn't high on his to-do list."

"I can sell myself as a freelance journalist and corner him for an interview. If he's out to pump his career, he'd probably jump at the opportunity. It's worked before."

"Yeah," said Gary unenthusiastically. "And we ended up almost losing our lives, more than once, if memory serves me."

The Darbys looked at each other in surprise, then turned expectantly to their guests, assuming that an explanation would follow.

Anthea shot Gary a warning glance and turned back to their hosts. "I do write for a couple of online news sites though mostly puff pieces to help promote my clients, which might stand me in good stead as being rather innocuous."

"Until they do an internet search and find everything you've written regarding the Nature's Wilds court mess."

Anthea brushed the thought aside. "Old news. I doubt they'd bother and any mainstream press has scrubbed that from their website. You'd have to go deep to locate those articles. People like that are hounds for what they think will be positive press. And folks flying the banner for the poor oppressed wildlife never consider that they could possibly be the bad guys. We see it everyday. Touting themselves as noble underdogs by calling anyone who disagrees a bigot, misogynist or nature hater, they just *know* they'll be loved."

Gary threw up his hands and half way laughed in his frustration. "I give up."

"Again…" Anthea smiled sweetly.

Ellie finally butted in. "Let's go back. What court mess? And did you say murder?"

Gary and Anthea exchanged the kind of glance that could only be defined as mutually accusatory with a tinge of exasperation, "Now you've done it."

Shrugging his shoulders realizing the cat was out of the bag, Gary went into his best Jack Webb, "Just the facts, ma'am," mode.

"I won't go into detail but Anthea and I tripped over a land scam up in Idaho a few years back that Nature's Wilds was closely connected to and benefited from. Unfortunately, it included some unwholesome characters performing illegal acts that led to farmers, ranchers and loggers losing their property. Property that was gobbled up by the NW. How it all came down, some folks died under suspicious circumstances. There were dubious land swaps involved, like what happened in Nevada with private and public lands, expanding the acreage under the control of the forest service. The court case against individuals is still ongoing and there have been gag orders issued to silence parties involved in the litigation. We made our statements public beforehand, so if you look it up, and like Anthea said, it means doing an in-depth search to find it, including checking her Facebook page. Our side of the story is out there even though we're constrained from discussing it further."

"But the bottom line is, Nature's Wilds is dirty and, maybe, dangerous," said Doug.

"*You* could say that," Anthea stated drily.

UNKNOWN PREDATOR

CHAPTER 19

Taking a meandering route along the valley floor, the ranging wolf stuck close to the road, crossing the river on the one-lane bridge. He felt fairly safe this far away from human habitation. Few vehicles passed as he jaunted beside the graveled stretch.

The pavement ending just five or six miles east of Nacqus, going all the way out to the Snake, the road serviced the ranches and homesteads that numbered less than a dozen. The final ten miles through the hills to Hells Canyon consisted of narrow dirt track that deterred rear-wheel drive trucks, cars and SUVs. It hadn't been grad - ed in years, making it hard going for firefighters in an emergency but a haven for horsemen and wildlife migration.

That wasn't the direction the wolf chose to travel. Slipping across the bridge's rickety slats, he trotted up the slope and continued west under the fringe of the trees that formed a canopy stretching a hundred feet from the rushing water. Instead of swimming through fast moving spring runoff, the manmade crossing suited him fine.

This side of the river was mostly open pasture bound by shelf after shelf of open fields forming basalt stairs up the cliff, cattle and deer dotting the hillsides. No buildings were around other than an occasional half-collapsed shack, the timbers left to rot over time.

None of this interested him as he moved west. Traveling on his own, his senses were heightened and he was wary of other predators roaming the area though he hadn't recognized any threat thus far.

He'd been a wanderer before grafting himself onto the off - shoot pack that had forcibly severed ties, sending him on his way. The young wolves of that group were from a previous litter and thorough - ly under the authority of the lead male, but he was a wolf of a differ - ent color and mature enough to cause a rift in the social fabric of the pack.

It wasn't the first pack he'd been attached to nor would it be the last. Hunting solitaire had its advantages but there were also drawbacks. Before joining the last group he'd had more than a year of loning it, his previous pack obliterated in a deadly encounter with the tallest four-legged beast he'd ever seen. After breaking in half it was still a mortal danger and the last of that pack bolted, never to reform.

Stringing alongside the river, he came to a wide spot where the waters were shallow. Deciding that only his feet would get wet, he forded the Nacqus and loped up the hill to stay in the trees that lined the top of a rocky bench. Down the way, he skirted a concentration of buildings, keeping a good mile between himself and the village.

Out of sight of the sporadic traffic trundling down the high - way, the wolf found himself circling an isolated homestead, miles away from where he'd been chased off by the alpha wolf. Pastures, corrals and one outbuilding stood near the house that sported a new paint job, not that he made any distinction between the structures or décor.

The few cows he saw chomping on the new grass were of peripheral interest to him. Although he'd participated in the hunt a couple days before, he wasn't enticed right now. He'd acted on his urges to kill for the sake of tasting blood in the past, but for now, he wasn't hungry or moved to attack. He was content to watch and wait having no reason to rush off upriver… yet.

Neither was he inclined to investigate the dog that was yap - ping around the base of the tree where he'd loitered for a time. Marking the spot before adjourning to this vantage point was plenty to trigger the runt canine to cause a commotion.

CHAPTER 20

Direct routes to Idaho from the Nacqus Valley were nonexistent without wings. Cutting a gash eight thousand feet deep, Hells Canyon was a formidable obstacle to crossing the state line. Available choices for Quint to reach his friend's place on the Salmon River came down to heading north a hundred and thirty miles or south for seventy, then east again in a scenic and circuitous journey. It was a coin toss since both ways took a good six hours drive time.

Time was short and Quint wasn't inclined to put his horse through twelve hours of a rough ride. Calling his neighbor, Howie Ketchum, he made arrangements to leave Hodey in a paddock just off the Nacqus Highway until he got back from his daytrip. This way, Hodey got a day off and Quint managed to avoid exposing the presence of his unauthorized passengers. The fewer people who knew what he intended, the better, and as much as he trusted his friends, he wasn't in the mood to defend what they would consider to be madness and indefensible.

Casting a glance over his shoulder, he saw the twin pups curled in repose, bored or tired of being boxed in with nowhere to go and nothing to see.

Frankly, he was still trying to understand his own motive other than being a sap. A few years ago he wouldn't have thought twice before destroying the two beggars in the back seat as potential dangers to stock growers. Now? Now he didn't know what to think and he'd prefer nobody else knew, either. He was committing one of the greatest sins known to ranchers - sparing the life of not one predator, but two.

His only redemption was ensuring they would never be released into the wild. Full-blooded wolves didn't make good pets no matter how well trained. They would never be fully domesticated. In the hands of a seasoned animal trainer who dealt specifically with dangerous species and had the resources to care and keep them safely separated from polite society, that was where they could survive without harm or causing harm.

Quint's buddy owned a facility that fit the bill to give these pups a chance. Had he left them on the range they probably would have made a choice hors d'oeuvre for a larger predator, or they might have managed to survive and become prowlers themselves. That left him two options, shoot them or deliver them to Rafe's compound. He could continue to berate himself for not putting them down in the first place or he could clear his mind and hand them over to a professional.

Back and forth, back and forth... *Cut it out, bub! You made your decision so drive and have done with it!*

Before he left the confines of Koyama and lost his cell signal for a good hundred miles, he called Rafe, told him he was coming for a visit and when he'd arrive on his doorstep. Hanging up, with finality he said aloud, "Done."

Long hours later and whipped from two days operating in physical and mental overdrive, Quint downshifted rather than ride his brakes down Whitebird Hill. Losing elevation with each sweeping curve, he closed in on the river weaving around the mountain's foot. A treacherous descent in winter, the steep grade still demanded alert piloting in the height of summer. Given his druthers, he preferred dry pavement and seeing meadows splashed with wildflowers to snow banks and dodging black ice in low gear.

Once he'd capitulated to his decision, good or bad, the rest of the trip was cathartic. Tired of wasting time worrying about his kids, his mom or the ranch, he unplugged, tuned in to his favorite music and blanked on the rest of the world. Life was good if he'd only take the time to recognize it, knowing himself for a fool if he didn't.

Forty-five minutes later, Rafe's compound came into view as

he rounded the last bend on Salt Lick Road. A few miles off the beaten path, the private refuge was isolated and self-contained, exactly how Rafe liked it. An Australian by birth, he'd become a citizen twenty years ago, the mountains beckoning him "home" on his walkabout in America.

Trekking foreign lands has long been a rite of passage to adulthood for many Aussies. A venture often accomplished in months, some took years to circumnavigate the globe, working their way along. Tempted by the world beyond the shores of his native continent, Rafe followed the example of other young people and spent a year overseas. Climbing in the Himalayas, Alps, Pyrenees, Andes and Rockies, he was continually drawn to craggy peaks. In the end, it was peering into the nadir of America's deepest gorge from the platform of Idaho's Seven Devils that captured his soul.

Never anticipating how an alien land would mesmerize him, Rafe had returned home for a spell only to expend every effort and dollar to immigrate to America. After six years his dream was realized, finally gaining citizenship a decade later.

Animal training originally brought Rafe and Quint in contact. Quint had landed a position working horses for a film crew during his after-college quest for direction in life. Rafe was on set as a handler for exotic and dangerous species.

A Western, the script called for scenes pitting a frontier family against ravenous wolves circling their snowbound homestead. By that time, Rafe had already developed an impressive reputation for working with wolves. During the month-long production, the two men became fast friends, keeping in touch after Quint had returned to the ranch and claims on Rafe's expertise grew in the entertainment industry. With his profits, he established Rafferty Animal Refuge and Training Center deep in the Salmon River Valley.

The sanctuary covered eighty acres of partially wooded land. Kennels on one side of the house, caged enclosures rising twelve feet high had been erected far to the opposite side where the more dangerous animals were boarded. Most of the species were native to America, but Rafe also raised and trained great cats from Africa and

Asia that had been illegally imported and confiscated. He was also licensed to breed wolf-hybrids that made their movie debuts as stand-ins for their full-blooded cousins.

Quint pulled into the empty parking lot. Leaving the truck in the shade close to the bungalow, windows open for the pups to bene-fit from the breeze, he started toward the porch. Before he walked ten feet, the front door flew open and a sturdy block of a man, 5'8" if he rolled up on his toes, clambered down the steps to grasp Quint's hand in a powerful grip.

Pumping his arm, Rafe burst out with a laugh, "Blimey, if it isn't great to see you, mate! It's been too long!" After all the years in Idaho, Rafe's accent had softened but not enough that he couldn't be pegged as a transplant from down under. Dark hair well peppered with gray now, he was in demand more than ever providing furry stars for the film industry. Business had expanded so much that he was grooming two full-time apprentices to work with his son who was pegged to take over the business when, and if, he ever retired. Not having reached sixty yet, Rafe figured he had another dozen years to go.

"Cryptic message you left, Quint. What's the to-do?"

"Found a couple of pups and although I should've, I didn't have the heart to put them down."

Rafe raised a querulous brow. "Lupus, are they?"

Nodding his head, Quint said, "Yeah. You know the trouble I've had with them, not to mention all the ranchers out my way, hell, over here too." He rolled his eyes skyward. "I'm going soft, old boy."

"You brought 'em?"

"I figured you'd be able to do something with them. They're not but eight weeks old by my reckoning."

"I won't ask for details. Less I know the better. Take me to 'em."

Waving his hand toward the Ford, Quint answered, "Back seat. They've been quiet as mice but really need to be let out." He opened the door and picked them up by their scruffs putting them down by a tree to do their business. "They don't travel far."

The pups immediately sniffed out a spot and did as expected then nosed around a large circle, too timid to inspect their surroundings beyond a few feet.

"Looks like you've already got 'em trained," Rafe guffawed and the pups stood stock still looking up where the noise had emanated. "Careful little buggers."

"I was hoping you could take them but I didn't want to say anything over a cell phone."

"Who knows about them?"

"No one but me. In fact, the sub-pack they came from ran completely under the radar. Nobody had ever acknowledged its existence, best as I can tell."

Rafe grunted, picked them up by their scruffs and examined their underbellies. "One of each." After a moment and 'hmm'ing a couple of times, he said, "Why not? This is supposed to be a refuge for wild animals and wolf pups lose parents to strange circumstances as much as any other species. Sure, I can take them. They're young enough to be trainable. You've proven that without trying."

Quint let out a "whew," taking off his hat and brushing his hair from his face with his forearm. "Thanks, Rafe. You've saved me in more ways than you know."

"Nor do I want to know," grinned Rafe as he strode over to the kennels to house the two new recruits. Quint followed him and stood aside while Rafe watered and fed the pups, leaving them to get used to their new lodging.

Stretching his back, he said, "I'll bet you need to stretch your own legs after that drive. How's a beer sound and a little grub, eh?"

"That'd be just about perfect. Thanks."

"Don't dawdle," and he marched ahead without another word.

By the time Quint rolled into his own driveway it was near midnight. Twelve hours behind the wheel to transport his illicit cargo after a day of tracking killers and manning a shovel had left him shot through and through.

Smart or not, he'd accomplished his purpose of saving the skins of two miniature predators from growing up to raid ranches like their sire, *Damn his hide*. Assessing their 'potential,' Rafe believed he could fashion them into film extras, providing them a good life and saving stock growers the pain of dealing with two more looters roaming the highland prairies.

Content with the conclusion of the whole affair, Quint climbed out of the cab, stiff from the road trip and ready to collapse onto his own bed. Ketchum had agreed to look after Hodey until he was ready to retrieve him the following day removing one more concern from Quint's overworked mind.

Still, there was an enigmatic element of this venture that had escaped his notice until he'd left Rafe's compound. Whirling through his head while he steered the winding highways home, was the oddity of that chewed radio collar he'd collected and dropped in his saddlebag. What was it doing there? None of the wolves he'd buried had any matted fur around their necks that would have been a telltale sign of being tagged. Yet that collar was old, showing years of wear. The more he considered that out of place detail, the more he realized that there must be something he missed - like another wolf… one that got away.

Temporarily setting aside the conundrum to be dealt with in the morning, he dropped onto the bench in the mudroom and removed his boots, blissfully wiggling toes liberated from confinement. With sock clad feet, he shuffled quietly into the den where his mother was encased in the old wing chair. Expertly working her needle through an elaborate quilt square, the television set on low volume so she could hear when Quint arrived.

"Glad you managed to make it home before sunrise," said Audrey, a ghost of a smile curling the corner of her mouth. "Not that I'd have waited up much longer."

"Always the night owl, aren't you Mom."

"Had to be with two wild boys in this house. You never know

what you'd be up to and I'd rather be sitting up to get the emergency call than have the ringer jolt me awake." She continued embroidering, azure thread creating a precise border on the center block of Shaley's graduation gift. "Your teen years jaded me. Hardly anything could shock me now." She lifted her eyes to half-challenge those of her son's, "Right?"

"Nothing so bad tonight, Mom. Just had an errand to run in Idaho."

Audrey quirked her brow in question and left it at that. She knew better than to stick her nose in his business. If he had something to say or that needed to be shared, he'd open up but he couldn't be prodded. He was like his dad who'd passed away at too early an age. She'd had forty years to get used to her husband's foibles that were echoed in their eldest son's taciturn personality. At this point in her life she'd learned to shrug it off. Nothing short of a major earthquake could shake her up.

"Kids in bed?"

"Long since, Quint. They were exhausted after being up most of the night keeping an eye on the stock, watching for wolves. Even with Del there, you know they wouldn't relax. Except maybe Cam. I swear he could sleep through an avalanche. Sounds like even he was twitchy and stayed awake, though."

"I don't blame them. They were eyewitnesses to the damage that pack had done. Must've been one of those phantom packs since ODFW hadn't recognized their existence."

"And do they exist?"

Quint chewed his lip. "Not anymore"

"Guess it's just as well the state passed them over, or Fish and Wildlife would be out hunting for evidence of their passage and then disappearance."

"I'm fairly positive this sub-pack had never been tracked or officially recognized." He added with a meaningful expression, "Nor will they be, at least not as far as we're concerned."

"That's good enough for me," said Audrey, tying off her thread. "Never heard anything about them before now and no need to mention it from here on out."

"Mmmmph," was all she heard from Quint as he went toward the kitchen.

"Thought you might be hungry so I left a plate made up for you in the oven. You can pop it into the microwave."

"Thanks. Mom. It's been a long couple of days."

Shaking her head, she decided it wasn't worth pushing her luck. She'd get nothing more out of him tonight.

CHAPTER 21

Winchester in a ready grip, Cressy stalked out to the pasture. Artie at her side, sniffing the air, ranging ahead and running back again, calmer now, he gave no indication that anything was amiss. No intruder was in the immediate area or the heeler would be antsy and squawking.

Determined to protect her own whether or not the dog sensed danger, Cressy wasn't about to let a mangy pirate catch her off-guard. That had happened one time too many to her family, leaving her child fatherless. The aftermath of dealing with unconscionable wildlife activists and government agents had pushed her to the edge. Reflecting on the hell they had inflicted made her blood boil with righteous rage all over again.

This time she didn't care what the state regs said, she had zero sympathy for the hairy vandals, however much the ignorant public idolized the beasts. Wolves had virtually confiscated her daughter's legacy and obliterated what could have and should have been a growing family. A single wolf attack had upended more than Tricia's future, it had killed two people.

Two years into recovery - which was the only way Cressy could describe her slow climb out of the pit of despair - Tricia began showing an interest in the prayer meetings held at the store. To get a feel for the church gathering and their teaching, she had attended a couple of them with her daughter.

One night, the group brought up verses referencing wolves in sheep's clothing and Jesus' disciples being sheep among wolves. Still burdened by the loss, she was struck by how the first reflected the government agencies' deceitful use of wolves, figuratively and literally.

What really caught her attention was where the frequently quoted sayings originated. Pondering how often people invoked axioms about wolves representing evil, including fairy tales like Hansel and Gretel or Little Red Riding Hood, she wondered about other common maxims. How many of them came directly from the pages of the Bible? Another study had discussed the Golden Rule, the "do unto others" bit that she learned was straight from the mouth of Jesus. It was a new perspective on a book she hadn't taken seriously for most of her life.

Throughout literature wolves were the epitome of evil, beginning with the most widely read book in history, and she had lived the truth of it.

For the moment, the subject of wolves revolved around a pile a excrement lying between the roots of an old cottonwood, evidence that at least one wolf was lurking in the vicinity. Keeping a wary eye open for the possibility of multiple prowlers, since they usually traveled in packs, she reached the metal gate of the fenced pasture. There she found the three pair and a young bull sidled up near the tubular railing. The three horses weren't far off, grazing calmly. No appearance of anxiety other than all the animals huddled in close proximity.

Not wasting any time to reason why they'd congregated at this end of the pasture, she opened the gate and sent Artie to round them up. A good working dog, he soon had the cattle hustling toward the corral by the old hay barn, Cressy bringing up the rear, leading the horses.

Relieved that none of the animals showed signs of distress, she still felt a need to pick up the pace. Dark was closing in, prompting her to move briskly. Within ten minutes she had secured the cows, bull and horses in the large corral. It didn't take her more than five more minutes to haul out hay to feed them and shoo Artie into the house. Before she crossed the threshold herself, Cressy thumbed through the contacts on her phone, landing on the number for Miles Crenshaw, the range rider.

Two hours passed before the phone jangled, catching Cressy in a fog, her thoughts a million light years into the future.

After cobbling together a temporary pen in the garage for the lamb, she and Tricia had eaten leftovers while watching some brainless television show for diversion. Tricia wasn't as perturbed as her mother, which suited Cressy fine. The last thing she wanted was to see worry cross a ten-year-old's face. *Kids are resilient*, she reminded herself.

Tricia was bedded down and Artie lay on his back snugged up against the sofa, legs flailing the air in his own dreamland when the generic ringtone snapped Cressy out of her reverie.

Touching the phone's face, she held it up to her ear. "Hello."

"Cressy, got your text. Sorry it took so long to get back to you. Just got in."

Miles Crenshaw could go either way in his conversation. Clipped and no-nonsense or loquacious if the subject suited him. They'd known each other for years, first as family acquaintances and later when she'd been a student in his biology class early in his career at Koyama High School. Circumstances flipped on him a few years back and he'd opted for early retirement when the school district went through a budget crunch, and he returned to running the family ranch.

Then the county came courting. The position of range rider had unexpectedly come open when the first applicant was compelled to leave the job. There were two stories circulating regarding his leaving, one that he was removed for negligence and the other that he left because of family obligations. More likely, it came down to differences of opinion and administrative pressure tactics. Politics as usual. Either way, the county was desperate and one of the commissioners, who'd also been one of Crenshaw's students, coaxed him into accepting the position.

In truth, it hadn't taken that much convincing. Crenshaw was eager to keep active after he'd delivered the lion's share of ranch business into the hands of his son. This was the ideal opportunity to get paid - meagerly, but it was still a paycheck - to do what he loved most, spending time in the backcountry. It meant tailing wolves, but nothing was perfect.

A gifted tracker, some of the oldtimers liked to attribute his skill to his heritage, spinning tales about the Crenshaw ancestor pioneering the valley with his bride, a local Indian. It was hooey as far as Miles was concerned but he'd occasionally draw on his grandmother's lore to good effect in his teaching career. Fact was, he was on the long end of retaining tribal membership having just made the "blood quotient" of one-eighth, which meant his children were ineligible because his wife was non-Indian.

Segregating himself by virtue of his Native lineage didn't interest him. He was part of both communities, preserving Indian tradition and working cattle, he did his bit in rodeo growing up. Describing himself first as a rancher and a teacher, he was exceptional at both.

"Hey, Miles, have you heard anything about wolves down this way?"

Detecting a twinge of concern in the question, he said, "There hasn't been any report coming across the ODFW channels. Nothing in terms of tracking from any collars. 'Course we know that doesn't cover all the possibilities of wolf traffic."

"Well, I just found - I should say Artie, my dog, just found a pile of steaming wolf crap not a hundred yards from the house. Snapped a picture of it and with my foot next to the spoor for size comparison. I texted them to you."

"So I see. You're pretty sure it was from a wolf and not a coyote?"

"Way too big and it looked like the animal had marked the tree quite high. No dog around here or coyote could match that."

"How'd you tell about the marking?"

"Artie had his nose pretty far up the trunk. After sniffing it he barked like crazy. Unusual for him to make such a fuss." Shrugging her shoulders to herself, she said, "I surmised."

"So, you want me too…"

"Check it out yourself before it's too late and the evidence, if that's what I think it is, decomposes. If there's a wolf or wolves around here, I want it documented in case anything happens to my stock... again," she added reluctantly.

Crenshaw knew her story. Terry's passing was still sharp in local memory. Two years is a blink of an eye when it comes to calamity so close to home that it could have happened on any of the neighboring ranches. Sightings had practically become common-place. Bitterness still affected the community after the state did zero to help her, instead taking an adversarial role following the incident, claiming it was an attack by an "unknown predator" in spite of what he considered was incontrovertible proof.

Because of Cressy's levelheaded assessment of situations, he wasn't about to disregard her call. Miles didn't know many women with her ability to set emotion on the back burner while dealing with a crisis.

"Can it hold 'til morning?"

"Probably. I doubt anything's going to come near a clear marking by a predator as daunting as a full-grown wolf. That is, if I haven't got my wires crossed."

"I'd be the first to vouch for your instincts, Cressy. Wolves are known to defecate where it will be noticed to make a statement like marking territory or boundaries. I'll be there first thing."

CHAPTER 22

At least the weather was cooperating.

Scratching his chin through a beard that he hadn't shaved since winter, he stood outside his truck where he'd spent the night in the back, the canopy providing cover from the elements.

He was on a rarely traveled ranch road that had put his four-wheel drive to task navigating over and through the partially washed-out track. Surveying the steep walls of the canyon, the grass tall, turn-ing gold as it ripened, he checked his GPS coordinates to find that he was in the right spot. Spring run-off had begun to subside and the creek was fordable as it rushed past him. But it wasn't necessary for him to cross the water to perform his hired duty and, silently com-mending his boss' site selection, he could tell that it wouldn't pose a barrier, impeding his objective.

Good enough, *he thought.* I'll finish stowing my gear, take care of business and I'm outta here. Easiest payday I've had in years.

Last night's sleep wasn't as tranquil as the previous night. Quint had turned the bedding inside out, his agitated thoughts twist-ing his body as well as his mind. It wasn't concern over the previous two days' activities. He was comfortable that he had done what was necessary. It was a beat-up, torn, masticated worthless piece of field equipment that kept clutching his thoughts.

That's it. He got out of bed and went to brush his teeth. *I'm not going to rest until I have an answer.*

Standing in front of the mirror in the bathroom, he imagined that the lines grooved his face deeper than they had a week ago. It had to be the churning of his mind and his stomach in dealing with the "problem." More than that, it was that stupid radio collar he'd collected. It didn't add up. Not one of those wolves he'd destroyed showed signs of wearing one, especially one as old and weathered as the collar he found. There was no way it could have been laying there by coincidence. It had to have bearing on the pack that he'd chased to that grove.

Getting dressed, Quint clomped down the stairs, his steps echoing the turmoil of doubt triggered by a tattered bit of plastic and metal.

The kids were at the kitchen table eating breakfast and his mother placed a steaming cup of coffee right between his hands, which he grasped appreciatively. A slow smile crawled across his lips as he inhaled the aroma, replacing the self-berating thoughts with simple gratitude for a cup of joe.

Chatter about school ruled the fifteen minutes they got to spend together, the majority of it coming from Shaley who anticipated her graduation with glee and a sprinkling of apprehension. She'd been accepted by three colleges and, overdue as it was, she still hadn't decided which one to attend in the fall.

"You'd better bite the bullet, girl," said her grandmother. "You're lucky they all have late admission but next week's the deadline."

"Are you any closer to making a choice?" Quint took a swig from his mug.

"I think so. It comes down to distance and flexibility in changing majors." She scrunched up her face in concentration. "Still not sure what I want to do."

"That's okay. The first two years are mostly taking care of general ed requirements and you can always transfer if need be."

"Yeah. I know." She swallowed the last of her juice and jumped up to get her books. "Coming Cam? Time to roll."

This year, Shaley could drive them to school having turned eighteen. The car she purchased with her 4-H savings for the past few years was a twelve-year-old Honda SUV that looked a little worse for wear but was reliable.

"Give your Grandma a kiss and scram, you two."

"See you later, Dad," was the greatest number of words strung together by Cam throughout the whole of breakfast.

Audrey watched them file out the door then turned to her son. "What's got your goat this morning?"

"Blunt as ever, Mom." He drank a little more coffee. "Just been thinking about a conundrum left over from the last two days' activities."

"And what's that?"

"I found a weather beaten radio collar where I confronted the pack but none of them showed signs of having been tagged."

"That *is* strange." She scrutinized his features, seeing his distraction. "And?"

Pushing away from the table, he stood up. "And, I need to find out if I missed something. These things don't just appear out of nowhere." Walking to the mudroom and collecting his hat and coat, he said, "I'll probably be out for most of the day. Give you a call later?"

"Sure, Quint. Just be careful."

"Yes, Ma'am."

Decision made, there was nothing for it but to get Hodey, saddle up and go back to where he'd found the collar. He'd have no rest until the area had been gone over yard by yard to see where this clue led, if anywhere. One more day to settle the issue wouldn't hurt.

Riding back to where he'd buried his enemies six feet under, Quint was struck by the parallel between him and a perp in a TV drama that's drawn back to the scene of the crime. That's where the similarity ended. He had no desire to revisit his deeds or double-check that all evidence had been destroyed. It was the quandary of the tagged wolf. Had there been one and where was he now?

Locating the place where he'd found the collar, he immediately recalled the signs of a scuffle. There they were, plain as day. No other animals or weather had blown through to disturb the scrapings in what had been soft and mucky earth a couple days ago.

Peering closer at the markings left by a fight, fluffs of hair that he'd noticed before were still present. Quint picked up a couple of clumps, again observing the distinct colorations indicating they came from two different animals. Standing up, he scoured the site for other signs and quickly came upon a line of tracks leading away from the skirmish.

Sure as sugar, I missed one. But only because he was already gone.

Discovering that he was right wasn't enough. A short walk following the tracks proved that they turned back west and Quint wasn't prepared to allow a confirmed killer free reign in his territory. After coming this far, he wasn't going to call it a day.

Mounting up, he resolved to catch the wolf that got away.

The a.m. arrived and so did Miles Crenshaw. Pushing sixty, his appearance didn't give away his age. Thick black hair only set off the few wild strands of silver around his ears, and his face was relatively unlined despite years of roundups, hunting, riding Harleys, snow mobiles and trekking the canyonlands. He was in his element when he was outdoors and being drafted as a range rider suited him perfectly.

Emerging from the Silverado that showed more wear than he did, Crenshaw strolled toward the Dillats' front door. Hearing him drive up, Cressy left her daughter to finish breakfast before catching the bus for school.

"Hurry up, Tricia or you'll miss the bus."

"You say that every morning and I haven't missed it yet."

"Because I remind you every morning," said Cressy, flashing a grin.

"Oh, Mom." Tricia rolled her eyes. She'd heard the refrain before and expected to hear it tons more in the future. *But not after this week*, she thought. *School's almost out!*

Tricia swept her plate off the table, more than half her meal uneaten, and into the sink. She ran to grab her backpack, stopped to kiss her mother and slipped out the door just as Miles was walking up the drive.

Barely uttering a brief "hi" and "bye" to the range rider, Tricia climbed aboard the bus just as it pulled to a stop in front of the house, the door opening with a whoosh and swallowing up the waif in quick succession.

Standing in the doorway, Cressy greeted Miles. "Want your coffee now or after?"

"After. Let's make sure everything is as you found it."

"All right. Let's go." Closing the door behind her, she slid her phone out of her pocket, intending to record everything 'just in case.' "This way," she said leading him to the cottonwood behind the house.

"Over here, next to the tree," Cressy pointed to a crusty pile of canine feces deposited in plain view by the massive roots. Artie trailed them out to the tree, snuffling the air and trotting around the vicinity, cautious but not on edge as he'd been the evening before.

"Your dog is calm enough. Not like yesterday, I take it?"

"You take it right. He was barking his blasted head off last night. He's pretty cool now but I'd say he's still being cautious. A little out of character. He likes to run and check things out but usually not with such care."

"Probably the intruder has vacated the area and the scent may have faded, lessening his feeling of threat."

"Could be," Cressy rocked back on her heels. "So, what do you think?"

He placed his boot next to the scat and took a photo just as Cressy had done, then knelt to examine the pile to see if he could identify anything undigested that might help identify the animal. "There doesn't appear to be anything odd in it that I can see without poking through it. But I'll forward some pictures and collect it as a sample for the lab. They'll fight me on testing it, but since they can trace DNA through feces now, let's see if they'll comply and do it."

"You're telling me not to hold my breath," remarked Cressy.

"Except for this minute. This may be twelve or more hours old, but it still stinks."

"Right," noting his attempt at humor.

Cressy stopped recording for a moment. "You're assuming they'll refuse to process the sample claiming 'budget constraints." She snorted derisively.

Straightening up, Miles agreed. "May as well suppose the worst considering Fish and Wildlife's history regarding your case. I'll just give them the address and location where you found the scat and spoor, see if I can sidestep identifying the property owner until absolutely necessary. I'd hate to think that prejudice could come into play if your name is connected to the specimen."

Finished taking photos, Miles pulled latex gloves and an evidence bag out of his pack and carefully collected the feces. "Money is always the binding factor and the go-to excuse. Frankly, if I could get into the lab, I could do the tests myself. It doesn't take a genius.'

"Just a biology teacher?" She chuckled.

"Pretty much." Sealing the bag he walked over to the truck and placed it in what would have passed for a tackle box.

"Ready for that coffee now?"

"You bet. But first I've got something for you."

"Really?"

Miles went to the back of the truck and dropped the tailgate. Reaching forward, he grabbed the end of a long tube thickly wrapped with rope strung with red plastic flags.

"Fladry," said Cressy, shaking her head. "Forget diamonds," she teased. "Who told you this is the way to a girl's heart?"

Chapter 23

Tracking the predator that escaped the showdown between its renegade mates and the hunter wasn't a walk in the park, but it wasn't exactly arduous. Time consuming, yes.

Mud stamped by passing paws had dried and hardened under the sun's steady rays since Quint had cornered the pack at the pine grove. Traversing what had been soft earth, the trail was obscured in places where it crossed rocky outcroppings, compelling him to dismount to comb through the brush for prints.

It was a slow go, turning the several miles of meandering tracks that spanned the river a couple of times into hours of travel time. Wolves can cover long distances in a day, but this one was rambling, lingering at times and marching ahead at others.

When Quint's quarry came near the village of Nacqus, it made a wide detour around the small population center. *Guess he isn't fond of crowds*, he thought, tracing the wolf's circuitous path that climbed up to higher ground on the journey west.

By noon, miles had been crossed without losing sight of the trail of spoor and Quint found himself on familiar ground overlooking the highway from the north side of the river.

He was staring down at the farm now owned by the Widow Dillat.

He knew the property well. It had been part of his family's holdings stretching back into the last century when the Corlers and Edwards had been neighbors with long adjoining fence lines. The two families' ranches ate up the better part of ten miles along the Nacqus back then, but ranching has fiscal hills and valleys like every business. Over the decades both outfits had been forced to sell off parcels to stay alive. Neither ranch was what it had been, property taxes and government regulations eating into the profit margin.

Despite that, Cressy and Terry had run a successful operation until the tragic accident that took his life, and the family's livelihood with it.

On Quint's side of things, the Edwards' ranch had been divvied-up between his father and uncle. The divorce then taking an additional toll on his own family. Being land poor, he had no choice but to partition and sell off some lots to settle with his wife.

The old house that was now Cressy's had changed hands many times over since it was first built and Quint was glad to know that it again belonged to someone with pioneer roots in Koyama County.

He wasn't thrilled to find that the ranging wolf had trotted right up to her backyard. Wolves had already caused her enough grief to last a lifetime.

CHAPTER 24

The summer season was kicking off with a bang. Bookings for tours were quickly filling the schedule at Terra Ferus' Gaston Buttes Preserve. As the protected landmass, the largest in the state, gained notoriety, eco-tourism was growing, hauling in Westsiders and non-Oregonians with a heart for conservation.

It was also filling the coffers of the land trust and its umbrella organization, Natures' Wilds, which connection was the worst kept secret in environmental circles. NW had tentacles in real estate markets all around the world, encouraging land transfers in sparsely populated regions where locals had a rough time contesting the trust's influence. Political gamesmanship and efficiently distributed funds overrode the provincial voice in the States and internationally. Not that opposition posed any real concern for Terra Ferus administration.

For this and other reasons, Director Ken Demetre was in seventh heaven.

Thousands more acres had been added to the scope of his management with the recent accrual of easement rights from a neighboring rancher. Cash was always an incentive, especially in an industry coming under harsher and more frequent pressure from environmentalists. Citing damage to grazing, natural wildlife traffic and fish spawn, the land trusts were making steady headway in the backwoods.

What land owners didn't grasp about easements - though he suspected some knew exactly what their actions precipitated - was that once they'd signed away their rights to develop their own property as they see fit, they'd actually given up those rights in perpetuity. Sure, Demetre assured them that the agreement could be revisited in a few years but, in reality? To date, no contract had ever been reversed.

Nature's Wilds, and Terra Ferus using NW's template, printed this in the financial statement:

"Conservation easements - intangible assets comprised of listed rights and/or restrictions over the owned property that are conveyed by a property owner to The Conservancy, almost always in perpetuity, in order to protect the owned property as a significant natural area, as defined in federal regulations. These intangible assets may be sold or transferred to others so long as the assignee agrees to carry out, in perpetuity, the conservation purposes intended by the original grantor."

Does no one bother to do their research? he wondered. Frankly, he was ecstatic that there were enough chumps under financial pressure, or willing to believe that Terra Ferus workers were motivated by the best of intentions, that they'd sign on the dotted line. He knew that there were indeed employees who truly accepted the land trust at face value, supporting its efforts to preserve the terrain. Among those, there occurred disillusionment to the point that they eventually left their jobs. But it was rare for any of them to speak up publicly about Terra Ferus or Natures' Wilds. Verbal threats weren't necessary. They were implied strongly enough to secure silence.

Demetre wasn't worried someone would talk. On the whole, they wouldn't be believed except by local yokels. Media refused to hear or publish sour grapes from former employees, which is how their protests were painted.

In the meantime, he added to the sway of Terra Ferus' control of more than fifty square miles of land that fenced out the ranching and hunting community. Researchers representing universities and environmental think tanks had relatively free access to the grounds. At this point, he was well on his way to ushering in federal oversight. Five thousand acres had already been approved as a National Natural Landmark, the first stage of creating a national monument and eventually a national park. How did Bears Ears and other national monuments get on track? By this designation that paved the way.

Demetre had every right to be self-satisfied. Years of graduate studies had led him to conclude that modern day ranching, farming and logging practices wreak havoc on the natural landscape. A longtime environmental activist, he prided himself on a triumphant record of assisting to lock up some of the most productive and scenic land west of the Mississippi. It was his passion to keep as much of that landscape as pristine as possible.

'Pristine' was the industry byword. Fortunately for him and environmental tacticians, average citizens still hadn't caught on to the fact that conservation was an industry, and a very lucrative one.

Thus far, he'd been successful at coalescing one of the largest protected private properties in the United States, if not the world. That was something he could hang his hat on.

Evidently others were acknowledging his work with well-deserved acclaim. Demetre had just received a call from a writer interested in doing a story on his achievements, including the expansion of Gaston Buttes. Dozens of articles had been published regarding Terra Ferus and its prominence among protected real estate, but this writer sounded like she was focusing on his accomplishments rather than the bunchgrass, disappearing weed or prairie chicken.

Capitulating to his stroked ego wasn't usual for him. In this case, who wouldn't enjoy a little publicity? And the timing couldn't be better since he was contemplating a run for office.

Feeling that he'd gone as far as he could working for Terra Ferus, he had two directions available. He could pursue climbing the ladder of corporate conservation, serving on multiple boards and raking in a boundless paycheck, or he could parlay his achievements into a congressional seat. The latter possibility was gaining ground when he considered how instrumental he could be in saving millions more acres of nature for posterity.

A career in Congress had much to offer in terms of distinction, notoriety and shaping national environmental policy, which was taking a beating under the new administration. After all he'd accomplished, there was now a possibility that the new Department of the Interior chief could put the kibosh on Gaston Buttes forming the core of a new national park in Koyama County. A man with his ambitions might find that problematic.

Demetre was looking forward to adding his name to a roster

of heroes that included Teddy Roosevelt, though he'd rather conquer D.C. than San Juan Hill. That was more his kind of battle.

CHAPTER 25

"Well, it's set."

"What's set? What did you do?" Gary queried his wife, whose mischievous grin belied her professionalism. "No, you didn't…"

Smiling like a naughty child, she turned back to her computer.

"Are you going to make me guess?"

"That's your prerogative," she said cryptically.

"All right. When's the interview." Figuring it was a done deal, his flat reply was as good as throwing in the towel.

"Ya got me," Anthea offered in faux surrender. "Since I wanted to talk to the director of Gaston Buttes before we leave the county, it's this afternoon. You coming with?"

Shaking his head in disbelief, Gary wondered if either of them had learned from past experience. "After what we've been through, no way on earth would I let you get stuck at the end of that dirt road without back-up."

"Spoken like true law enforcement."

"You expected another response?" He arched an eyebrow at her. "Who knows what's out there beside some paper-pushing administrator. That is an apt description of the director, isn't it?"

"More or less. I'd call Demetre a suburban outdoorsman. You know, the typical weekend hiker who rides a mountain bike and camps in a yurt. But he's also a big player involved in corporate money behind environmental causes. Working state and federal officials, he's earned a reputation for putting together major land acquisitions. Swaps, too, though from what I can tell, they've mostly gone under the radar. He knows dough and how to compile lots of it."

"What a guy."

"We're going to meet him at the Terra Ferus office in Rory and he'll ferry us out there."

"Did you really think I'd let you drive sixty miles to the middle of nowhere without an escort?"

"Hardly, I know you too well," she smirked. "And you may have pegged the lack of accommodations at the preserve because I don't think they have any real improvements on the property other than a few utility buildings. Maybe some ramshackle, uh, shacks."

"Isn't that kind of strange on a preserve the size of Catalina Island? Should be fascinating." Under his breath he added, "Not."

"I heard that," she laughed.

"Then hear this. It better not be Yogi Berra's 'déjà vu all over again.'"

Terra Ferus' office in Rory was an inconspicuous storefront wedged between a computer consultant and a real estate office on the main drag of which there was only one. The town was incorporated with a population of less than a thousand, but it serviced the surrounding community with the basic necessities - a local grocer, specialty shops, hardware store. Outnumbering the churches were bars and eateries, the majority of restaurants limiting their hours to tourist season. The bars stayed open year 'round, of course.

Perched on a less trafficked block at the end of town, TF headquarters stood kitty corner from the gas station with a few oblique parking spaces out front. Gary parked the truck and in the adjoining space was a decade-old Toyota SUV, dinged and pockmarked from back roads. It had recently been washed and the trust's decals decorating the front doors were legible, though faded.

"Guess that's our ride," observed Anthea.

"Yeah, but I'd rather make the trip in that," said Gary, pointing to a gleaming black Hummer parked in a driveway that separated the trust's office and the property broker. "Real estate must be booming."

"I've heard it's getting to be a rare commodity in these parts unless you have the capital to purchase sizeable tracts, kind of what Terra Ferus does." She leaned over to take a closer look at the fancy wheels. "Makes you think about the amount of cash that changes hands and... who that really belongs to."

"Talk about a suspicious mind," said Gary. "Come on, let's get this over with."

"Please, restrain your enthusiasm," she chuckled as he opened the door for her.

Like the company vehicle, there wasn't much to recommend the interior, either. A couple of desks in the narrow room with a battered bench for visitors, and walls lined with photographic displays of the conservation and research projects ongoing at the preserve. Obviously the work of professional outdoor photogs, they showed what could otherwise be bleak landscapes in their best light, literally. Using the last of the sun's rays or the first at daybreak, the subjects were augmented by natural amber, rose and pink tones creating pleasing views.

The wall exhibits were virtually the only objects of interest in the office. If any artifacts had been unearthed from that vast preserve, they weren't on display for visitors to inspect. Anthea found it puzzling that the trust didn't entice tourists and support with more than images of the vistas pasted to the wall. If this is such a great conservation effort, why not have something showing what and how they're doing their job with fifty square miles of unspoiled land.

A door at the back of the room swung wide and a wiry man, maybe 5'10" stepped out of the private office that Gary and Anthea only glimpsed as he quickly secured the latch. Reaching forward, he first grasped Anthea's hand and briefly pumped it before doing the same with Gary.

The greeting had all the warmth of shaking fins with a dead fish, despite his plastic smile. Anthea was tempted to check her fingers to see if she needed to wipe off loose scales. Okay, not everyone has charisma, though he must have appeal in order to raise the mil - lions he does. Whatever it is, he's charming somebody out there... or does he know how to make the right offer to the right people?

"Thank you for coming over. We do have a great day to travel up to Gaston Buttes! Couldn't ask for better weather," he said. "Oh, sorry, I should introduce myself. Ken Demetre."

"Glad to meet you, Mr. Demetre," said Anthea.

"You must be Anthea Keller," he cut her off before she could add another word to her greeting. "And you must be... Again, I'm sorry, I know I wrote down your name but between all the calls today, I've forgotten."

"Gary, Gary Mathers. Mr. Keller to some."

Puzzlement flashed in Demetre's eyes before he caught himself and laughed politely at the joke. "I assume that would be due to your wife's celebrity."

"Hardly," smiled Anthea. "More likely it's that people often meet me first.
We're all guilty of making assumptions on first glance." She looked around, "For instance, I assumed you'd have some intriguing objects collected from the preserve for visitors to paw through. You know what a tactile bunch we tourists are."

"What finds that we collect are generally transported to the universities that work with us. Makes sense since students are usually the ones who come across items but, in case you're interested, most are related to the pioneer era rather than ancient Indian artifacts. You know how large the land mass is. There's still plenty that could be out there that hasn't been discovered yet. I expect more will continue to be unearthed by the researchers who collect these things."

"So you're saying that we probably won't stumble across some fascinatingly important, eon's old relic today."

If he could tell that Anthea was playing with him, he didn't let on. Except to crack a half-smile at her jibe. *I seriously doubt this guy has a sense of humor.*

"And you'd be right. As you'll see, it's a great prairie with few prominent features."

"Except the buttes, I presume," cut in Gary.

Demetre just continued with his thought as if he hadn't heard the joking remark. "But the importance in preserving what's left of native plants and animal life that's been endangered is beyond calculating."

"That's why we're here, Ken. May I call you Ken?" asked Anthea.

"Certainly."

She continued, "I've heard a lot of chatter about Gaston Buttes, especially its size. It must be something to manage a preserve of this scope."

"That it is. Are you ready? We'll take the company vehicle. Some of the roads aren't much better than deer paths."

He ushered them out the front door, flipped the 'open' sign to 'closed,' turned the lock and led them to the Toyota.

Driving out the long stretch of highway, Demetre periodically directed their attention to points of interest. He also began explaining how the preserve is protecting an indigenous plant from extinction. "Though you're not likely to see any on this trip."

The odd comment gave Anthea the cynical idea that perhaps the rare catchfly didn't really exist. She cracked a smile at the absurd thought. *But wouldn't that fit with enviros peddling unprovable theories like climate change?* Then she remembered the 2001 story of how USFWS scientists had planted hairs from captive lynxes on central Washington forest lands to create "evidence" of the endangered species' presence. *And no one was fired, either. So, no, not out of the question.*

It took over an hour to reach the gate spanning the gravel road at the entrance to Gaston Buttes Preserve. There was an unmanned security kiosk on the right side and the metal gate was gaping open.

"Is the property generally left open to visitors?" asked Gary.

"As you can see, it can't be fenced in. It'd be like erecting a fence around Disney World, except this is larger and the preserve doesn't charge an entry fee to cover costs."

"Your organization also doesn't pay property taxes, to speak of," Anthea tossed out. Gary looked out the window and rolled his eyes heavenward. *Didn't take long for the lioness to bare her claws.*

"No. We have an agreement with the county that gives us

flexibility when it comes to that."

"That's interesting. I expect Terra Ferus must have preferred status due to being nonprofit. I'd read that the tax is voluntary and the rate is much lower than surrounding properties such as the neighboring ranches pay."

Demetre kept his countenance blank though his temples twitched. "Something like that, though more complicated." He was beginning to think he'd been bamboozled.

They were quiet for a while as he drove them a few miles onto the property. There were a few odd-shaped chain-link enclosures.

"What are those fenced areas?" asked Anthea.

"Yes. That looks curious," remarked Gary. "I don't see anything inside."

"That's where the largest concentrations of bunchgrass remain," explained Demetre. "They're fenced to keep the ruminants from destroying them."

"How much bunchgrass was still on the prairie before Terra Ferus took possession? It must have already been pretty sparse compared to after you acquired the land." Anthea awaited a cogent answer, knowing there wasn't one.

The director hedged before answering because the amount of the native grass had actually diminished greatly since Terra Ferus started its conservation project.

Letting him off the hook, Anthea provided an answer of her own. "My research showed that bunchgrass needs to be processed through the stomach acids of ruminants to actually help the seeds germinate. That's according to the old time ranchers I've interviewed who grazed cattle on the buttes for generations. I was given to understand that there was never any dearth of the high-protein grass which made it perfect for feeding their herds in summer."

Now she's done it. Gary could see the director's visage darken knowing his reply would be inadequate.

"That's not the whole story. We have continued to run cattle on a limited basis on the prairie. The university research projects have determined that there are other factors contributing to the reduction of bunchgrass proliferation but that grazing practices of the past were largely at fault for the steady shrinkage of native grass growth. Much of it is due to the manure from cattle also containing other grass seed that is steadily overwhelming the bunchgrass." Barely perceptible beads of sweat had appeared at Demetre's hairline as he searched his brain for plausible justification for what was obviously an ineffective treatment to save the bunchgrass. The pathetic areas fenced off from the elk, deer and few cattle they raised were proof enough.

Anthea didn't refute his argument. There wasn't any point since she'd already encountered this feeble and unsupported claim. She'd even read that stomping and scuffling by stock hoofs was killing the grass. At least he didn't go there.

"Considering that the elk and deer also roam, wouldn't they be as much to blame as domestic stock?"

"That's why the fields are fenced off, as a deterrent to the ungulates," said Demetre.

"That's not a word I've encountered much," said Gary. "You mean anything 'on the hoof'?"

"Yes, that's the definition, in fact. Hoofed animal." The crack flew right past their host. Anthea reminded herself, *Yep, no sense of humor.*

"It's too bad the fencing is such an eyesore," observed Anthea. "Why is that water hole also enclosed?"

"They're called 'wildlife exclusion fences' and they serve to keep elk and deer away from plants so they can regenerate," explained the director. "And, often, those plants grow near the water."

"Doesn't this cause another problem?" Anthea was drilling for oil. "That when you block off the water from, what I hear are huge elk herds, those same elk and deer and what have you are forced to find water elsewhere?"

"That could be assumed," concurred Demetre, though he was thinking that was the land trust's purpose in drying up the water sources in the first place. *Could she know that?*

"And the only other water in the region is what the local ranches have to supply their own stock, as I recall. Doesn't that put your protected herds in direct competition with the ranchers' stock, applying undue pressure on your neighbors to water the ungulates that are being denied water on the buttes?"

"They have the option of hazing the animals to get them off their property."

"How well does that work?" asked Gary.

"It's fairly effective. We also have guides who conduct annual elk hunts to thin the herds."

"I gathered that you sell a limited number of tags. I assume the money goes back into your coffers as well as to a few preferred nonprofit causes." It was not a question from Anthea. "Have you thought about using the proceeds to assist the neighbors by installing or repairing fence to keep the elk contained? Maybe add watering holes for them?" She'd done her homework and heard that Terra Ferus had done the exact opposite of removing fence and backfilling ponds.

"We're actively working with the surrounding land owners to alleviate the problem." He cleared his throat, glad that she didn't inquire how many tags were auctioned off. Until recently, the number was so few it made no dent whatsoever in the herd sizes. He also realized that she probably already knew the answer.

"Does that include offering to buy them out or set-up conservation easements?"

"When the advisory board deems it appropriate." His discomfort was becoming evident and Gary was trying not to chuckle. Anthea was on a roll.

"As a matter of interest, I ran across a witness of how a rancher, fed up with the elk overrunning his water pond, hazed a couple hundred elk down the road because he couldn't get them to go back up to Gaston Buttes. Instead they swarmed a neighbor's water source. Here's the odd part. It caused a real problem for the locals and a lot of enmity, especially since Terra Ferus had hired the guys to haze the elk for the first rancher that resulted in pressuring the second with the elk invasion." She let that sink in not expecting a response.

"It didn't seem to be a particularly neighborly act." She arched an eyebrow and Gary about blew a fuse knowing that their pleasant afternoon jaunt, spiced with some targeted questioning, had switched into a hostile interview.

"Which brings me to ask about a curious change in policy regarding elk hunts. Whereas Terra Ferus seemed to be working diligently to build the herd size to what, over thirty-five hundred head I think your website said, and restricting tags to a minimum, now I see that there's a complete switch in management strategy. That there have been three hunts alone this year where ninety hunters each participated. Why the contradiction?"

Demetre hadn't expected to be under the gun to explain the total flip-flop of elk management and supplying the truth was absolutely out of the question. "It turned out that the elk population has grown beyond the capacity of natural predators to keep it under control and the movement of massive numbers across the prairie was damaging the native grass renewal. As well, ODFW was registering increased complaints from area ranchers about elk overrunning their fields. Thus, the state recommended we institute more hunts to thin the herd."

"Without appearing too adversarial, Ken, but it seems to conflict with your stated purpose to protect both wildlife and endangered flora on the preserve. If the herds are whittled down to less than a third of what had preciously been encouraged to grow, won't that add another and different stress to local ranchers?" Anthea was going somewhere on impulse, a notion that had just occurred to her.

"I don't follow," said Demetre, who was afraid that he did.

"Well, since Terra Ferus is working with ODFW to pare back the number of elk so dramatically, but not diminish the number of predators, won't the wolves be forced to look elsewhere for sustenance? I mean, if you're successful in taking the herds down to nominal numbers, then there not only wouldn't be enough elk to sustain herd size for replenishing as well as human consumption, but also nowhere near enough to feed the protected wolves." Stepping over the edge, she said, "Too many wolves are already habituated to preying on cattle now, but wouldn't this policy encourage more stock depredation?"

Trying not to appear as if he were caught with his pants around his ankles, which is exactly what he felt like, Demetre spouted an anemic answer. "Of course not. Stock growers wouldn't be engaged in the herd thinning process if that were the case."

"You know," said Gary. "She has a point. I doubt that anyone addressed that as a possible consequence when proposing increasing elk tags to handle the immediate problem."

"Because the idea is absurd," Demetre shot off too quickly to be believed.

Anthea realized she might have hit paydirt.

Changing tack as smoothly as he could to avoid the direction she'd taken her questions, Demetre said, "As you've noticed, most of the preserve is composed of windswept prairie that is home to all kinds of wildlife. The trust's efforts are to sustain the land, including partnering with government agencies and universities to develop scientific research to implement solutions that improves grazing practices which will be shared with the ranching community at large." Demetre took a deep breath and let it out slowly through slightly flared nostrils.

"Assuming that we've satiated your interest, that's about all there is to see up here, so I'm going to turn around and head back to town. You'll want to get back before it's too late in the day." It was a good thing she had gotten as many photos as she needed on the ride up to Gaston Buttes. There wasn't likely to be any stopping on the return trip.

Anthea had taken the precaution of digitally recorded the conversation and as soon as they reached a place along the road where she had a cell signal, she uploaded everything to the cloud. She'd learned her lesson years ago when her hotel room had been burglarized and all her notes stolen by Nature's Wilds operatives after a potentially damaging interview at their corporate headquarters.

After she had done so and they were about to part company back in Rory, she informed Director Demetre that all her notes had already been forwarded to back-up systems, hoping he wouldn't contemplate any illegal or untoward action. "I've lost information too many times in the past, so I take extra care now. You know how it is when a hard drive crashes. I wouldn't wish that on anyone," she said genially, not that her smile carried much weight with their host. She'd already burned that bridge.

After her announcement, Demetre took another look at Gary and decided entertaining any thoughts of intercepting recordings would have been out of the question. Mathers may be in his mid-fifties but he had a military bearing that, if he wished, could be intimidating. He wondered why he hadn't done an online search of her husband but then recalled that Keller's bio didn't mention being married, only that she was a part-time college instructor and a freelance writer for a number of magazines.

What he'd seen of her work had been pretty tame, giving him the impression he'd be in safe hands. He certainly got that wrong. He'd been hornswoggled by a dwarf of a PR agent. The realization cut into his otherwise expansive self-image. This Keller gal was more of a scorpion than a pushover writing puff pieces, making him speculate whether a negative story would damage his political ambitions.

Taking leave of his guests, he pasted a superficial smile on his face, doing his best to put a positive spin on an episode that he'd prefer disappear.

Unlocking the office door, he let himself inside and watched them drive away. Setting the afternoon aside as a waste of time, he realized that the danger was probably minimal. The media was on his side, environmentally aware and loyal to fighting the same battle to save the nation, no, the world's natural landscapes from man.

Coming right down to it, Keller'd probably never find anyone to publish her tripe.

CHAPTER 26

Concerned about her animals, Cressy had asked May to come and spell her at the mercantile for an hour during lunch. She told May that a predator had been prowling around the house and she wanted to double-check on the stocks' safety, make sure nothing had changed since she and Miles had walked the property that morning.

When the diminutive widow slipped through the front door, Cressy thanked her for watching the shop.

"Not a problem, dear," reassured May as she sat down behind the counter, her accent softening the words to match her friend's worry. "You need to go home and look after your cows."

"See you in a bit."

Driving up to the house, Cressy was surprised to see a horse tethered to the rail that wrapped her front porch. Thinking, *Don't think I know that horse*, she climbed out of the Jeep, Artie jumping down behind her. Since May was only able to cover for her for a short while and not having the option of keeping him home, she'd taken him with her to the store. She refused to leave her dog at the house with a wolf or wolves running loose in the area.

The lamb was in the garage, penned up in the crude stall she and Tricia had thrown together, but there wasn't much she could do to protect the cows. Pointless as she considered fladry, Cressy was thankful that Miles had thought to supply a roll of it when he'd come earlier to investigate the wolf tracks. Before he took off, the two of them had strung the flag festooned rope around the corral as the only safeguard available on short notice. If for no other purpose, she'd be able to demonstrate compliance with policy should anything happen to the horses or cows.

Artie bolted past the horse, circling the house and barking a few times before he quieted down. Following the blue heeler around back, Cressy saw a cowboy poking around the cottonwood shading the creek, Artie had already moved on, unconcerned by the man's presence.

"Hello!" she called to the man stooping near the spot where the wolf droppings had been before the range rider had collected it hours ago.

Looking up from his inspection, he tilted back his hat to see who was hailing him.

"Hey there, Cressy. How're you doing?"

"Quint? What are you doing out here? I haven't seen you in ages!"

"Yeah, I know. Things have been running me ragged the last couple years. Haven't had much time for socializing. Same for you, I suppose." Even as he spoke, he knew they both had steered clear of old acquaintances to avoid fielding the inevitable and uncomfortable questions. Death and divorce did that to people, made hermits out of them.

"True enough. What brings you out here? And right to the very place Miles and I were checking this morning?"

"The range rider, hunh? That makes sense considering it also looks like you had another visitor. An unwelcome beast, at that."

Initially taken aback at his accurate conclusion, her reaction didn't last long. Knowing Quint from growing up as neighbors, she remembered how he'd always been a quick study. Quiet but sharp, a lot of people underestimated his critical eye. A good eight years older than her, she'd ascribed his aloofness to arrogance when they were young.

"If you mean the wolf, you'd be right. That's why I called Miles. He came by to collect the excrement sample it left as a gift... right about where you are. The scent drove Artie nuts when we got home last night.

"That's not surprising." Crouching down, he circled the area in the air with his index finger. "His prints are obvious."

"Yup, I recorded Miles inspecting the sample and bagging it for the lab."

"Smart. Have to document every damn thing if you want to get action out of the authorities, for all the good it does." He caught her eye. "No one knows that better than you."

Cressy bobbed her head in agreement. "But how did you know about the wolf? I didn't tell anyone besides Miles."

"I've tracked this wayward male - I'm pretty sure from the size of his spoor - for quite a distance," said Quint as he straightened up.

"Really. Now why would you be tracking a wolf…" It wasn't so much a question as adding voice to speculation.

"If I told you, I'd have to kill you," he smiled in a weak attempt to be jocular.

Half-smiling back at him, she said, "There was a time I might have thought that was funny."

Taking off his hat, he combed his fingers through hair that showed more salt sprinkled through the natural yellow than she remembered. "You're right," he responded contritely. "I didn't mean to be insensitive."

""Of course not. And I don't mean to be so touchy. Tell me what's going on then. I'd hardly call the cops after all the good they did for us, or anyone else for that matter."

Glancing at the ground feeling a tad sheepish, he brushed his fingers around the brim of his hat, deciding how much to tell her. He knew if anyone was trustworthy, it was Cressy. Their families had known each other for a couple generations.

Relaxing, Quint shifted his weight to one hip. "Had a wolf attack a couple days ago out on the Ketchum lease. The kids were with me when we discovered two dead calves and a dying cow. You know the scenario. She was ripped apart and I had to put her down while Shaley and Cam tried calming the rest of the herd."

Artie came back around and rubbed up against Quint's leg until he got what he wanted, a good back scrubbing. "That's one determined dog," he said as he scratched Artie's head.

"He's good at getting what he wants, though he doesn't warm to strangers that much."

"Yeah, well..." he trailed off before continuing his tale. "I didn't have long to decide what to do. Wait around for the mounties to show up and go through the rigmarole that wastes everybody's time - something you understand better than a lot of us - or say the hell with it and go after the wolves myself."

"You said this was a loner, though. Just now you talked about "wolves" plural, What about the others? Did they get away?"

He hesitated a moment. "That's the part we don't need to discuss because you can guess well enough. This one headed off by himself after what appeared to be a fight with the alpha male of the pack. Or so I assume."

"I don't doubt you. You've always been an exceptional tracker." She cocked her head to the side. "But Miles didn't mention anything about a pack in the area. In fact, he specifically said that he'd heard nothing about one."

"Best I can figure, this one was off the grid. No collars, at least none that worked, and so, no signal to follow. Apparently, this particular group hasn't been sighted or reported anywhere to my knowledge."

"So," said Cressy, finishing his thought, "as far as the State's concerned, they didn't exist. And if they didn't exist then, I don't suppose they do now."

He dropped the corners of his mouth pensively and agreed with her logical conclusion as if the thought had just crossed his mind. "That'd be a pretty good bet."

"Then this is the one that got away."

"Not for long if I have anything to say about it."

"In for a penny, in for a pound?" Cressy queried.

"Sounds about right."

"Okay, tell me what you got."

Quint gave her the rundown of finding the banged up radio collar and how he surmised that there was a wolf cruising the region that had managed to stay unobserved, perhaps for years. He told her how he'd trailed the animal to her yard where she'd found him poring over the signs for an indication of where the wolf had gone from here.

"It's not clear whether he'd fed much at the last kill, being at odds with the alpha that finally chased him off. At least, that's the way I read it." He considered his next words before speaking. "Once they've begun preying on cattle, you know there's no reason to quit. He may be ready to make a meal of easy targets and that could be your little bunch of cows."

"That's not good news." She paused to let his words sink in while scrutinizing the ground by the tree, which had been pretty well trampled by her, Tricia, Artie and Miles. "Can you make anything out of the mess we made? Miles didn't really check any further than this because, well, it hadn't been confirmed the stool was left by a wolf."

"I can't tell much… yet. But we can take a good look around."

Stepping carefully to avoid mucking up the scene further, Quint led the way as the two of them hunted for telltale signs of a wolf's passage.

Realizing the process was going to take more time than she anticipated, Cressy called May to ask her if she could handle the store for a while longer. As usual, May was delighted to hold the fort until Cressy's return.

Widening the search, Cressy trod cautiously in one direction while Quint went another. Having gotten a feel for the wolf's habits after tracking him all morning, he was drawn to explore along the brook that ran through her property. Fifty yards away, he came across a couple of paw impressions in the spongy earth.

"Over here, I think we've got something."

Cressy abandoned her pursuit to join him where he hunkered down next to the watercourse.

"See these?" He was pointing to two clear prints. "Notice how deep they are in the mud? This canine must weigh at least a hundred pounds, if not a fair bit more."

"That's definitely not any of the local dogs. Most of them are working dogs,
border collies and the like. The closest neighbors have a little schnauzer that'd be a snack for this mutt." She placed her foot next to the print to compare for size. "That looks like the size of the tracks by the tree, see?" She pulled up a photo she'd taken the day before showing her boot beside the print. "Too big for the dogs around here."

"Agreed." He nodded his head toward the base of the hill. "It looks like he was headed off to that little stand of pines at the back of your property. Doubtful that he's still there. After all the activity around here and the fact that the animals aren't making a fuss."

"You think he's gone, then."

"For now, but if he's hungry and he hasn't traveled far, your cows might look like dinner. Fladry is hardly a deterrent."

She sighed. "Don't I know it."

Surveying the property from the standpoint of where the wolf prints were preserved in the hardening mud, Quint made an offer.

"Things at the ranch are handled, barring any emergency, and Del's overseeing operations to free me up for a little down time. If it works for you, since I've already taken the day off to track this guy, why don't you let me do what I can to find out where he went. That way, you can head back to work and I'll make sure nothing happens to your stock."

At first Cressy hesitated at the suggestion. Never being good at receiving, though always ready to assist someone else in need, she had trouble accepting help. "I couldn't impose on you to do that."

"It's not an imposition if I offered out of the goodness of my heart," he winked, remembering how headstrong she'd been as a girl when he'd worked for her folks as a teenager. Cressy had been a stubborn child, and spoiled as he recalled. After they both married, they hadn't seen much of each other except at community or stock grower meetings. Daily life got in the way. "You know what a compassionate guy I am," he jibed.

"If you say so," giving him the once over to nettle him. *That's not working. As ever, the cool cucumber dude.* She relented. "Okay, since you insist and I do have to get back before May gives away the store. That woman has a heart of gold but for all the business savvy she tells me her grandmother had, it bypassed her generation. Promise me you'll call or text me if anything happens."

"Of course, but I think the wolf's long gone. What's your number?" She told him and he entered it into his contacts on the phone. "If you want, you can leave Artie here. An alarm barker isn't a bad idea."

"He'd much prefer that to hanging out in the office. Thanks, Quint. This takes a load off my mind."

"Happy to be of service, Ma'am," he doffed his hat.

After she drove away, Quint turned his attention back to the brook. He walked the length of it scouring the sides to locate the errant wolf's trail. Repeated trips up and down the watercourse revealed nothing. It appeared that the wolf had used the water as a path for some distance. Why, Quint didn't know. He hadn't come across any data that showed wolves being wise enough to hide their scent in water, not that it meant they weren't capable of doing so. They were clever animals that operated on intuition and, for all he knew, that might be instinctual.

He covered the area thoroughly, Artie often trotting along behind him, but he couldn't find a point where the predator had exited the stream. The tracks entering the water had been impressed in muck that had since dried so he expected to see similar prints leaving the creek bed.

Scanning the horizon, he removed his hat and scratched his head. Wherever the wolf had left the water it had been at a place where the ground was dry or stony, making it unlikely that he'd leave marks behind. *Unless this one was canny enough to slog through the water for a mile or so before exiting the creek.* It was a possibility given the water was only running a few inches deep.

Much as he hated to give up, he'd call Cressy and tell her that neither he nor Artie found any clues to where the wolf went. One thing was certain, he was gone.

CHAPTER 27

"Gotta say that was about as much fun as I could stand," Gary remarked as he opened the passenger door for his wife to climb into the Dodge.

"What, a little confrontational journalism got you on the run?" asked Anthea impishly.

"Hardly. You had Demetre on the defensive, which is where he belonged. You brought up policies that his organization has instituted on its properties that are more detrimental than they are helpful." He walked around to the driver's side, got in and started the engine.

Anthea picked up the conversation. "He didn't have plausible answers, did he."

"Plausible? It was all he could do to dance around the issues you raised. He exuded the arrogance of your average career environmentalist. So proud of the empires they've built, blocking out the public with their fences, restrictions and know-it-all attitude. Supposing the rest of us are morons if we don't hop on their bandwagon and fawn over the studies fabricated by elite university research teams."

"Exude. I like that image, as if the arrogance was secreted from their pores, sort of like skunk musk."

"After all my huffing that's all you got from it - exude?"

Laughing, she said, "I got the gist, Gary. But you get used to their huffiness if you interview politicians or attorneys very often."

"This Demetre guy qualifies as both, if I remember what you told me. He certainly has the personality for both, if you can call that personality."

"Right on all counts," agreed Anthea. "He's put it out there that he's interested in running for Congress, though not in this district. I don't think he could con the folks out here, though he's done a good job so far with big money donors for Terra Ferus."

"He wouldn't get far in this county even with the influx of liberals hoping to displace the ranch community."

"Still, they're making inroads with as much land that's ending up in the grip of these oversized land trusts." She tried to lighten the dismal mood brought on by the hours spent with the director of Terra Ferus, "Isn't that why we're here? To put the brakes on them creating a new national park or monument at the expense of agriculture?"

"If only we had those super powers," lamented Gary. "I hope it's not too late," he said as they drove back toward Nacqus.

"Yeah, I'd hate to see this beautiful landscape end up the disaster area that Yellowstone has become. The government's done so well there that half of it looks like a moonscape."

Stopping in town, Gary and Anthea thought they'd scrape off the pomposity of their earlier encounter with a cup of coffee at the one and only public house in Nacqus. Unpretentious conversation with authentic people was appealing after enduring a tour of radical environmental doctrine at work.

The Nacqus Grill's menu was typical of most small diners in the northwest. Baskets with burgers, fish, sandwiches, fries; homemade apple, berry, rhubarb pies; beer on tap, wine, coffee and the usual array of beverages. All served with a congeniality that wasn't standard in most uptown restaurants and bars. This was where the community convened and the stools and booths were occupied by neighbors yakking about everything under the sun, including the sun.

The Mathers lived in a city of 35,000 that had numerous family-run cafés, but friendly chitchat was becoming a thing of the past with the disappearance of regulars and oldtimers. Nacqus' restaurant and bar was a haven from small-city big talk that drove both of them to distraction. Sure, every town had a person of consequence, but putting on airs wasn't what gave them distinction in a place like this. They had to earn it.

Hobnobbing with the locals for an hour, they picked up relevant information about the area directly from individuals who knew the history because they were part of it. If Anthea were collecting background for her story, she couldn't have picked a better source for local color.

Feeling as if they'd been welcomed to the family, they thanked the owners and patrons for the convivial exchange. "No wonder visitors rave about your town," said Anthea to the proprietor. "You blow away the city smoke."

"That's good, because it isn't healthy," he grinned, "and it doesn't belong out here. We're always glad to have good folks stay awhile. I hope you come back."

"Who could turn down an invitation like that?" said Gary, shaking his hand.

Leaving the establishment, they saw Cressy in front of the mercantile straightening a display that had been knocked over by one of the deer that made a habit of nibbling on her flowers.

"Keeping up appearances?" Gary asked jovially as they converged by the shop's steps.

His upbeat note was lost on her. "Cleaning up after the riff-raff.

"Deer," she elaborated, answering his quizzical look.

"Right, the denizens of the wood…" he began facetiously.

"That can't keep their nose out of my planters," finished Cressy.

"So much for their nobility."

"Royal pains," grumbled Cressy. "That's as noble as they get." She stood up. "Sorry, that's some 'how d'you do,' isn't it? The deer just get under my skin sometimes."

"They do the same at home. We have them noshing through our garden on a daily basis. Hardly worth planting it," commiserated Anthea.

"At least we get our revenge by eating them," smiled Cressy. "Our fruits and vegies make for tasty venison."

"Hah! There ya go," said Gary. "Never thought of it in that light."

"What sightseeing have you been about today?"

"A guided..." started Anthea.

"Boring, tiresome, tedious..." interrupted Gary.

"...tour of the Gaston Buttes Preserve with the...

"Supercilious, snobbish..."

"...director, Ken Demetre," concluded Anthea.

"By the description I'd have known him anywhere," said Cressy. "Was quite the learning experience, eh?"

"Sure, if he'd had a straight answer to any of my questions," said Anthea.

"The guy was dancing around the issues so much you'd have thought he was doing a jig."

"Obviously entertaining, too," added the shop owner.

"You can apply a lot of adjectives regarding Mr. Demetre, but not that one," chuckled Gary. "How's your day been? Had to be more enthralling than ours."

"I suppose you could say that. We had a visitor last night of the quadruped variety."

"We've just been discussing deer so it wasn't that, nor are they worth special recognition," Anthea thought aloud. "No," her eyes widened. "A wolf?"

"You're good at this," replied Cressy.

"It didn't do any damage, did it?" asked Gary.

"Sent my dog Artie into paroxysms of barking when he smelled the wolf's scent. Had the range rider out this morning to collect the evidence and make a report."

"What kind of evidence?" Gary's interest was piqued.

"What many don't know about wolves is that they will defecate in a public place, for lack of a better term, as a kind of challenge."

"That's a new one on me," said Anthea.

"That's what he left us. Cute, huh? I went back to the house at lunch to check on the stock, that they were okay. A neighbor had come by and is keeping an eye on the place for now so I could get back here." Cressy was starting up the step to go back inside the store when she turned to the Mathers'. "What are you two doing for dinner tonight?"

Gary looked at Anthea who shrugged her shoulders. "We haven't made any plans yet. We're flying on autopilot. What d'you have in mind?"

"If your schedule is open, why don't you come over for dinner? We could use some company... other than wolves."

Quint had texted Cressy earlier to update her on the wolf quest, or the lack thereof, telling her that he hadn't located where it had traipsed off. What he did know, was that it had vacated the premises and was nowhere near the property. He and Artie had taken an extended walk through the surrounding area, stopping to chat with the neighbors. None of them had seen hide nor hair of the trespasser.

After closing up shop, she and Tricia arrived home to find Quint parked out back in one of her lawn chairs, Artie keeping him company chewing on an old bone he'd dug up.

Tricia immediately went to release her lamb from the makeshift enclosure in the garage, leading him to the outside pen to graze. Closing the gate behind him, she asked her mom if he had to go back inside for the night.

"I don't know yet, Honey. Let me talk to Quint and see if he's found anything else. Go ahead and finish your chores. We have company coming for dinner tonight."

"You mean Mr. Edwards?"

"I hope he'll stay but that nice couple I took out to the old place are coming over."

"Okay." Spinning off to attend to her own business, Tricia didn't seem to give a second thought about dinner guests.

Before Cressy joined Quint in the matching lawn chair, she went into the kitchen and brought out a couple of glasses of iced tea. Handing him one, she asked, "Or would you prefer a beer?"

"Nope, this is perfect. Thanks," he lifted the glass in salute and drank down half of it in a few gulps.

"I figured you'd have gone back home by now," said Cressy. "What are you thinking?"

"Already called to tell the family what I'm doing. Depending on your input, I'll let you in on my plan."

"I'm always interested when someone has a strategy. I've shelved the idea of planning anything for the immediate future. Fewer disappointments that way."

"That could either be wise or shortsighted," observed Quint.

"You don't pull any punches, do you?"

He opened his arms, gesturing with his hands palms up. "No games here. What you see is… you know the rest."

"Gotcha, just an open book. So what's your vaunted plan, master tactician?"

"Let's not blow it out of proportion," he chuckled. "Simplistic covers it. I propose to camp out tonight and keep a watch."

Cressy immediately objected. "You've got better things to do than look after my few pair and some horses."

"Not really. I've got a vested interest in finding this wolf and if he comes back, I want to be here."

"And do what? Shoot him?" she asked skeptically.

"Maybe," he was enigmatic.

"You're sure this is what you want to do?" She was hesitant to accept his offer.

"Sure, it's a perfect night to be outside and I came prepared to do exactly that."

"Okay. With one caveat," she said, getting up.

"And what's your counter proposal?"

"Come in for dinner. I've got a couple coming over and if you're staying, we may as well make it a party."

"I don't turn down a homecooked meal," he said finishing off the tea. "You are cooking, aren't you?"

"Yes. Whether that's a good or bad thing will be decided once you taste it."

"I'm game if you are," he handed her the empty glass.

"I thought you said that games weren't your *thang*."

Quint shrugged his shoulders, "Depends on your definition of 'game.' There's 'Twister,' then there are wolves."

Turning toward the back door, a corner of her mouth upturned, she said, "Have it your way."

In a tone she couldn't hear, he said, "I will."

He followed Cressy into the house and went over what was needed while she rummaged in the fridge for dinner makings.

"The pasture nearest the house is already grazed over and I can't leave them there," her voice was muffled as she dug through the vegetable bin. "I need to move the animals back to the north ten where I had them before the 'visitation.'"

"You make it sound like the place is haunted," he grinned while he watched her empty an armload of greens on the counter.

"Could be for the way the whole incident gave me the creeps," she said as she opened the cupboard to examine the contents. "At least it didn't seem to phase Tricia."

Quint kept his mouth shut, he'd already stuck his foot in it.

"So the camp-out will have to be over there. Have to rotate the stock in the pastures whatever the safety circumstances. They can't eat dirt and extra hay isn't in the monthly budget. I get to make the choice between which inventory gets fed, the store or the stock. And since I have grass, that decides the issue."

Cressy turned around and queried him one more time. "Really, you don't need to stay, Quint. It's not your responsibility and you've your own to look after."

"Like I said, everything at home is under control barring any emergency, which isn't going to happen." He wasn't worried since he'd done away with the threat by destroying the pack. The wolf that showed up at Cressy's wouldn't be backtracking. As far as the loner knew, the pack was still roving the territory he'd vacated.

"Besides, I've got a bone to pick with this wolf."

She bored her eyes into his, "You mean, you're dedicated to getting the only surviving member of the pack no one knows about."

"No one ever said you weren't scary smart. But I wouldn't word it quite like that. Others in the area have an inkling this sub-pack existed, or exists, depending on how you look at it. We're not the only ones who suffered predation from the no-name gang whether or not ODFW tried to pin the incidents on another pack."

"That's right, come to think of it. The Lakens said they've had trouble lately but got nowhere with Fish and Wildlife when they reported it. Officials kept saying that the Nacqus pack couldn't have done it, too far away. So they accused some other predatory animals... that they never found, of course."

"No wonder there. After botching the investigation with Terry, ODFW isn't going to come close to acknowledging another pack could be operating on your old ranch. That'd be as good as admitting they might have been mistaken, poking a hornets' nest after denying compensation or even an apology for their muck-up."

She looked up from the deep drawer where she kept baking pans, "Government never apologizes. Don't think they have to. Just government at its best, or worst... I don't know which anymore."

"Both. Government policy is so bad, its best is its worst. If that makes any sense."

"There must be something wrong with me because it does."

Quint went outside to see to the horses, putting Hodey in the corral with them for the time being. While Cressy worked in the kitchen, he made the rounds of the property one more time to ensure that he was correct in his assessment of the wolf's departure.

He was off in the field west of the house when he saw a truck pull into the driveway and a couple exit bearing a bottle of wine and what looked like a pie box.

Guess the other guests have arrived. Don't think I've seen them before.

As he strolled toward the front of the house, Cressy welcomed the couple, ushering them inside. Quint stopped by the Dodge and noticed that it carried Idaho plates. Interesting. *Not like we can't have friends from other states. Duh, where was I yesterday?*

Cressy having already brought her visitors inside, Quint figured it was probably a suitable time to make his own entrance and walked around the house and knocked on the back door.

Tricia came running to answer the door and flung it wide in her haste and enthusiasm. She couldn't remember anyone coming over to visit other than her grandparents and cousins, and those times were rare.

Her mother had been a social butterfly before her dad died. Young as she was, Tricia'd been very aware of her mother's grief and how she'd locked herself away, becoming a recluse except for dealing with business that couldn't be avoided.

During the period that her mother had been haggling with the authorities and wolf advocates, Tricia had been shuffled off to her grandparents on a regular basis. She saw her mother struggling to keep an outward show of being in control. Kids are sponges when it comes to adults bottling up their emotions and Tricia wasn't fooled. She'd soaked in her mother's turmoil. Neither did she know what she could do to help. That's the other thing about kids, they feel utterly powerless when it comes to consoling parents.

Tonight, all of a sudden there were three people at the house for dinner. It didn't matter to Tricia that none of them were her age, they were company and that signaled a change in living conditions. Cressy may now be the owner of the mercantile, but there was a complete difference between her interactions with customers and the isolation at home. One was obligatory and the other was a hideaway.

Quint was surprised to be invited in by Cressy's gleeful daughter. He assumed Tricia would be more annoyed than happy to have a table full of gabbing adults. At her age that's more how his kids would have reacted, knowing they were about to be bored to tears by grown-up drivel like neighborly gossip, or worse, politics.

"Well, thank you, Tricia. I see your mom has some other guests for dinner. Do you know them?" he asked as he scraped his boots on the bristly back of an iron hedgehog.

He was about to remove them when Tricia said, "That's okay, Mr. Edwards. Mom said you should keep your boots on in case there's an emergency."

Taken aback at first, Quint nodded, "You can call me Quint, Tricia. I know it's been a long time since I've seen you but you're grown up enough to use my first name, don't you think?"

Beaming at his compliment, Tricia said, "Sure, Mr., um, Quint. Come on in. Mom's got dinner ready."

"Thank you. I'm going to go wash up real quick," which he did at the sink in the mudroom while she went back to the kitchen. He was appreciative for being able to keep his boots on, supposing that Cressy's other guests were still shod. Being introduced in his stocking feet wouldn't really bother him but it was considerate of her to think of such a detail.

When he came into the kitchen, Cressy was about to extract a casserole from the oven. Tossing him the mitts, she said, "Here, make yourself useful and bring this to the table while I get the side dishes."

"Surely, Ma'am." He donned the mitts and carried the hot pan to the dining room. If he thought he'd been spared ignominy by having boots on his feet, that was dispelled as he greeted the other guests while his calico gloved-hands were full with a steaming casserole.

Cressy introduced them, "Gary and Anthea Mathers, this is my longtime neighbor, Quint Edwards. He dropped by this afternoon looking for, of all things, a wolf."

If she was expecting to get a rise out of the three of them with that bit of information, it worked. Gary's forehead crinkled, Anthea's eyes widened and Quint nearly dropped the bubbling main course.

Quickly depositing the hot dish on the table, Quint removed the quilted mitts and shook hands with the couple, feeling exposed, boots or no boots. His hunt wasn't common knowledge, especially considering the circumstances that had put him on the wolf's trail. "Good to meet you both," he said without allowing his discomfort to show.

"Anthea and Gary are visiting from Idaho. They're staying with the Darby's at the inn."

Okay, I wasn't really prepared to tell a couple of strangers what I was doing, especially since some might consider my intent to be criminal. On top of which, this guy has 'cop' written all over him. Quint caught himself. Cressy was no fool and if she opened this door there had to be a good reason.

"I hope you're enjoying your visit here," offered Quint. "Is this your first time in Koyama County?"

"Yes," replied Gary. "Seems strange that this is only a few hours from home and yet we'd never been here before."

"The surprise was..."Anthea stopped herself. "Actually, it wasn't really, considering what we've learned in the last years about hardships confronting ranchers and farmers." Realizing the comment made no sense, she clarified. "Cressy and others have been filling us in on the problems folks have had with wildlife advocates. Not that it's anything new to us. We encountered a similar circumstance in Idaho. Kind of got caught in the middle of it."

"Is that why you're here?" Quint was curious now.

"It wasn't our reason for vacationing here," said Gary. "We'd heard about the area - we live mainly in Lewiston - and having an opportunity to get away, we opted to check out the countryside. Purely by accident did we find out about the issues you're having with wolves."

"And how bad it is," added Anthea.

Cressy stepped in while she laid the rest of the table and took the salad bowl from Tricia who was half listening. Glad as she was for her mother to entertain, she was really tired of hearing about wolves. "Let's sit down and eat. We can talk shop later. Right Tricia?"

"Hm-hmmm. I'm kind of hungry and I'll bet Mr., um, Quint is too." She grinned as she took the oven mitts from him and sat down in her usual place.

"Please," said Cressy, her hand open to indicate the chairs on the left side of the table. "Have a seat. I'll let you do the honors," she said, holding out an opener to Gary for him to decant the wine.

Accepting the tool, Gary said, "Certainly, it would be my pleasure."

The table was set, the guests were seated and the wine was poured. For the next forty-five minutes, tales were told, and Quint and Cressy replayed childhood memories for the Mathers but mostly for Tricia's benefit.

"I don't suppose you have any homework tonight," said Cressy as dinner was winding down.

"Not in the last week of school," replied Tricia, stretching her arms over her head and grinning with her best impression of the Cheshire Cat. "All done for the year."

"It's a good feeling, isn't it," said Gary. "That's why we're here for a week, because I got out of school, too."

"Really?" Tricia was incredulous until it struck her, "Oh, you're a teacher."

"Even teachers are relieved when summer rolls around."

Tricia was interested. She didn't talk to her teachers much outside of class except running into them around town. "What grade do you teach?"

"Well, I teach college, mostly online these days."

"I wouldn't have pegged you for a college professor," observed Quint. "I figured you for law enforcement."

"You've a good eye, Quint. I'm retired." He looked at Tricia, "Talk about being glad to get off work. That's a job that'll wear you out even more than a classroom full of fourth graders," he winked at her.

"I guess. We're not busy breaking the law. Usually."

Gary glanced at Cressy. "How old is she?"

"Takes after her mom," cut in Quint. "Precocious."

Cressy rolled her eyes. "Okay, girl. Time for you to get yourself upstairs. Unless you want to help clear the table."

"Are you giving me an out so you can have adult conversation?"

"Don't blow it by talking yourself out of a gift from heaven," warned Cressy.

"You don't have to tell me twice," Tricia popped out of her seat. Before rushing up to her room she made certain to properly say goodnight. "It was nice meeting you!"

"It was a pleasure to meet you, Tricia," said Anthea. "Have a good night."

"Thanks!" and she was gone.

"Let me help you with the dishes, Cressy." Before her hostess could refuse Anthea put her hands up to cut off any argument. "Come on, we'll finish it in a flash and the guys can yap about whatever guys yap about."

"Yeah, all they need is brandy and a cigar."

"You forgot the dinner jackets."

"That'd be a hoot." Cressy looked over her shoulder at the guys. "Nah, I can't picture it."

Kitchen duty was complete and Anthea and Cressy returned to the dining table with a pot of coffee and four mugs. "Anyone interested?" asked Cressy holding the carafe on high.

"Only if it comes with another slice of pie," said Quint.

"Done. Besides you've earned it today. In fact, you can take the rest with you to satisfy midnight cravings on your vigil tonight," said Cressy.

"Pie or coffee?"

"Both, if you like," she grinned.

"Vigil?" Anthea asked.

"Back to the whole wolf thing," explained Cressy. "Remember I said Quint was looking for a wolf? I wasn't kidding. Just so happens the very wolf that showed up on my property is the one that Quint tracked here. He's going to keep watch over the stock tonight… only because I couldn't talk him out of it."

"Chivalry isn't dead?" Anthea said lightheartedly.

"If that were my only reason, I might agree but I do have an ulterior motive," said Quint. "I want to catch him and my best chance, at this juncture, is if he's still in the area, which, unfortunately, I doubt."

"What would you do if he does turn up?" asked Gary.

"That depends on whether he's threatening the stock, which I can pretty much guarantee. After all, it is my word, and gun, against his being where he doesn't belong."

"I get it, but after hearing all these horror stories, I wonder if you're not flirting with taking up residence in a jail cell," said Gary.

"The losses are piling up. I expect you already know Cressy's story. ODFW is unresponsive and operates according to its own rules that hold wolves' lives as more precious than ours. Face it, their policies are a conflict of interest advocating for wolves literally *against* us, we who pay their salaries to protect us from wolves." Quint leaned back in his chair, cradling his mug. "I'll take my chances."

"Besides, he'll have corroboration," said Cressy. "Not that ODFW ever wants to see my face again."

"They don't know what they're missing," said Quint, raising the cup to cover his mouth before anyone caught his expression.

Chapter 20

Bedded down for the night, Quint rolled the day's events through his mind while he watched Hodey muzzle through the grass in the dying dusk.

After the Mathers' had taken their leave, he and Cressy had moved her cattle back to the north pasture. Again, she protested his decision to stay with her stock, something she felt she should be doing.

"I hate leaving you out here alone. I'll feel guilty."

"Okay, if it eases your conscience to lose sleep while I snore blissfully under the stars, go for it."

She was tempted to elbow him in the side as if they'd never passed puberty. "There's the other part of it. How are you going to know if a wolf is nosing around if you're out like a light?"

"Don't give me that. Like you've never stood watch before. Between Hodey and the cows no wolf is going to be able to sneak up unnoticed. They'll sense him."

"Or he'll scent you," she sniffed mockingly.

Quint played along, raising his arm and faking a whiff of his shirt. "That bad, hunh?"

Shaking her head, she said, "Nothing gets through to you, does it?"

"If it does, I'm not about to share," he said with finality. "I think this will be fine right here," and he dropped his bedroll next to a couple of aspens someone had planted ages before. "The likelihood of the wolf even coming back is slim but we want to comply with as much of the administrative nonsense as we can. Human presence is required since there's no place to drape those flippin' flags. I suppose we could have brought a sheet and hung it like a ghost for Halloween. I'm sure that'd do the trick."

"Except that device isn't on the official list of deterrents," she deadpanned.

He checked out the scene. The cows were quietly moseying nearby so Quint indicated it was time to walk Cressy back to the house. "All seems copacetic so let's get back and see you two gals locked in for the night."

Enjoying the mild weather, they walked to the house without further objection from Cressy. Accepting his thanks for supper, she closed the door after watching him lead his horse toward the spot he'd chosen to camp. At first uncomfortable accepting Quint's offer to spend the night in the field with the cattle, she got over it knowing she was actually going to sleep soundly because he was out there.

Before lying down to get some rest, Quint leafed through social media sites on his phone to see if anything had been posted about wolf activity in the area. Half the time, news found its way online before the authorities bothered to inform property owners.

Tonight there was nothing.

The sun having dropped behind the mountains almost an hour before,
the sky was gradually mellowing into the dulcet tones of evening. The darker it grew, a dim yellowish glow became more visible above the northwest horizon.

Quint kept his gaze glued to the line separating the highlands from the sky, thinking it was a trick of his eyes and he was imagining the glow to be intensifying against a blacker backdrop.

He noticed what could have been smoke plumes when he'd made his run to Idaho, assuming they were mare's tail clouds reflecting sunset colors. At the time, it briefly crossed his mind that there might be a small fire, probably started by dry lightning.

This was the season when there was apt to be a fire someplace at any given time. Always hoping the fires would be quickly doused, some years proved to be devastating when high winds whipped the flames across hundreds and thousands of acres of dry brush.

The brighter the stars shone, increasingly contrasted against a darkening sky, the golden radiance became more distinct above the line of mountains. Quint was now sure a fire was burning.

For the time being, there was nothing he could do other than check a few websites on his phone for information. Sure enough, after revisiting social media he came across someone who posted about a fire spreading fast up the slopes of the Hiller Range on the other side of Koyama, the county seat, a good forty miles away. The fact that even a faint light was visible from that distance said much about the size of the blaze. Either that, or another grass fire had ignited closer to home.

Already committed to keeping watch for a wolf that was unlikely to show up, Quint decided to shelve concern about the fire. In small communities like his, locals remained prepared to jump to the aid of neighbors in the event of a fire, but tonight he wasn't in a position to abandon his post. He'd made a promise that he needed to keep.

With Hodey occupied munching grass and the cows unperturbed, Quint settled back on his sleeping bag to catch some shuteye. Tomorrow would be another story.

A day after stopping by that farmhouse where his passing trig - gered the resident dog into a fit of barking heard across the canyon, the wolf had traveled miles.

He had spent the night under the branches of a thicket of vol - unteer plum trees a couple miles from the speckled noisemaker before moving out of the district.

Nothing else in the vicinity to distract him, he padded along a deer track winding across the bottom of an arroyo that cut into the mountain, taking him up to the rimrock. Topping the height, the wolf hadn't bothered to look back as he continued through the tall grass covering the prairie extending in front of him.

As the wolf loped across the fields, steadily gaining elevation, the smell of burned hay wafted across his sensitive nostrils, the acrid odor making his nose twitch. Every animal, wild or domestic recog - nized the smell as a sign of peril and he became more wary as he forged ahead. In the past, he'd seen the fur of small animals set alight by a spark carried on the wind. Singed hair was probably the most unpleasant stench to him. Rotting meat meant food but burning hair spelled threat.

Transient most of his life, his instinct for self-preservation was more honed than wolves that had matured in the confines of pack dynamics, reaching adulthood within the group.

Milling around the vicinity, he'd seen nothing besides a few mule deer that bolted as soon as they detected the wolf's presence. Lacking direction other than to keep moving, the reek of smoke com - pelled him to circle back around to the gully. Crossing the stream he'd followed up the incline, the wolf retraced his steps from earlier in the day. A few miles later, the stench of burnt grass had lessened, allow - ing him to relax and locate a resting place before continuing to trav - el. Fire would determine where he'd go from here.

Hunkering down by blackberry brambles, nothing could be discerned of his coat, the color blending in with his surroundings. An occasional glint of yellow eyes might have been visible to nocturnal creatures passing by but even they were scarce, perhaps warned off by telltale signs of fire.

Peering out from the cover, the wolf made brief note of a horse in the distance where a strange light flickered now and again.

Having no impetus to budge from the protection of the thorny overhang, the wolf settled in for what remained of the night, eyes closing out the dormant world.

Chapter 29

Morning dawned with an ochre pall hovering over the northern ridge of mountains, fingers of smoke slowly drifting east and spreading across the lightening sky. As the wind picked up, smoke saturated the air making it hard to pinpoint where the fire originated.

Whump, whump, whump, whump, whump...

Whirring blades beating the air caught Quint's attention as a helicopter flew overhead steering for an alpine lake, orange bucket trailing in the wake of its airstream.

A few miles outside Rory was where county fire control set up the regional command center year after year. On site was a parking lot that was roped off to serve as a temporary helipad. The aircraft would lift off from the asphalt, bearing south to the nearest large body of water, a lake high in the Koyamas, to scoop up the liquid in monstrous buckets. Throughout the day, helicopters continued the rotation of collecting water, flying out over the blaze and dumping the hundreds of gallons in an effort to quench the flames.

Rolling up his bedding, Quint saddled his horse before checking the surrounding area for any sign that an uninvited guest might have dropped by during the night. He'd already expected to find nothing since the night had passed without disturbance, the stock remaining quiet through the dark hours, indicating that the wolf was either gone or maintaining a healthy distance from human habitation.

Picking up his gear and tying it to the back of the saddle, Quint led Hodey the quarter mile back to Cressy's house, examining the turf as he went, just in case he'd missed something the day before.

Coming up empty, he wrapped Hodey's reins over the fence rail and turned toward the farmhouse. He was ready for a good jolt of java.

Cressy didn't disappoint. She appeared at the open door to the kitchen holding a steaming mug as he strolled in her direction, a smile scrolling across his face as he approached. Climbing the step, he removed his hat with one hand and accepted her offering in the other with a hearty "thank you."

Waving him inside, Cressy said, "Come on in. I've got breakfast on the table." She pinned him with a look, "I assume you're hungry."

Noncommittal, he replied, "I could eat." Winking, he went through to the kitchen, sat down and proceeded to pile his plate with a bacon, potato and cheese scramble. After the first swallow Quint paused just long enough to commend Cressy on her culinary skills before digging in with alacrity.

"Glad you like it." A corner of her mouth turned up in a slight smirk, sitting down across from him and taking a smaller portion. "It's nice to have someone around for once who enjoys a good meal. Tricia's appetite could satisfy a finch on a diet."

"When you find a bird worried about weight loss, let me know. That'd be one for the record books, all right."

"I'm more concerned about Tricia's lack of interest in food."

Chagrined, he put down his fork. "I'll bet you are. I noticed that she didn't eat much last night even though she said she was hungry. That girl is just a wisp of a thing, would blow away in a stiff breeze." He drank some coffee. "Been going on long?"

"More than a year. Started after Terry died so it's no surprise really. It took me a good long while before I could eat much, either."

"Kids are sensitive... and different. You never know how they're going to react to things."

Cressy lifted her eyes from her plate. "You'd know. How'd Cameron and Shaley react when, hmmm, things changed?"

"The opposite of what you'd expect. Shaley could eat but Cam lost his appetite when Kim took off. I think he internalized a lot of the disillusionment, but I also think he blamed himself in a way for his mom leaving. It was my mother who finally got Cam to realize it had nothing to do with him and everything to do with Kim. And I'd be lying if I didn't admit to being part of the equation." He took another sip of coffee. "Guess you never know with boys, do you?"

"If you're any example, then, no," she said, trying to

lighten the mood.

Shaking her head, she stabbed a chunk of egg and changed the subject. "Anything happen last night? Yipping coyotes or howling wolves split the air?"

"You'd have heard that yourself."

"Nope, I slept like a contented baby. First time in weeks."

Quint gave her his attention, surprised but guarding his expression. "Is that so? Good thing you didn't lose any sleep because not a thing stirred. I double-checked the area this morning and didn't see any evidence of critters in the neighborhood that didn't belong there. The wolf must have moved on but I'm still going back out to do a more thorough sweep before calling it quits. The last thing we need is this lone ranger to peel off a female from another pack and beget one of his own." He refocused on his breakfast.

"On that I'd agree. I've had enough of wolves to last me five lifetimes."

Quint felt empathy but said nothing.

As he finished up, Cressy popped a slice of bread in the toaster, buttered and spread jam on it before going to the foot of the stairs and calling up to her daughter. "Hurry up, Tricia, the bus will be here any minute."

"Okay, Mom," floated the answer from the top of the landing.

A moment later Tricia came crashing down the stairs, making Quint wonder how so much noise could be generated by such a little girl.

Tricia would have ignored the toast on her way out if her mother hadn't stopped her and insisted she eat something.

"But I'm not hungry."

"I know, but you need something in your stomach, so take it and eat it. I'm not going to have you fainting for lack of sustenance," and she shoved the breakfast, such as it was, into Tricia's hand.

Without further argument, Tricia grabbed the toast and took a bite while running out the door. "G'bye, Mom!"

"Have a good day!" yelled Cressy, watching Tricia reach the side of the road, the bus pulling up as if on cue. The door whisked open, Tricia disappeared inside and the bus trundled on its way.

Cressy returned to the kitchen, collected the plates and deposited them in the sink for washing up. Brushing crumbs off her hands, she told Quint, "I have some time before I need to open the store. Do you want company inspecting the property for clues about the wolf's whereabouts, see if there's something we missed?"

"You mean, 'I missed?'" he grinned. "Sure, another set of eyes is always a benefit. If he's smart, though, he's gone. But they are unpredictable, clever or not."

"I can finish here later. Do whatever you need to do and I'll go saddle my horse. Meet me out back in a few."

Quint tipped his hat and dropped his head in a mini-bow, peering at her from under his brow with a jocular half-smile. "Yes, Ma'am."

Taking their time, Cressy and Quint rode well beyond the perimeters of her acreage, fanning out onto neighboring property and making a mile-wide circle. Dismounting occasionally to examine questionable signs, they still found the wolf had left nothing that was less than two days old. And that was a single smudged paw print that might have pointed off toward the northwest. Their tour didn't tell them much aside from the fact that the wolf was no longer in the area.

"Looks like you may be out of the woods for now, Missy."

"Until the next marauding band of hairy beasts roves through here."

"You make it sound like pirates on the high seas."

"As good as," said Cressy as they rode back to the barn. "Hunting for booty and stealing what isn't theirs. Pirates, raiders, what's the difference?"

"None to speak of but we haven't heard of any other packs operating in the area aside from the one that's now gone," he said as she allowed him to carry her saddle to the tack room.

"Caveat: almost gone. What were we looking for if not the last member of that pack? And we know how informed the wolf coordinator kept you, or anyone else, for that matter."

"Point taken." Walking with Cressy, he led Hodey around to the front of the house. "You can only share what you know and for that no-name bunch, the authorities didn't know anything. It might be a longshot, but I'm even thinking that this wolf is a nomad that has attached himself to more than one pack along the way. By the looks of the collar I found and considering the decrepit condition it was in, this guy could have come from as far away as Yellowstone.'

"Why would you think that?"

"That's one place where it was well documented that the wolves chewed off the collars and this one was gnawed to pieces, old, and I don't think the transmitter ever worked properly," he said.

"And you believe this is the one that wore it," she stated.

"None of the other wolves' hair was matted around the neck. They'd never been tagged. It had to be this one which has to be full-grown to have posed a threat to the pack's big dog."

"So the evidence seems to say." She stopped at the driver's side of her Jeep, ready to go into town and open the mercantile. "What now, Quint?"

"Looks like there's not much I can do about the wolf I tracked here." He settled his hat back on his head. "May as well go on home and get back to work." He caught her eye before mounting his horse. "You call me if that 'pirate' shows up again, or if there's anything else I can do for you. I'm not that far away."

"Thanks, Quint." Facetiously, she added, "If I come across a mislaid eyepatch or lost parrot, I'll do that."

CHAPTER 30

Riding toward home, now that Quint had his gaze aimed up the canyon rather than scouring the ground, the smoky veil he'd noticed earlier hooked his attention. Cresting the rocky cliff, the extent that the murky plumes had broadened across the plateau was wider than he'd supposed.

Studying the northwest, he could see the base of one cloud originating from the other side of the round-topped Hiller Range and another, larger smoke column rising from beyond the Gaston Buttes. He checked the horizon in all directions and saw a tower of smoke billowing from beyond the Koyamas, probably centered across the Snake River in Idaho. As he'd thought when he woke that morning, the likely culprit was the storm that blew through a couple days ago, lightning strikes sparking the blazes.

The fire season was off to a gangbuster start.

Deciding not to wait until he got home to talk to Del, Quint dialed him right away. As the call connected, a helicopter swung overhead making its way to Tyre Lake to fill the dangling bucket. The noise overwhelmed the phone's speaker as it flew past so Quint couldn't hear Del answering the call.

"Sorry, Del. Helicopters on water detail flying by."

"That, I could hear from up here and over the phone. Not a good sign this early in the year."

"No, it isn't. It's why I'm calling, to see if you've heard anything about the fires. I couldn't get much from the phone apps."

"As usual, Quint, your timing is impeccable."

"How's that? No emergencies with the family or the stock, are there?"

"Not here. We got a call from Joe Taylor, though. They're trying to round up cattle from the bench out by Emville. That fire is raging through the brush so fast they've already lost around twenty-five head. They need extra hands as quick as they can get 'em.''

"I'm not fifteen minutes from the house."

"Good. You'll want me to wait for you." It wasn't a question.

"Yes. I'm on my way." Shutting down the phone and pocketing it, Quint spurred Hodey into a gallop.

Anthea and Gary watched smoke darken the sky to the north. They'd been planning to head for home, their getaway at an end. At least, that had been the plan. Anthea was from fire-prone Southern California where the autumn Santa Ana winds propelled flames across the chaparral practically on an annual basis.

Moving to Idaho brought a whole new perspective on the concept of "fire season." The inland northwest wasn't criss-crossed with highways and freeways allowing accessible egress when the swift moving blazes leapt across river canyons and prairies. Evacuations were difficult and communities had volunteer fire crews to fill the gap while waiting for professionals to arrive. She'd been impressed by their skill and coordination fighting arson fires when she and Gary had been researching the land conservancy a few years back. Fire awareness for remote towns and ranches was a constant concern because it was hard to flee, let alone stay and fight to save property and livestock.

Seeing the orange-tinged plumes rise and fill the northern horizon decided the Mathers to check road conditions. Home lay in that direction up a lone two-lane highway and there was a strong probability that it may be closed to through traffic.

Outlying houses, businesses and ranch and farm operations made it a habit to keep abreast of fire reports and the Darbys were true to that practice. They told Gary and Anthea about the Emville blaze, detailing how local ranchers were converging on the Taylor lease to help round up cattle that were dispersed over miles of open range. Describing the rough terrain and deep canyons the cowboys needed to cover to rescue cattle was an unfamiliar scenario to the city-bred Anthea, not that she couldn't grasp the breadth of the ranchers' dilemma. Doug and Ellie had been through similar circumstances and effusively depicted the crisis.

"The Rory Creek drainage is rugged land and steep. Getting those cattle out of there ahead of the flames is gonna take a miracle," Doug predicted. "But those cowpokes know what they're doing."

"What have you heard?" Gary asked.

"About the roads," said Ellie, "It was posted that the fire's on both sides of the highway, closing it for now. They're using it as a main artery to move fire equipment in and out of the area. What's interesting is this... One person said the fire crossed the road but there are a few posts saying that fires started a little ways east *and* west of the road *about the same time and then joined.*" She looked up from her phone's screen. "The funny thing is that there wasn't any storm activity at the time and some folks think the origins are suspicious. There was another fire, though, that was sparked by dry lightning out to the northwest, past the Hillers, a couple days ago. These other two, that are now one blaze, came up out of nowhere overnight and spread faster than whipped by a gale."

"There's more smoke to the southeast," said Gary. "Any mention of that from your network?"

"Not much that I've found other than it's coming from Idaho, but, as usual, there's nothing yet about the fire's origin." Eleanor looked at Gary and Anthea, "I assume that's what you wanted to know."

"A mind reader, too," said Anthea. "Seems as if every year the fires have been getting worse and more pervasive. We had a number of friends that were evacuated from their homes along the Clearwater River last year. One family lost everything while our other friends' home, a half a mile away, was untouched. Of course, conspiracy theorist that I am," she said half-joking, "I'd like to know how many of the really devastating fires have been traced back to arson."

"Like the huge fire that burned through the Yarnell, Arizona area a few years back where all those hotshot firefighters were killed," Anthea continued. "The mainstream press didn't pick it up, or ignored it more likely, but an Al Qaeda connected terror cell claimed responsibility for setting it."

Doug shook his head, "That's hard to believe."

"We need to keep an open mind about terrorism, whether it's eco-groups, Islamic or some other political or grievance organization, methods have grown beyond the stereotypical Molotov cocktail," said Gary. "Biologics, poisons, machetes, guns, trucks and vans, anything that can be used to inflict harm and property damage is being used for terror purposes. Fire is one of the most destructive methods. Think about how much damage is done to natural resources, agricultural industries and homes."

"The thing about the Arizona fire," cut in Anthea, "is that I located a credible source that linked to the terror group's website that claimed credit. Be assured you were never going to hear about it from the network news, nor did you. After what we've seen in Idaho and other instances where eco-terrorists like EarthFirst! set fire to car dealerships in California and housing tracts, I think that was Arizona too, over the last twenty years, it's reasonable to consider the possibility of questionable origins behind some of these fires."

"We hear about arson now and again but I hadn't thought about fire being a terror tactic," considered Eleanor. "From what you've told us about your experiences, sounds like you ought to know."

"Would that we hadn't been through them, as far as I'm concerned," said Anthea. "Scared the snot out of me and I'd rather not do it again." Gary just nodded in agreement. "Like I said, I'm naturally skeptical but terrorism isn't out of the question." She shrugged her shoulders, "Just saying."

Once Quint reached home, he saw Del waiting by the horse trailer, ready to load up and be on their way. Taking a few minutes to change clothes and check in with Audrey, Quint moved quickly, feeling the pressure of knowing that wildfires wait for no one.

Ten minutes from arrival to jumping into the passenger seat, Quint buckled in as Del fired up the truck and started down the mountain. The Taylor Ranch wasn't thirty miles straight across the plateau except the only route to get there wound seventy miles around the mountain base. There was nothing for it but to be patient and drive.

The last ten miles of road was gravel pitted by washboard from the spring runoff. Trailering the horses, Del kept his speed in check. There'd be enough rough riding once they got to work rounding up cattle.

The staging area lay east of Emville in a wide spot along Rory Creek. Trucks and trailers lined the road with a number of semis standing ready to load cattle and drive them to safer pastures.

Del parked the Ford and he and Quint immediately dropped out of the cab to talk to the ramrod and find out where they were needed.

Georgia Taylor was working out of a weathered motorhome coordinating wranglers, dispatching them to different quadrants. With her was a representative from County Fire keeping her updated on the movement of the flames, climbing and descending three thousand feet of canyon wall. Her husband, Joe, had just ridden in and finished loading steers onto one of the cattle trucks that was now pulling out of the parking area.

Catching up with Taylor, Quint and Del walked with him to the RV to receive their marching orders. This wasn't a haphazard operation. Cowboys had two-way radios and cell phones with them attempting to stay in contact with Georgia, but the terrain posed a major obstacle for communication. Adding to that the heavy smoke that cut visibility, the complications of the roundup were tremendous.

It wasn't long before Quint and Del were mounted and heading toward an arroyo on the south side of Rory Creek. Cattle were strewn across the face of the steep hills, making their way to the gulch, a stream running down the center. Shielded by the smoke, the encroaching fire was evident by the intensifying heat and the ash swirling through the air, carried in every direction by the flames' draft.

The riders were told that the blaze coming from the buttes was still miles off to the east with another front high on the north slope, seven miles behind them. The danger was if the two blazes joined creating a firestorm that could cut-off retreat to the west. Quint and Del, like all the wranglers driving the cattle to the trucks, were aware of the fires' proximity but the ranch community was tightly knit and ready to support one another in dire circumstances such as this.

As they forded the creek at a wide, shallow spot, the two men from the Edwards Ranch saw what they didn't expect. A brief rift in the smoke gave them a glimpse of the flames jumping the banks of Rory Creek half a mile away, much closer than had been reported.

The situation just got more desperate.

CHAPTER 31

Tricia hopped off the schoolbus, the last child to descend the steps before they retracted and the door closed. Running in the front door of the Wild River Mercantile, her book bag was hanging off her shoulder. Not seeing her mother right away, Tricia called out in her excitement, "Mom, have you seen all that smoke. It looks like there's fire everywhere!"

"No, I haven't been outside for awhile. Been too busy around the shop, though it's been slower than usual. But I can smell the smoke now that you mention it."

"Come look!"

They went outside and scanned the sky in all directions. The sun was high and shaded a vibrant orange behind the haze. Nacqus was near the bottom of the valley and the smoke hemmed them in, coloring the sky a grim yellow making it impossible to tell where the fires were located.

Cressy was surprised as she skimmed the hilltops. "That was fast. There were only smudges of smoke on the horizon this morning.

"Yeah, it looked scary coming down the canyon and all you could see or smell was smoke," said Tricia with the exaggeration of a ten-year-old.

"It's bad enough that I'm going to check to see what I can find out about the fires," Cressy said as she walked back in the store to access the computer. "I don't think any of them are close to us here but we need to know what's going on."

"All I heard at school was that there's a big fire out by Emville and another one the other side of the Koyama Mountains."

"Well, your information may be pretty accurate knowing how many kids have cell phones," she commented as she sat down at the counter and started typing on the keyboard. "And that would account for the smoke coming from more than one direction but the fires must be moving fast to generate so much of it."

Pulling up social media first, Cressy checked her timeline knowing that people living in the region would quickly post reliable information when disasters loomed, and fires qualified for that category. Not two posts down she saw orders regarding evacuations from Emville to the highway heading north out of the county. Growing up in Koyama County, she knew all the families out that way, how large their operations were and what a mess it was going to be to take care of their stock. Swift moving fires posed huge dangers to the animals, especially at this time of year when they had already been taken to summer pasture.

Cressy didn't want to think about what her friends and acquaintances might be up against. She and Terry had run thousands of head of cattle and she didn't even want to imagine what it would have been like trying to save them in the midst of a wind-whipped wildfire.

Scrolling down, she came across a map that showed the fire moving both south and north at the same time, which didn't make a lot of sense to her assuming the winds were blowing in one direction. Then she recalled that really hot fires could create their own weather patterns, except the map showed hot spots and approximate start times as being on the heels on one another in three different places. They also said the origin of the fires was unknown, which wasn't a surprise since there hadn't been any lightning storms lately that she knew about or that were mentioned.

There was always the possibility of some careless hikers sparking a blaze. There were plenty of those, most visiting from the Westside of the state and lazy when it came to managing a campfire.

Then there was arson. There'd been more and more instances of that over recent years, a fact that didn't improve her disposition any. Fire was particularly dangerous in a vale like theirs with only two ways out - one back up to Rory and the other a forest service road southeast to the Snake River. At least both were paved, the rest of the routes were basically Jeep trails.

"So far it looks like we're in the clear, including the road back to Rory," she said half to herself despite having Tricia peering over her shoulder at the computer screen. "Nothing to worry about, okay?"

"Okay," agreed Tricia, some relief ringing in her voice.

"We'll keep normal hours today and see what's up tomorrow." She turned around to look at the concern on her daughter's face. "Does that suit you?"

"Sure." Always ready to squeeze her mother's compassion for a boon, she suggested, "Can we have pizza tonight?"

Cressy cocked an eyebrow at Tricia, knowing she was being played but just as happy to go along, "Yep. Got one at home with your name on it."

Time was running short after Quint and Del saw the fire vault the creek and speed up the canyon wall, engulfing newly leafed-out trees and shrubs lining a gully, sap-filled pines exploding like thunder.

Climbing the steep flank of Rory Canyon, constantly aware of the fire's progress downstream, they followed the switchback trail in an effort to circle behind the fleeing cattle and direct them down the slope away from the advancing flames. Sensing the danger, most of the stock were finding their way into a streambed carved into the mountainside, corraled by a couple of Taylor cowdogs expertly doing their job.

The Taylors trained working dogs and kept a kennel a couple miles from where Quint and Del were located. As the fire had approached, Joe and one of his cowhands had released the dogs only hours before the fire roared through, destroying the complex which included a bunkhouse and hay barn. The rescued dogs were taken to safety where some of them were then returned to the field to assist in the roundup, these two among them.

Billowing smoke and heat from the searing flames challenged the two cowhands as they ascended the canyon. They'd made it halfway up when the wind changed, sweeping the smoke away from them and opening a view of the bench to the east. Cattle careened past them, fighting to stay on the cow paths heading down the slope, a sense of panic in their flight.

"Look!" yelled Quint as he reached for his rifle, pulling it from the scabbard. Del caught sight of what his companion had spotted, responding by grabbing his own gun.

It wasn't the blaze that stopped them in their tracks. Running down the hill were four wolves, close on the heels of two calves bolting sideways in fear while scrambling to keep up with the herd. The cowdogs turned to face the much larger wolves, growling and snapping, trying to protect the stock as they made their escape.

One of the wolves moved in on the border collie, snatching the dog by the neck and clamping down. Before his powerful jaws could sever an artery, Quint sent a bullet into the predator's own neck, instantly dropping him in a heap. The other three wolves darted back up the mountain and out of sight, Del missing his shot as they ducked around a thicket of blossoming elderberry. Released from the dead wolf's jowls, the valiant dog collapsed next to his attacker.

"You're getting good at this," said Del as he holstered his gun and quickly hopped down to collect the hurt dog.

"How is he?" asked Quint, sheathing his rifle.

"I think he'll be okay. The bite is deep but not life-threatening. Joe will be glad to know that Tater will heal. Good working dogs are worth their weight in gold."

Lifting the dog and laying him across his horse's shoulders, he remounted. Together with Quint and the remaining dog, they hustled the rest of the stock down the arroyo. Feeling the prickling heat behind them and hearing the distant roar of flames, they collected a couple of scared strays to rejoin the herd moving toward Rory Creek and the ford.

Relieved that they were able to round up this batch of steers ahead of the swiftly approaching blaze, Quint, Del and the Taylor dog got them across the shallow water and onto the gravel road. Driving them another mile down the road, Quint and the cowdog guided them into the temporarily erected corral at the rescue headquarters, joining hundreds of head that were rapidly being loaded for transport.

Del immediately took Tater to the RV where Georgia had a triage station set-up to treat minor injuries. Fortunately, no one had been seriously hurt until Del arrived with the wounded dog.

"What happened?" Georgia laid down the radio receiver and instantly ran over to examine Tater, taking him from Del's arms and rushing him to the dining area where first aid supplies were ready for application. The dog was conscious but moving very little. The fact that he was able to twitch his tail was a good indicator that there was no spinal injury stemming from the bite on his neck, though his hair was matted with blood.

"Four wolves came rushing down the canyon chasing a couple of calves running for their lives to catch up with the herd. Tater and Yokie turned and confronted them, not taking any notice they were half the size of the wolves and one of them caught him by the neck. Quint saw them first, pulled his rifle and shot the attacker before any more damage was done. Saved old Tater's life."

Georgia listened while she tenderly laid the dog on the dining table and began washing away the blood to see how deep the bite was on his neck. "Looks like a lot of blood but the puncture wounds hadn't penetrated deeply enough to cause permanent damage, I think. Though we'll need to get him to the vet. There's one at the other station back at Emville." She petted the dog's back, smoothing his fur, "What happened to the wolves?"

"The one that attacked Tater is dead. We left it there, the fire was less than a mile away from us and as we moved the steers down the mountain, we passed a crew of sawyers on the way who were cutting a firebreak. The other three wolves beat it back up the canyon."

She took care of the dog's wound, treating it with antiseptic and temporarily wrapping it with gauze. Then she turned to reach the door, Del already having backed down the steps to let her through. Calling the older of her teenaged sons who'd been helping load cattle, she told him to get the small pickup and drive the dog down to the vet. As soon as he'd carried Tater out to the truck, Georgia sat back down at the post to inform the other wranglers of the wolves' presence and continue directing traffic gathering cattle and shipping them to safety.

Del and Quint hardly missed a beat receiving new instructions to move further upstream and collect more strays that had bolted from the herd in terror. This time they knew to expect the possibility that other wolves from the pack might make an unwelcome appearance.

CHAPTER 32

Weather became firefighters' adversary.

Brief rain showers that had periodically broken the string of uncommonly warm days had only added to extreme fire conditions brought on by a dry spring. The snow had already melted from the mountains, leaving the Koyamas with only a remnant of winter's white speckling the heights.

The afternoon wind picked up, sending sparks in all directions, pressuring the ranchers around Emville to evacuate the cattle as fast as they could ride out on horseback and four-wheelers to get the herds to safety. Flames shooting up the canyon walls of Rory Creek that flew through parched underbrush edging the Gaston Buttes Preserve produced smoke that pervaded the whole region. Moreover, the thick film lying across the landscape made it difficult to pinpoint where new fires might be cropping up.

Sweeping across acres of ripening hay fields and prime pasture, the blaze left in its wake swathes of burnt stubble and blackened tree trunks, a few scorched and shriveled leaves dangling from dead branches. Carcasses of fleeing animals that couldn't outrace the swift flames lay in ditches, tainting the air with the putrid stench of charred flesh and smoldering fur.

Helicopters made clockwork runs from the reservoirs to the smoke-cloaked prairie, dumping load after load of water. At intervals planes releasing fire retardant sailed overhead between water drops. All the herculean effort firefighters expended from the air and on the ground setting backfires and cutting firebreaks hardly made a dent in the fire's rapid advance.

As the fires raged, night seemed to arrive early, the sky masked by an umber haze that transformed the sun into a shadowy red disk.

When Cressy and Tricia left the mercantile in Nacqus, they

walked out into a darkened world. The smell of smoke permeated the air even though the fires were dozens of miles distant according to the most recent accounts Cressy could access online. As usual, social media posts carried the most current information, county fire officials opting to use Facebook and Twitter to circulate data even before they updated the forest service or local government websites. Individuals working the firelines were constantly uploading new pictures and directions the fires were shifting.

Friends living closer to the firelines were on top of the changing evacuation orders and consistent in posting the information as quickly or quicker than official channels, an anomaly that bewildered Cressy. Because they were so dedicated to keeping pertinent information flowing, she was able to keep abreast of the evacuation stages in the county and was relieved to see that the Nacqus Valley was in no immediate danger.

Once the fires began burning, however, Cressy knew that it would be foolish to assume they were beyond being threatened. Whatever started these blazes, whether dry lightning, errant campfires or other origin, new blazes could pop up anywhere at anytime. That prompted Cressy to undertake preparation as soon as she and Tricia reached the house.

After parking the Jeep, Cressy took Artie with her to bring the cows close to the house just in case something happened and they needed to bug-out with little notice. Having so few evacuation routes available meant being ready to leave at the drop of a hat. It didn't take long to bring the cattle back to the pasture that she and Quint had just moved them from the night before. While driving them back across the property, it occurred to her how much had happened in the last couple days. Calling it an emotional rollercoaster would be an understatement.

Guiding the Mathers through the events that comprised her worst nightmare only to return home and find a wolf stalking her new house, it was as if the nightmare had never ended. Quint's appearance triggered a mix of happy memories and tragic events all wrapped up in the setting of her childhood home, making her wonder if she'd ever get past all of it.

Shaking the cobwebs from her head, she closed the gate behind the cattle and went on with her duties.

Tricia was taking care of her lamb when she saw her mom pull the old pickup around and hitch it to the horse trailer. As Cressy climbed down from the driver's seat, she came around to ask, "What are you doing, Mom? Are we going somewhere?"

"Not so far as I know, Sweetie. I just want to be ready if we need to leave in a hurry."

"You think the fire might come close?" Tricia's eyes widened with worry.

"No, Tricia, but you know it would be silly not to have everything prepared just in case something did happen." She walked to the back of the trailer and opened it up. "You want to help me haul some hay?"

"Sure, Mom." She followed Cressy into the barn and they pulled out a few bales and loaded them into the trailer. Having only one truck and one driver, she'd have to make a couple of trips to move all the stock but she didn't believe that it would come to that. More than once in the past the smoke seemed to portend disaster but fire never came close, for which she was grateful. Having a few things in order for a quick getaway was something she'd been taught to do and it eased her mind to prepare as much as possible.

Finished with the truck and having fed the animals, Cressy was at the back door when she called over to Tricia who was putting up her lamb for the night, "Are you ready for dinner?"

"Are we having pizza?"

"Yes. We're still on for pizza. Come on in and get cleaned up."

Barely stepping inside the kitchen, Tricia blasted through the door and up the stairs. *What is it about kids and pizza?* Pulling a hand-tossed pizza from the freezer, Cressy turned on the oven and decided this would be a good night to chill, maybe have a beer after Tricia went to bed. Or maybe not. It promised to be a fidgety evening, keeping tabs on the fires and an ear attuned to the phone in case circumstances unexpectedly changed.

CHAPTER 33

Dim was the best adjective that could be assigned to the new day. The orange-tinted sky, gloomy with smoke, was filled with floating flakes of gray ash that settled on the ground, carried by the heady breeze that couldn't quite be categorized as wind. Unfortunately, even a blush of air current was detrimental to gaining control of the blazes now dotting the county. Calm was what firefighters needed but not what they were getting.

Quint opened his eyes to unchanging dusk. The morning light looked the same as when he'd rolled over in his sleeping bag, housed along with Del in a ten-man tent at a makeshift firecamp pitched on the outskirts of Emville. They were living on the edge, the closest firelines having been drawn not three miles away.

Regular fire crews may have been inured to crashing for a fortnight in a danger zone but it took work for Quint to get comfortable enough to doze off for a couple hours. Concern for his family kept him awake thinking about his proximity to a fire less than ten percent controlled. Not so much for his own safety but worry about what they would do if anything happened to him. It was the same kind of unease he had felt when weighing whether to go after the wolf pack. If he were found guilty and carted off to jail, his family would be in a world of hurt.

Brushing aside the pointless musings, he sat up, pulled on his boots and joined the rest of the wranglers for a cold breakfast as there hadn't yet been time to set-up a proper kitchen. Del walked out of the tent right behind him, shoving his fingers through his spiky hair. "I hope there's coffee."

A crew member, putting his arm into the sleeve of his heavy fireproof jacket, replied in a gravelly voice, "One thing you can count on around here is coffee. And it isn't bad, either." He pointed toward a pavilion, "Over there."

"Thanks."

The two cowboys strolled over to the table where a stack of disposable hot cups stood next to a sixty-cup urn that had just finished percolating a fresh batch of caffeine. It was plugged into a portable generator that provided emergency power to the kitchen that was under construction. For this morning, breakfast consisted of fruit, packaged baked goods and sandwiches donated by Koyama businesses. Quint and Del weren't choosy, they were hungry so everything was appealing. Frankly grateful that the morning meal wasn't MREs, they each grabbed a piece of fruit and cellophane-wrapped bearclaw. Because their job was basically done and they were packing up, they left the sandwiches for the firemen and women.

The day before they'd been able to round up the majority of Taylor cattle, losing far fewer than expected to the fast moving flames. Today they only needed a skeleton crew of wranglers to hunt up strays that had managed to avoid the burning embers. The danger was that there were too many places where fire had skipped through, leaving smoldering hotspots that could flare up unexpectedly.

In a twist of fate, because Terra Ferus had denied grazing access within its perimeters to local ranchers for some years, none of their cattle needed to be evacuated from the preserve. As fire scorched ribbons of grassland across the edges of the prairie, the only cattle endangered was the meager herd owned by Gaston Buttes management. Luckily, the land trust had been able to employ a canny old cowboy to run the herd and he'd been quick to move them to protection.

Their job being done, Quint and Del went to load their horses and head for home and a long hot shower.

Peering outside, the murk dismayed Cressy. Smoke had penetrated the house despite closed windows, stinging her eyes. Getting out of bed, she pulled clothes haphazardly out of the closet, not really concerned with what to wear except to be prepared for action, which she hoped wouldn't be necessary.

Tricia came into her bedroom still in her pajamas. "Mom, it looks like the sun isn't up yet but the clock says six."

"I know. I don't think we've seen fires this bad since you were a baby and then we lived up on the mountain so the smoke wasn't as concentrated like it is down here in the canyon." She laid aside her clothes and picked up the phone to check fire conditions and make sure they weren't in any imminent danger.

While waiting for her mother to collect information, Tricia ran her fingers over the bits of finery and keepsakes in the jewelry box open on the dresser. Pulling out a delicate cameo on a gold chain, she held it up to the dusky light coming through the window. "What's this, Mom? I don't remember you ever wearing it."

After a few moments of scanning posts and forest service websites, Cressy looked over at the piece of jewelry Tricia was examining. "That's a very old coral cameo that belonged to your great-grandmother Dillat. Your father gave it to me on our wedding day and it will become yours when you get married."

Turning over the heirloom in her hands, Tricia said, "But what if I don't get married?"

Cressy glanced up from the phone, "Why do you say that? Do you know something I don't?"

"No. It's just that things happen," she said dreamily. "You never know when something might happen."

A little disturbed at Tricia's solemnity, she set it aside as a consequence of the fire and the threat it represented. They've had smoke from fires before but not so bad that she went through the preparations of hooking up the trailer like she had the night before. The concern probably influenced Tricia's thinking.

"Nothing's going to happen. It looks like we're fine. Everyone in the area confirms that there are no fires around here, blocking us in or chasing us out. So quit worrying."

Tricia replaced the necklace. "That's good, even though I can hardly breathe."

"Sometimes breathing's overrated," said Cressy.

"Mo-om," Tricia rolled her eyes.

"Go on. Get dressed. We have plenty that needs to get done around here, and I still have to go into the shop. Remember work? Someone's got to bring home the bacon."

Tricia closed the lid of the jewelry box and went to get dressed, whatever somber thoughts she'd had were as quickly dismissed. Cressy shook her head. *Kids.*

Donning her own clothes and getting ready for the day, Cressy went downstairs to start breakfast.

Just as she was about to pick up the coffee carafe and fill it with water, Cressy heard the horses raising a ruckus, neighing and stomping. Without missing a step, she redirected to the back door.

Tricia had gone into the garage to get the lamb and take him outside, the peculiar thought popping into her head as she went, *Why? It's almost as dark out there as it is in here. Reminding herself that, smoke or no smoke, outside is where he belongs.*

Just as Tricia rounded the corner of the garage, leading the lamb on a rope, Cressy shouted to her, urgency in her voice, "Quick, Tricia! Take the lamb back inside!"

"What's wrong, Mom?"

"Not now! Go back inside!"

Obeying without arguing, Tricia moved her lamb back to the garage and into the pen, grumbling about her mother's tone at first. But then, listening to the hubbub from the horses and cows, her brief snit switched to anxiety. Had she thought about it, she'd know that her mother didn't raise her voice unless there was a real problem, like the other day when they found the wolf dung. A light went on in her head... *Wolf!*

Cressy ran out to the corral and saw that the horses were standing against the side of the barn, eyes wild with fear. Over in the pasture, a couple hundred feet away, she saw a cow was down, sprawled unnaturally on the ground and a wolf was tearing at it.

Cursing the air for not having thought to bring the rifle she'd left beside the shotgun always kept by the door exactly for this kind of emergency, she stayed where she was for an extra moment, knowing that the cow was done for and nothing could help it now. Seeing the worthless fladry flapping in the breeze, her mind immediately whirled to collecting evidence. She pulled her phone from her back pocket, taking a few extra seconds to record the beast in the midst of its hellish work before dashing back to the house to grab her gun.

The other cattle had rushed as far from the injured cow as they could get, bawling as they jostled trying to get through the unforgiving fence rimmed with red plastic flags. By the time she re-emerged with the rifle in hand, the wolf raised its head from the bowels of the cow, maw dripping scarlet with blood. In that instant, it became aware of the figure running toward it, halted feeding and bolted in the opposite direction.

Cressy gave chase on foot then stopped in her tracks, swiftly lifted the stock to her shoulder and aimed at the dark gray animal speeding up the hill, readying to jump the creek. The wolf was fast and, shaking slightly with pent-up rage her shot skimmed past, ruffling his fur. Striking the ground inches from him, she saw the dust kicked up by the bullet as he fled.

She had one last hope of catching the killer before he was out of range. Standing her ground as if she were back in competition, she fired off one shot. Seeing the wolf flinch and falter before he regained his stride and fled up the hill, she was sure she hit her target. Time would tell how critically he was wounded.

Running over to the cow to determine the extent of the injury, she was flooded with anger. Blood had pooled all around its hindquarters and there were entrails strewn from its slashed and torn gut.

Tricia, who'd been in the garage the whole time, arms wrapped around the neck of her lamb, heard the gun discharge more than once in quick succession, confirming her fear that there was a wolf in the yard. She was about to go to the door and call out to her mother when she heard another shot ring out.

That sent her into a tizzy of worry after hearing the caterwauling of the cows and the gun being fired. Tricia couldn't stay still any longer and opened the side door just wide enough to yell, "Mom! Are you okay?"

"Yes, Tricia! I'm fine!" she answered her daughter immediately, knowing the racket must have frightened her. "Stay put and I'll be right there!"

Cressy trotted back to the garage after dispatching the suffering cow. As she opened the side door, Tricia leapt from the lamb to her mother and grabbed her around the waist. Cressy took a few minutes to hold her close, brushing her hair with fingers trembling slightly from an overload of adrenaline. "It's okay now, Sweetie. He's gone and we're all right."

Tricia was a tough little girl and rarely cried but the sounds emanating from outside had crushed her with a fear that something might happen to her mother. A few tears dribbled down her cheek in the aftermath of the tumult as she was calmed by her mother's presence.

"We're okay," Cressy repeated. "There was a wolf attack…"

"I thought so," interrupted Tricia.

"Right, I knew you'd figure it out." She looked down at her daughter and caught her eye, sorry that Tricia had to experience another incident that could raise the spectre of her father's death. "So, you know that I have to make a few phone calls now."

Tricia nodded.

"Go on into the house, Honey. We'll have to steer clear of the pasture since we can't disturb anything before the authorities get here." *Not that I'm going to wait for them.*

Tricia released herself from her mother's embrace and patted the lamb's back on her way into the house.

"You can go ahead and turn on the TV if you want. I'll be there in a few minutes."

"Okay," Tricia's answer was subdued as she closed the door behind her.

Without losing a beat, Cressy texted Miles, attaching the video. She hoped he was in a location where the message could get through. Then she called her mother whose usual schedule had her up and running early most of the time. It wasn't seven yet but Fran would already be dressed for the day.

"Mom, I need you to get here right way," Cressy dove right in, not bothering with any pleasantries.

Hearing haste and distress, she asked, "What's wrong, Cressy?"

"I don't have time for long explanations but we just had a wolf attack..."

"No! Not again!

"There's not much time. I need you out here ASAP. I had to put down the cow that was mangled and I need you to pick up Tricia and take her back to your place because I think maybe she should skip school. The scene in the pasture is too gruesome and I don't want her getting it into her head that she needs to go take a look."

Fran was grabbing her keys and pocketbook as Cressy gave her a quick rundown of the events. "I'm getting into the car now."

"Good because I'm certain that I wounded the wolf with the last shot. I'm going after it to finish the job..."

"What? No, Cressy, you can't take off after a dangerous predator, especially a wounded one. That makes it even more unpredictable..."

Cressy cut her off. "Please just get here as soon as possible. I've already contacted Miles Crenshaw with a video of the attack..."

"You're kidding! You got it on video?"

"Mother!" she said, exasperated. "Just listen, please. If we want to catch this wolf, I can't let him get too far ahead of me. Look, he's operating alone, so it's not like I have to worry about a whole pack that could get the jump on me."

"How do you know that? There could be others that you just didn't see."

"Believe me, I know. This one's been here before and it was alone."

"Honey, why don't you let Crenshaw and the sheriff handle things?" As soon as Fran opened her mouth, she regretted the comment. She could practically hear Cressy fuming on the other end of the phone. Knowing full well that the official response had been absurdly deficient in the past, letting the pack escape after Cressy's husband was killed as a direct result of their idea of wolf management. In her daughter's shoes, she might have gone after the beast too, just to make sure it was eliminated and could cause no more damage.

"Will you just get here?"

Knowing that she had lost the argument with her hardheaded daughter, Fran capitulated. "All right, all right. I'm already on the highway. It shouldn't be more than twenty minutes."

"Great. Take lots of pictures when you get here. The cow's still in the pasture and the others need to be calmed. I'll have the neighbors walk over now to stay with Tricia until you get through with that and can take Tricia home with you.

"And thank you, Mom! Sorry I'm being so curt. FYI, the wolf headed northwest. I'll call the sheriff once I'm in the saddle. I'm taking Minuteman since he's kept his head before and the four-wheeler is limited. There's a wounded wolf out there and I can't wait for officials to putter around with a dangerous animal on the loose." She hung up.

While she was on her way into the house, Cressy called the Thompsons next door. They'd heard the shots and were more than willing to run right over to stay with Tricia.

Before putting her plan into action, if you could call it a plan, Cressy went to talk to Tricia. She knew that her daughter wouldn't be happy about her decision, but if she stopped to think it over, it would be too late to take action. She quickly explained that George and Yvette were coming over until Franma arrived and then she'd be going home with her until Cressy got back.

Kissing Tricia on the top of her head, she squeezed her and hurried out the door, calling, "I love you!"

Running into the tack room, Cressy grabbed her saddle and hauled it over to the fence rail, whistling softly to Terry's horse that trotted over without hesitation. The big chestnut had stood his ground, protecting Terry from the wolves after the brutal attack.

Minuteman was a stalwart workhorse that wasn't easily spooked, especially following the incident at the ranch.

Cinching the saddle and shoving the Winchester into the scabbard, she vaulted onto his back and rode in the direction she'd last seen the wolf escape.

Tricia stood at the kitchen window watching her mother run to saddle her dad's horse, ram the rifle in the saddle boot, hop up and gallop off across the creek. Although her mother hadn't said what she was doing, it was obvious that she was going after the wolf. There was no other explanation for the hurry to leave and take her gun with her. Her mom had tried to keep her as much in the dark as she thought necessary, believing that Tricia didn't need to view the hideous nature of wolf attacks, how vicious and grisly they could be.

Since she'd been sequestered in the garage, Tricia had only heard the stock crying and bellowing and, of course, the shots. She knew that her mother was an exceptionally good marksman and she'd been training Tricia to shoot. The fact that she took off on Minuteman made Tricia sure that the wolf was still on the loose and her mother was not going to let him get away. If she had missed her shot, that would have made her even more determined to go after the wolf and kill it. It wasn't so much a guess as it was that she knew her mother.

Tears sprang up in her eyes when she remembered the last time they had wolf trouble. She had been at her grandmother's house and when she got home the thing that hurt most was when her mom told her that her dad wasn't going to be coming home… not just that night, but never again.

The memories hadn't faded over the last two years. Tricia still felt the bitter loss of her father and her home. And now her mother had ridden out in pursuit of another wolf, and on her dad's horse. She couldn't bear the thought of losing another parent to the dreadful wolves.

Still, there was one thing she had learned that she could do when she felt the most helpless. She couldn't physically intervene for her mother, she was too small and young. But size and youth didn't make a difference when it came to praying, And that's what Tricia decided she could do - pray for her mother's safety because she knew her mom wouldn't think to do it for herself.

Cressy wasn't one to ever pray aloud. In fact, she wasn't sure if her mom prayed at all, but Tricia had a different perspective. This year, she'd been feeling especially empty after moving to the new house and watching her mother try to start over. Packing up and leaving the ranch house was bittersweet for both of them. It was a house full of warmth but, at the same time, bereft of it. Everything there reminded them of how much they missed her father.

When the Sunday night study group began meeting in the store's conference room, Tricia liked to sit in and listen. Some of it was over her head but most of what they said was sensible, even to a ten-year-old.

She'd been learning about things that her mother avoided talking about, especially after her dad was killed by wolves. Tricia may have been young but she could tell how disappointed her mother was in God. It was to the point that she would hardly mention God.

What caught Tricia's attention at a couple of the meetings were the leaders discussing how people sometimes blame God when terrible things happen to them, and Tricia was pretty sure that was how her mom felt... like God had let her down.

Tricia had actually spent a lot of time thinking about that, whether it was God's fault that her father was attacked by wild animals. What she'd been hearing and reading in the Bible (she'd found the one that had belonged to her mother as a girl) made her question that idea. If God is love like the Bible said, and she'd memorized that verse in 1John, then it made no sense that he would want people to die awful deaths. She was finding more in that book that made her believe God was there to help them through rough times, not create trouble to hurt people, teach them a lesson and make them suffer.

Over time, Tricia had become more certain that God wasn't

the problem because the more she talked to Him, the calmer she felt. So she made a conscious decision to pray for both her mom and herself. If nothing else, it gave Tricia that little bit of courage when she was really struggling with fear - like now, when her mother had just ridden off to shoot a vicious wolf and fires were roaring all around the valley making things look bleak and scary - it was a perfect time to pray. So she did.

CHAPTER 34

The first half-mile of tagging the wolf's escape route was easy, the direction it had bolted was obvious because she had watched it run with a hitch in his gait. Arriving at the point where she had lost sight of it, Cressy slowed down to scour the ground to be sure that she was still dogging it. As wound up as she was from fury and adrenaline, she was determined not to botch this by running headlong in one direction only to lose the trail in her haste. If the wolf was hurt - and she knew that he was, she'd seen it stumble when the bullet hit - there was no way he could travel at top speed for long. He'd run out of steam after the initial shock wore off.

Cressy understood the mechanics of a body, human and animal, but a callous predator would never receive an ounce of compassion from her. These wolves never belonged here but were transplanted by manipulated fools who had more reverence for beasts than for their own kind. The fact that people actually believed men ravaged the earth or should even be exterminated in favor of wild beasts literally boggled her mind. When she thought of her own daughter constantly having to block these ideas that were being perpetuated in school, it raised her ire more and enforced her resolve to do what is right... kill a dangerous killer.

Reining in Minuteman from hurtling across the field and losing track of the wolf, she pulled her phone from her pocket to call the range rider.

"Did you get my text?"

"Yes, Cressy, I did. I was way out by Emville where there was a wolf sighting and attack as they were evacuating cattle in Rory Creek. It looks like the Big Elk pack is to blame. With the fire roaring there's nothing I can do about it right now. The upshot is, I won't make it to your place for a couple hours with all the fire equipment on the road. Firefighters rightly take precedence."

"Absolutely. Just so long as you get there."

Crenshaw was no slouch and he could hear that she was moving, let alone catch her use of language. "What do you mean get "there?" Where are you?"

That slip of the tongue might get her in trouble but, at this point, she didn't care. Done with sitting on the sidelines and letting the authorities twiddle their thumbs, this time she wouldn't be restrained. "I'm following the wolf. I'm positive that I wounded it with the last shot and I'd be an idiot to let him get away. You saw the video."

Not bothering to address the obvious because they both knew he had viewed the recording of the wolf disemboweling one of her cows, he asked instead, "Are you alone?"

"Of course."

Listening to her put herself in danger, he wasn't willing to pull any punches. They knew each other too well, "You just may be an idiot going off on your own."

"You know anyone who could've gotten here soon enough to catch this guy? You said yourself that you were dealing with a sighting past Emville. How much should I bet that the sheriff and ODFW were out there too?"

"You got me. That would be a winning ticket. Most of the ranchers who could get away have been out here rounding up Taylor cattle besides."

"The reason I called was to let you know that my mom will be with Tricia when you show up. She's been through the drill before and, aside from taking pictures, is leaving everything as is for you to bring in ODFW and the sheriff to document the scene. I had to shoot the cow. You do what you have to do and I'll do the same."

He hesitated before telling her, "As much as I don't like the fact you're out there alone, just be careful. If that's the wolf we took a sample from, he's been around. He's a survivor. You've got a dangerous wounded animal on your hands."

"I *would* be an idiot if I didn't acknowledge that and act accordingly."

Nothing more to be said, he hung up reluctantly.

Keeping her eyes on the ground hunting for crushed grass and other signs of the wolf's passing as she rode over a hill, Cressy made one more call.

"Mom, are you there yet?"

"Just pulling in. The Thompson's are here and Tricia's okay. George has been out tending to the horses and the cows while Yvette has been inside with Tricia. I'm going out to take photos now."

"Good. I already called Miles and he's on his way from Emville but he won't be there for a while with all that's going on with the fires." Cressy knew this was gutting her mother but both of them understood that she had to act. "Okay, I don't want to announce my presence if I'm going to close in on the wolf, so I'm putting the phone on vibrate and will be texting from here on out."

"You'd just better be careful." The worry in her voice was covered by a bravado that she'd also instilled in her daughter, making it even harder to keep her cool while talking to Cressy, knowing exactly how obstinate she'd been growing up. Fran didn't add what she'd wanted to about the fact that her granddaughter couldn't afford to lose another parent. She knew her words would be wasted because the idea wasn't lost on Cressy.

"Love you, too, Mom."

Cressy's farm occupied the valley floor, a creek running through her property fed into the Nacqus River. The level dale converged on rising ground that quickly gained elevation that met rock walls incised by gullies and deeper arroyos. The cuts in the mountainsides connected step after step of grassy flats ascending more than two thousand feet. Knolls broke up the incline in uneven planes that blocked the line of sight as Cressy followed the trail upward.

More than once she whispered "thank you" to the air as she found a blood-smeared twig or crimson drops on a grassy mound left by the injured wolf in passing. Stopping to test a spot, she touched it with her finger. Rubbing it between the pads of her thumb and fore-finger, she felt that it was still wet. Unless another wounded animal had come this route within the last half-hour, which was highly unlikely, she was as positive as she could be that she was on the right trail.

Like most ranch kids growing up, she'd hunted deer and elk but after a few years of marriage, Terry would usually go out with his friends during the season, leaving her a hunting widow. With a young child at home, Cressy had gotten out of the habit of joining her hus-band in the fall though she had expected to pick it up again when Tricia was old enough to accompany them.

After Terry's death, she hadn't been hunting, or engaged in much else with friends and family for that matter, and her knack for tracking game had gotten rusty. Years may have intervened in prac-ticing those skills, but as she tenaciously followed the wolf, it came back to her little by little.

Just as she was gaining confidence in resurrecting what she'd thought to be lost skills, she hit a block wall in a literal sense. The face of the canyon was splintered basalt rising from a stone base that had no grass or vegetation within two yards of the rock expanse. Before getting too close, she halted and gazed at the scene in front of her. There was nothing to gauge which direction the wolf had gone. Turning either right or left led to gullies and she couldn't discern any disturbance in the grass edging the stone flat.

Sliding out of the saddle, Cressy carefully absorbed every bit of the site with her eyes, seeking any indication of the slightest dis-turbance of the surroundings, including the dust on the pitted rock floor abutting the basalt wall. Back and forth she searched the area looking for the tiniest clue.

It was critical that she made the right decision which way to go. If she chose wrong, the wolf might be impossible to catch and, for her, that would be an unpardonable mistake.

The wolf was knocked sideways by the impact.

A bullet lodged itself in his shoulder making his front right leg useless for a beat, going out from under him as he barreled ahead. Not knowing what hit him and not caring, the instinct for self-preser - vation overcame the momentary loss of function and, persisting, he immediately put weight on the leg, making a dash for the trees a half-mile away...

After being turned around by acrid smoke from a brush fire that sprang up, the wolf had headed back the way he'd come the day before. Initially covering almost twenty miles when he'd been forced to retrace his steps, pushed hard by rising winds, the flames had rout - ed the wolf, landing him back at the little homestead by the road.

By the time he'd arrived at the place where he'd spied a few cows and calves two days earlier, he'd gained an appetite. The heat, dogfight he'd had with the pack leader and constant travel had depleted his energy, leaving him with little to spare.

Emerging from the copse on the south-facing hill in the first blush of dawn, he had seen the cattle spread out in the pasture. The smoke had irritated the wolf as he sniffed the air but hadn't appeared to trouble the cows or bull as they ambled aimlessly around the field.

One cow was isolated from the others, lying down and quiet - ly chewing its cud, heedless of its surroundings on a calm morning. A perfect target. The fence that separated the predator from the little herd was strung with harmless objects fluttering in the breeze. The wolf didn't consider the barrier an impediment to his need. Prey was all that concerned him and he stalked the cow, crouching until he was ready to spring, the smell of smoke working in his favor by covering his own scent.

Tired, hungry and wanting a kill, the wolf crawled under the lowest rail of the three-runged fence and leapt onto the cow, snagging its flank before it could get on its feet. Taken completely by surprise, the cow barely had time to bellow before the wolf tore open its stom - ach.

Engrossed with rending the bowels and feeding on the entrails spilling out, the wolf paid no attention to the other stock running from *the violent attack and bawling at the top of their lungs.*

That's when everything went south for the predator.

He looked up from his victim and saw an approaching figure with a long arm pointed at him. Intuitively knowing it spelled danger, he bolted and cleared the fence in two bounds. A bullet whizzed past him, ruffling his fur and strafing the earth next to him. Two more strides toward the creek and the next shot caught him in the shoulder. That's when he stumbled but got up and ran out of the range of the shooter, racing for the trees and escape.

...The wolf was now back on the same path from whence he'd come, making a getaway up the mountain. Knowing there was fire in one direction, he swerved to the left, keeping to the lower ground until he was forced to turn up one of the ravines splitting the canyon side. Bushes lined the trickle of water running down the crevice and he veered around them, the branches scratching at the wound causing enough pain to make him balk. He climbed through the grass and brambles, working his way onto the flat wherever he could.

At a point hundreds of feet up the slope, the wolf found a spot where the land flattened out and he dashed across the open field until he came to a rock face that thwarted his uphill climb. Without a thought, the wolf turned aside and traced the foot of the basalt forma - tion, reaching another cut in the mountainside to take him further up the canyon toward the prairie.

CHAPTER 35

Del was loading his horse in the trailer when Quint decided to give Cressy a call to ease his mind that there'd been no other alarming episodes. He'd been concerned that the errant wolf might have resurfaced looking to gorge his mangy hide on her cattle.

He knew that once wolves become accustomed to taking advantage of quarry that can't outrun them or don't have the capacity to fight back, they won't change the habit. Why work to eat if you don't have to? It's not so different from people who get used to being coddled and lose their willingness to take care of themselves. Ease begets laziness and animals are as susceptible to falling into bad habits as are humans. *If you want a cat to be a mouser, don't feed him so much that he won't hunt.*

Checking on the status at Cressy's house wasn't his only motive for calling. He'd enjoyed their ride, making the rounds of the neighboring properties to discover where the wolf had disappeared and he wanted to keep in touch.

Taking a quick minute while Del secured the tailgate, Quint thumbed through his contacts and dialed Cressy's number. It took a couple of rings before she answered and when she did her voice was subdued, almost a whisper.

Feeling the phone vibrate in her back pocket, Cressy extracted it, and put it up to her ear, quietly saying, "Hello?"

Immediately speculating why the undertone, he skipped a proper greeting, "What's going on?"

"Quint? Hello to you too."

"You're keeping your voice down, makes me think something's up, which I'd hoped was not the case when I called."

"Sorry to burst your bubble, bubba, but something did happen."

"That vile animal came back, didn't it." It wasn't a question.

"'Fraid so. Attacked one of my cows and I had to shoot her. But I also got the wolf with my second shot as he escaped."

"He got away?"

"Not for long."

"You went after him? Who's with you?"

"No one. No time to wait around for back-up, Cowboy."

Incredulous at first, Quint buried his worry before he spoke. Remembering that Cressy was a deadeye shot, it still didn't lift his unease about her tracking a wounded wolf by herself. He'd just gone after five grown wolves on his own and realized how foolhardy he'd been. After the fact, of course. In the moment, he'd been convinced it was the right thing to do. Taking that into consideration, he fully understood where Cressy was coming from, but the difference in this instance was she was following a desperate animal. The level of peril rose astronomically when dealing with a wounded wild predator.

"All right. Promise me you won't take any chances and keep me updated on your location."

Cressy released a sigh at his obvious concern. "Okay. I'm sticking to text from here on out."

"Good enough. Be safe."

Turning on his heel, he caught Del's elbow as he was jawing with one of the firecrew, waiting on his buddy to close his call.

"What now?"

"We gotta roll. I need to get back as soon as possible." Holding out his hand, he said, "Keys."

"Your ride, your prerogative," he said dropping the ignition keys into Quint's open palm. "Let's go. You can fill me in on the way."

As Quint maneuvered his rig around the fire equipment and the parked cattle trucks waiting to transport the last of the steers to safety, he told Del what Cressy had done. What he didn't say was that he was planning to stop at Cressy's and follow her. Somebody had to have her back.

CHAPTER 36

Halfway through the day and Cressy's adrenaline rush was waning.

She'd jumped onto Minuteman without taking the time to eat or grab any provision. The fight or flight impulse had been in full gear when she reacted without hesitation, completely forgetting that circumstances can change in an instant and she could be hunting this rogue killer for days rather than hours.

Though Cressy wasn't really hungry, digging in the saddlebag she found a bottle of water leftover from her trot around the property with Quint. That would have to suffice. Furious at being victimized by another heartless killing machine fueled her resolve. This gray wolf was her great white whale, the coalescence of all her nemeses rolled into one predator that had no conscience.

She knew very well that animals didn't have the moral directives that did mankind, but that could not excuse this one senseless kill or the hundreds more that this wolf would perpetrate over its lifetime.

The thing people refused to understand about wolves is that they often kill for the sake of killing. They will rip open the throat or pelvis of an animal and feed a little on the calf, deer or horse while it's still alive. In the wild there are few beasts that eat their prey while it's still breathing. Even lions kill their quarry before they feed. Wolves are clever animals and once they'd become habituated to preying on cattle and sheep, they rarely bothered to hunt deer or elk that were swift on their feet and a challenge to bring down.

Relying on Minuteman to give her warning if he felt the presence of predators, she continued to examine her surroundings. Wolves weren't the only dangerous animals in the region. There were bears and cougars, for which the Koyama Mountains were named. Both were daunting enemies if encountered under perilous conditions, especially those that had become accustomed to the proximity of humans.

Cressy had been gradually ascending the canyon for five or six miles and the wolf wasn't bothering to be crafty about hiding itself so much as just moving. Having no idea if the wolf knew it was being followed or was simply running from necessity, it didn't matter.

In the end, there'd never been an option for Cressy but to go after the wolf. Partly because she still struggled with wondering whether Terry would have survived and the killers destroyed if she'd just been told where he was going and been there to assist, exactly as they'd always discussed about handling wolf sightings.

Since his death, there'd been no end of self-recrimination, that she should have known where he was and done something to save him. The truth was the hardest thing to accept, that she couldn't possibly have arrived in time simply because he responded to the crisis without thinking to call.

Cressy's current dilemma was that she had virtually copied her late husband's example. Sure, she called Miles and talked to Quint but all they knew was that she's out trailing a vicious wolf that she'd wounded, perhaps not mortally, making this escapade even more foolish and risky.

What is it I said to Quint, 'in for a penny, in for a pound?' Well, I'm really in it now and there's no going back until I've either killed this SOB or lost him. Taking a deep breath as she pored over the stone slab at the foot of the basalt columns, she thought, *but I'm not going to lose him. I'm tired of the Dillats being abused by wolves and their spineless protectors.*

Finally seeing a disturbance in the dusty coating on the stony ground, Cressy took a closer look. It could be paws had brushed aside the thin deposit of dirt that was barely perceptible atop the surface.

Got you now, you coward! You're dead meat.

Quint did his best not to overdrive the road conditions, which consisted of plain old bad roads shrouded in smoke, in his rush to get back to Nacqus. Blocking from his mind why he was concerned about Cressy's safety, he acknowledged the simple fact that he was worried. As stupid as he'd been to ride out after a pack of wolves, she was making the same mistake by tracking a wounded one that had proven it wasn't afraid of approaching people.

Quint, usually a patient man having managed outward calm through the whole mess when Kim had walked out, was surprised that staying cool about Cressy was taking
effort. Without expressing it, Quint could tell that Del was curious about his friend and boss' hurry to get home.

He'll have it figured out before long.

Hoping he'd be able to catch up to her before daylight died, that the sun hung in the sky for seventeen hours at this time of year was some consolation. It also lessened the sting of traveling at a snail's pace that made the drive seem to take forever.

Passing the turnoff for the road to his ranch, Del finally piped up, "Going to the Dillat's?"

"You guessed it. Any comments from the cheap seats? I'm sure you have an opinion, Del."

"Other than the fact that, if what you told me is true that Cressy took off after a wounded wolf, I expect you to go after her. It doesn't take a genius to put the pieces together that this is the wolf you were tracking," he looked at Quint who was slowing as he approached Cressy's driveway. "Am I right?"

"Proof that I don't hang out with imbeciles," said Quint as he cranked the wheel to the left to make the turn.

Pulling the rig and horse trailer around the circular drive, Quint noticed both the range rider's battered Silverado and an SUV he didn't recognize parked next to Cressy's Jeep.

"At least Miles got here," observed Del as Quint popped open the driver's door.

Before he rounded the front of the truck, Cressy's mother emerged from the house, surprised to see someone other than the authorities.

"Quint! What are you doing here?"

"Hello, Fran. It's good to see you," he said walking forward and getting sucked into an enveloping hug from a woman who'd practically served as a second mother in his teen years. "I talked to Cressy earlier and she fessed up that she'd gone after the wolf."

Fran looked up at him querulously. "I didn't think you two had spoken in years." She hesitated, having waded into muddy waters, "What with everything that's happened to both of you."

"There are no secrets around here and, though mine wasn't, Cressy's life has been on Page One."

"Sadly," she said, stepping back. "You look well, Quint, even if you do reek of smoke."

"No surprise there. Del and I were out in Rory Canyon helping Joe Taylor round up stragglers with a fire breathing down our necks."

"Oh my! I'd heard that a lot of folks had rushed out to Emville. Did he lose many head?"

"Nowhere as many as he originally thought. The last estimate was around thirty, which is thirty too many." He scratched his two-day growth of beard. "We also had a run-in with the Big Elk pack."

"Guess they were running from the fire, too," said Fran, suddenly reminded of the problem at hand.

"Killed one of them that attacked a Taylor dog. So a good day's work." Changing the subject, Quint said, "How long has Cressy been gone?"

"Hours. I was supposed to take Tricia home with me but I had to stay and talk with Miles once he got here."

"How is Tricia?"

"She's a trooper, that one," Fran said with a sorrowful smile. "I kept her home from school even though it's the last day, which she didn't complain about. Tricia wanted to stay as close to home as possible to know that her mother is safe."

"Which brings me to answer your first question. I'm going to find Cressy and make sure she has back-up." He turned to get Hodey out of the trailer. "I want to get going as soon as I can but I should talk with Miles first." Taking his leave of Fran, he collected his horse, told Del he'd catch up with him as soon as he could and walked around the house to find the range rider.

It wasn't hard to locate Miles. He was standing by the dead cow in the pasture closest to the house, the enclosing fence draped with useless fladry that was flapping in the smoke-drenched breeze. He was on lone duty. Not a shocker considering the sheriff and wolf coordinator had been called out to deal with the wolf encounter by Emville. After Quint and Del had driven the steers back from the ridge, they'd heard that another one of Taylor's working dogs had been killed by the Big Elk pack. It would be a while before they arrived to deal with this incident.

Pressed as Quint was to get on the trail and find Cressy, he wasn't about to go off half-cocked. He needed to have as much information as he could gather to be of any value to her.

Dropping Hodey's reins over the rail of the corral, he quickly strode over to the range rider, "Guess you're "it" today."

"You might say that. No one else is available to do an investigation since they're all dealing with the fire and the wolves up north." He noticed the traces of ash on Quint's clothing. "Looks like you already knew that. You were out at Emville rounding up cattle?"

"That obvious, huh?" He checked his shirt where Miles had been looking. "Thought maybe you were impressed with my sense of style," he brushed off some of the ash on his sleeves. "Just got back. Talked to Cressy a while ago. What do you know?"

"Aside from the fact that that girl worries me, not much. She blew out of here before I or anyone else could get here. Managed to wing the wolf."

"So I heard. If she says she got him I'd believe it. She's a crack shot with that rifle. If Cressy had a clean shot she'd have killed him outright."

"I looked and saw some blood in the tracks that got mucked up with her horse's. She was back here by the house, I found the spent casings, so it had to be a four hundred yard shot, easy."

"What now?"

"Still waiting for ODFW and the sheriff to come out to bag this cow for a necropsy, then make a report. At least they can't wiggle free from calling this a wolf kill."

"Yeah? Why?"

"Cressy had the presence of mind to record a quick video of the wolf ripping up the cow before she ran and got her gun. She texted it to me. This is a clean predation and the state can't pull the rigmarole they did two years ago," said Miles.

"Good, that's good," said Quint as he started to walk off.

"Where are you going?"

"To follow Cressy and make sure she's okay and has support. I doubt she took the time to pack any supplies, so I need to get a few things and get going." Quint looked toward the house and saw Tricia peering out the kitchen window at him and Crenshaw. He decided that he needed to say hello and reassure Cressy's daughter that he was going to help her mother.

"See ya, Miles. Make sure they wrap up this one right."

The afternoon was on the downhill run and Cressy was miles from home carrying only a bottle of water that she had refilled at one of the swift-running brooks she'd crossed, an emergency kit she always carried in her saddlebag and her gun. Night was cool on the prairie this late in the spring but not too uncomfortable. With the warm temperatures and the smoke functioning like a blanket holding in the heat, exposure wasn't a concern.

The wolf had been steadily gaining elevation, sticking to the rocky bottoms of streams cutting through the precipitous slopes and deer trails winding up the inclines. Certain that she was on its tail, Cressy still hadn't glimpsed the wolf leading her to high ground. Despite the injury and an evident limp that she detected in a couple of muddy spots where all paws had imprinted the soft earth, it was still traveling with speed.

At places, she'd been forced to dismount and lead Minuteman up a rockfall that the wolf would have been able to negotiate with comparative ease, giving it an advantage. But Cressy was confident that she'd be able to catch up once she reached the flats stretching toward the buttes.

There was one hitch - if the wolf made it onto Terra Ferus land before she could execute it. Then she could expect to suffer the full measure of environmentalist wrath backed to the hilt by government. It'd mean jailtime because no quarter would be given for a wolf murderer.

Cressy laid that aside as a bridge yet to be crossed. In the meantime, her main fear was whether she could find and kill the beast before dark fell creating a whole other set of problems. At the top of the list was staying awake through the wee hours to keep her and her horse safe. Wolves were capricious and she had been assuming that it was the same lone male that Quint had tracked to her yard. If that were so, this one had proven itself to be arbitrary, changing course on impulse. She didn't know for certain that was the case but she also had not uncovered any sign that this wolf had company. *Thank God.*

Dropping out of the saddle, Cressy crouched down to probe the ground along a well-used cow trail. There were a couple of solid prints in the dust and some specks of blood on the tall grass, probably left as the wolf brushed by. Remounting, she clucked her tongue to cue Minuteman forward, relieved to know that she was on the right track.

Just as he thought, Cressy's direction was plain as day. Being concerned with keeping tabs on the wolf, she left an obvious trail of her own making Quint's pursuit fast and effortless.

Out of the gate, she'd galloped after the predator, her horse's hoofs tearing the grass as he went. Reaching the place where she'd slowed to check for wolf sign, the course she traveled pointed northwest. In its hurry, the wolf didn't deviate in its heading other than skirting impassable boulders, skree slopes or treacherous crevices, allowing Hodey his head to run and catch up with Cressy.

Clambering up ravines and over rocks, Quint could discern where she had to dismount to chase her quarry over rough ground and he was forced to follow suit. Because he had the advantage of a clear route, it didn't take as many hours as he expected before he found himself watching Cressy break from a stand of pines a quarter mile away as he cleared the canyon rim.

The wind was driving out of the northwest, carrying sound past Cressy toward Quint's position. Downwind of the wolf, it worked in her favor but it also meant that she wasn't aware of Quint's approach from behind.

Good thing I'm on her side.

She couldn't hear Hodey's hoofbeats until he was within fifty yards of her position.

Hunching over her horse's shoulder, Cressy was poring over the earth looking for signs of disturbance in the long grass. Preoccupied with her search when the pounding caught her attention, she sat up instantly and turned to see a rider bearing down. A smile broke across her face as she recognized her new companion.

"Hardly expected to see you out here!" she called as he closed the gap.

"You didn't really believe that nobody would come after you and offer a little support?"

"More like handcuffs."

He laughed as he reined in next to Minuteman.

"But I certainly wasn't going to wait around for Turlow or the sheriff to arrive. Aside from having their hands full with the fires out on the county line, under normal circumstances they'd be late for dinner." Prescott Turlow was the area wolf coordinator and, much as he considered himself impartial, it was like pulling teeth to get him to commit to calling an evident wolf predation exactly what it was. Whether or not Turlow purposefully took his time, arriving late on the scene had a way of allowing evidence to deteriorate in favor of the wolf.

"And it didn't cross your mind what kind of trouble you'd be asking for riding out after a wounded animal on your own." Almost wincing, it was hard for him to rebuke her after he'd done the same thing and she knew it, but his concern spoke before his brain engaged.

"The pot calling the kettle black?" she raised her eyebrows in reproach.

"I asked for that. But you might be giving Tandy short shrift. She just took office and neither of us have seen her on one of these calls yet. Sheriff Swifter just might surprise us. She's indicated her support."

"I sure hope so," Cressy said preparing to ride forward.

"Speaking of which, I'll bet you didn't bring any."

"Any what?" She looked at him quizzically.

"Energy support. Dinner. Bet you're hungry."

"Haven't thought about it. There's more need to catch that wolf before doing anything else," with which words she turned to head off in the direction she was sure the predator had gone. "Besides, that's your job," and she trotted ahead of him.

"My job?"

Looking back at him, she said, "Picking up the tab. You coming?"

"Right behind you."

Conversation halted as they cantered across the prairie, knowing the wolf might either hear them or sense the tread of the horses closing in on him. Having broken through the grass and left prints on patches of bare ground, his track was unmistakable. Quint examined the spoor, concluding that it was leading them by long minutes rather than hours.

Darkness would descend soon, applying even more pressure to finish the hunt. If they couldn't corner him by nightfall chances were that they'd lose him. They could tell that the wolf was favoring the injured leg to the point that his paw was barely making contact with the earth, indicating a worsening limp. If the wound wasn't mortal - and it appeared not to be considering how fast and far he'd been able to travel - he'd be out of reach just to show up later ravaging another rancher's stock. Not only had he developed a taste for beef and the easy kill, the injury would now require it.

CHAPTER 37

It was an hour from sunset when Sheriff Swifter arrived at the Dillat farm. Miles Crenshaw had taken it upon himself to cordon off a quasi-crime scene to protect the evidence from scavengers and the other animals.

He'd stayed at Cressy's out of loyalty, determined not to allow another subversion of justice. She'd already suffered too much at the hands of bureaucratic policy wonks.

Fran had finally taken Tricia and Artie home with her, handing over the keys to Miles, in a manner of speaking. He made the kitchen into a temporary office. From that perch, he was able to keep an eye on the pasture where the carcass lay and wait for the authorities to make an appearance.

When Tandy Swifter parked beside his dented rig, Crenshaw went out the back door and walked around the house to meet her.

"Where are the rest of the troops?" he attempted to inject some levity being reticent to tell her that Cressy wasn't on the premises and had gone in pursuit of the perpetrator. Miles knew Swifter wouldn't be thrilled to hear it.

"You ought to know. You were out at Rory Creek with everyone else." She strode forward and shook his hand. "Can you fill me in? I only got the sketchiest background from Dispatch."

He waved her around the house and they walked out to the pasture where he'd roped off the area.

"Looks like a murder scene. This your doing? Sort of outside your job description."

"Yes on both counts. I didn't want anything to be disturbed after what happened with the last Dillat incident," he said gravely.

"That was simply wrong the way Cressy was treated." She removed her hat for a moment and scratched an itch behind her ear, careful not to muss the bun nestled at the nape of her neck. Swifter was a stickler for maintaining a sharp appearance to the point of austerity in a generally laid-back county. She believed that dressing casually created the impression that she or her deputies approached the job with a casual attitude and she took her job seriously. "Tell me what you know."

"Here, I'll show you." As they approached the carcass that was looking the worse for wear after sitting in the heat all day, not to mention the rising odor, he played the video for her on his phone.

"I'll say Cressy had real presence of mind to capture that image. Incontrovertible, as far as that goes." She looked around having noticed that they were the only two in attendance at the scene. "Where *is* Cressy?"

"She had to leave and I'm not sure when she'll be back. Her mother took Tricia home with her and basically left me in charge."

Tandy pinned him with unreadable green eyes. She'd cultivated the art of masking emotion after twenty-five years in law enforcement. It was a proven intimidation tactic that worked against even hardened criminals. "I noticed that her Jeep is still in the driveway."

"I wouldn't know about that. She was gone before I arrived." He was thankful that he hadn't actually witnessed her departure.

Eyebrows rising almost imperceptibly, Swifter said, "That's interesting." Turning her attention back to the carcass, she said without inflection, "So, what have we got?"

"A cow mauled while it was still alive, you saw the recording, and subsequently shot once through the head. Obviously to put it out of its misery. Cressy's mother gave me the basics and texted me all the photos she'd taken. I've forwarded all the photos and the video to Scott." Crenshaw looked at the sheriff, "Have you talked to Turlow?"

"Not really. We were both out at the fire, as you know, and he told me he'd been informed of this but said he didn't know when he'd make it here."

"Great," he said, disheartened. "Does he have anyone coming out here?"

She puffed her cheeks, slowly releasing air between her lips allowing her displeasure to slip through her stoicism. "Mikey

Stromberg from Wildlife Services is supposed to be on her way."

"Terrific." Neither one needed to say more. USFWS' Michaela Stromberg was well known for her lack of sympathy for ranchers and their losses to depredation. In comparison, Turlow could be considered a compassionate advocate for stockgrowers. As impartial as he worked to be, that description would hardly be accurate which showed just how adversarial Stromberg was to the ag community. "What about a vet to examine the carcass?"

"No idea. I'm just the county grunt as far as Fish and Wildlife are concerned. Scott tries to be fair. I'll give him that." Changing the subject, Swifter said, "Can you send me the photos and recording?"

"Sure, I'll do it right now while you do your own documentation."

She gave him her official email address as well so he could forward the information to both places. In the meantime, the sheriff used the digital camera to record the evidence, including the wolf tracks since Cressy and then Miles had kept other traffic at a minimum to preserve the scene.

Then, they waited.

CHAPTER 30

The wolf stopped for a moment under the cover of a stunted white pine to lick the wound on its shoulder. Flight from the enemy that was able to inflict pain from a distance had kept him on the move. Shock that had blocked the pain had worn off miles back and he need-ed to take a break to apply the salve canines carry in their tongues... saliva.

Hearing a horse neigh once far in the background and the occasional clatter of shod hoofs on rocks that he'd already traversed, he sensed that the danger hadn't passed but was catching up. That his right leg could hardly bear weight didn't impede the drive to keep moving. He had enough of a natural sense of self-preservation to intuit that whatever had attacked him would finish the job if trapped in the open, so he hid to take a breath.

It didn't matter that the wolf was thirsty. There was no water nearby, having left the course of the nearly dry streamlet that, earli-er in the season, had fed the creek he'd followed up the canyon. Feeling pressed by the hunter, he hadn't dared to stop and drink other than a splash or two that got on his tongue miles back while climbing the arroyo.

This region was new territory to him, having only recently connected with the pack that had turned him out. The distance he'd come before that had taken a year to navigate.

Always, there had been something that kept him moving toward the setting sun, over lofty mountains and across swift and sluggish rivers on their thousand-mile trek to the sea.

Each time he'd find a pack, the leader put up with him for only so long before forcing him out as a threat. Acquiring a gamey shoul-der that will permanently hamper his gait would, ironically, make him more acceptable to a pack, relegating him forever to a submissive role, overlorded by a dominant male.

Headstrong enough to get him booted from other packs, changing his behavior wasn't apt to occur. Gimp or not, he'd still be ranging from place to place, seeking a mate who was ready to break away from her family group.

For now, only two things mattered - water and escape.

Cressy and Quint continued to find markings on the prairie floor that kept them close on the wolf's trail. It was running on blind instinct, not stopping for anything as far as the pursuers could judge. Behind them was rolling grassy plain, ahead was more of the same riddled with empty watercourses cutting ditches around hillocks and sparse groves of scraggly trees.

The wolf was adept at staying under their line of sight by sticking to low ground and ducking around bushes, but its route was visible through the trodden hay that hadn't time to unbend and regain its height.

The sun was hovering over the horizon, ready to sink beyond the string of foothills to the northwest that edged the higher ground of the round-topped mountains. The buttes lay off to the east, already bathed in the tawny glaze of the last rays of daylight.

Under other circumstances, Cressy would have noticed the beauty and serenity of the landscape, maybe even taken a couple of photos. Today, however, her eyes were glued to the ground and trying to capture an inkling of motion ahead.

They knew the wolf wasn't far away.

As they rounded a bluff, they spied a flash of dark gray sprint from a cluster of bushes toward a pair of puny trees, trunks permanently leaning east from a lifetime of battering by unforgiving winds.

The wolf felt the earth shudder with the two horses' approaching hoofbeats, and fled toward the nearest cover it could find. Cressy was in the lead, Minuteman holding back nothing even after a full day of arduous climbing up thousands of feet through some of the West's roughest cow country. Quint brought up the rear, ready at her back but keeping clear of her fight.

Exhausted and injured, the wolf had lost the race to escape. Slowing, he turned in readiness to attack the advancing horse and rider. No recourse left, the wolf snarled, bared its fangs and, open jaws slavering, leapt toward the horse as it closed the distance.

Pulling Minuteman up short, Cressy cleared her rifle from the saddle boot, grounded the stock firmly against her shoulder, steadied her hand and, without pause, drew the wolf in her sight and pulled the trigger. Nailing the lunging wolf in mid-stride, a hundred and twenty pounds of wild, wounded, matted gray pelt and wiry sinew was dropped in his tracks.

A scant few yards to her side and slightly behind, Quint was prepared with his own gun to take a shot should Cressy have missed. Just as he expected, the bullet went straight home and Quint dropped from the saddle, keeping his rifle in hand in case the shot had some-how not delivered a fatal blow and the wolf was only stunned.

Cressy dismounted as well and the two of them cautiously approached the wolf to make certain that the animal was dead. Getting within ten feet of the predator, it was obvious that she'd got-ten a clean shot through its heart. This raider would never steal any-one's stock again.

"We got this one," said Cressy, "only a few hundred more to go." She exhaled relief but fatigue was fast taking hold. Her hands were jittery as the last drop of adrenaline was used up, leaving her limp with exhaustion.

Quint, who'd been running full bore for the last week himself, wrapped an arm around her shoulders as they gazed at the carcass of their wily adversary, his left hand gripping his gun while Cressy still held the Winchester in her right hand.

"This boy will have to do for now," he left her to bend over the wolf and take a good look at his neck. He was right. The fur was matted above his shoulders where a radio collar had been attached probably for years. All the scratching the wolf had been doing since its loss couldn't comb out the knots. "Looks like we both got our wolf."

She shook her head to focus on what he said, "What?"

"This is the same wolf that escaped the pack that was but wasn't and now isn't."

"If I were any more woozy from this hunt, I'd shoot you for being so irritating with your riddling. Lucky for you, I'm too tired to haul two carcasses back down the mountain." She leaned in to look at what he was talking about. "Ah, the enigmatic untracked wolf. Yep, you pegged it." She straightened up. "Could he have wasted any more of our time?"

"You know as well as I do that this is only the beginning of our time being literally thrown to the wolves…"

"Ain't you funny."

"Yeah, but state and federal Fish and Wildlife, the county and Lord knows who else is gonna be breathing down our necks looking for hell to pay for offing one of their precious babies."

"That's no joke," she said humorlessly. "But it's not going to start tonight. Looks like we're stuck out here 'til morning. You did say you brought provisions, right?"

Quint stood up and went to replace his rifle in the scabbard. "So *now* you're hungry."

"And you're not? Face it, it's been a helluva ride. Especially for you, Quint. You've been doing nothing but for a week."

Putting one arm over Hodey's neck, he said. "That is oh so true. This guy has been plodding every side of the canyons from here to Emville and never was there a better soldier."

"Is that where you were yesterday? Moving cattle for Joe Taylor? I thought I smelled smoke but I couldn't tell if it was you or just the general atmosphere," she managed the slightest grin.

"I can understand your confusion, the fragrance of the day is prairie grass embers." He held his sleeve to his nose then out to her which she slapped away, "Like it, do you?"

She couldn't help but smile. "Okay, enough. It's getting late. We've got a dead wolf, two tired horses and us, whipped and hungry. What's our next move, hotshot?"

"You know the drill, make a camp of sorts and call in the kill."

"I think there are a couple of things we'll need to iron out for when we're confronted by the wolf police," Cressy was definitely not looking forward to that episode. "I'm assuming no one knows about that collar or can tie this wolf to you and your other, uh, exploits."

"Let's get settled since dark's coming on. You can call in the basic information to Miles and then we'll decide what to do from there. Deal?"

"Deal."

The sun had dropped out of sight, lighting the smoke-filled sky with copper streamers that were beginning to fade.

Watching the sunset dissolve toward dark, Cressy had an opportunity to appreciate their situation, "I'm taking you at your word that you came more prepared than I did. All I've got is my emergency kit."

Quint grinned in satisfaction that he'd done the right thing chasing after her. "Yep. I had more time to gather the basics in case we needed to spend the night. Nothing lavish but at least we'll have ground cover and a sleeping bag."

Cressy's reply was a suspicious arching of an eyebrow.

"We may have to share the ground cover, but I will make the gallant offer of giving you the sleeping bag. I also grabbed a blanket. I'll use that. Will that do to protect your virtue?"

"It'll have to, won't it," she said, starting to walk toward the nearby bracken to collect branches and twigs to build a fire. Then she stopped herself putting her hands on her hips, rethinking her intial intention. "Bet they'd haul us in for an illegal campfire if nothing else would stick."

"Especially if we're on Terra Ferus property," added Quint. "Be prepared to fight from every possible angle. They're gonna come at you without mercy."

"I know," she let out a long, slow breath. She didn't have to iterate what they were both thinking - *Been there, done that.*

They unpacked the slim supplies Quint had colleccted in a hurry, including a jacket he'd had the presence of mind to ask Tricia to get. After Cressy's revelation about a campfire in fire season, they planned to sleep cold. But it also meant they had to take turns on watch to keep scavengers away from the carcass. It wasn't going to be a restful night.

While he disgorged what food he'd filched from her kitchen along with some water bottles, before calling Crenshaw she first talked to her mother to let her know that she was fine and that Quint was with her. Fran's sigh of relief that Cressy wasn't alone was loud enough Quint heard it as he opened a couple of containers of "lunchables" and pulled out some crackers.

Hanging up after reassuring Tricia that she was fine, Cressy tried not to laugh as she watched him make dinner with items purchased for Tricia's box lunches.

"Thank goodness for having kids in school," he said as he handed her the pre-packaged meal. "One look in your fridge and I had enough to get us through the night." Reaching back in his saddlebag, he extracted a bottle of red wine and a couple of half-crushed paper cups. "I figured red since it's best served at room temperature."

Cressy couldn't hold back anymore and hooted her laughter.

"Shhh, you might disturb the dead." Which only made her laugh more, releasing the tension she'd been feeling since finding out a wolf had been stalking her cows.

"I've known you all my life, Quint, and truthfully, I never knew you had it in you."

"Wha-at?" he asked, elbows bent and open, flat hands out in his best Jack Benny impression.

"If it weren't for Mom and Dad watching all those videos of ancient television shows, I'd never know who you were imitating. Bob Hope, right?"

"Never mind. I know you're playing me. Before we pour the wine, I need to make my calls home."

As they relaxed and sipped the cabernet watching the stars gain intensity against the darkening, smoke streaked sky, Quint raised the battered cup, "This stuff isn't half-bad."

"I'll take that as your stamp of approval."

"Perfect with string cheese and smoked turkey chunks, don't you agree?"

Her only response was, "Hmm-mm."

Turning the conversation back to the conundrum at hand, Quint asked, "Miles said you texted him a video of the perp in action. I'd like to see it."

"Sure," and she brought her phone out of her pocket and found the recording, playing it for him.

"Pretty irrefutable, I'd say." He handed back the phone. "You have photos too?"

"I had Mom take photos and she did. She also sent them to Miles."

"Let's take a look at what little evidence we have to support your claim. You do have the video, which is the best part. Everything else is after the fact but photos of the wolf's prints, which I assume your mother took…"

"As well as Miles and he said Tandy Swifter did and Mikey Stromberg when she showed up. So there are lots of photos."

"Not to mention the ones we have of the wolf here, even though we couldn't get a recording of its attack. I kinda couldn't put down the gun to shoot video and neither could you. But we do have corroborating stories."

"Always nice to have a witness," said Cressy. She raised her cup to him, "Here's to the witness."

"Which ODFW will do everything in its power to make it sound like we concocted some outlandish tale. We'll need to be prepared for anything. Just because the video and photos were texted to Miles doesn't mean they might not be deleted. He carries a government-issue phone and, crazy as this sounds, there's always a possibility it could be messed with. I'd like you to send me whatever you have, including your mother's pictures."

"Okay, she sent them to me so I'll forward all of them to you," which she did immediately.

But Quint didn't leave it at that. "Is there someone else you can think of not connected to government or anyone involved with this issue? If you can, I think you should email them all of it, too. The wider the information is disseminated the less likely it is to disappear,"

Cressy took a sip from her cup as she thought about it. Quiet for a few moments while she scanned her memory for everyone she could think of, she then reached around to her back pocket and removed the little wallet she always carried with her. Opening it, she remembered that she'd stuck a card inside when she'd first met the newsgal and her husband who'd come over for dinner the other night.

Her eyes brightened as she extracted Anthea Keller's business card. "Here," she said handing it to Quint.

"Right, she was the one you invited over with her ex-cop husband." He looked at Cressy in the faint starlight. "Isn't she doing some kind of research on the wolf problem?"

"Yes."

"Perfect. Email or text everything to her and ask her to safeguard it."

CHAPTER 39

It wasn't just another sunrise.

Cressy had been sleeping so soundly that Quint hadn't the heart to wake her to take her turn for their agreed swap at standing watch. Although he'd dozed off now and again, there hadn't been any alarm raised by either horse as they grazed and rested, allowing him to feel secure at their cold camp.

Lying on his back, fingers entwined behind his head as he watched the sky change color, Quint waited an hour after the sun had cleared the horizon before nudging Cressy awake.

At the slight pressure applied to her arm, she rolled over and did a double take, having blissfully forgotten where she was and the nightmare that was hours from commencing.

"This is not the dream I envisioned," said Cressy, blinking away the sand from her eyes.

"Sorry to be such a disappointment," Quint frowned, slightly offended at the inference.

"That's not what I meant," and this time she did elbow him as he lay less than a foot away. "Nice enough to enjoy the great outdoors again, but not under these circumstances with a dead wolf a dozen feet away, probably crawling with all kinds of repulsive insects," she winced. "And I'm hardly looking forward to dealing with the lupus doofus patrol."

"That's no way to describe our well-meaning wolf advocates," he chided. "Anti-humanity green goons might be more kindly."

"Right," she said pushing off the hard ground and sitting up. Then she remembered, "You didn't wake me to do my stint at watch."

"Nah, who could poke sleeping beauty out of a well-earned slumber? Not me," he tossed out as he rose from the ground and dusted off bits of weeds and ash. Standing up, he said, "There, all ready to receive the wolf enforcers. How 'bout you? Prepared to meet your fate?"

She climbed out of the sleeping bag and, undoing her half undone ponytail, she combed her fingers through her hair before replacing the band. "No time like the present. What do you think? Should we bury the bottle so they don't think this was a joyride?"

"Nah, it goes in my saddle bag, with the remainder of the contents to show we weren't drunk in case they decide to sift through my goods, which I doubt they will." Regarding her with compassion, "I'm afraid they will not be so sweet in their dealings with the shooter, and I presume that you will not allow me to take the blame for that."

"No way, Buster. This is my kill. Not only will I own it but after these last few years of living through hell because of wolves, I'm thankful for putting one of the perps down." Cressy cocked her head, "Who knows, this may be one that got away more than once."

He bobbed his head considering the thought. "There's always the possibility."

Taking a long look at the horizon, Quint said. "We'd best figure out where we are before alerting the authorities. I think we lucked out and didn't cross the boundary onto preserve property."

Standing beside him, Cressy scanned the horizon in all directions. "You're right. I'd say for certain that we're on Echo Trails' land. Been a while since I was up here but, by the looks of it, we cut it close."

Echo Trails Ranch was the largest landowner in the county other than Terra Ferus' Gaston Buttes Preserve. Thousands of acres were owned by the ranching consortium out of California whose majority shareholder, Howie Ketchum, was a rodeo personality originally hailing from Texas. Chalking up close to a hundred head lost to suspicious circumstances over the last couple years, he was symapathetic to the local outfits that had suffered wolf depredation and harassment by virtually unmanaged deer and elk populations.

Protected elk had been causing additional strain on ranchers from conservation trusts and non-producers buying up land then purposefully removing fencing and water resources. That activity set-up the expanding wild herds to compete with cattle and sheep by seeking water and fodder on independent ranches in the region.

This was the modern range war.

"I really hadn't paid attention how far we'd come last night after climbing Esther Creek, but now that I see the landscape, we can be certain that this is ETR's property. You recognize Little Butte that abuts Terra Ferus' land. That bugger really covered some miles yesterday."

"What are we, ten miles across from your ranch, Quint?"

"More or less. Talk about a roundabout route." He thought for a moment, then said, "I'm going to put in a call to Howie and let him know what happened and where we are."

Quint and Ketchum had developed a friendly working relationship over the years since Echo Trails began purchasing land in the county. Quint leased grazing land from ETR and they had long since instituted reciprocal permission to hunt, the latter of which Quint blithely alluded to during their chat. Hunting is hunting, right?

When he closed the call he told Cressy, "The regulatory storm may be brewing but at least we have the solid support of the landowner where the *incident* occurred."

Taking it upon himself to roll up the bedding, "Time you called in the *murrrderrr*," he said rolling his tongue with the worst Scottish brogue she'd ever heard.

After noting that they were only a quarter-mile from one of ETR's ranch roads, Cressy supplied Sheriff Swifter with directions to reach their location, leaving it to her to contact the other agencies.

It took three hours of Quint and Cressy cooling their heels before the sheriff arrived, followed within fifteen minutes by Prescott Turlow, ODFW wolf coordinator, and his trusty, perpetually unhappy sidekick, Mikey Stromberg from Wildlife Services. Stringing along was a veterinary consultant from Washington State University who happened to be in the county, having been called in on the wolf depredation at Emville.

Cressy could think of few things she dreaded more than having to deal with any Fish and Wildlife reps. Especially after the appalling treatment she'd received at their hands when Terry had died on the scene of the horrific wolf attack that forced him to shoot two predators, one as his life was cut short. Vestiges of the battle with the state over irreparable damages and compensation hung over her head, though nothing on earth could replace what she'd lost - her husband.

Sheriff Swifter was as compassionate as possible while maintaining her professionalism in handling this new situation, not having served on "wolf duty" as a deputy. She and her husband, one of the local pastors, knew Cressy well from the Sunday evening prayer meetings. Being familiar with the abominable accusations and subsequent fines that Cressy had endured, the sheriff did what she could to deflect some of the regulatory blitz that was likely to be unleashed. As expected, the animosity would come from Stromberg who had often voiced her disdain for ranch and farm culture as infringing on the rights of wildlife.

Trying to relegate Quint to the background wasn't working particularly well for the state and federal representatives. As a direct witness to the final events leading up to the killshot, he didn't exactly interfere in the proceedings but he did make his statements clear, doing what he could to protect Cressy without actually getting tagged for obstructing justice. In the meantime, he was recording the proceedings on his phone, having guarded its battery life for such a necessity.

Cressy had steeled herself for the onslaught, thankful that Quint had taken it upon himself to track her down and support her in what was turning out to be a battle of wills, and one in which she'd have to control her temper. After two years of burying her emotions in order to maintain equanimity amid unjust charges from ODFW, Cressy was having a more difficult time than two years prior. Quint could see how she was struggling to be civil and attributed the difference to the fact that this time she wasn't in deep shock. For this reason, Cressy also wasn't about to be blindsided again.

Circumstances took an unusual turn when the Oregon State Police showed up.

Cressy turned to Tandy, "Why are they here? Doesn't the county handle these calls?"

"I've been informed of a change in policy since the last time you went through this. ODFW has, for lack of a better word, contracted with the state police to enforce their regulations," the sheriff explained, frowning at the direction the handling of the incident was heading. "Prepare yourself, Cressy. I believe they're going to arrest you for killing a wolf without a permit."

With an unusual shrug of her shoulders and misplaced half-smile, Cressy said, "I expected as much, to tell you the truth."

Standing right beside Cressy and the sheriff, Quint was on the edge of losing his composure as Tandy told Cressy why reinforcements had arrived. When an officer approached Cressy with handcuffs, Quint was recording it all blow-by-blow, including her offhand remark to Quint, "What did I tell you? Another prophecy fulfilled."

As Cressy was marched off to the state police SUV, the other officer handed Quint a citation for his complicit action in the so-called crime. Before being helped into the rear seat, Cressy winked at Quint, "Bail me out, would ya?"

CHAPTER 40

Watching OSP shackle Cressy's hands in front of her and stuff her into the Durango's back seat, Quint bit back anger while Tandy Swifter bit her lower lip in frustration.

As the police drove their prisoner down the mountain, leaving Quint with two horses to get home, Sheriff Swifter said, "What next?"

"Let's see, I'm ten miles from home and the quickest route is to ride rather than have Del come get us." He turned to face her, "How long before I can bail out Cressy?"

"Processing will take hours and they'll probably do it here in county rather than heading to the jail at Cleric County right away. You know we don't have any overnight facilities here, don't you?"

"Actually, no, I didn't know. But you think I can get to the county lock-up to post bail before they transport her to Alder?"

"Yes, I think you can make it to Koyama if you head out now." She looked at her watch, "It's just eleven now. But you'd better get there before four or they'll take her in and you'll have trouble getting her released before Monday. Courts close down on weekends." As he gathered Minuteman's reins and mounted Hodey, she added. "I only wish I could post bail myself."

"You've done your best, Tandy. Thanks for being here to at least run interference. I don't trust that Stromberg as far as I could toss her and if she could have incited anyone to mistreat Cressy, she would have."

"Our OSP officers are professionals, Quint. That would never have happened."

"If you say so." Quint turned to face home. "Looks like I'll be seeing you later, Sheriff."

Riding up to the corral closest to the house, Quint jumped off Hodey, tossed the reins of both horses over the rail and immediately pulled his phone from his pocket. As he strode toward the house, Del emerged from the barn and signaled Quint to get his attention.

"Whose horse? Cressy's?"

"You've already heard they arrested her," he said matter-of-factly. "Is Mom inside?"

"Yeah, Audrey's the one who told me."

"Would you mind seeing to the horses, Del? I need to find out what's being done to get her out of the hoosgow."

"No prob. Keep me updated."

"Sure will."

Running up the back steps and into the house, Quint called, "Mom, do you have Fran Corler's number?"

"Yes." With a touch of irony, she added, "Glad to have you back, Quint." Scribbling the number onto a post-it, Audrey gave it to her son. "Last I heard she was heading to Koyama, though I don't think she knew how they were going to raise bail."

"That's my concern. We only have a few hours before they transport Cressy to Alder and it's Friday. That's going to make it tight."

"Do you know how much that'll be?"

"Well, Mom, last I heard the fine for killing a wolf without a permit is over six thousand dollars on this side of the state. But Tandy told me that it's ten percent paid directly to the sheriff's office. If there are other charges that might up the bail."

"I expect she might be stretched thin like the rest of us this time of year. A thousand dollars isn't going to be easy to raise," Audrey said. "Hasn't the government persecuted that girl enough?"

"My feeling exactly but ODFW doesn't consider that. I frankly believe that they don't think it's their job to care about the people who pay their salary. Sorry, Mom, gotta call Fran and see what's up."

Guilt was part of the equation for Quint shouldering responsibility to assist with bail money. It was a fluke of circumstances that landed Cressy in jail instead of him. If he'd taken out that wolf as he'd planned, she'd never be in this jam.

After talking to Cressy early in the morning, Fran Corler had been waiting to receive a call from her, which didn't come through until after Quint had gotten back to his ranch and phoned to check in. As far as Fran could tell, processing Cressy into the system was taking an inordinate amount of time. It made her wonder if Wildlife Services had managed to draw it out, expecting to make an example of her daughter by delaying her induction just long enough that she'd end up spending the weekend behind bars. Just the thought made her livid.

The pressing problem was how they'd raise the money to get Cressy home before she was stuck in an Alder jail cell.

Of all people keeping a cool head, it was one little girl listening to her grandmother who was desperately struggling to keep emotions in check. Papa was as upset as Franma and as frustrated by time and financial limitations.

Hearing that her grandparents weren't sure that they'd be able to collect enough to get her mom out of jail sent her thoughts spinning. Who could help?

Then it clicked.

Tricia had a cell phone without the bells and whistles that did other kids she knew. Her mom had insisted on her having one only because they lived so far out of town. It was a matter of security to Cressy.

Digging into her backpack, Tricia found the handout from the last prayer meeting she'd attended. On the back were phone numbers for the pastors. She remembered them talking about how important it was to help one another and how often they had mentioned families in need and had pulled together to assist them.

Maybe it was time to see if they could help her mother, though she also knew her mom would probably decline the help because of pride. Turning over the options in her head and realizing she was playing with both her mother and grandparents' disapproval, Tricia decided someone had to act.

Ann Foster, one of the pastor's wives who had shown nothing but kindness to her, was listed as a contact. Entering the number into her phone, Tricia defied her status as the overlooked, overprotected child and placed the call.

Within the hour, Fran was opening her car door in front of the bank in Rory. Hoping to be able to talk to the president, whom she'd known since he'd been in 4-H with her daughter, she was preparing herself to beg a loan against their house. Except for the dire position Cressy was confronting, Fran wasn't all that confident she'd be able to convince him to sign off on a property that already carried a second mortgage, which had

funded Cressy's previous fight with the state and her husband's healthcare. Thankfully, he'd recovered after timely surgery and was well on the way to mending but it had left them seriously strapped.

Twisting in the driver's seat and planting her feet on the asphalt, her phone rang. Checking the number, it was local but not one she recognized.

"Hello?"

"Hello, Fran? This is Ann Foster. I know it's been a while since we talked but I've been informed about Cressy's dilemma."

Fran's first reaction was, *No, not now. I don't have time for friendly commiseration.*

"Let me get right to the point, dear. You probably know Jerry is the pastor of Nacqus Community Church and that we meet at Cressy's on Sunday nights. I put out a call to our members on the prayer line with your need for Cressy's bail."

Her attention captured, what Ann was saying was not what

Fran was expecting to hear.

"We've collected over five hundred dollars that I hope you'll accept in order to get Cressy out of custody. She's been a pillar of courage and has already dealt with so much tragedy we wanted to do what we can to help. Where are you that I can get this into your hands? I understand that there's a real time crunch."

Flabbergasted and speechless, Fran's mouth worked without a sound escaping her lips. Clearing her voice to utter words of gratitude that were momentarily stuck in the back of her throat, Fran finally croaked out her heartfelt thanks. "I'm at the bank now, Ann. I was just going in to try and wangle a loan," she choked back tears of relief.

"Perfect. I'll be right there so you can make the deposit. Don't move!"

Completely overcome with emotion that people she hadn't spoken to in years except in passing at the grocery store or around town, Fran succumbed to allowing a few tears to trickle down her chin. She'd closed the car door for privacy in an attempt to regain composure before Ann arrived. As she wiped the wet from her face with a tissue, her phone rang again.

Swallowing first and seeing who was calling, she answered, "Hello Quint."

"Are you all right, Fran?" He could hear the tremor in her voice.

Coughing briefly, she said, "Yes, I'm fine."

"Good. I was calling to see where you are. I assumed you'd be on your way to town."

"I'm in Rory now. What do you need?"

"It's not what I need, Fran. I was hoping to catch up with you to make sure you had enough to get Cressy released today. You know she asked if I'd spring her so I was on my way to the bank."

"It so happens that I'm parked there now with the same intention."

"That's great. I'll meet you there." And he rang off without another word.

Leaning back against the headrest, Fran was completely

blown away with how Cressy's neighbors had stepped up to help. She knew that the community was tight, she and her family had been part of it for decades, but this was much more than delivering a casserole or plate of cookies. This was emptying pockets to stand up for what's right. Dabbing her cheeks with the tissue, she just whispered, "Thank you," again and again.

There was one minuscule, barebones holding cell at the county sheriff's office that served multiple duty as retention facility for Koyama City, County and Oregon State Police. Currently, Cressy was the sole occupant of a space designed for short-term incarceration, no more than a few hours and one tenant at a time.

Fingerprinting and the paperwork grind long since completed, Cressy had been striving to maintain patience. Expecting at any moment to be grilled about the whole episode, she'd been left alone, no one even bothering to say 'boo.' Uncertain whether ODFW and its enforcement arm were dragging their feet, the closer it came to five p.m. the more she resigned herself to being transported to overnight accommodations. With Cressy's history with the state, she could be considered a scofflaw that the court would view as disqualifying for being released under her own recognizance.

Stromberg had made it her business to hang around dropping comments within earshot about the inadequacy of Koyama's jail facilities. Cressy could swear that the Wildlife Services rep was literally rubbing her hands together in gleeful anticipation of OSP carting off the prisoner to a proper jail. Having been read the charge of committing a Class A Misdemeanor, Cressy overheard (as she was meant to) Stromberg alluding to the fine, knowing full well the hardship it would cause.

Temporarily twiddling her thumbs behind bars, Cressy could indulge her errant thoughts about how she had ended up in this place. Was it being a hothead, vengeance or, the more she considered what drove her to track that wolf, drawing attention to a growing danger?

Cressy was being reminded that people like the gloating Stromberg reserved their compassion for plants and animals, forgetting why they were paid, which wasn't to elevate protection of wildlife above the public, but to protect it for the public's benefit. And giving predators a pass at the expense of the public was completely upside-down. Government had done one thing in regulating every aspect of commerce, which conservation affected: it had skewed the concept of vulnerability by redefining it to apply to any life form except its human boss.

When Terry was killed as a direct result of a brutal wolf attack, it was this backward mindset that led the government to posthumously impose fines on him for shooting two wolves that were in the act of mauling his cows. Remembering the humiliation the authorities had piled on top of her grief, Cressy was scarcely keeping a lid on the resentment that threatened to spill over with the authorities processing her through the system. It crossed her mind that might be why they had avoided unnecessary contact, helping her by restricting interaction and not allowing her the opportunity to blow her stack and make the situation worse.

That didn't affect everyone's favorite Wildlife Services rep who prided herself on her ability to goad the offender into digging a deeper hole. Stromberg's contrary nature was the agency's worst PR nightmare and the reason she was usually stuck in the field when the press was around. Today, however, she had insinuated herself into the middle of the Dillat arrest after being the sole government representative that had initially documented the predation at Cressy's farm. She would be giving evidence in the trial that Stromberg was eager to see go ahead.

Hearing the ragged voice of Mikey Stromberg continually seeking an opening in conversation to denigrate Cressy and the Dillats' lawless history was grating on the officers at the station. But as a representative of one of the agencies pressing charges they were having trouble getting rid of her.

Rolling the events of the last two years through her mind,

Cressy still fumed at how the court disallowed introduction of evidence that she and Terry had complied with every possible guideline instituted by the state. In the end, it hadn't mattered how much fladry they'd strung up or the hundreds of hours of lost sleep keeping watch in the field or relying on ineffective hazing. None of it had deterred wolves from taking dozens of head at Cripple Calf Creek Ranch. Compounding the denial of compensation for livestock on top of the fines, wasted money defending her case was the last straw that had forced the sale of the ranch.

Reporting every wolf sighting, encounter and depredation; following every bit of administrative procedure required by ODFW and EPA or Endangered Species Act regulations; none of it halted the bureaucratic steamroller that crushed her business and, ultimately, her life. All because the facts didn't fit the narrative that wolves were beneficial to the ecosystem, which Cressy and every serious rancher in Eastern Oregon knew was a lie. The reaction to the majority of their reports was the same - the state refused to acknowledge wolves were involved and, alternatively, she and Terry were saddled with the blame of instigating the tragedy that took his life.

Cressy's response to this last predation at her home that landed her in a jail cell occurred less than a dozen miles from the earlier attacks at Three C. They were part and parcel of the ongoing wolf problem all the ranchers had experienced in that sector. The range rider had investigated numerous reports in the area though it was uncertain if they were related to the same pack that attacked Terry.

Despite all, Cressy had continued to employ the standards set by the state's wolf plan to cover the eventuality of encountering problems from the roving band and is why, when she saw the stool left by a wolf, she immediately reported it.

Learning from the atrocious treatment she and others had experienced, Cressy made sure she had her ducks in a row, following procedure until she was confronted with a situation that escalated out of control within minutes. Under the law, she had every right to shoot the offending animal caught in the act of rending her cow, catching it on video, no less. And she did shoot. The only problem was that it didn't kill it.

Allowing an unpredictable wounded wolf to roam free would have put her neighbors at risk, giving Cressy no choice but to pursue it. It didn't matter that doing so would put her in conflict with regulations. Waiting for authorities to arrive was not a viable option. The wolf would have been lost to hunters (not that a hunt would have immediately been approved, because it wouldn't) and could conceivably attack humans, other domestic animals or die of its injury. All choices were inhumane. By all reasonable standards, Cressy's actions were necessary.

The state had proven time after time that adhering to reason was not government's strong suit. Protecting wildlife, any wildlife, above serving human needs had proven to be paramount, even if it meant placing children and families in danger, physically and financially.

Cressy wasn't having any of it. Her husband had died because government favored predators over her family. Her daughter's life would have been in jeopardy had she walked outside first, her lamb in tow.

No.

As Cressy sat in solitude, waiting to learn her fate, she concluded she'd do it all over again. She's already lost her husband.

This was one fight she didn't plan to lose.

Time was growing desperately short for Cressy's redemption as office hours approached closing time, building Stromberg's exultant expectancy of imminent transfer to Alder. The OSP officers, on the other hand, dreaded the extra eight hours required to transport the inmate. Not one of them was sympathetic to the dead wolf, and less so toward Stromberg who was rapidly wearing on their last nerve.

With fifteen minutes to spare before the lock-up was depopulated, Cressy's mother flew frantically through the door held open by a somber, visibly displeased Quint Edwards.

Tandy Swifter was back in the office and anxiously waiting Cressy's rescuers to arrive, having no wish to see her spend the weekend caged up with real criminals.

Catching a glimpse of Fran and Quint through the glassed-in entry, Swifter came around the barrier and greeted the flustered mother and unsmiling cowboy. Glancing at her watch, she said with a touch of relief, "That's cutting it close. I'm glad you made it in before your daughter was escorted out of here."

"It's a miracle that we were able to raise bail at all," whispered Fran, unwilling to create any more of a spectacle for the consumption of unsympathetic noseyparkers, including the press, which she had seen a reporter from the regional paper sitting in his car.

"If it had been up to me, things would be handled differently," said the sheriff. "If I really wanted to push the jurisdiction issue, it would guarantee more press than anyone could stomach. Frankly, I didn't think Cressy would be interested in this going national."

Quint cocked his head with interest. "Are you saying there could be a jurisdiction dispute between the county and the state and Feds?"

"Yes and no. ODFW have less say in this because wolves are no longer on the endangered species list. USFWS is operating under federal regulation which, for the moment, hasn't been challenged in court by any county, though, in my opinion, it should be."

"No matter now," said Quint. "Fran has the bail to release Cressy and we can get her out of here. She's endured more injustice than anyone rightfully should."

"I'm just thankful we got here in time so I can take my daughter home to her daughter," breathed Fran.

"I'll get the process going. You can relax now," and she disappeared into the back.

To which Quint added under his breath, "Yeah, it's Miller time."

CHAPTER 41

Assisting Fran into the driver's seat of her car, Quint acknowledged the two women's thanks before climbing back into his own rig and heading home. The weeklong rush that had constantly spurred him to action slowly dissipated into a bone-deep weariness that left him hollow.

Guilt succeeded the brief triumph of bailing out Cressy, knowing full well that he should have been the one handcuffed and tossed into a cell, the evidence of his hunt buried on the edges of the rimrock. He also realized that she had a better possibility of beating the system than he did.

As a sympathetic widow who had been browbeaten by government, Cressy stood a chance of victory whereas he would have faced serious jailtime withour reprieve. Not that the wisdom of the facts alleviated the shame he felt for allowing Cressy to take the brunt of censure and punishment at the hands of self-satisfied bureaucrats. The one thing he could do was make certain that he supported her every step of the way.

The ride to pick up Tricia at her grandparents' passed in silence. Preoccupied by the stress of how the day had unraveled, Cressy's expression of gratitude to Quint had been genuine but distracted. Fran explained who had pitched-in to provide the funds that rescued her from spending a dispiriting weekend in detention, which only weighed further on her conscience. These people had come forward to help without a second thought for their own financial strain. The personal need to do away with a killer wolf had engulfed her, overpowering the sensible part of her brain that ought to have considered fully how her actions would affect others.

That the community had gathered in support should have eased the self-condemnation but it wasn't working out that way. When she thought about what was to come, Cressy began questioning if it would be worth the guaranteed anguish. Past experience left nothing to the imagination.

It had already been proven there wasn't an attorney worth their salt in the county, or the state for that matter, that could conscientiously handle Cressy's case. Every one of them that she'd dealt with regarding the suit arising from Terry's tragic death had been unwilling to think outside the box. Their perception of legal redress for damages was colored by assuming regulations that doom the victims of predation couldn't be challenged, rendering their counsel useless to Cressy and every other casualty of environmental policy.

When government hid behind surrogates like protected species to penalize average citizens for protecting their rights and property, the knee-jerk reaction from victims in their frustration was to assume they must immediately file suit against the offending agency. Too many had learned the hard way that it 'just ain't so.'

These last years of battling ODFW and US Fish and Wildlife's endangered species protocols, Cressy had gained invaluable understanding about how officers of the court - attorneys, prosecutors, judges - worked as a unit in tandem with government agencies that created the regulations and enforced them.

What it confirmed, for all practical purposes, was the lack of adversarial action in a court of law, nor was there real advocacy for a petitioner or defendant standing in opposition to government. Generally speaking, it was a family of lawyers scratching each other's backs. Backroom deals consummated with furtive handshakes occurred to avoid upsetting the apple cart, and Cressy had been on the receiving end of that kind of justice.

Sure, she was seeing the process through a jaundiced eye, but until Cressy witnessed something different, she couldn't be convinced otherwise.

When Quint finally walked through the door, he was swamped by girl gab. With everything that had happened during the last week he had completely forgotten that Shaley was graduating on Saturday.

Audrey was fussing over preparations for the next day, having hustled weeks ago to procure reservations for a late lunch at the one and only snazzy restaurant in the area. Walking into the midst of a grandmother fussing over the first of her grandchildren to graduate high school, Quint realized just how much he'd neglected his family. Not knowing if Shaley's mother would bother to make an appearance, he felt even worse.

"Good, you're home," Audrey greeted him. Discerning the slightest reproach in her voice, Quint knew she was actually relieved that he was back, knowing that he'd be available for whatever Shaley needed.

"Like I'd miss anything to do with my girl's milestone? Not on your life," he said hanging his hat while Shaley swept through the doorway to kiss her dad on the cheek. She was practically floating on air with anticipation of starting a new chapter in her young life, not that she had a clear picture where that story was going... yet.

He couldn't help but grin as he let the other concerns take a back seat for now. There was nothing more to be done to assist Cressy this weekend. She was home with her family where she needed to be, so Quint let the angst dissolve amid the hubbub that swirled around him.

"I don't suppose there's anything I can do to help..." he hoped desperately to receive a negative answer.

"Nope," said Audrey, to which he audibly sighed. "The women have it all under control," which was hardly what it looked like with feminine attire and other beauty accoutrements strewn across the living room furniture.

"Where's Cam?"

"Hiding in his room," said Shaley. "He'd hardly be interested in this stuff, would he."

"I suppose not," agreed Quint. "Maybe we boys need to make ourselves scarce while you, uh, do something with all this fluff," and he swung his arm out to indicate the ordered mayhem his mother had coordinated.

"Not a bad idea," said Audrey. "Dinner's in the kitchen and the den is free."

"I'll take that under advisement," and Quint went up the stairs to see his son.

Collecting Tricia at her mother's was heartrending in a way Cressy hadn't anticipated. She hadn't really thought that spending the better part of one day in the cooler would affect her so deeply until Tricia ran out of the house to capture her mother in an embrace that was more like glue.

Blinking back tears, Cressy hugged her tightly for a moment before speaking. "Are you ready to go home?"

"Uh-huh!"

"Good, I'm famished," lied Cressy, who really had no appetite. "I could use some dinner and I'll bet you could, too."

"Sure. Papa and I had a little lunch but I could eat... now."

"That's good news. It's not often you admit to being hungry."

Tricia looked up at her mother as she opened her left arm to hug her father who had followed Tricia out of the house. "I guess worrying can do that."

Brushing Tricia's hair back behind her ears, Cressy said, "I hope you didn't worry too much."

"No. I knew the church people would come through."

"You did? How so?" Cressy was intrigued.

Tricia immediately blushed with guilt realizing her mom might get angry when she heard. Knowing she had to fess up, Tricia winced, "I called Mrs. Foster when Franma seemed so upset about you being stuck in jail for the weekend."

"What did you tell her?" Cressy held her alarm in check, not knowing what her daughter might have said.

"Just that you'd been arrested for killing a wolf and that we needed prayer. I hope that was okay."

Cressy just pulled her daughter closer and smiled at her own mother, whose jaw had dropped at the disclosure that it was Tricia who'd taken the initiative.

"Honey, that was absolutely okay. It definitely helped get me out. Didn't it, Mom?"

"Yes, dear, it did."

CHAPTER 42

Friday night was spent munching burgers and fries from Tricia's favorite take-out restaurant and watching a fifty-year-old slapstick comedy that had absolutely nothing to do with anything. Chortling at the same jokes that made them howl every time they followed the ridiculous storyline from silly beginning to victorious end, by the time the TV was turned off they were spent from laughing, sides aching from the emotional release and ready to hit the hay.

Packing it in for the night, Cressy saw her daughter fall into a deep sleep within seconds of crawling into bed. Relieved that Tricia was relaxed enough to drop off so quickly, sliding under the covers of her own bed, Cressy fell into an exhausted, dreamless slumber.

Saturday morning arrived and nothing could break through the oblivion to which the girls had succumbed.

Smoke haze still permeated the atmosphere, obscuring the dawn and allowing Cressy to sleep in, undisturbed by morning's usual light flooding her room. Ironically, the fires that supplied the Dillat women a reprieve, continued to consume the grasslands, winds and grueling topography stymieing containment.

It took effort to pry open her eyes, stuck closed from a residue that could have been generated by tears in her sleep. Cressy didn't remember, nor did it make a difference. She was just grateful for a peaceful night's rest in the midst of what promised to become a legal maelstrom.

Deciding it was time to greet the day, whatever was in store, Cressy threw back the covers and stretched.

A half-hour later she was downstairs and making breakfast for herself and Tricia, hoping that her daughter was ready to start eating again. Despite the demoralizing events that followed the triumphant end to the hunt, Cressy was enjoying an odd calm, somehow sure that this time things would be resolved in the favor of ranchers like herself. *Maybe this is what the Sunday group calls faith,* she mused. *I guess Tricia must be rubbing off on me.*

She wasn't fooling herself that it was going to be a lark taking on the establishment, but there was a spark of hope lighting the way. All she needed was some levelheaded guidance and she was fairly certain that her new acquaintance, Anthea, might have a good idea about where to find it.

Tricia tripped down the stairs in a chipper mood but rubbing her eyes.

"Are we awake yet?" Cressy downplayed her amusement.

"Uh, yeah. Too bad I don't like coffee."

"I don't recall that I've ever served you any, young lady."

"Papa has let me try some of his. It smells good but taste awful."

As Cressy took a drink from her mug, she said. "It's what we like to call an acquired taste."

"Sounds like you have to work at it. I'll pass. Except everyone says it helps you wake up, I don't see why you'd drink it."

"Then it's lucky I poured you a glass of orange juice."

"Thanks Mom," Tricia plumped down at the kitchen table and guzzled half the glass.

"Does this mean you're ready to eat?"

"Hm-hmm," was the only response available as she swallowed.

Smiling about one more step forward, Cressy dished out their breakfast and joined her daughter at the table.

After cleaning up the kitchen, the two girls got back to business as usual taking care of animals, further worries allayed of a wolf making an unwelcome appearance. As Cressy watched her daughter move the lamb back to his permanent enclosure next to the garage, she marveled at Tricia's ability to bounce back. *Another lesson to be learned from my little girl.* With that thought ringing through her head, Cressy went about her own chores leaving the wolf issue to marinate until she was ready to make some calls later in the day.

The afternoon sped by as the Dillat ladies whisked through a Saturday of staying home. This was the third day that the mercantile was closed and Cressy had carefully weighed whether or not to unlock the doors for trade. She could have called May at any time but decided against it knowing she'd be peppered with questions she couldn't answer and that the phone would be ringing off the hook with calls from a hostile press as well as wellwishers. Monday would be soon enough to confront the public.

In the meantime, she had contacted May to let her know everything was under control, relieving her friend's mind. May had also volunteered to open the store for the Sunday night prayer group but Cressy had demurred, knowing that it was necessary for her to greet and thank them for their invaluable help and friendship. Doing so would be uncomfortable because Cressy had always been reticent to receive assistance, but this went far beyond accepting a bouquet or other benign gift. She would be remiss if she didn't come forward and acknowledge their generosity with earnest thanks.

As well, Cressy called her mother and asked if she and her father wouldn't mind attending the prayer service to offer their gratitude. Fran agreed even though she had as difficult a time as her daughter accepting kindness, but were it not for this congregation, Cressy would be languishing in a lock-up surrounded by chronic offenders. Absolutely, she'd be there.

After tying up those loose ends, Cressy put in a call to Anthea Keller hoping to pick her brain before engaging legal representation. From what they'd discussed during the meetings they'd had thus far, she had a feeling that this woman just might have some innovative ideas. If nothing else, Cressy knew the status quo in the county, or the state, didn't offer a viable answer to her problem that could rapidly devolve into a farce if she relied on regional lawyers.

It turned out that the Mathers' were still in Koyama County, the road north not yet opened for through traffic. They could have taken the long route around, adding on another four hours of travel time but there was no rush to get home. Cressy found that the Darbys continued to host them at their river lodging and when she talked with Anthea, she was pleased to hear that they'd be happy to help in any way possible.

It was set - a Sunday brunch confab had been added to the social calendar.

Quint's Saturday was crammed with inconvenient sensations that he'd effectively buried for years. Witnessing the graduation of his firstborn was a frontal assault on his composure, especially when he couldn't find his ex-wife anywhere in the mob of neighbors, friends and family attending the ceremony.

His heart broke for Shaley knowing how much this would affect her. Shaley had outdone herself, earning the title of salutatorian, and her mother couldn't be bothered to make an appearance to hear her address the graduating class. Just in case she showed up, Audrey had included an extra seat in the reservations for lunch, not that she'd told her granddaughter about her plans. Audrey was hoping Kim would be there but didn't want to rain on her triumphant parade in case she was a no-show.

Kim's absence couldn't dampen Shaley's mood, assuaging Quint's concern. She'd worked hard and reveled in the culmination of all the toil that rewarded her with three prestigious colleges vying for her attendance. Just before going to the commencement ceremony, she divulged her choice to her dad, telling him that she'd submitted her registration information while he was chasing down a rogue wolf.

The declaration weighed more on his conscience. She'd finalized one of the biggest decisions of her life without any further input from her father. In contrast, his chest swelled with pride that she'd made the choice on her own. That was his first sign of letting go, knowing his little girl was capable of taking responsibility for her life.

From beginning to end, when he saw her off for the grad night celebration with friends, he realized how the conflicting emotions drained him more than the last week riding dozens of miles over precipitous terrain.

Confident that she was safe for the allnighter chaperoned by people he trusted implicitly, Quint kicked back in the living room, settling in for vacuous boobtube viewing with his son. They weren't half an hour into a program when his phone rang. Checking the caller ID, he answered with another flash of remorse.

"Hello, Cressy. How does freedom feel?"

"Peachy. Tricia and I had a perfect day. I assume you did too, listening to Shaley give her speech. How's that feel, proud papa?"

"Pretty awesome to know that she didn't just make it through, but did it with total class." He sighed, "Yeah, I'm proud of my girl."

"That is terrific. Life can go on, can't it."

"Yup. So, what's on your mind?"

"I just talked with Anthea Keller about moving ahead with a plan of attack," she said.

"Attack? I thought you needed to design a defense."

"Remember that old adage, 'offense is the best defense?' That's where I'm going and I believe that Anthea has contacts that will help develop a strategy."

"That's good news," Quint encouraged her.

"Are you in?"

"Sure, if there's anything a broken-down cowboy can do to help."

"Don't think you have a choice, bucko, being a witness and maybe even complicit."

"You're already sounding like a lawyer. Thinking of representing yourself?" he jibed.

"Lord, I hope I don't look that stupid," she chuckled.

"No one could accuse you of that, believe me. What do you need?"

"Can you come over tomorrow at noon? Anthea and Gary are going to be here and we'll have a brainstorm brunch."

"Can't turn down good home cooking. Shaley will be back and I'll be free."

"See you then."

Cressy's dining room table was cluttered with a pile of dirtied dishes pushed to one end that had been replaced by notepads, Anthea's laptop and coffee mugs. The discussion was as dull as the dishwater that was yet to be drawn for washing up - administrative process.

Everyone had been through it but Quint and Cressy had never properly assigned a name to the plodding protocol that both of them and fellow ranchers had been forced to follow if they wanted to make a case for loss. They were familiar with the mounting number of regulations that governmental agencies had been continually devising and instituting since they were kids. But it wasn't until the wolf debacle that they'd begun to realize the need to document every dang thing they did if they were to have recourse, and they certainly hadn't called it anything except a pain in the neck.

What Anthea and Gary were helping Cressy to get a grip on was that she would have no case if she hadn't followed the guidelines, however worthless or idiotic, and documented her compliance.

"I've seen so many folks who believed they were in the right, and, in fact they were, but hadn't followed every procedural hiccup laid out by bureaucrats because, frankly, they were a waste of time. But you see, it's the heart and soul of administrative agencies to create those time wasting regulations. That's what keeps them in a job for the rest of their working lives; spinning webs that tangle citizens in red tape that only administrators can sort through." She wagged her head, "Yes, it's a con to grow government at the expense of you and me who pay their wages to thwart our efforts to, well, pay their wages, if you know what I mean.

"The deal is, people get so frustrated that they don't dot all their 'i's' or cross their 't's' and they can go nowhere in court when they want to sue, which is their first inclination - to sue the government. Well, it doesn't work that way and when the state came after you when your husband died, Cressy, they used that to their advantage. You were railroaded because no legal counsel in this area, maybe the state, was either conversant enough to know how to approach the case or they were uninterested because they would become a pariah in the courts. Whatever the reason, it's unconscionable how you were treated."

"That doesn't sound like I've got much of a chance this time, either. Could it be any more dismal?"

Gary cut in, "Chin up. If you know your adversary, you have a strong possibility of winning. That's a leg up. You know more now and did a lot of things right that can sway the system to your advantage."

"That's heartening," said Quint who, alone of the foursome was leaning back in his chair, legs outstretched and cradling his coffee cup on his stomach. He figured if he acted laid back maybe it would magically manifest in his mind.

"What I'm getting to is that you did what you needed to do. You complied with the rules and you documented it so it's not a 'he said, she said' situation, though the state's attorneys will try that tack," said Anthea.

"Not to mention, twisting the facts and, if it suits them, even lie," added Gary.

"Terrific. Even ex-law enforcement considers the opposition to be underhanded and untrustworthy," noted Cressy.

Gary shrugged his shoulders, "Don't like to admit having seen it done, but I have. You already know what to expect, now you prepare for the onslaught."

"But," said Anthea, perking up, "we have someone on our

side who knows how to use their tactics against them and win."

Quint's attention was arrested but he kept with the sarcasm, "We have a secret weapon?"

Anthea's head bobbed appreciatively, taking his interpretation into consideration, "You could say that. Toddy's had more wins applying the written word against administrative agencies without ever having to go to court. I've never met anyone who manages to grasp procedure and unravel it, putting bureaucrats at a disadvantage using their own weaponized regulations against them."

"But we have to warn you, as much as you may not think so, what you're undertaking can actually be dangerous," said Gary. "You're not just bucking the government and its toadies, but you're taking on the land trusts and ecology freaks who are doing everyting in their power to minimize human footprints on their wild-eyed concept of a pristine earth."

"We're familiar with Nature's Wilds and the behind the scenes real estate swaps with US Forest Service… even their pressuring landowners to sell," said Quint soberly. "They've tried their tactics on both of us."

"I supposed as much," said Gary. "I rather doubt, however, if you know how far these folks are willing to go to get their way."

"I'd agree to that," said Cressy. "It's fairly certain that the wolves' proliferation is tied to illegal importation of breeding pairs. There are credible sources who say they've witnessed it, so we know they'll go that far."

"True. James Beers outed his own agency for doing exactly that in the Yellowstone area when the US Fish and Wildlife Service was denied funding for their pet project. Here's one article from 2013 and I contacted him to ascertain the authenticity of the story," Anthea pulled the paper that Doug Darby had copied for her that she had followed up.

"According to whistleblower Jim Beers (former USFWS Chief of National Wildlife Refuge Operations), after Congress denied funding for his agency to carry out the Northern Rockies Wolf

Recovery Project, the agency acted illegally as it brought the Canadian wolves into the Yellowstone ecosystem.

Speaking in Bozeman in May 2010, at the Gran Tree Inn, before Congress on wolf recovery issues in 1998 and 1999, and in October 2013 to the Montana Pioneer, Beers insisted that, after Congress denied USFWS funding for wolf recovery, the agency illegally expropriated Pitman-Robertson funds (federal excise taxes required by law to be distributed to the states as reimbursements), helping themselves to tens of millions of dollars.

When contacted by the Montana Pioneer for this article, Beers further stated, "The General Accounting Office verified that at least $45 to $60 million was taken, diverted, by USFWS from P-R funds."

Beers went on to say that the Pittman-Robertson excise taxes, by law, could only be used by State wildlife agencies for their wildlife restoration projects. "These funds were then used primarily...to pay bonuses to top USFWS managers that had no right to such funds [and] to trap wolves in Canada, import them, and release them into Yellowstone National Park."

Beers, a 32-year veteran USFWS biologist, whose job included overseeing the Pitman-Robertson funds, alleges that the agency misappropriated monies for the trapping and transportation of Canadian wolves into the U.S. To conceal its misuse of the funds spent on the project, the true number of wolves imported, and the subspecies brought in, USFWS intentionally did not file mandatory paperwork, according to Beers, that would have established a paper trail. Or, he speculates, somehow that paperwork mysteriously disappeared.

Beers also alleges USFWS failed to file an appropriate and accurate Environmental Impact Statement. In recent comments to the Montana Pioneer, he elaborated, saying, "The EIS was and remains a document of lies, misinformation and woefully incomplete coverage of the matter."
(https://montanapioneer.com/non-native-wolves-illegally-introduced-says-whistleblower-2/)

"So it's probable that a similar operation could have been carried out in other regions," said Anthea. "But the illicit activities can be far more egregious than transporting dangerous predators."

"We've heard about eco-terrorism threats, if that's what you mean."

"I don't like to be a harbinger of ill news," sighed Anthea, "but we've been in the thick of it and nearly lost our lives more than once dealing with individuals connected to Nature's Wilds."

"To be fair, not all people involved with them are crazy enough to do violence, but it only takes a very few ruthless sociopaths and the extreme environmentalist movement draws them like flies, to, um, dung, to be polite." Gary's eyes hooded with not-so-fond memories of the life-threatening predicaments he and Anthea had been subject to for opening the land trust can of worms.

Quint was skeptical, having a hard time believing eco-nuts were that nuts. But catching Gary's eye, he said, "You're not exaggerating, are you." It wasn't a question.

"No," Anthea cleared the air further. "If Gary hadn't been a trained law enforcement professional, retired or not, the likelihood of our having survived to tell the tale is pretty slim."

Neither Cressy or Quint were inclined to respond to that. What could they say?

"It's not our intent to scare you off, besides the fact that I don't think either of you are lacking courage. We just want to warn you that this could be a much bigger fight than you expect. It's a battle to retain your way of life and, as far as the agencies, environmental groups and land trusts are concerned, they're winning. But they're cowards hiding behind protected species to get their way - wolves, elk, spotted owls, snail darters, bunchgrass or blue butterflies - and it's not beyond some of them to resort to violence." Anthea paused a few seconds, "We know what they're capable of."

All was silent while Cressy dropped her head back to examine the ceiling paint and take a deep breath. Lowering her gaze to capture Anthea's, she said calmly, "My daughter already lost her father because of something that is absolutely wrong. I've gone this far and it just isn't in me to back down now. Somebody has to choose this fight… it may as well be me."

"I know the community will support you, they've already proven that, and so will I," stated Quint evenly, masking his determination to stand by his longtime friend and neighbor. "Skirting unjust regulations and laws to save what's left of ranching in Koyama County is not the answer. These agencies have to be gutted."

"With the right guidance and representation, I think Cressy's case could be the one to crack things wide open, maybe even the test case that could go as far as the Supreme Court, not that I'm any expert." Anthea sat back from the table, "But I know someone who is."

CHAPTER 43

Monday was arraignment day.

As much as Cressy hoped she'd be able to slip through media cracks, her wish was not granted. She'd been forewarned that the environmental contingent would be visible and vocal as soon as news leaked about her arrest, and Anthea was certain someone would blab. Nor would it be difficult to pinpoint the culprit, knowing how vehemently the federal Wildlife rep opposed destruction of her furborne wards for any reason.

Time had been too short to retain competent representation before the rushed court appearance and Cressy stood for herself at the bail proceeding, but Anthea was determined to get that changed ASAP. She'd already placed calls on Cressy's behalf but was still waiting to hear back. Since the only thing that was to be done was to accept the court's decision to hold the bail already posted, Cressy was thankful that the judge didn't add to the financial burden at this juncture.

The worst part of the day was leaving the courthouse and unexpectedly being swarmed by regional media, including Portland television reporters. Flooded with memories of how she'd been treated two years ago by many of the same crew, Cressy's countenance darkened, unable to keep her expression bland amid the ambush.

Topping off the humiliation was a grandstanding appearance by Ken Demetre, positioning himself at the top of the courthouse steps where he had convened a presser.

Cressy's eyes widened in spite of herself, seeing the man confidently addressing the press corps with his version of the charges filed against her.

"How'd he know to be here?" Cressy whispered to Anthea who was with her for moral support.

"Probably the first call your buddy Stromberg made. I wouldn't be surprised if they've been colluding on land trust issues for some time. He's been casting his political bait among the enviros, it seems."

"That's to be expected. Fits his character, I guess," acknowledged Cressy as she hustled through the crowd that threw demeaning questions in her wake.

Demetre had the gall to point a finger at her back while she descended the steps with as much dignity as could be mustered under the circumstances. "This is what comes of antipathy for nature. Ranchers wiped out the wolves generations ago and are attempting to thwart re-establishing a token population in this region where they once thrived."

He continued a diatribe on how the noble wolf had been eradicated by invading cattlemen, using Cressy's example of hunting an injured, defenseless animal with the intent of killing it.

"Damn right," Cressy muttered through gritted teeth as Anthea and Quint hustled her into Gary's rig. Finishing her sentence inside the Dodge, "I intended to kill that beast, and every other one that has attacked my family, my life and my neighbors."

"It doesn't matter what this guy says," said Anthea. "Yes, the press will eat up his performance but you actually do have the law on your side. You will win… but it's not going to be a cakewalk. This is proof."

As the defendant drove away, the media returned the cameras to center on Demetre and his planned assault against Cressy as representive of the whole beef industry. It wasn't so much that he hated stock growers, they were the convenient stepping stone to office in a widely liberal state.

Given a heads-up of the downed wolf by a crony working with Fish and Wildlife, he had parlayed that into a rapidly generated press release to Westside news outlets. His roots were in Portland where he'd formed strong connections and Demetre was assured they'd send a flock of junior reporters to tiny Koyama, tucked away in the far eastern corner of the state. This was his first blatant foray into the political arena hoping to get compassionate coverage for the downtrodden wolf that had been ruthlessly depopulated by intruding cattlemen and, as a byproduct, capture the spotlight for himself.

Demetre had been preparing for this day, knowing that some-time someone would slip-up and shoot one of these stunning creatures fleeing for its life. What he hadn't banked on was the perpetrator being an empathetic character like a widow who'd lost her husband in a nasty wolf attack a couple years prior. Still, he was fairly certain he could twist the tale to make the dead Dillat look like a villain in the previous wolf caper, painting the surviving wife as a vile vigilante.

This narrative would steel him for a congressional run against the wavering republican that had held the northcentral Oregon seat, where Demetre's primary residence was located, for twenty years. The region had been overrun by Westsiders for a decade and by focusing on their sympathies for nature, he could see light at the end of the tunnel.

One of the local press reps watching the proceedings from beginning to end was the new publisher of the long-established County Koyama Weekly. Aris Nolan had purchased the paper the year before from the original publishing family after the death of the elderly patriarch whose grandfather had started it in the early 1900s. Heritage had lost its meaning to the younger generation who gladly sold off the publication to the Midwest transplant. They were more enthralled with Portland city life and eager to leave the boondocks behind them, so they sold the paper lock, stock and barrel and headed west to a life of sophistication.

Nolan hailed from a Missouri city that was equally divided between black and white citizens which created something of a culture shock for him, arriving in an old-fashioned ranch community where his color was unusual. He'd grown up dogging the local news scene, working his way up the ladder by learning the journalism trade from seasoned professionals rather than acquiring a fanciful communications degree from university.

His idea of news coverage was to gather information from as many credible sources as possible before fitting it together in a tight fact-driven story. Those kinds of priorities put him at odds with the journalism majors who saw the field as a route to promoting social justice.

A widower with grown children who were pursuing their own stars, Nolan took a chance with his hard-won savings and purchased the small paper serving the outlying burg. Moving from the city to a ranch town slowly being turned into a tourist destination was a leap of faith, but he'd earned his stripes as an editor and was looking forward to the slower pace in a quiet backwater.

What he hadn't anticipated was the antipathy many of the left coast visitors had toward the ranchers who'd opened this wild country for them to eventually visit and enjoy. Except the urbanites had started buying up properties, bringing their curious ideas of country living with them, determined to see Koyama County transformed into an idyllic paradise for retirees and tourists - basically, a proctectorate for wildlife and its patrons. He found it odd how they also barely considered the Indians, who had utilized the land for centuries, other than to occasionally remark on Native history. The interlopers' mindset was disparaging of any human interference with the flora and fauna that, frankly, included tribal claims on the land unless they could twist the treaties to further the eco objective of preservation.

Listening to the director of Gaston Buttes lambast Cressy Dillat as a gun-toting Annie Oakley who would shoot anything that moved, Nolan wasn't convinced that Demetre's coloring of the incident was the whole tale even though he could see the other media slurping up his rhetoric.

As the local paper of record, Nolan's publication had received Demetre's announcement about this press conference purposely timed to coincide with Mrs. Dillat's arraignment. He had also received a press release from the defendant's camp attempting to head-off exactly the kind of malicious condemnation currently being spouted by the Terra Ferus' administrator standing on the courthouse steps.

Unwilling to accept anything at face value, Nolan weighed the difference between the language of the two communications and decided he would delve into Dillat's legal challenge. It was obvious to him who was spinning a tale and who was detailing facts as they knew them.

Thinking he'd seen enough major stories in the St. Louis area to know what's news and what's not, Nolan recognized the potential for this case going national. A final ruling, that he could see going as high as the appellate courts, would either button down the ranchers in favor of the land trusts and protected wildlife, or lock-out the government from regulating individual land use. This was a property rights issue and Nolan was savvy enough to grasp the scope of the government versus the Widow Dillat.

Researching and writing this story, in another life he'd look for a Pulitzer Prize, but that was before he'd lost all respect for the institution.

CHAPTER 44

Evening news shows broadcasting from Portland and Spokane all had segments devoted to the press conference conducted by Ken Demetre at the Koyama County Courthouse. Without turning off the television, there was no way for Cressy to avoid seeing an odious shot of her clenched jaw and then her stiff back as she walked down the courthouse steps, ignoring disrespectful questions denigrating herself and her dead husband. Fran hadn't brought Tricia home yet, for which Cressy was grateful, having a difficult time holding her tongue even though the personalities on the screen couldn't hear her talk back to them.

She fumed at the mischaracterization of the facts as presented by the Gaston Buttes director in his quest for fifteen minutes of fame. What made it worse was when the ODFW wolf coordinator appeared by Demetre's side and made a statement about the case when he hadn't been at the site of the depredation in the first place and only showed up where Cressy had shot the wolf and was subsequently arrested.

Prescott Turlow had no firsthand knowledge of the wolf's mutilation of the cow on Cressy's property, but was more than happy to weigh-in on her culpability for tracking the wolf and killing it without a permit.

As if a permit would have been issued, Cressy didn't bother to say it aloud to nobody, being alone in her living room. *It was a now or never situation, not that he would know, arriving after it was waaay too late.*

Cressy contemplated turning off the TV when the camera zoomed in on good old Mikey Stromberg. Whereas Turlow didn't really say much of substance, though the fact that he had attended the presser lent support to the irrational charges made by Demetre, that was not the case with the USFW Services representative. Her clear prejudice against Cressy was plain and the media loved every bit of it. Painting Cressy, who Stromberg referred to as the 'perpetrator,' as craven and deceitful supplied sound bites that would go national.

Before the segment was finished, she texted Anthea about the unjust portrayal of the whole affair. The answer wasn't exactly heartening when Anthea told her to expect it to get far worse including the press pestering her nonstop in attempts to trap her into making a statement that would be characterized as incriminating. "Beware and don't answer phone calls from numbers you don't recognize."

Tell me something I don't know.

Just before the segment closed, one of the news anchors made it a point to note that Twitter was alive with hate posts against Cressy. What the anchor didn't mention was that the majority of tweets came from bots not real people, though he felt it necessary to focus on posts bewailing the loss of a regal wolf, symbol of the unspoiled wilderness that should be admired for its tenacity.

They're lucky I'm not on Twitter. Those twits wouldn't know what hit 'em, Cressy was so mad she could spit nails but laughed when Anthea texted, "What, no lamenting the evils of guns? How disappointing the lefties didn't go to their gun control safety zone. Did they forget that you shot the wolf?"

Demetre made the splash he'd hoped for and couldn't help but grin as he wandered from one end of the house to the other, reliving his moment in the sun, certain that it successfully launched his public career. It didn't take long before major media outlets began calling for on-air interviews. Receiving two calls before he reached home, he decided he was going to have to call his assistant at the Terra Ferus office to help him schedule bookings.

Elated, he punched the air as he contemplated leaving the next morning for Portland to make midweek appearances on cable and network morning news shows.

Demetre's victory celebration was cut short when, in all his excitement about finally throwing his hat in the political ring, an individual he'd practically forgotten about showed up.

He wasn't happy about the guy turning up at his home. *At least he was discreet enough not to waltz into the TF office in Rory*, thought Demetre as he answered the door. His assistant had told him that a couple of reporters had staked it out for the rest of the day hoping to get some new angle on the story. And their prayers would have been answered if this bozo had trotted right past them and in the front door. Luckily, he had more brains than Demetre had figured him for.

The Gaston Buttes director owned a property in a heavily wooded area on the north-facing slope of Marshall Peak southeast of Rory. He kept it as a second home that he planned on selling at a hefty profit as soon as he was elected to office, his primary address more centrally located the other side of Pendleton.

Generally, the traffic by his home was minimal, having so few residences on the road that dead-ended half a mile beyond his property. When the nondescript truck rolled past the houses that were set back a fair pace on their own acreage, no one paid much attention.

Pulling around to the side of the house where Demetre maintained a neatly graveled parking area near the front entrance, the visitor's rig was masked from the closest neighbor's view behind manicured shrubs and a thick stand of Ponderosa pine. Not that they'd be interested. Most of the residents on Marshall Peak had moved there for privacy and solitude. Climbing out of the truck, the man strolled to the front door and rang the doorbell without observation.

Demetre answered the door himself, his wife gone for a couple weeks to visit their daughter in Seattle where she worked at the regional Nature's Wilds office, keeping business interests in the family, so to speak.

Without comment, Demetre opened the door and let in the visitor. The fellow looked a little the worse for wear after camping for the past two weeks in the Hiller Range and out by Emville. Washing up in a creek, his clothes weren't filthy but not as fresh as his host would have preferred, ushering him inside to seating that was soil-repellent.

Once the man had crossed the threshold and entered the foyer, Demetre turned to him, scowling, "What are you doing here?"

"Pretty simple, really. It wasn't likely you'd be able to find me in my current digs down on the Nacqus, so I came to collect," he shrugged as if to say, *no big thing.*

"Were you not listening when I outlined the arrangement to deposit the rest of the payment for your services directly into the account?"

"Look, what I want is a shower and to sleep in a real bed and something's come up. I can't wait around for you to transfer funds and have the bank hold them for a week. Besides, I would have thought that you wouldn't want to leave a trail. Everything's digital these days."

Demetre gave him a hard look, his arms crossed. "Do you think I keep that kind of cash lying around out here?"

The man wasn't cowed by his host's lack of hospitality. Standing just an inch or so shorter than Demetre, he was in good shape, used to working outdoors logging and construction. Pulling on his ear, he said, "Yeah, I do. You're a cautious kind of guy. I'd say you're prepared for any emergency and this would be one."

Grumbling about being placed in a precarious position but realizing the danger of not complying with the man's wishes, Demetre flicked his hand toward a leather settee by the entry. "Have a seat and I'll see what I can do."

Not in the least intimidated by Demetre's frosty welcome, before sitting down he said, "Do you happen to have a beer? I could use a little refreshment after being out in the woods for a week."

"Yeah, why not." At this point, Demetre was only interested in satisfying the guy enough to get him out of his house. He walked into the kitchen and grabbed a bottle of a local microbrew. When he came back through the den, he found his visitor wandering around the room, idly picking up knickknacks and admiring the genteel opulence of the furnishings.

"Tasteful," he said as he reached for the beer. Turning the bottle to read the label, he remarked, "Nice. Designer ale." Demetre had already opened the bottle and the man lifted it in salute to his barely civil host, "Cheers."

Trying not to appear rushed in retrieving the man's payment, though he wanted nothing better than for him to be gone, Demetre made sure the guy didn't follow him into his study. Sitting down at a birdseye maple desk, he unlocked a drawer and accessed a small metal cashbox.

The visitor was right in assuming that Demetre kept a stash on hand. Mostly he used it to pay the gardener and other laborers but he kept a sizeable sum available for contingencies like this one, not that he often had dodgy chores to be handled. On the whole, he kept his business aboveboard. This situation arose as a necessity to rock the boat in a provincial county. Terra Ferus and Nature's Wilds weren't revered household names, but he had plans to change that as champions to save the environment from itself, let alone outmoded agriculture.

Unfortunately, Demetre didn't have enough on hand to take care of the full bill. Only half what he'd contracted to pay the man was in reach. *It will have to do for now.*

Removing the bills from the cashbox, he locked it back up and returned to the den where his visitor had deposited himself on the sofa facing the fireplace.

"I figured you for one of those who had a safe behind the big painting on top of the mantel," he grinned at his own wit.

"We don't live in a movie." He handed the cash to the man who hadn't bothered to stand up. Counting it, the guy said, "Where's the rest?"

"You show up out of the blue just expecting me to have that much money under my mattress?"

"A guy can hope." He stood up and pocketed the funds. "It'll have to do for now. When can I come back to get the rest?"

"I'm afraid it'll have to be next week. I travel to Portland tomorrow for important business." He wasn't about to tell the man that he was going to be doing television interviews. He'd been out in the woods until now so he probably hadn't heard anything about

Demetre's press conference, though he would before long if he was headed to a motel. "I'd suggest that you head out of the area, maybe Alder, for a room. We don't want you being noticed around here. People know the locals and pay attention to out-of-towners."

"Gotcha. I'll be back next week. Have the rest of the money," and he swilled the rest of the beer, plunked the bottle onto the coffee table and sauntered out the front door.

As Demetre closed the door behind him after watching him get into his truck and leave, he muttered, "Good riddance."

CHAPTER 45

In more ways than one, representation for Oregon Department of Fish and Wildlife and US Fish and Wildlife Services weren't precisely thrilled with the press attention the Dillat case was receiving. As much as they worked in concert with Terra Ferus, Ken Demetre had received a phone call from Salem expressing their concern and Prescott Turlow was not exempt from their dissatisfaction after he'd made a statement at the press conference. From here on out, Turlow was to keep a low profile but Demetre was a free agent to do what he saw fit even if it was paradoxical to the state and federal legal team's better judgment.

As sympathetic as defenseless wildlife could be made to appear, when the adversary is a disenfranchised widow, government and quasi-governmental agencies could rapidy lose their charm. Public opinion is a fickle thing and no matter how adamant mainstream media may be in tarring the shooter as callous, social media was capable of turning the tables in a blinding minute.

Despite their arguments that Demetre's strategy could backfire the whole case making the government look like the heavy, he was on track to make points for a congressional run and wasn't about to be deterred.

The answer to that was to fast-track the trial to limit the ranchers' collective arguments against the so-called repatriation of wolves in agricultural zones, keeping them out of the courtroom and, in so doing, out of the public eye. The presiding judge, generally acknowledged for fairness in the average civil and criminal case, was on board for dispatching the Dillat affair as quickly and quietly as possible and the county district attorney concurred.

The pressure was on.

Anthea and Gary exended their stay to supply what support they could to Cressy. They were determined to see a different outcome for her this time.

The morning after the arraignment there was another huddle at Cressy's only this time it included an online conference call with Toddy Littman. He wanted to be updated not only on the current charges against Cressy but he felt it was important to gather background information on the previous incident involving her husband's death.

He and Anthea hadn't seen one another in a couple years and the call had commenced with the usual remarks about graying temples on both counts, Toddy ascribing the aging to the stresses of parenthood. Anthea retorted that a family addition should guarantee he turns silver in a couple more years. She could have sworn his eyebrows brushed his hairline in surprise before skewering her with suspicion, asking who betrayed the secret. Shaking her head, she had said, "For a genius, Toddy, you just blew it. I only suggested what an extra family member could do. You confirmed that one's on the way." She grinned at the screen, "Congratulations!"

Abruptly ending that conversation and attempting to hide his embarrassment, Toddy immediately went into Cressy's history with the question about the timeline. "How long has it been since your first go 'round with the authorities?" He asked through the computer connection that gave them face-to-face communications.

"It's been two years since the wolf attack that killed my husband," was her answer.

Tilting his head sideways for a moment, he said to the wall, "Did you ever file a formal complaint against the government?"

"What do you mean? Terry was the one charged with a crime, even though he died and I lost the ranch fighting their case."

"Did you countersue?"

"No one ever suggested that. All we did was try to defend his good name," Cressy was puzzled.

"So nobody told you to file a claim for damages," Toddy was contemplative.

"No. Could I have done that?"

"Yes, and you have two years from the incident to do so but because a death was involved there's no statute of limitations. Let's see," he had been typing and reading all through their conversation. "Oregon statute 496.270 (5) says the following: 'The limitation on liability provided by subsection (3) of this section does not apply to claims for death or personal injuries.' And it lists the references."

"You're saying that I could still do that?" said Cressy incredulously.

"Yes. In fact, you really need to file an SF-95 against the federal agency and file an equivalent claim against the state's agency," said Toddy. "To make sure you have standing to sue the government you must exhaust the administrative process. Government employees operate under sovereign immunity, meaning that you can't sue them for instituting the regulations of the agency they represent. But if you've exhausted the administrative process and received no relief then you can file suit in a court of law. Government agencies bank on people not knowing how to work the process and jumping ahead with the idea they can win a case brought against them by the government. It doesn't work that way. Plodding through the system must be the first order of business."

"I was wondering, Toddy," said Anthea, "Is there any way of combining the two cases into one when it comes to claiming damages?"

"Are you reading my mind? That's exactly what I was thinking. This current loss is related to the loss two years ago. When you called me yesterday, I started hunting through the Oregon statutes and I'll tell you I've never seen anything like it. All other states I've dealt with, and that's the majority of them, publish their laws in a way you can access them. Not Oregon, oh no. They actually try to hide the statutes. It took me three hours of combing the state websites to find the claim form."

"Talk about something unheard of," said Anthea. "It's practically impossible to hide information from Toddy if it's anywhere on the web."

"Thanks for the vote of confidence," he said, half-smiling. "And I did find it in ORS 30.275 'Notice of claim; time of notice; time of action.' However, these guys have a clause that you have to claim wrongful death within a year of the incident so, combining the claims is necessary.

"First, Cressy, you lost your husband and all his future earnings due to a wolf attack. Secondly, you were forced to sell the ranch and two years later you lose another animal to a wolf that could very well have been part of the original pack."

Cressy was quiet for a minute then said, "It's a longshot but there was DNA taken from the original attack and we have DNA from this wolf, so... what if this wolf had been involved in both attacks?"

"That'd be a miracle if it could be proven but it would be another tie that binds," said Toddy. "It would add to the argument making this latest attack an extension of the first. What you're going to need is supportive legal representation and, from what I gather, there's no such thing to be found in your area."

"You can say that again," moaned Cressy.

"I'd think the way she was bulldozed before would be a clue," added Gary.

"The first thing the prosecution is going to do is try to push you to accept a plea agreement that will waive jail time and lower the fine for killing a wolf without a permit but they'll add in some dishonest and irrelevant requirements."

"That's what they charged my husband with because they hadn't changed the rules yet and you couldn't shoot a wolf even in the midst of an attack. They were still protected as an endangered species. They still are on the west side of the state by the feds."

"Even though they've been delisted in all other states?" asked Toddy.

"You got it. Oregon is special and the advocates want more than a thousand wolves in this state, which means double that since they under-report their numbers now."

"I can't even conceive how asinine that is," said Gary.

"Either way, they know this is a tenuous case and the tactic of getting the defendant to buckle under pressure is purely an effort to avoid a court battle that isn't a sure-fire win for them," said Anthea. "Or so it looks to me."

"You're partially correct," said Toddy. "This case is open and shut for the prosecution."

"What?" Cressy lost her composure. "You're saying I'm guilty?"

"Well, didn't you shoot the wolf without a permit?"

"Yes, but…"

Toddy cut her off. "This is going to sound counter-intuitive but hear me out."

"O-kay," said Cressy thinking she may be making a terrible mistake.

"We've already talked about playing out the administrative process. This is part of it however much it galls your sense of justice. First, you shot the wolf without a permit and a fine has been levied, right?"

"Right. We paid ten percent of the total to get me out the slammer."

"The option now is to pay the fine, do the time or plead not guilty and go to court when they can prove you did the deed. Am I right?"

"Yes, but there are extenuating circumstances," said Anthea.

"I would agree," said Gary.

"This is true, but because the evidence and the court is stacked against you, you'll lose. Sorry, but that's what will happen if you fight the charges. You've seen it happen before, correct?"

Cressy nodded, still flabbergasted that she was being counseled to fold when all she wanted to do was beat the snot out of the self-satisfied wolf advocates and their court representatives.

"This is how it needs to go if you want to win in the long run and make a challenge that could go to SCOTUS."

"SCOTUS?"

"Supreme Court of the United States. One - you shot the wolf. Two - you pay the fine and get the receipt. Three - now you're set to make a claim that your rights have been violated by Fish and Wildlife, both Oregon and federal agencies. This is the claim: that your livelihood is being destroyed, that you can't manage the land because of these regulations, and that it appears the state is trying to cause you as a rancher to alienate your land to the state."

"I can't say that I fully understand that," said Cressy.

"See if I have this right, Toddy," said Anthea. "The law has restricted her ability to manage her own land because it prohibits her from protecting it from federally and state protected species which is, and actually has since she lost the ranch, destroyed her livelihood."

"Yes…"

"And by alienating her land to the state, you mean that the government has by proxy taken control of her property making it impossible for her to manage it according to her prerogative," said Gary. "Is that right?"

"Essentially."

"Oddly enough, I got that," said Cressy.

"Now, you go forward with something like this, 'I discovered a tort claim in administrative remedy as of this date and am filing this claim for the injuries accrued since - start it at two to three months after the time that the wolves were introduced into the area and/or treated to special protections. The amount of this claim is subject to standard tort amounts for denials of use of property since depredations began without just compensation pursuant to the Fifth Amendment by and through the Fourteenth Amendment of the US Constitution.

"By and through the application of the State's easement through the ODFW my property has been constructively seized and present cattle lost - the list does not include the breeding over X generations - which is legalized, state-endorsed cattle rustling.'"

"Good thing I'm recording this," said Anthea. "I don't know about the rest of you, but I'd never get all this down."

Toddy grinned in spite of the gravity of what they were discussing, which was years of Cressy's life set aside to battling the mammoth government. "From there you request a hearing, putting forward that you want a waiver to shoot wolves - of which I assume there isn't one - that the law is written to protect wolves. Question where is the law to protect the landowner? They'll deny a hearing and that opens the door so you can go directly to federal court because you called in the Fifth to Fourteenth Amendments."

"Whew. Is that all?" asked Cressy facetiously.

Toddy simply went forward per usual without dropping a beat. "This is how you set up the tort claim. Run the gamut of procedure so you can win on your turf rather than trying to fight a case that's rigged against you.

"It will set-up a prime challenge to government regulation of private land use and avoid a local court case where they will fight tooth and nail to limit admitting evidence in court of your tragic loss because it would introduce prejudice in your favor. No way will the state allow that. This is how the two cases can be rolled into one. And it could very well be the test case that makes it to the Supreme Court and I can guarantee that ODFW and USFWS are not interested in going there.

"They have strong misgivings they'd lose a constitutional challenge that would set back what appear to be plans to gain federal ownership and legal control through regulation over the majority of private property in your county. Dreams of a national monument or park would be permanently dashed."

"Sounds good to me," agreed Cressy.

"It could also create a precedent building a hurdle to the continuing seizure of property by government nationwide, essentially closing down the rapid expansion of so-called public lands. The USDA and Department of Interior bureaucracies have grown so grandiose in their vision of *conservation* that their gobbling up of private lands has become nearly unstoppable. They operate on their own agenda now, irrespective of who was voted into office. They're a headless, immoral government inside the government."

"This is why I know that I don't have a choice but to go all the way in this. I've already lost everything once," said Cressy, a breath of vehemence underlying her words. "We might have to live with my parents for a while but my daughter, and I hope others, would learn a valuable lesson that sometimes we have to take a stand for a rightful cause whatever the consequences."

The daunting problem confronting her was locating competent legal representation with knowledge and experience fighting government bureaucracies administratively as well as in court.

"The prosecution is on a tear to take this to trial before you have a chance to blink. So-oo," said Toddy pensively. "There has to be someone we've come across that's capable."

No one spoke as thoughts buzzed running through cases and counsel that have been through the process and won in appellate courts.

Then Toddy's brown eyes sparkled and he chuckled. "I think we've got a winner. There's a lawyer I've spoken with who fought the EPA in a case of literal life and death for a distant cousin of my wife, Solana."

"I remember," perked up Anthea. "Lainie - she's a good friend," she explained in an aside to Cressy, "donated a kidney to the little girl in Wyoming. The child's lawyer, right?"

"Yancy Collings. She worked at an outfit called the Constitutional Legal Fund in Billings, Montana. I'll bet she'd be interested in your case, Cressy."

A spark of hope lit Cressy's face, "Really?"

"Yes, she's one of those windmill-tilting protagonists who had enough of corporate law and now mostly represents ranchers in property rights issues. She'd be perfect."

"Do you still have her number?" asked Gary.

"Actually, it hasn't been that long since I spoke with her, maybe six months to a year." He started typing. "Yes, I've got her contact information right here." He looked at Cressy, "If you want, I'll give her a call and explain your situation."

"And pray that she's interested," added Cressy.

Meaningfully, Anthea said, "Prayer is always in order."

Anthea immediately got to work supplying news releases to the media, concentrating on the conservative outlets, websites and agriculture industry press. The history of the Dillat story was moving up the chain to becoming viral, especially since the Gaston Buttes director was making the rounds of media on behalf of the beleaguered wolf population.

Demetre, working the press for his own ends, only pushed the story more to the forefront, so when Anthea got a funding site set-up for Cressy's legal bills the money started coming in quickly. Constitutionalists around the country were taking notice and putting their money where their mouth was.

Due to the building intensity of the media, the prosecution upped their game to move the case along rapidly in an attempt to keep the press off-kilter.

Toddy didn't have to cajole Yancy into representing Cressy. She was in-between cases and arrived in Koyama County in the nick of time to advocate for her new client. The only hiccup was finding an Oregon legal firm to serve as co-counsel while Yancy received her temporary license to practice law in the state. Fortunately, Toddy located a respected firm out of Bend.

Between the state, which had delisted wolves as endangered but hadn't moved to allow unpermitted removal of offending animals, and the feds who still held wolves to be protected on the west side of Oregon, Cressy was fighting charges relating to the illegal hunting and killing of a wolf.

The case was gaining national attention because so many states were suffering depredation from introduced, re-introduced and recognition of unverified breeds of wolf. The Canadian Gray Wolf in the Northwest and Upper Midwest, the Mexican Gray in the Southwest and the so-called Red Wolf in the Carolina region were all coming under scrutiny.

CHAPTER 46

It was becoming obvious to Ken Demetre that the Dillat woman was worse than stubborn.

She had everything to lose - again - but wouldn't be coerced by the state. A court date had been set that was rapidly approaching and Demetre was feeling desperate about getting this resolved in such a way that the blasted woman was looking at time behind bars or vilification to the point she'd have no credibility. He needed a platform for his congressional run and protecting wildlife and wilderness in his home district was a choice ticket.

Weighing his options, Demetre wasn't encouraged. It was looking less and less likely that Cressy Dillat would succumb to pressure from the court to take a reduced punishment and go back to her life of relative anonymity. He was surprised that she was able to find counsel willing to take what should be a slamdunk case for the prosecution. The district attorney had generously offered to waive the fines if the woman would agree to undergo grief counseling and submit to substance abuse treatment.

Frustration rising, he thought, *Just get it over with*! even as he waltzed onto the sets at Portland and Seattle television stations with a concerned smile slapped across his long face.

Cressy flatly refused the plea deal. Hitting the ground running, her attorney, Yancy Collings, responded to the opposition with heat. There was no basis to demand her client enter treatment programs for emotional and alcohol or drug abuse problems that she'd never demonstrated any symptoms or been diagnosed. Yancy outed the offer as an obvious ploy to smear Cressy as unstable, maligning her character and destroying her veracity in lieu of future legal action or public statements.

When Cressy declined the offer, the judge showed his hand by siding with the prosecution and levying a hefty fine. Waiving the one-year jail time and instead imposing another fine for reparation, the judge gambled that slapping the defendant with more money rather than incarceration, the public's compassion for her might be reduced. Sending her to prison would only fuel the rebellion, much as it had with the Hammonds and Bundys in the Malheur Wildlife Refuge case.

Yancy assisted Cressy through the first part of the process that Toddy advocated, concurring with the wisdom of the strategy. They were in this to win not ruffle a few bureaucratic feathers or make headlines to garner attention and sympathy. Her story went to the core of saving a way of life in the face of government introducing crushing control, sliding toward prohibiting individuals from using their property as they saw fit.

With the court more than doubling the fine, additional pressure was applied to accept a plea deal that included all the reprehensible caveats designed to undermine Cressy's credibility. Time was of the essence to resolve the issue financially and extricate her from the fast-aproaching trial that could result in disaster.

Anthea immediately put out an appeal for help and the community heard the call, supplying every penny necessary to appease the court.

Feeling as though she'd been blackmailed, Cressy was relieved to be able to pay the full fine, which was only possible due to the donated funds. From here on out, she and Yancy were empowered to move forward to counter the bully tactics of the county DA who wasn't ecstatic about the developments in the case but was leashed to the state and federal agencies' suit.

Following up, Yancy lost no time filing the claims for damages and setting the stage for what promised to be a fierce showdown.

CHAPTER 47

It was taking an effort to adjust to being at home without the constant worry of having to appear in court, but Cressy wouldn't have it any other way. The stress of preparing herself to run the gauntlet of hostile protesters bussed in from the nearest universities tested her resolve, and her temper. Hearing the students' ignorant spoutings egged on by a few professors was a lesson in the foolishness disseminated at modern institutions of higher education.

Fifteen years removed from her own college graduation, Cressy recalled how environmentalists breathed down the necks of animal science and ag students, utterly oblivious about who fed them. To this day, she couldn't fathom people who seemed to think food was created out of thin air. Could they possibly believe meals magically appeared in *Star Trek*-style cafeteria cubbies?

During the ten days of wrangling with the prosecution about a deal that would save her weathering a brutal trial, was a trial in itself. It was prayer, in which Tricia was proving to be an inspiration, the diligence of a team of good people whom she'd just met and the fortuitous gifts of cash that literally bailed her rear end out of a deplorable situation. When she considered these things, Cressy was bowled over by what she was beginning to see as God's intervention.

Trying to settle back into a routine, Cressy had been at the store for a couple of days straight. May had picked up some of the slack when Cressy was called to the Koyama County Courthouse but it felt good to be re-entering what she'd dubbed 'real life.' Because her attorney was staying at the bed and breakfast where Anthea and Gary had lodged, official meetings outside of court were either there or at the farmhouse.

The Darby's had insisted that housing Yancy at the Nacqus Rocks B and B would be their contribution to the cause, which lifted an enormous burden from the defense team that was operating on a negative budget.

Yancy was in her room late in the afternoon researching the case that she was putting together on Cressy's behalf. She'd learned the ropes of suing government agencies the hard way, but precedent had been set in the last few years proving that there's hope when it comes to butting heads with bureaucrats. With luck, they'd be able to force the issue of damages and hogtie some of the worst offenders, though it had become a toss-up between agencies with EPA, BIA, USFWS, IRS, DHHS, Department of Education or Energy and every other administrative acronym, as to which earned that title.

The internet signal was slow at the inn located as it was at the end of the paved road, and Yancy was waiting for a PDF of an appellate court opinion to download when her phone rang. Mirroring the languid attitude of the server, Yancy answered with a yawn.

"Hello."

A distraught voice came through with an echo. The reception was often spotty out there as well. "Is this Yancy?"

"Yes. What can I do…"

She was cut-off midsentence by Cressy's mother who gave her name and said, "Hurry…" before the call was dropped.

Nothing seemed to be working to break the spirit of the wolf killer determined to buck the combined strength of state and federal agencies' power play. Making an example of the Dillat woman wasn't turning out to be the sure bet Demetre had expected to catapult him into office as the champion of wildlife. Instead, his ticket could be punched before he ever boarded the train. The only way to ensure success was to sideline the one obstacle that could appear more vulnerable than an injured wolf, and that was a widow protecting what little she had from the ravenous government hiding behind it.

Demetre was interrupted in the midst of mulling over his next step, startled out of his reverie by his vibrating phone.

Business had been brisk.

Cressy was bushed after serving dozens of customers during an unusually lucrative day at the mercantile. Even Tricia was kept busy running errands to help her mom take care of the buyers browsing the aisles.

News of the legal battle had drawn Rory and Koyama residents down to Nacqus to support the owner by shopping at her store. Online sales and special orders were also burgeoning, giving Cressy a boost of morale and vitally needed funds.

Swinging around the palisade on the road home, the two girls were ready to relax when Tricia spotted smoke upriver.

Cressy had been on edge since a grassfire that swept the southern tracts of Gaston Buttes may have been what drove the wolf back to her farm. Not knowing which direction the minimally contained blazes could swerve in the shifting winds added to her jumpiness. Dry as the weather had been, anything could spark a wildfire, even the rare scraping of metal fittings on farm equipment.

As officials continued to investigate what triggered the two fires that had decimated the Rory Creek watershed near Emville, no natural causes had yet been identified. The county fire marshal was leaning toward human origin, though he hadn't pinpointed whether it was purposeful or accidental, such as an unattended campfire.

Driving toward the thick black plume, Cressy saw the flash of yellow flames leaping skyward from her barn. Grabbing the phone from her back pocket, she handed it to Tricia as she entered her driveway.

"Call 911, Tricia. I'm going to get the hose. Stay here!" Cressy said, emphatically making her point by stabbing her forefinger into the driver's seat as she dropped out of the Jeep.

She ran to open the barn door to make sure no animals were caught inside though they'd taken the horses out to pasture in the morning and the lamb was back in its paddock by the house.

Swallowing her panic, Tricia did as she was told and reported the fire without delay, then she called Franma and Quint as their nearest neighbors came running from their rig after noticing the smoke from their house a quarter-mile away. When Tricia got through to the dispatcher, she was told that the fire had been reported ten minutes before and fire crews were on their way, but even Tricia could tell it was a lost cause.

Everyone pitched in and did what they could spraying down the burning building, but by the time the volunteer fire crew arrived on the premises a few minutes later, it was a done deed. They all had to step back as the blaze swallowed the wood structure, leaving nothing but charred timbers.

Fortunately, no animals were harmed and the farmhouse stood untouched. For the moment, there wasn't any wind stirring the air and as the firefighters dampened the last of the flames they saw no evidence of blowing cinders that could be blamed for starting the fire. The origin was immediately suspect. Something must have kindled it.

Quint, who'd dropped everything and headed down the mountain, asked if flammable material was ever stored in the barn.

"No," Cressy tried not to snap at him in her shock. "Not with hay and animals. Anything like that is in the shed, where it belongs."

"Good," he soothed. "Be prepared for the authorities to ask you the same thing."

Yancy drove up just in time to view the smoldering ruin. Watching as the fire crew hosed down the embers, she and Quint got what Cressy knew of the story, which wasn't much.

"It had to be a message," Yancy lowered her voice so she wouldn't be overheard by the neighbors. "I don't see any other realistic explanation."

"Seriously?" Quint didn't want to believe it.

Cocking her head to one side, Yancy earnestly considered the circumstances, "I don't see any of the state or federal guys doing anything like this. They may want your case to go away but they don't have a personal or vested interest. Besides, government workers are too lazy or unmotivated, on the whole, to take this kind of action. Ununh," she shook her head side-to-side, blonde hair swinging slightly, "It was someone else, but it was surely arson."

CHAPTER 48

It was a waiting game now.

Oregon Department of Fish and Wildlife and US Fish and Wildlife Services had a limited time in which to respond to the formal claims submitted by Cressy with Yancy's assistance. Stating that Cressy just discovered an administrative remedy for the initial damages and death of her husband, due to state obfuscation of statutes by regularly changing website access, there was an additional argument in favor of Cressy's claim. All in all, it came down to the timely, or lack thereof, of the entities' response to the claims.

From there, the next step would be requesting hearings on the claims. If they were refused, then they'd be off to the races in federal court asserting constitutional rights were violated by the agencies' actions.

Once more, Ken Demetre opened his front door to admit the unsavory visitor who'd be out of his life as soon as they finalized their covert contract.

This time around, the man's hygiene was much improved. Cleancut with a freshly shaved jaw and his clothes were new, spiffing up his appearance considerably. Moving aside to allow the man entry, although the transaction was distasteful to Demetre, at least his counterpart no longer looked disreputable.

"Let's get this over with so we can go our separate ways, shall we?" With that brief overture, Demetre reached into his pocket to remove a thick envelope.

"No need to be so hasty," said the man who walked past his host into the living room. Without invitation and irritating his host, he sat down and crossed one clean booted foot over his knee, draping his arms along the back of an overstuffed leather chair. "You don't happen to have another one of those brews handy." It wasn't a request so much as a passive order.

If it'll placate the guy and get him out of here for good, fine, he can have his beer. Without answering, because Demetre didn't want to blow his cool exacerbating an already deteriorated liaison, he fetched the beer.

Returning from the kitchen and extending the bottle toward his guest, Demetre said. "It's time to close this deal."

Leisurely examining the bottle before chugging a quarter of it, the man sighed with satisfaction. "That is premium stuff," he lifted the ale in salute to the homeowner. "Yes, time for a powwow."

"I doubt we need to 'powwow.' I have your cash and you can move on with your life."

"Not quite."

Demetre was getting closer to losing his composure but didn't respond.

"There is one other point of business to discuss," he said before taking another swig.

"Not as far as I can see. You performed your duties as arranged and here's the final installment," Demetre replied through a clenched jaw, handing the man the envelope.

Setting down the bottle, the visitor took the envelope and flicked through the bills inside. "You're missing some."

His misgivings coming to fruition, Demetre's face reddened with annoyance and rising anger. "This is the full amount, as agreed…"

"Except I did you another favor and you owe me for that."

"What are you talking about?" Demetre was standing by the mantel, attempting to calm his temper by running his fingers up and down a smooth-sided trophy, the action usually relaxing him.

"First, I believe that the little blazes you had me set out by Emville earned me a raise after all the damage they did, just as you predicted."

Here it comes, the blackmail. I really didn't think this guy was ambitious enough to go this far.

"Hey, I went out of my way to take care of another problem for you. This afternoon, that Dillat gal's place went up in smoke."

"What!?" Demetre couldn't control his response. This was beyond the pale. "I didn't ask you to do anything else! And why her?"

"I saw your little performance at the courthouse and a couple of your interviews on TV. It was obvious this woman is one of your enemies like the rest of the ranchers." He smiled slyly, "You made it clear that you wouldn't complain if the bunch of them went out of business."

"What was the point of torching her property? That doesn't do me any good."

The guest pursed his lips and bobbed his head side-to-side as if he were considering the goal, "Maybe not, but it helps me," he said smugly.

"Come again?"

"I'm sure folks would be real interested in how you happened to pay for setting the fires that are still burning up thousands of acres and lots of cattle, all to make those poor ranchers lose enough that they'll be forced to sell off more of their land to, guess who?"

"You'd only implicate yourself," said a nervous Demetre, knowing that this guy was a transient, unknown to anyone and who could virtually up and disappear. He could also reappear at any time to continue the blackmail.

"Let's look at it from this angle. The only one who could benefit from both the wildfires in Rory Creek and the Dillat fire is, well, your little organization. You guys have been buying up land wherever you can get your hands on it." He took another swallow of the beer. "I'm not as dumb as I look, *Mister* Demetre. Anyone can use the internet these days and you want to run for office. Seems to me that if your personal enemy, which is what the Dillat lady seems to be, is attacked and it's connected to all those ranchers that are approached to sell land to your TF group, uh, it could kind of crash your future. Don't ya think?"

That was the last straw and Demetre lashed out without thinking. Swinging the heavy glass trophy wide, he clocked the arsonist as he tipped his head back to glug the last of the beer. He hit him so hard, that the guy fell backward, taking the chair over with him.

Immediately frightened by his own unchecked anger, Demetre stood there holding the environmental excellence award in hands that quivered with rage, waiting for the guy to rollover and get up.

Except he didn't.

Lying there perfectly still, bleeding from a gash on the side of his head, the would-be extortionist was still unconscious. At least, that's what Demetre thought until he looked at the guy's face and saw that his eyes were wide open and glazed over in surprise.

It took a few minutes before Demetre came to himself. Realizing that his caller was dead, he went into a fullblown panic, cursing the guy for being such an evil ass, that his death was his own fault for not leaving well enough alone.

Replacing the award on the mantelpiece, all Demetre could say was, "Now what? Oh hell, now what?"

His wife was due back in a couple hours and he had to come up with a solution to this disaster - fast. He couldn't call 911. How could he explain the body with his head bashed in that couldn't possibly be an accident or self-inflicted? There was no way to make it look like he'd fatally banged his head on the end table.

No, Demetre was stuck with a lifeless body in the living room and a beat-up truck in his driveway. There was no choice, they both had to go.

CHAPTER 49

Recognizing the address on the Nacqus Highway where Dispatch had radioed that another fire had broken out, Sheriff Swifter rolled up to the scene close to an hour later. The one deputy that wasn't tied up with another call had shown up moments before his boss pulled in front of the Dillat farm.

To Tandy's relief, the house seemed to be untouched by flames but the barn was utterly decimated, nothing left but scorched ends of old two by sixes poking up from a bed of cinders and ash.

She found Cressy surrounded by family and friends, her arm wrapped around her daughter's shoulders. The sheriff spotted her attorney with her, some ace land use advocate out of Montana. She was the only blonde in the crowd, unless you included Quint who Tandy thought was graying too rapidly for his years.

Having an inside track on the recent proceedings regarding Cressy's case, albeit unorthodox, Tandy thought the attorney, Collings, was doing a bang-up job, because, in all honesty, she assumed Cressy would be bludgeoned into submission or serving time. She didn't know how they'd gotten a hold of this Collings gal, but deep down Tandy was thankful for her presence. Cressy deserved a break but surveying the damage confronting her as she approached the clutch of friends, it didn't look like she was getting one.

"I'd say 'good evening' but it's not really looking that way, is it," Tandy said, bringing attention to her arrival.

Cressy looked over her shoulder and Quint stepped back, opening a space in the group. "And I'd say 'welcome' but, truthfully, I'm not feeling all that hospitable. You'll have to make your own coffee," said Cressy, making light of the situation.

"It might not be much consolation, but at least you'll be sleeping in your own beds tonight."

"You know, Tandy, that actually means a lot. This house could be on the auction block if it weren't for the community coming through for us," Cressy gave Tricia a squeeze as she spoke. "Losing one house is enough for a while."

"Which brings me to the current issue. Do we have any idea what happened?" asked the sheriff.

"No. Tricia and I were driving home and as soon as we rounded the bluff we saw the smoke, though I've got to tell you it scared me silly. I'm just glad all the animals were outside and it didn't reach the old house. That would have been more than a loss to us, it's almost as old as this county."

"It hearkens back to the first of my family settling here, anyway," said Quint. "We were really glad to know that it was a Corler moving in to keep the ownership local." It was his diplomatic way of stating that he didn't want any liberal neighbors, which Tandy appreciated having herself moved to the county to escape what she considered crazy Westside politics.

"Do we know if any of the neighbors noticed anything?" The sheriff scanned the other individuals standing around the smoldering ruin.

"None of us has asked, Sheriff," Yancy addressed her. "It went up so fast and I gather that most of the people here had tried to help fight the fire."

"That's right," added Cressy. "The neighbors got here when I did and Quint and Yancy arrived a little while afterward. I think George and Yvette said they called in the fire first and then came over. Tricia called it in when we arrived."

"As you'll probably need to know," said Yancy. "I was at the Nacqus Rocks B & B when Fran Corler called."

"And I was at the ranch, about fifteen minutes up the mountain, when Tricia called me," continued Quint.

"Thanks. I'm going to check with the neighbors and the fire crew to see what anyone knows. I expect the fire marshal will show up sometime soon." Tandy walked over to join her deputy who was already talking to the others.

Tandy queried the closest neighbors about whether they'd

noticed anything out of the ordinary from their perch on the highway, a quarter mile west of Cressy's place. At first they said 'no,' having been busy with household chores and paying little attention.

"What about traffic? Was there much this afternoon? Anything different or unusual?"

The older couple thought about the afternoon's traffic stream. "It's been pretty much what you see most days. A number of tourists coming down to the village, but also a lot of local vehicles today. You get to know a lot of the rigs, seeing them in town and around. Really, it was busier than normal, wasn't it George," Yvette deferred to her husband.

"Yea-yup. I'd say you're right. There was a lot more folks traveling up and down the highway today. Better than normal," he bobbed his head affirming his thoughts, thumbs in his belt. "Wonder why?"

"I don't know. Cressy may. She was in town at her shop."

"Oh! That's right," enthused Yvette. "Cressy said that she was busier than a bee at the mercantile today. Couldn't figure it out but lots of people from town were shopping there."

"Might be they're supporting her and building her business is a good way to show it," offered Tandy.

"Now, that makes sense," said George. "But there was one truck that came by kinda slow and pulled over by the river a couple hours ago. I figured he was just taking pictures."

Tandy scanned the river and the general panorama. As beautiful as the general area was, this wasn't a particularly good spot to get photographs. Too many trees blocking the view. "What did the truck look like?"

"Oh, it was a nineties model Dodge Ram, 1500 I think. Kinda dirty and had lots of use."

"You didn't happen to get a plate number?" the sheriff knew that was a longshot.

"No, but it was a gray and blue two-tone paint job." He thought about it a little more. "I almost forgot but at the time I was trimming hedges in the front yard and noticed that he came back by a while later." George shrugged, "But that could mean anything.

Maybe he got his pictures then went back to town."

"But you didn't see the driver or what he was doing," Tandy didn't really ask, assuming he'd say 'no.'

"No. But I did hear Cressy's dog barking now and then. Figured it was just some deer going through the yard."

"Okay. That's good. Can you think of anything else?" She assumed this didn't mean much but, then again, it might.

"Not really. You, Yvette?"

"I'm afraid I was inside most of the afternoon doing things around the house. Sorry, Tandy."

"Don't trouble yourselves. You've been very helpful." She shook their hands and went to see what her deputy had learned from the fire crew.

There wasn't much information to be gained from the volunteer firefighters. By the time they got there, the barn was fully engulfed in flames and all they could do was keep it from spreading to the other buildings.

Tandy found out from Cressy that there'd been some hay stored inside, which made the fire burn hotter. She also asked what Quint had earlier about whether she kept any flammable materials in the barn and the answer was the same. All the gas cans, paint and any other combustibles were in the shed. As the sheriff walked back to her rig, Quint nudged her and said, "Expect the same question again from the fire marshal."

"So don't cop an attitude, is that what you mean?"

"Sorta," he gave her a half-smile. "Though he'd probably understand. It is your first fire, after all."

By all accounts, the fire was deemed suspicious.

The anti-Cressy contingent was vocal trying to pin the guilt on her with the argument that she lit the fire herself to seek sympathy. One of her most vehement detractors was Ken Demetre. He was working every side of the issue he could to paint the wolf killer as a scofflaw willing to break all the rules to turn public opinion in her favor.

That strategy became an uphill battle for the environmentalists and wolf advocates since every one of Dillat's friends and family had solid alibis for the time of the blaze. Not that they let that stop them from claiming she could have hired an arsonist, though Demetre wasn't the one selling that story. Interestingly, it came from Mikey Stromberg who evidently hadn't received the memo to back off the issue and shut up.

Between Anthea's continued press releases and Yancy's plying the media, the winds were shifting in Cressy's favor. Arson had been confirmed and officials were leaning toward eco-terrorism as key to the crime. The close brush with rabid environmentalism that Anthea had experienced in the past powered her words to make them count where it mattered for Cressy - earning the public's trust.

And that didn't sit well with the future candidate Demetre. That was *his* job.

CHAPTER 50

Unlike most cases levied against government that dragged on interminably, Yancy had picked up a few tricks over the years to push things along. Attorneys representing the state and federal agencies were unprepared for her actions, being inured to the slow pace that most cases advanced. In contrast to the rapid strike strategy they tried in their first blitz against a defendant Cressy, delay tactics were the general modus operandi of government lawyers, expecting to wear down the complainants until they collapsed under the weight of overwhelming odds and looming bankruptcy.

Between Yancy's bar experience and Toddy's unconventional insight, they weren't playing by the usual rules. Cressy's counsel was relying on procedure that average attorneys had been tamed to ignore.

Anthea was a busy woman further disconcerting the state and feds' defense. The optics of Cressy's case captured the attention of both sides of the issue - fanatical environmentalists and property rights advocates - fueling another news cycle every time court documents were filed.

Tying to the case increasing attacks on the beef industry, Anthea had unending fodder for press releases. In another attempt to damage stock growers, activists were climbing on a United Nations bandwagon. Climate change worrywarts renewed the outlandish idea that bovine flatulence endangered the planet and lauded the Danish scheme to tax meat in supermarkets.

Blaming animals for CO_2 overload wasn't a new assertion. Anthea recalled a decades-old claim that moose in Scandinavia were equally guilty of methane overproduction, an oxymoronic assault against wildlife by environmentalists who were supposedly protecting it.

Noting how the EPA was still operating at out-of-control levels, Anthea included backbreaking rules upheld by the courts such as the 2015 requirement for 45,000 farms and ranches to report how much manure is produced each day.

Relating these stories to the full-fledged war on meat producers that Cressy's case embodied kept the media dancing on the edge of reason.

Courtside, utilizing arguments in accordance with Toddy's suggestions, Yancy explained how injury stemmed from the agencies' violation of Fifth, Ninth and Fourteenth Amendment rights. Outlining the claims for her client's family and Anthea's efforts, they grasped how Constitutional rights were obstructed:

Amendment 5 - Compensation for Takings... No person shall be... deprived of life, liberty, or property, without due process of law; nor shall private property be taken for public use, without just com - pensation.

Amendment 9 - Construction of Constitution. The enumera - tion in the Constitution, of certain rights, shall not be construed to deny or disparage others retained by the people.

Amendment 14 - Citizenship Rights. All persons born or nat - uralized in the United States, and subject to the jurisdiction thereof, are citizens of the United States and of the State wherein they reside. No State shall make or enforce any law which shall abridge the priv - ileges or immunities of citizens of the United States; nor shall any State deprive any person of life, liberty, or property, without due process of law; nor deny to any person within its jurisdiction the equal protection of the laws.

"It's a wonder to me that Constitutional lawyers think average Americans can't understand the language of the Bill of Rights," Cressy shook her head in bewilderment as Yancy went through the amendments with them. "I can see how you make the argument that the amendments can be applied to the Endangered Species Act. How obvious does it have to be that regulations openly protect animals *against* citizens' guaranteed protection of life and property!" Cressy was exasperated how far the government had gotten out-of-control and what she'd gone through was being inflicted on others throughout the United States.

To demonstrate, Yancy had shown her cases where it was happening. "*Life* being an operative word in the Fifth and Fourteenth," said Yancy during one of their meetings at the farmhouse where Cressy's mother, father, Quint and Tricia were in attendance. Cressy saw no reason to exclude her daughter, who would probably benefit most from the experience, learning first-hand what the Constitution meant to every citizen. "Specifically in how Terry's life was cut short indisputably due to federal regulations that coddled killers; brute beasts that were then free to roam, accost, maim and kill stock all the while endangering the lives and livelihood of your neighbors."

"Are you saving that language for oral arguments?" asked Quint. "I sorta like the 'brute beasts' bit."

Yancy laughed. "I do get carried away when it comes to this kind of injustice."

"I liked it," piped up Tricia. "Makes you think about how scary wolves really are."

"Yes, you do," agreed Fran, giving Tricia a hug.

Aside from the periodic meetings regarding the case, Cressy's life had normalized - to a point. Unasked for, the community bestowed her with minor celebrity because of her audacity in taking on the government, though state and federal attorneys tallied it up to cheek, treating her as someone might an impudent child. It went without saying how that attitude fired-up the locals to stand yet more firmly with Cressy, drumming up business at the mercantile and building her legal fund.

Quint came by when time allowed, often bringing Cam along to continue the neighborly history of their two families. Riding down the mountain a couple times a week on his own, Cressy employed the teenager much as her mother had done with Quint at that age. Shaley spent her time working around the ranch and preparing to attend college so she rarely made the trip with her dad.

Yancy traveled back and forth as necessary for court apearances while she kept a handle on her practice and personal life in Montana.

Terra Ferus was scrambling to keep ahead of the media, churning out pro-wolf propaganda as often as possible. Because the regional land trust functioned with a skeleton crew, its unofficial umbrella organization, Nature's Wilds, picked up the slack. The monster real estate conglomerate relied on a Madison Avenue advertising agency it kept on retainer to supply regular releases on TF's behalf.

Demetre was openly targeting a seat in Congress as an independent having assumed that a democrat wouldn't have much of a chance crossing the finish line in what he considered a backward, slightly republican majority constituency. He had weighed the options carefully before making a final decision to drop the democrat party despite the number of liberal thinkers flocking into his home district. Listening to the mainstream media, independents were being attributed with a more progressive outlook than historically speaking, motivating the direction of his campaign strategy.

It was becoming a contest between who derived more compassion in the press - a young widow or an endangered wolf - and Demetre was determined to rule the airtime and land his place in D.C.

Late August, a peculiar development occurred at the sheriff's office.

One blistering afternoon, a woman wandered in to report a missing person. Sheriff Swifter couldn't remember when, or if, she had handled such a report the whole time she had worked at Koyama's department. Among such a small county population everyone knew everybody's business and a person disappearing into the ether was unheard of. But here it was, some gal from another part of the state was parked at Tandy's desk telling her story.

"Why was your brother in Koyama County? Has he been out here before?" Tandy queried the harsh looking mid-fortyish woman with stringy brown hair. The lines in her face and heavy upper body indicated a life that probably included some hard drinking. Tandy had learned to recognize body types that implied certain health issues. In this case, it looked like a lifestyle that stressed heart and liver. Her rough voice and tiny lines etched around pinched lips signaled a smoker, adding to the sheriff's assessment of the woman.

"Last I talked with my brother he said he was coming out here to do some hiking around a place called Gaston Buttes. I had to look it up 'cause I'd never heard of it before. And then he texted me that he'd made some good money while he was there and was coming home soon but he never showed up."

"How long ago was it that you received the text?"

"Oh, I don't know," she said gazing into the distance as if she were scouring her memory. "Maybe a month?"

Tandy's mind did a doubletake. *A month?* Aloud she said, "Why did you wait so long to make the report?"

"Well, we're not real close and I've been working. But when I tried to text him a couple of times about a week ago, he didn't answer. So, I tried calling and it kept going to voicemail. That's when I started to get worried so I looked up this buttes place. I was able to get a few days off so I came out here yesterday."

"Is there anything else that he might have told you that could help?"

"Well, the last text he mentioned some weird name that I couldn't figure out," the gal pulled out her phone and scrolled to find the message. "I can't pronounce it but it sounds foreign. Here," she held out the phone for the sheriff to read it for herself.

"It's Latin. Terra Ferus. It means wild land or earth and it's the name of a non-profit organization out here." Tandy looked at the woman who appeared only mildly worried about her missing brother. It was a relationship she didn't want to figure out. "They're the ones who own and manage the Gaston Buttes Preserve."

"Really?" She genuinely seemed relieved that part of the puzzle was solved. "So I'm in the right place after all."

"As far as it goes, yes," agreed Tandy. "But that doesn't mean he's still out here. It's been a month, he could have gone anywhere."

The woman shook her head vigorously. "No, he would have told me if he wasn't going to come home."

"I thought you said that you aren't close. What makes you think he would have contacted you?"

"We had an agreement and he was supposed to come back and take care of some, uh, business."

Tandy didn't really want details as to what kind of business. She could guess that it was probably sordid at the least and possibly illegal. From what the woman said it didn't sound like it was directly relevant to his vanishing act, other than him making a big score that he preferred to pocket and not to share with his sister. If that's who she really was.

"Give me a complete description of your brother. Name, address, what he drives and anyone he might know out here and we'll see what we can do."

"Like I said, the only thing he ever said about this place was that wild land name and the buttes."

"He never mentioned any names of individuals?"

"I'm pretty sure he didn't."

"We'll have to make do with what information you can give us then," said Tandy while thinking that this guy made his money and ditched his 'sister.' *But I wonder what it was he collected a big pay - ment for and who made out the check.*

It had already been a month since she'd heard anything from her 'brother.' It suited the woman to adopt her ex-boyfriend as a family member to justify hauling the cops into her search. Both their family histories were sketchy at best, neither one having much in the way of traceable relations.

As she left the sheriff's office she began rethinking the wisdom of reporting him missing. They could demand some real paperwork that didn't exist. But they couldn't disprove her story either. At first she thought she should have said he was her husband, but tossed out that idea since she couldn't produce a marriage certificate. Nah, she was right to call him her brother. What with families being so broken up and scattered these days, it was harder to disprove.

If they did find him, though, the cash would come to her one way or the other, she thought. If he's alive, she'd be able to collect and if by some chance he wasn't, she figured she could claim his property, which ought to include any cash that's found.

Climbing into the road-weary, quarter-century-old Subaru, she decided that her best bet was to go to this Terrus something office herself. *Sounds like a weird kind of dog, not a nonprofit group.* If her 'brother' was anywhere around here, they ought to know. The sheriff probably wasn't going to bother much with a guy who was just passing through. Putting the car into gear, she realized she was going to have to do this herself.

Tandy didn't give the report much credence. She scented a scheme of some kind between the woman and the guy who was missing and the probability of him being found in the county was scant. She'd place bets that he'd made some score with the resident biker band that had a camp a number of miles outside of Koyama. They'd been a thorn in the side of local law enforcement for fifteen years and they had a tendency to draw nasty characters from all over. This guy the woman was looking for? Tandy was sure he was long gone and the money with him. That gal was definitely out of luck.

Ken Demetre was on his own at the Terra Ferus office in Rory closing up shop before he loaded his Hummer to head for Portland.

The schedule for the rest of the week was filled with personal appearances and testifying for the defense in the Cressy Dillat claim against the feds. TF's lawyers had supplied supporting rationale for protecting wolves that allowed removal only by permit and special circumstances in accordance with the wolf plan still in effect. In which case, the widow would be liable for illegally killing one. Although not directly named as a defendant in the suit, Terra Ferus had been implicated as colluding with the federal agency in knowingly promoting and protecting notorious wolves that cross onto their property, forbidding the taking of offending wolves while on the preserve.

As he loaded the last of his papers in his briefcase and readied to walk out to the car, the door swung open and a woman he didn't recognize walked into the waiting area. She didn't fit the description of the usual tourist who found their way to the office. No walking shorts or hiking boots. This one was dressed in an oversized knit cotton tunic decorated with a spangly deadhead design covering a heavy bosom and thick middle, calf-length leggings and well-worn platform sandals.

Not now. I don't have time for a cat-collecting armchair environmentalist.

Belying his derogatory thoughts, Demetre greeted the woman pleasantly, "Good afternoon. What can I do for you?"

She didn't have a lot of patience left after poking around for a couple days and running out her time off from a job she couldn't afford to lose. She'd lived a tough life and needed a little comfort that was her due after her so-called brother ripped off the last of her stash. He'd promised to pay her back and she was determined to find him and her money.

There'd be no beating around the bush. It didn't take a genius to see that this guy, who looked like the boss with his swanky briefcase, thought he was a big fish in this little pond, which meant he'd have answers. And if he didn't?

Nothing more to lose, she blurted out, "Where's Randy Giles?"

CHAPTER 51

The case was moving rapidly to the next stage requiring Cressy and counsel to appear before the U.S. District bench in Pendleton.

Arriving a day before the scheduled hearing, Cressy and Yancy took an evening off to enjoy a quiet dinner before the storm that they were prepared to encounter. U.S. District Court was the stepping stone to the Ninth Circuit, well known as the most liberal of the appellate courts, and the most overturned by the U.S. Supreme Court.

No matter what tomorrow's outcome would be, the case was guaranteed to move up the ladder. Neither side was going to allow a ruling against them to go unchallenged, whether the feds lost or it was Cressy who was defeated at this level, an appeal would end up before the Ninth Circuit. Yancy was sure this was going to be a precedent setting case and she was determined to see a win for the landowner.

As much as she wasn't interested in doing interviews, Yancy had booked Cressy for one, planning to travel to Portland after court. In no uncertain terms, Yancy had turned down every major network and cable news show except this one. Cressy had been through the wringer as recently as two years ago where the liberal media excoriated her despite the tragic loss of her husband and Yancy refused to allow a repeat of that experience. Cressy's heart was still raw despite her stoicism before the court so they consented to a single interview with a sympathetic national host after the court appearance.

When Yancy and Cressy arrived at the courthouse, they had expected to be met with the ever-present Ken Demetre, who managed to show up with his media flunkies wherever there was a scheduled court action. He wasn't about to let any opportunity escape him to confront his rival, his appointed scourge of wildlife, while the press did his dirty work of hanging the widow for him.

Surprising Cressy and Yancy, and to their relief, Demetre was nowhere to be seen though his minions had arrived en masse. Two reporters from Portland news networks had the gall to ask Yancy if she'd seen her client's outspoken adversary.

"Why don't you ask them?" retorted Yancy pointing at the attorneys for the feds whom the press practically ignored as too milquetoast. They needed their firebrand activist to quote and slink after.

When the opposition lawyers were queried about their unofficial spokesman they did what attorneys do, equivocated and turned to walk into the courthouse.

Standing in the crowd of press was Aris Nolan. He'd assigned his stringers to handle the day-to-day reporting back in Koyama to free him up to travel. This story had him riveted. Not one to assign blame before all the facts were in, it astounded him that the director of Terra Ferus had painted such a huge target on a bereaved wife. Demetre's political ambitions were obvious but thinking compassion for a wolf overshadowed that of a widow?

The culture shock was turning out to be more than Nolan expected. How vicious the left was didn't throw him. The last few years in St. Louis had proven how this brand of liberalism muscled out common sense in something as basic as community safety. But demonizing a young mother in favor of a wild beast? It didn't compute, not yet anyway, which was why he was spending extra time on this story.

That Ken Demetre wasn't anywhere in sight on this day when his proclaimed enemy was appearing in district court was peculiar. It was rumored that he was a witness for the defense and he hadn't snubbed a single occasion to promote his conservation mission. Between television, radio, youtube or rallying unemployed millennials at federal buildings, Demetre was a pro at tantalizing young people with a righteous cause when they should be working a real job.

Nolan didn't hang around for the parties to depart after court. There wouldn't be a ruling today and he wanted to find out what happened to the wolf's best advocate. There had to be a damn good reason why he wasn't in Pendleton pumping up the protesters and giving the media a piece of his mind.

Next day, the interview went a different direction when Yancy and Cressy made their remote television appearance on a New York newstalk show from a Portland studio.

Before they were asked any questions regarding the progress of the case and Yancy's impression on which way the ruling might go, the host brought up the absence at the courthouse of their usual greeter, the wolf cheerleader. Always one to keep her composure in public, the query was unexpected, all the same. She hadn't time to open her mouth when he went further to inform them that Ken Demetre had also been scheduled to appear with him preceding their segment.

"My producer informed me that Mr. Demetre was a no-show at the courthouse yesterday. Did that throw you for a loop, him not being in attendance receiving the lion's share of the press?"

"The strange part of our arrival for the court proceedings was when the media asked us what might be holding up Mr. Demetre," replied Yancy. "In all truth, we have no direct interaction with him. He's more interested in delivering his brand of rhetoric straight to the media."

"It was my hope that we'd be able to pigeonhole him on some aspects of your case against the government so you'd have the chance to respond afterward," the host went on. "What's really interesting is that we've been informed that Mr. Demetre not only stood us up but three other programs, too. Nor did he cancel his appearances."

A little nonplussed, Yancy answered, "Your guess is as good

as ours. As much as he's made it a habit of dogging Cressy and inserting himself into the proceedings of this case, making it into his personal political platform, it seemed unusual that he wasn't present at district court. Truthfully, we've become accustomed to seeing Mr. Demetre on-air or in the flesh when there is a development in the case."

Turning to Cressy, the host asked her about the up-and-coming politician's absence.

"I agree it's uncharacteristic of Mr. Demetre not to take advantage of media exposure," added Cressy. "Although he's targeted my family and me over the last months, we still wish him well."

"Can you tell me why Mr. Demetre is so adamant about this case, going so far as to attack a grieving widow? Couldn't the tactic turn on him in what looks like a lead-up to his running for office?"

"There are some aspects of this issue that are related to Cressy's situation but not part of the case itself. The greater implications of the case have to do with the pressure that the presence of wolves has put on ranchers in Eastern Oregon and in other parts of the country. The testimony of Cressy and neighboring stock growers is how they've suffered such enormous losses to their businesses that they've been forced into selling off stock and, as in Cressy's case, the ranch."

"What do wolves have to do with that?"

"Using wolves and other protected wildlife as a smoke-screen," replied Yancy, "ODFW and the feds have forced beef growers to implement budget-busting regulations. In one case, a rancher was refused assistance from the state wildlife agency to remove a herd of elk, numbering around two hundred head, from their land. The elk decimated their hayfields, eating the food they were growing for their cattle and destroying the fields during the rut but the landowners weren't allowed to remove the elk. The ranchers followed all the rules, dumping thousands of dollars into accepted methods to rid themselves of the elk but none of the methods worked. They weren't intended to work."

"Are you saying that the regulations were meant to harm the

landowner?"

"In so many words, yes. This particular family is hanging on by the skin of their teeth while the land trusts are drooling over the prospect of snapping up the property at bargain prices," said Yancy. "The fact is, Terra Ferus, which is little better than a subdivision of Nature's Wilds, has been instrumental in sponsoring the massive elk herds and other wildlife that invades and damages surrounding ranch operations. They willfully protect animals that make forays onto neighboring land, refusing to cooperate with them. Not only have they back-filled essential water ponds on the Gaston Buttes Preserve, forcing these herds to compete with private cattle herds but, until this year, they haven't encouraged thinning wildlife herds except to issue nominal hunting licenses.

"The result is the failure of surrounding smaller ranch operations, though the Dillat's was actually quite large. The forced sale was the consequence from the wolf attack that killed her husband, the fight with the state and the loss of his participation in the business damaging the finances beyond repair. Terra Ferus stands in the wings ready to buy out the ranchers and expand the land trust's sway over the county, further pressuring the remaining operations. They already manage a preserve that is more than fifty square miles of prime grazing land. Land that was historically used by local ranchers for summer pasture from which they are now banned."

"Cressy, this sounds like some kind of nefarious cabal," said the host. "It's almost hard to believe."

"Believe it. They tried to buy our ranch but I continued to hold out as long as possible and we were lucky. A ranch family that is keeping the land in production came forward to purchase the property," Cressy's eyes became moist recalling the ordeal. "Terra Ferus did not win despite my family's loss, thank goodness."

"Land confiscation comes in many forms," said Yancy. "And it begins with regulating wildlife to the point that private landowners are stripped of their prerogative on how to use their property. This is a land rights issue that must be resolved in favor of the landowner. If not, more land will end up in the hands of these land trusts that sell the property to the government. The end result is the creation of National Natural Landmarks, which Gaston Buttes has officially begun to implement, that have become National Monuments every time without fail."

"You're saying this is the first step in nationalizing private property," said the host, a trace of righteous anger telling in his voice.

"That's exactly what I'm saying."

Chapter 52

Sheriff Swifter got sidelined from filing the missing person report by a drunk and disorderly call that swallowed a few hours of the afternoon. By the time she made it back to her desk and picked up the paperwork, she was ready to call it a day. Instead, she began leafing through the documents and one of the facts triggered a cloudy memory.

The truck. What was it about this lost "brother's" rig that bothered her? The gal said it was a twenty-year-old Dodge.

Tandy double-checked the description. Blue and gray. Why did that sound familiar? There'd been a lot going on that summer from the fires to Cressy's wolf case that had picked up national attention. Then there were all the annual promotional events that fill up the summer tourist season.

Sitting at her desk, hunched over the report, Tandy massaged her temples. *There's something weird here. What is it?*

A light flicked on in her brain. Truck. Fires. Cressy. The fire that burned down Cressy's barn. *That was it.* Tandy leaned back in her chair, staring up at the fluorescent lights without seeing them.

Cressy's neighbor said something about a nineties era Dodge that had driven near their place and then come back a short while later. Not enough time to go into Nacqus and turn around. Tandy had distributed the information about the truck but nothing ever came of it so she had shuffled it away as a dead end.

So what if this truck was really there? I have no reason to doubt George and it just could be that this Giles character was driv - ing it and immediately left town, which is why the hunt came up short. As she pondered the loose connections, pieces began falling into place.

Dodge truck. Fires. Cressy's fire. Terra Ferus. Gaston Buttes. *This might be the arsonist who set fire to the Dillat barn. I wonder what else he might have lit up in this county?*

Immediately, Tandy went to pull the files on the Emville and Dillat fire reports. *There just might be something there.*

"Excuse me? Have we met?" the Terra Ferus director asked the woman who had walked through the front door of the office and without preamble threw a name at him that made his heart lose rhythm for the briefest second.

"No, but I'm pretty sure you know my brother." She wasn't exactly belligerent but she had taken an immovable pose blocking the exit. Although not tall, the woman was hefty enough that physically removing her wasn't something he'd consider. It was evident she wasn't going anywhere until she got a satisfactory answer and he wasn't about to call law enforcement to have her ejected.

"Ma'am?" He needed to give himself a little wiggle room in case he was caught in the lie.

"You should know him. He did some work for you about six weeks ago." She was bluffing, putting what little she knew to use and hoping he'd take the bait. She'd been in tight spots before and had learned how to work a mark with just a few choice bits of information. This guy's ego was a plus for her because he was sure she wasn't very bright. *He'll find out I'm smart enough to handle him, fancy boots and all.*

"We have a lot of volunteers seeking to help our nonprofit, and I'm afraid I can't recall all of them. Most are college students and we've been inundated with them this summer."

"Randy's no college kid and he doesn't do volunteer work."

Demetre's only response was to raise one haughty eyebrow.

"You hired him for a project at the buttes." This was pushing the envelope of her knowledge but she jumped in with both feet. "It was for good money too."

"Is that right. We've a lot going on here this summer between our regular conservation studies that brought all the college contingents. There've been the fires and other pressing issues. I did employ some people dealing with fire cleanup. He may have been among them. I don't recall all the names." He reached for his briefcase, "If you'll excuse me, I'm running on a schedule.'

That answer made her pause with momentary uncertainty. Quickly running through her mind what Randy had said, knowing he wouldn't boast about a score if it was just some pick-up job, she said, "The point is, he texted me about a whole lot more than that. We were supposed to meet up and then, poof, nothing." She settled a haunch on the corner of the front desk. "I need to know where he is or I'll have to make a missing person report to the sheriff and they'll be visiting you here, which has got to mess with your plans." She sure wasn't going to tell him that she'd already seen the sheriff. That might screw up this whole thing because he was acting shifty. *Oh yeah, he knows where Randy is.*

"Look, Mister D," betting it was his name she'd seen on the door but couldn't pronounce it. Just as well, now he'd think Randy had told her about him, too. "I only have a couple of days off and I need to see Randy. You know what happened to him…" Seeing his reaction to this last comment, she knew he was covering for something or someone. Closing in for the kill, so to speak, she added, "Don't you."

This interview was not going in Demetre's favor. This woman could very well be related to the Giles fellow. Though there was no resemblance they both had an instinct for blackmail and he had to come up with an instant plan of attack. She couldn't know that her brother was dead but she certainly had an inkling something was wrong. She wasn't letting on how much she really knew about his firebug antics, but it sounded like Giles had told her more than he should and she was obviously expecting a payday.

Well, maybe he could provide one.

Demetre's mind whirred. He was expected in Pendleton and the arrival of Giles' sister was interfering with his schedule, not to mention his future aspirations.

He looked at his watch. There was still time.

"Since I don't have an assistant here to help you, what I can do is take you out to where the work was being done on the preserve. I believe that some of the guys we hired are still out there finishing some of the reclamation work. They may know your brother and his whereabouts."

"Can't you just call them? They must have cell phones," she wasn't thrilled with the idea of going out to the boonies. This town was as far as she was interested in traveling.

"I'm afraid there's no cell service out there. It's a good way out on the buttes. You can leave your name and number and as soon as they check in, we'll contact you." Demetre started to pick up his brief-case to leave, her hesitancy to drive out there signalling he was free to go.

"Okay. It's really important to find him and if it means going out there to look," she stood up and straightened her tunic, "Let's go."

That was not the answer he expected, being certain she would backoff. Seeing the determined look on her face, Demetre realized he was stuck with her. He was not happy with off-the-cuff decisions but he was boxed in. He wasn't looking forward to what promised to be an unpleasant drive to Gaston Buttes.

Unwilling to be seen with a disreputable looking woman in the passenger seat of his Hummer, Demetre put his briefcase back inside his private office then ushered her out to the company Toyota. Not having seen his other ride, she didn't complain getting into a vehicle that was still an improvement over her car, which she left sit-ting in front of the Terra Ferus office.

Pulling out into the street, Demetre cringed when he saw the dilapidated Subaru parked next to the TF SUV. It was an eyesore that he preferred were parked down the street rather than at the office. Nothing to be done about it now, he turned north on the main drag and headed for the preserve. It was going to be a long hour and a half. As encouragement to get this situation controlled, he thought, *At least it'll only be one way.*

Unable to get Ken Demetre on the phone to answer why he skipped making an appearance at the courthouse before the all-important hearing, Aris Nolan went with his gut and ditched the rest of the press gaggle. What he'd learned of the Terra Ferus administrator over the last year was that he'd never willingly pass up a photo op. He had big plans for himself, there was no doubt. Following his newsman's intuition, Nolan turned his back on the other reporters and skipped down the steps to reach his rig, driving the few hours back to Koyama.

When he came up the valley and into town, Nolan bypassed his office and continued directly to Rory with all intention of discovering Demetre's whereabouts. First stop was the Terra Ferus office on Main Street.

Pulling up in front of the building, Nolan parked next to a Subaru that had seen better days and, if he didn't know any better, looked like an abandoned vehicle. Climbing out of his SUV, he approached the front door and tried to enter. It was locked but the 'closed' sign wasn't displayed which he knew was out of the ordinary for the meticulous Demetre. But then, it could have been locked up by a less fussy assistant. He decided to take a look around the building to see if any other cars were there since the trust's Toyota wasn't occupying a space out front, which it did half the time.

After circling the office, he saw that Demetre's personal vehicle, the tricked-out Hummer, was sitting on the side of the building, the engine cold. *So it's been here for a while, anyway.* The company car was gone, though.

Nolan had interacted enough with the director that he knew the Toyota was used to take visitors and run errands out to the office miles out in the middle of the preserve. It wasn't here but Demetre's rig was which, to Nolan's thinking, meant that he had made a trip out to the buttes.

To go or not to go. Nolan was divided as to whether he wanted to engage in what might be a wild goose chase out to Gaston Buttes. Except for the fact of Demetre missing a golden opportunity to harangue the press at the biggest development thus far of the Dillat versus the government case, Nolan might call it a waste of time. But Demetre being a no-show just wasn't in character and if his car was here, it would indicate that illness or accident wasn't the answer to his absence.

Nolan decided to trust his news nose and log another couple hours onto his already long day on the road. Squirming in his seat as he headed back the way he'd come, the journalist went in search of a story and hoped it wouldn't be a bust.

Silence prevailed through most of the trip to the Gaston Buttes Preserve. Discomfort between the two occupants of the vehicle was palpable but each could sense minds working overtime trying to figure out the other's game.

Having covered quite a few miles after entering the preserve, the woman broke the quiet in the cab. "This place is huge. Where is it we're going?" Nervous the farther they traveled, the empty terrain seemed to close in on her rather than be liberating. She knew city streets and was more secure in back alleys than out here where the vacant landscape felt oppressive.

Vindicating his decision to drag this hag out to the prairie, Demetre found it satisfying to hear uncertainty creep into her voice. She wouldn't be so confident about trying to extort money from him when all she could see was endless grass. They passed the outlying office that had the old farm pickup parked in the back.

"Don't we need to stop there?"

"There's no one there. It's just a couple miles more to where the guys were working."

She said nothing. All she could think about was when they were going to turn around. This entire place made her skin crawl, which she realized was probably his intent. She wasn't stupid. Though right now, she was beginning to doubt how smart a move it was to push this guy into bringing her out here. Patting her purse, she reminded herself that she carried backup. Luckily, he hadn't thought it necessary to go through her shoulderbag, small as it was.

Demetre turned off on a dirt track that seemed to follow the rim of a ravine. She couldn't see into the depths because the dropoff was on the driver's side, but it looked deep.

"I don't see anything burned. Didn't you say that the guys you hired were cleaning up from a fire?"

"The fire was down the side of the gorge. It didn't come up over the top."

"Wouldn't there be some cars or trucks out here? I don't see anything," she said craning her neck to see out the windshield.

"Like I said, they *were* working at this location. It looks like they may have finished up and packed it in. I told you it was a shot in the dark to see if anyone was still out here." He stopped the SUV and opened the door. "We're here now. May as well see if there's any sign of your brother."

She hesitated to get out of the Toyota but climbed down anyway, walking over near to where he went to check out the canyon below, she kept her hand in her purse for security.

Peering over the edge, he said with shock, "Oh my god. There's a truck over the side here!"

"What? No!" She didn't think before rushing over to see if it might have anything to do with Randy.

As she approached, he pointed to a blue and gray Dodge flipped upside-down a couple hundred feet down the defile, "Look! I don't know whose that is, but I can't tell if anyone's in there."

"That's Randy's truck!" She looked at him. "You have to check to see if he's in there!"

That wasn't at all what Demetre was planning to do. He'd gotten her close enough that he leaned out to push her over the edge to share the same fate as her larcenous brother.

Moving quicker than he thought possible, she pulled a sap out of her shoulderbag and whacked him hard on the shoulder, knocking him off balance and sending him tumbling down the slope, arms and legs flailing in an uncontrolled fall. Nearly slipping over the rim herself, her left ankle buckled in the platform sandal, collapsing her leg under her. Twisting her ankle ended up saving her from rolling over the brink too.

All she could do was sit where she'd fallen, losing track of time staring at the limp form of her driver lying within twenty feet of the truck's broken frame.

Not knowing what else to do as the initial shock began to wear off, she replaced the sap she'd been clutching back inside her purse and fished out her phone. Holding it up to check for a signal she saw that he hadn't lied about that fact, not a single bar showed up in the icon display.

Dropping the phone back in her purse, she tried to stand up and cried out in pain. She'd done a helluva job on her ankle, but she couldn't bring herself to be angry. The sprain had saved her life. Slowly crawling away from the edge she managed to get herself upright and hobble back over to the Toyota. When she got there, she hung onto the rearview mirror for balance while she opened the driver's side door.

Thank god! He left the keys in the ignition. Using every ounce of strength she had left, she pulled herself into the driver's seat, adjusted it to her shorter stature and turned over the engine. Giving in to the vestiges of terror, her arms wrapped over the steering wheel, she wept in relief as her panic slowly dissolved. Still physically shaking with fear but grateful she wasn't the one who went over the edge, she put the vehicle in gear and turned it around.

CHAPTER 53

Bumping over the rugged road that led to the outlying office on the Gaston Buttes Preserve, Aris Nolan switched between berating himself for following a flight of imagination and scanning the miles of grassland for any sign of activity. He'd forgotten just how isolated the building was and how long it took to get there.

I've come this far so there's no turning back now, even if I make an ass of myself.

Finally, Nolan saw the dilapidated shack on the horizon. To a degree, he understood them retaining the impression of unchanging landscapes, but as much as Terra Ferus discouraged cattle it didn't make a lot of sense to save a ranch setting. Shrugging his shoulders at his own thoughts about the contradictory nature of nonprofits, as he approached the building in question, he noticed the two vehicles parked there. Coming closer, he could see that the company Toyota was pulled in haphazardly which, knowing Demetre, was definitely out of character.

He was just a couple hundred yards out when he saw a woman struggling with the office's front door until she heard his approach and turned toward the sound of his car, waving her arms wildly. Frantic as she seemed, she didn't run toward him as he pulled up. She was disheveled, hobbling and obviously in pain.

Jumping out of his car, Nolan ran over to her and caught her as she crumpled in his arms, blubbering about an accident. There was no place to sit and since she'd been banging on the door, he assumed it was locked so he half-carried her to the passenger side of his own vehicle.

"Calm down, ma'am. Catch your breath and tell me what happened." He tried to be reassuring but wanted information right away if someone else was injured and they needed help.

Gulping air in between fits of uncontrolled tears, the woman began to regain control of herself. "I can't get in and my phone won't work."

"I can see that." He tried again, "Tell me what happened. Is someone hurt?"

"Yes. Yes! He's out there," she swept her hand in the opposite direction from where Nolan had just come. "He fell down the cliff! I don't know if he's okay. I don't know if they're dead!"

"They? Who's out there?"

"That man who runs this place and Randy. They're both out there." She was running out of steam and listlessly waved her hand in the same direction.

"Let me see if my phone works," said Nolan, trying to keep his cool though his newsman's instinct was screaming at him to get the story. Letting go of her, he pulled his phone out of his pocket and held it up. He had a local carrier and a signal was available.

"Okay, I'm calling 911 right now."

She just nodded and let her head drop into her hands, trying to get a grip. Always believing she was a tough chick that could handle anything, when confronted with a real disaster, she couldn't cope. Right now, she could barely understand what had just occurred, let alone worry about what would come next.

Nolan got a hold of Dispatch and gave what information he had, which wasn't much. They said that an ambulance and a deputy would be out there as soon as possible. Considering they were so far out of town, he was warned that it might be as long as two hours.

Thanking the operator, he hung up and tried to soothe the woman sitting in his passenger seat. She wasn't dressed for a day on the prairie in leggings and sandals that had gotten ripped up in whatever had happened out there.

"Quick, tell me. If we go out there, can I get to them?"

At first she just looked at him, uncomprehending, eyes glazed, shocky, making Nolan wonder how she'd driven back to the office. She shook her head, stringy hair loose from where it had been tied back. When she peered at him, she was more lucid. "No, they're halfway down the cliff. I don't think Mr. D is alive and I think Randy's been there for weeks."

Standing up, he put his hands on his hips knowing there was nothing to be done but wait. Gazing out in the direction she had pointed, he realized that he had more than an hour to get an exclusive on what was bound to be an explosive story. Turning back to the occupant of his passenger seat, Nolan told her to sit tight while he checked out the building.

Going over to the front door, he tried it and found that she'd been right. It was locked. After hunting around for a hidden key and finding none, the newspaper publisher decided brute force was called for and going to the woodpile, he chose a hefty timber. Walking back to the building's face, he saw that a window was close enough to the door that he could break it and gain entry, which he did. It took some effort to climb through the window. Even though he kept himself fairly fit, this kind of stretching and crawling over furniture hadn't been part of his job description for years. Unlocking the front door, Nolan walked back to his car to lift the woman onto her feet and help her inside.

Sitting her on the couch in the cramped quarters, Nolan was rather proud of himself for completing his first breaking and entering criminal endeavor. He could, however, already tell he'd feel the impact from the atypical exertion tomorrow.

At the sink, he filled a glass with water and took it over to her. As she swallowed the liquid he checked out the interior, recalling that Demetre kept a spendy single malt tucked away for his private use. A good reporter, Nolan made note of numerous details when he'd interviewed the director there some months ago.

He found the liquor and poured a little into another glass. Positioning a chair in front of her, he offered her the whisky and sat down to get the whole tale.

This ought to be good.

Sheriff Swifter was walking the perimeter of the Terra Ferus office in Rory when she got the call from Dispatch.

Exiting her rig, Tandy had noted she parked next to the same paint-blistered Subaru that the roughcut gal owned who had reported her brother as missing. Evidently, she'd gone off to do her own investigating. Not a surprise. The woman didn't appear to be particularly patient. Nor did it look like she was here, the office locked-up tight despite Demetre's Hummer sitting idle in the drive beside the buildiing

Thumbing the control on her shoulder set, Tandy acknowledged the call as she returned to the cruiser, turned on the light bar and sped back toward Koyama and out to the preserve.

Arriving at the Gaston Buttes outpost, Tandy saw that she had beaten all other first responders to the scene. The Terra Ferus Toyota was parked at a crazy angle while she recognized the County Koyama Weekly publisher's rig also parked at the building. She had assumed that the call-in had been made by the preserve's director, so she wondered what Aris Nolan was doing here.

Immediately approaching the front entrance, Tandy didn't have to open the door, it was already standing ajar. Pushing it all the way open, she saw the back of the woman's head, hair mussed and dusty, like she'd been rolling on the ground. Across from her was Nolan, his dark face stern with compassion as the woman answered a question.

Hearing the sheriff's boots hit the flooring, Nolan looked up from his interview, for clearly that's what it was, and said with relief, "Thank goodness you're here, Sheriff. There's been quite a ruckus and it looks like you have your work cut-out for you."

Raising an inquiring eyebrow, "Are you involved with the events that occurred here, Aris?"

"No, I was following up a hunch and found this lady trying to get inside the building to reach a phone since hers didn't have a signal."

"Well I see she managed it," Tandy indicated the broken window.

"Actually, that was me," he admitted sheepishly. "She was acting shocky so I called in the incident and broke in to get her a place to calm down."

"And tell you what happened."

He shrugged in chagrin, "Well, you all weren't going to get here for more than an hour and I am a newsman. It's to be expected of me."

"No real harm done, I suppose, but I need to know what's going on," she said catching the woman's eye.

"You'd better tell her what happened, Lucy," he said encouragingly. "First, Tandy, you need to know that one of the victims involved in the accident needs emergency attention. We've been waiting for the EMTs to show them the way to the site since there was nothing that I could do. From what she said, a rescue team is necessary."

"So I heard. One has been called. Who is it that needs help?"

"Ken Demetre. He apparently fell over a precipice."

As she was getting the basic information, the ambulance drove up followed by fire rescue, at which point, Tandy hustled both of them out of the office and loaded Lucy into the back seat of the cruiser.

Just as she was about to drive off, signaling the other crews to follow, Nolan held open the passenger door of the cruiser. "Do I go with you or drive my own rig out there?"

Shaking her head, Tandy said, "Get in. We don't need any more vehicles out there than necessary to mess up a crime scene."

"Crime scene?" came Lucy's squeak from behind the cage. "I didn't do anything except defend myself!"

"I'm sure we'll be able to determine that but someone also said there was a vehicle that went over the side at an earlier time. Is that right?" She said it over her shoulder as she backed out and drove down the main road.

"Yes, Randy's truck was down the cliff. Could have been there for weeks."

"Okay. Now, can you remember how to get there?"

"Yes." And she gave the sheriff directions as they drove out to the location as fast as the miserable condition of the road allowed, answering Tandy's questions as they went.

As soon as they reached the scene, Tandy popped out of her rig and made sure the other responders parked the vehicles a way back to avoid disturbing evidence. Then she let Lucy out of the cruiser and had her show her where Demetre was as the med techs unloaded their equipment.

Reaching the edge of the ravine, they could see the land trust's director lying at an odd angle more than a hundred feet down the incline.

"Oh," hissed Lucy, "He hasn't moved." Looking at the sheriff, "Could he be unconscious?"

"It's more likely that it's worse than that. It's been at least two hours since he fell over the ridge, from what you said. Let's get the recovery crew down there." And she waved them forward.

The rescue team went to work and Tandy questioned Lucy about where the Toyota was parked and where the scuffle took place, writing notes and taking pictures. Nolan kept his distance, trying not to be intrusive, which was killing him because he wanted to be in the center of activity so he didn't miss a thing.

From what he'd already gleaned talking to Lucy, Demetre was into some dirty business. If anyone was going to put the pieces of this yarn together it was going to be Nolan. The idea that he came all the way to the literal end of the road to stumble across what might be the story of the decade blew him away. *Who'd a thought ranchville could harbor an archvillain?*

CHAPTER 54

When the story broke, it ripped into the environmental community like a Cat 5 tornado, blowing up the rafters and tearing off the roof of a carefully constructed house of cards.

Arson had long been suspected in the Emville fires that scarred thousands of acres of picturesque Northwest canyonlands. The rub had been proving it... until now.

Providence had manipulated time and circumstances to drop Aris Nolan in the middle of the quandary's unraveling and he took full advantage of the opportunity, spilling the tale in his paper that served a tiny media market. That didn't stop the story from swiftly circulating and being picked up by major press outlets, except the few hardcore leftist arms that had learned to ignore inconvenient news rather than report it.

Nolan briefly became the toast of national news shows for all the wrong reasons. The story should have been covered for the treachery that charred prime grazing land abutting a monstrous private conservation preserve with barely a spark touching it.

Instead, the questions centered on his exclusive about the untimely death of an outspoken leader in the environmental movement. Rarely referenced was evidence pointing to arson as part of an orchestrated plan to rob ranchers of land that neighbored the expanding Gaston Buttes Preserve. Not that the omission stopped Nolan from turning the conversation in that direction. He continued to unwind more of the scheme in a series of in-depth investigative pieces that was turning the county inside out but disregarded by major media markets.

Hounding law enforcement for facts was the meat that sustained the big city reporter now running a small town paper. Every scrap of information Nolan retrieved was published to the embarrassment of the state and federal agencies defending against Cressy

Dillat's case for damages.

Conservative talkers turned their attention to Cressy as the darling of the beleaguered ranch community despite her unwillingness to appear on their programs. The wolf advocates came out of the woodwork to fill the shoes of Ken Demetre but the more they talked, the more appealing Cressy became as the victim du jour.

Terra Ferus was called out to explain about instances of shady funding for land purchases, including state lottery money, and pressure tactics applied to local landowners to support increasing the size and number of wildlife refuges. In Demetre's absence the hunt for documents forged ahead, no longer benefiting from his painstakingly constructed façade. Land swaps and sales to the US Forest Service began to come under scrutiny by some press while remaining largely ignored by legislators and completely sidestepped by mainstream media.

One unexpected development occurred when Mikey Stromberg left Fish and Wildlife to assume Demetre's mantle as director of Gaston Buttes. What she lacked in finesse she made up for in aggressively shielding Terra Ferus business of which, interestingly, she had an extensive knowledge. That set-off alarms for Yancy who immediately went after the conspiracy angle of USFWS and Terra Ferus colluding to profit from wildlife incursions on private land.

As part of the information dump, documentation came to light of the tight connections between Terra Ferus and Nature's Wilds, drawing speculation on cross-case involvement with ongoing litigation of the latter's alleged illegal activity in Idaho some years prior.

Aris Nolan's digging deeper into the Emville fires tied together some very loose ends that, at first blush, seemed unrelated. Unsanctioned wolf releases, wolf population misreporting and agencies' refusal to protect landowners, willfully disregarding the few beneficial regulations, influenced the Dillat case.

The other side of the coin was the criminal investigation of Demetre's involvement in land acquisition schemes that included arson, possible murder and covering up all of the above.

Sheriff Swifter had put the puzzle together from the beginning point of the infamous blue and gray Dodge pickup. Linking the truck containing a dead body with the Dillat barn fire and finding it weeks later slung over the side of a canyon at the same place where Demetre had attempted to dispose of another inquisitive person, was plenty to fire off an investigation.

Evidence gathered was in the form of paper trails and corroborating interviews that painted an appalling picture of the ambitious nature of the Terra Ferus director.

Demetre's wife unwittingly provided much of the insight that closed the case. Informing Swifter and the state's detective about her husband's odd behavior the night she'd returned from Seattle, forensics was called to examine their home. It was a shock to her when she was told that traces of blood had been found on a glass trophy and in the floorboards behind a leather chair. Samples were collected and the DNA later matched to that of the body found in the derelict Dodge dumped over the remote cliff on the buttes.

Tidying up the tales of the wife and the woman Lucy, the story came together. Mrs. Demetre had followed her husband to the Rory office the next day to drop off the battered maintenance vehicle that was usually kept out on the preserve. For reasons unknown to her, he had brought it home late the night before, arriving a couple hours after she'd gone to bed exhausted from her day traveling from Washington's westside.

He had transported the body of Randy Giles, whom he'd killed in the living room of his home, in the back of Giles' Dodge to Gaston Buttes. There, he'd set up the body behind the wheel, disengaged the truck's gear and rolled it over the rim of the ravine. Then he'd hiked the few miles back to the Gaston Buttes onsite office and driven the maintenance truck back to his house where his wife saw it the next day.

When the so-called sister of the arsonist arrived looking for him and/or a payoff, seeing disaster in every direction, Demetre plotted to have her join Giles in his rock-strewn grave. A dire miscalculation ended up sending Demetre into the chasm instead of his intended victim. What was unknown was whether Giles' death had been accidental or intentional. Either way, had the incident become public, Demetre's political career would have ended before it had launched.

Every bit of the grisly affair fed into coverage of Cressy's case and the far-reaching implications of systematic complicity that pervaded relations between government wildlife agencies and the land trusts. Unlikely that involvement of the state and federal bureaucrats in Demetre's underhanded and illegal dealings could be proven, the inference was enough to create an atmosphere of conspiracy.

What the consequences would be from reporting these details was anyone's guess. Landowners across the nation were paying close attention to the Dillat case. Environmental organizations, federal and state land use agencies were coming under fire from fair-minded news outlets, which were few, pressing the legal system to step up their game and Nolan was leading the charge.

CHAPTER 55

Yancy didn't leave it up to a phone call when the ruling was to be handed down from district court. As soon as she heard it was coming, she caught a flight to Lewiston where Anthea and Gary collected her and drove to Nacqus the same day she arrived.

Cressy had done her best to separate herself from the legal proceedings knowing that thinking about the progress of the case would drive her mad with frustration. The developments in the investigation of Ken Demetre's death didn't help her state of mind.

With every installment of the arson case that Aris Nolan printed in the local paper, some of which was covered in the regional press but not disseminated much further, the implications of what had been perpetrated on county landowners was magnified. As Cressy's case had already been argued at federal district court, the discovery couldn't be presented regarding the decision about to be delivered. Moving forward, should the court rule against her, which they all knew was likely, Yancy hoped it could be admitted as new evidence but she wasn't counting her chickens.

For now, Cressy stayed occupied with running the business and trying to live as normal a life as possible. It was a daily battle to keep her sanity while fending off gatecrashing correspondents more interested in trashing her reputation than reporting facts. But she was managing pretty well thanks to her daughter's extraordinary ability to focus on the simple things, keeping a down to earth perspective far beyond her years. Cressy chalked it up to Tricia's paternal DNA, Terry and his dad always being able to find pleasure in the mundane and peace in the storm.

As the time approached that they were expecting to hear how the court would rule in her case against the behemoth, Cressy did her best to rearrange her priorities and shuffle apprehension to the bottom of the deck. Concentrating on day-to-day activities was working, to a point.

It wasn't surprising then, to see her core support group unload from Anthea's SUV after dark on a shortening fall day. Yancy had been successful in fast-tracking the case through administrative channels, leapfrogging it into federal court without delay. It could have been that the government switched directions and, instead of holding up the process, assisted moving it through the channels, assuming that a quick win for their side would put the whole controversy to bed. But that was before the breakthrough relating to Terra Ferus' seedy activities. Whether the late land trust administrator's deceit would influence the case in the long run was yet to be seen.

Welcoming them into the house, Cressy teased, "I thought there were four in this posse."

"He's on his way," said Gary.

"Well, are we breaking out champagne or am I putting on coffee for a work session?" quipped Cressy as she moved to close the door behind them.

"Anything, as long as it comes with a slice of homemade pie," said Quint as he grabbed the edge of the door, preventing Cressy from shutting it on him as he blocked the entrance.

"Revealing your hidden agenda for joining this intrigue against the government." was Anthea's greeting to the almost latecomer. "Do you have a preference?"

"Everyone's favorite, apple or berry or pumpkin or…"

"Whatever happens to be on the menu tonight," Cressy cut him off.

"Which is, considering we're here unannounced, very possibly none of the above," said Yancy, pulling off her jacket and hanging it on the hall tree.

"The deal is, Quint's known me far too long and also knows that I bake when I've got something on my mind. In answer, you have a choice between apple and peach," said Cressy ending the controversy. Turning to Yancy, she asked again, "So what is it, celebrate or commiserate?"

"No champagne tonight but no crying, either," was her reply.

"Coffee it is then. Come on in and make yourselves comfortable,"

Cressy waved them into the living room.

After settling where the Mathers' and Yancy were staying for the night, the five of them dove into the reason three of them had just driven hours for a not-so-casual visit.

"As everyone's figured out," started Yancy, "they ruled against us in district court."

Leaning back into his chair, a generous piece of apple pie filling his dessert plate, Quint asked what everyone wanted to know, "What now? Cressy's the plaintiff so she can't appeal, can she?"

"It's a federal case, Quint, so yes she can. What we do next is appeal to the Ninth Circuit."

"We all know how that will end," foretold Gary. "The most liberal of all the appellate courts will certainly rule against you."

"Probably," agreed Yancy. "But I believe that this case will make the grade when we petition for a writ of certiorari."

"And that is?" asked Cressy.

"A request for the Supreme Court to review the decision. This was not a jury case but judged by a federal district judge, who decided against Cressy's claim that her Constitutional rights were violated. Opinion from the Ninth will likely be in favor of the defense, too. Their leaning usually denies expression of rights they deem to be conservative in nature. We've seen it time and again. Certiorari is the next step, along with lots of prayer that four of the nine justices consent to review the case."

"How much of a long shot is that?" asked Anthea.

"Truthfully, the odds are huge since they only take around a hundred and fifty of approximately seven thousand cases submitted, but..." and Yancy paused for a moment, "this is a unique case that will set precedent and I have a strong belief they will give it consideration."

"You mean like the Hobby Lobby or wedding cake cases?" asked Cressy.

"Along those lines. Also because your case addresses protecting private property and, of even more importance, life, particularly since a person actually lost his due to the actions of the state." Yancy sipped her coffee. "I think we've got a chance. But it's not only me. The legal foundation I've gotten to partner with us thinks so, too."

"You won't be handling this on your own, then," said Cressy.

"I can't and neither can the firm in Bend. We need someone experienced and certified to argue before the Supreme Court, and lucky for us, one of the best constitutional law groups has volunteered to help us."

"So maybe champagne wasn't completely out of the question," said Gary. "Seems to me that tidbit of knowledge is worth a little celebration."

"Yes, it's good news but we'll hold off popping the cork on the bubbly for when we win," Cressy said, holding up the coffee pot. "Anyone need a refill of tonight's beverage of choice?"

"Sure," said Anthea as Cressy poured until everyone had a full cup. Raising her mug, she added, "A toast to winning the final round and *then* the champagne!"

They spent the evening discussing the protocols and strategies of the appeal and probable petitioning of the Supreme Court of the United States. The idea of taking her tale to the most august judicial body in the country made Cressy catch her breath. The courts were supposed to be where justice is delivered but she'd seen the seamy underside of the legal process and how all the determination in the world to set things right won't guarantee a just outcome. The process had squeezed and wrung her out so much that she'd abandoned hope of recapturing what it felt like to have a full life.

The loss of Terry and their baby had blasted a hole in her heart that she thought could never be repaired. Having neighbors, the community and virtual strangers give generously of their time, possessions and finances to help her family was, at times, beyond her comprehension. Cressy had always been a do-it-yourself girl and accepting the kindness that had come her way posed a greater obstacle to moving on than she'd realized.

How the prayer group had stepped up with physical and spiritual support had opened a whole new perspective on what it meant to believe. Looking back over these months made her recheck her definition of the spirit, that it wasn't some nebulous, sanctified entity that was beyond human reach, and hers especially.

And fellowship. Cressy had no idea what that was all about until she'd experienced it with Quint during the wolf hunt and then with the comaraderie of the Mathers', the support of the prayer group, Toddy's partnership and Yancy's leadership. In an obscure way, she caught a glimpse of what bonded combat veterans together - the mutual reliance in the midst of a battle, understanding that a single soldier can't win a war by himself.

Her war wasn't comparable to a mine-cratered battlefield with bombs exploding and bullets flying. But the need for interdependence to forge a path through a firefight was driven home.

At the government's first onslaught she'd tried to do it alone. Not only had she lost the battle but she'd withdrawn from the field, hiding in the trenches to lick her wounds. This time around, Cressy was forced to accept aid and comfort from allies and she could see how far they'd come. Victory *was* possible; her cohorts could taste it. But could she? Was she ready to let the future triumph over the pain-filled past?

That was going to take a different kind of fortitude, not just the staying power to slog through another day, month or year. Whether or not they win in court, the ultimate feat would be embracing new days with a lot of hope, a little joy, a risk of love and a foundation of faith.

Listening to the options Yancy was laying out, Cressy reflected on how these four people had triggered a fundamental change in her attitude, altering her life in a way she'd never expected.

Today's ruling was a temporary setback for a resolute team.

Stout hearts, that's what her Navy dad had called his shipmates. Considering her companions seated comfortably around the living room planning future salvos, Cressy smiled, *Yes, they are.*

EPILOGUE

This is it.

Standing before the steps of the Supreme Court, Cressy gazed up through the swirling snow at the massive Corinthian columns supporting the pediment under which was engraved "Equal Justice Under the Law."

Previous experience had taught her otherwise and she'd be a fool not to admit she was daunted by the majesty imbued in a temple built to house the priests of American jurisprudence.

Not alone in her response, she could feel the mixed anxiety and anticipation radiating from Yancy next to her. The culmination of a blistering battle of will against immovable bureaucracy was at hand.

For this final episode of the case, Yancy was as much a spectator as Cressy, as only members of the Supreme Court Bar could argue before the Bench. Months of preparation for this day had been spent in the company of the legal team who had partnered with them and they were about to enter the courtroom to watch and hear reasoning that would set precedent.

Having been an integral part of the sojourn to state her case in the highest court in the land, Anthea and Gary joined Cressy, filling out their contingent of four. Taking a few moments, allowing Cressy to gather courage to enter the premises, Yancy scanned the courtyard, pulling her overcoat close to block the frigid January air.

"What are you looking for?" Cressy had taken notice of her lawyer swiveling her head to examine the mass of people milling around the building.

"Nothing really. I'm just a little antsy," she looked at Cressy. "You know how it is. You work and plan for something and when the time finally arrives, you wonder if you got it right. And then there's the part where you hand it all over to someone else to carry the burden."

"That, I understand. You've been pulling my weight for a long time and it's been awful letting go so you could do your job... with amazing skill, by the way. I really don't know how to thank you."

"Don't just yet. We still have months to go to see how this will all play out, though I'm confident of our chances," she reassured.

"If nothing else, this will be an occasion to remember," replied Cressy.

"With elation, is what I think," added Anthea.

To which Gary agreed, "I've said it before, the odds of a win are excellent. This top-notch legal group wouldn't have offered to represent you if it weren't."

"I'm gonna go with that," perked up Cressy. "Shouldn't we go, even if we do have reserved seating?"

"Yes," said Yancy, still hunting through the crowd. "But we're missing one."

Cressy was about to ask who when she saw a tan cowboy hat floating through the clusters of tourists crossing the quad.

"Sorry I'm late. The flight was delayed because of weather and I was afraid I'd miss the cattle call."

Cressy's eyes widened in surprise but couldn't find any words, her mouth forming a perfect 'O'.

"I'm just glad you made it in time," said Yancy. "We need to get going," and she led the way to the building entrance.

Forgetting to move, Quint hooked his arm through Cressy's to nudge her along. "You didn't think I'd let you have all this fun without me, did you?" Planting a quick kiss on her lips, he turned her to follow Yancy and the Mathers' before she could do anything but smile.

-30-

AND WHAT MORE SHALL I SAY? I DO NOT HAVE TIME TO TELL
ABOUT GIDEON, BARAK, SAMSON AND JEPHTHAH,
ABOUT DAVID AND SAMUEL AND THE PROPHETS,
WHO THROUGH FAITH CONQUERED KINGDOMS,
ADMINISTERED JUSTICE, AND GAINED WHAT WAS PROMISED;
WHO SHUT THE MOUTHS OF LIONS,
QUENCHED THE FURY OF THE FLAMES, AND ESCAPED THE EDGE
OF THE SWORD; WHOSE WEAKNESS WAS TURNED TO STRENGTH;
AND WHO BECAME POWERFUL IN BATTLE
AND ROUTED FOREIGN ARMIES.

HEBREWS 11:32-34

Afterward

As much as I would have liked to add a full reference list of links to websites where I acquired information for this book, it is notable that many of those dozens of articles have been deleted from or relocated on the internet. Luckily, I have screenshots and downloaded pdfs of original articles so I know that it wasn't my imagination. Wolf advocate sites are easily accessed and not censored by internet search engines, thus I won't bother to list any. They're easy to find.

The excerpt about conservation easements in Chapter 24 was lifted directly from the 2010 financial statement of The Nature Conservancy.

Below are a few sites that I was still able to access online though some links may have disappeared:

http://www.wolfed.org/
http://www.wallowa.com/wc/editorials/20150317/guest-column-wolf-attack-a-cow-mans-worst-nightmare
http://www.cattlenetwork.com/news/industry/cows-witnessing-wolf-attacks-suffer-ptsd-symptoms-new-research-shows
https://www.epa.gov/sites/production/files/2015-07/documents/manuremanagementinformationsheet.pdf
http://www.beefmagazine.com/outlook/new-epa-rule-stinks-manure
www.foxnews.com/food-drink/2016/04/27/denmark-considers-tax-on-beef-other-red-meats-to-combat-climate-change.html
https://montanapioneer.com/non-native-wolves-illegally-introduced-says-whistleblower-2/
http://agenda21news.com/2015/01/kudos-north-carolina-wolves-never/
https://www.environews.tv/122017-governments-co-ut-nm-az-deliberately-derailed-mexican-wolf-recovery-documents-reveal/
Wolf attacks in Israel:

http://www.haaretz.com/israel-news/1.813362
http://sbaa.ca/assets/attachments/cms/wolf_telemetry_activity.pdf
http://www.azgfd.gov/w_c/wolf/documents/MWNon-
agencyTelemetryStatementofUse.20081031.Final.pdf
Feds spend $815M on land but no one knows how much:
http://dailysignal.com/2017/08/03/feds-have-no-clue-how-much-
land-was-bought-with-815-million/
Lynx Hoax:
http://archive.sharetrails.org/node/8480

A few articles regarding The Nature Conservancy:

http://netrightdaily.com/2011/04/how-the-nature-conservancy-
secures-government-land-grabs/
http://www.wallowa.com/20130411/zumwalt-prairie-preserve-desig-
nated-as-national-natural-landmark
http://www.oregonlive.com/pacific-northwest-
news/index.ssf/2011/05/so_many_elk_eating_trampling_grass_on_z
umwalt_prairie_that_hazers_are_now_trying_to_run_them_off.html
https://www.nature.org/ourinitiatives/regions/northamerica/united-
states/oregon/placesweprotect/elk-hunting-at-zumwalt-prairie.xml
http://www.webpages.uidaho.edu/css385/Conservancy_part_one.htm
http://netrightdaily.com/2011/04/how-the-nature-conservancy-
secures-government-land-grabs/
http://www.newsnet1.com/electricnevada.com/pages96/collude.htm

Appendix A

The column that nudged me to go whole hog and work the following information into a book. Never published, it is still in its draft form from November of 2012:

Zumwalt - A Microcosm of the Public Funding Scheme
- Draft 11/12

Where are public tax dollars and lottery funds ending up in the bureaucratic and public-benefit scheme of things? These are questions being raised by individuals attempting to preserve their independent livelihood, a livelihood that is rapidly shifting out of the control of farmers, ranchers and "agripreneurs" who rely on the land to produce, but see their access to that land, their own property, severed by single-minded legislation and administrative regulation.

It is this term "production" that has been mistreated and twisted to refer to anything that seems to have a report attached to it. A major misnomer that underlies this whole story is the concept of research being a productive activity, generalized scientific research more specifically. That the definition of production and producing are herein receiving attention is due to the millions and billions of dollars being spent to preserve otherwise productive land (in the original sense of the term as harvesting a crop or raising livestock) for the purpose of conservation and/or research, which appear to be the same regarding goals of the ecologists and researchers.

This is Oregon, a state that teeters on the edge of a $3.5 Billion deficit for the 2011-2013 fiscal biennium, http://sunshinereview.org/index.php/Oregon_state_budget. Although this seems paltry in comparison to the federal deficit of $11 Trillion for 2012, it is a symptom of the overall spending mindset of government. While doomsayers worried the golden population by threatening cuts in entitlements for the elderly, or families with budgetary slashes to education, the regular underwriting of budget items (middle management, i.e. union jobs) and grants to private concerns and holding companies continue to leech the economy of hundreds of millions.

One example of these projects is the Zumwalt Prairie conservation project in the extreme northeast corner of Oregon, a rural farm and ranch community that has seen land title move from productive hands into those of the government, conservation organizations and land trusts at an alarming rate. Already, Wallowa County is 70% under public purview, and now, inhabitants are encountering further limitation of land use by expansion of protective regulation along with land conservation ownership, removing property from productive tax rates, if not the actual rolls.

The vision of some, the numbers adding up to minority interest groups with a majority voice, is to restrict farming and livestock on private lands by designating them as harmful to the natural habitat. The assumption being that individual landowners haven't the education or knowledge to understand the viability of their property without destroying the ecosystem of which it is a part, in this instance, Wallowa County. Irregardless of individual opinion, it is imperative to trace land ownership and influence in the region to grasp how state and federal funds - public trust funds - are being utilized.

April 7, 2006, the Oregon Legislative Emergency Board passed a number of budgetary items including a $700,000 grant, written through the Oregon Department of Agriculture, toward the retroactive purchase of 6065 acres of Wallowa County land by a private concern, Nature Conservancy. This added to the land acquisition by the holding company, creating a block of 33,000 acres (52 square miles) that would no longer be in efficient production, nor paying taxes at the customary rate. In fact, a tacit agreement was arrived at between the county and the non-profit where the Conservancy agreed to voluntarily pay property taxes.

Two problems here. One: it was a voluntary agreement, which indicates the private organization could also decide to no longer pay taxes and; Two: the tax rate was one much lower than that of a working ranch or farm, thus significantly lowering the assessment owed and further creating fiscal hardship for a county already struggling to meet its budgetary responsibilities.

There are further irregularities about this transaction. The fact that a state agency (ODA) operated as a fiduciary for a private land acquisition by applying to U.S. Fish and Wildlife for a federal grant of federal funds, some would say is cause for concern. Read the minutes of the meeting to see how public funds were allocated in this one circumstance:

"The Oregon Department of Agriculture (ODA) applied for a $700,000 grant from the U.S. Fish and Wildlife Service for a **$700,000 federal grant to purchase 6,065 acres in Wallowa County on behalf of The Nature Conservancy (TNC).** *The pur - chase will protect a plant community that now provides habitat for the federally threatened, Spalding's Catchfly. The U.S. Fish and Wildlife Service require that a state agency be used to apply for these grants. The total purchase price of the property has been estimated at $3 million. The grant requires at least a 25% match.* **TNC indicates that it will attempt to secure $1.2 million in public funds** *for the purchase of the property, with the remainder coming from private donations.* **TNC will apply to the Oregon Watershed Enhancement Board (OWEB) for a $1.2 million grant to acquire the 6,065 acres** *during OWEB's next Capital Grant Cycle, with final grant action occurring at OWEB's September 2006 meeting. If TNC's grant application is successful, they will reduce their OWEB funding request to $500,000, thus keeping the* **total public financing potentially used for the acquisition at $1.2 million.** *The grant project falls within the Department's mission to protect natural resources, and would allow ODA to continue progress towards its goal to remove plant species from threatened and endangered status."*
(emphasis added).

What you see here is $1.2 Million of public funds set aside to purchase private land for a private holding company, where access to the public, who paid nearly half the purchase price, is restricted, even to the point of trespassing should they arrive at any time other than that permitted by the new private owner.

This is, of course, not a singular instance of public funds paying for private enterprise. Reading through a report from the ODA, http://www.oregon.gov/ODA/docs/pdf/project_summary_FY2010.pdf, note the nearly $2 Million allocated in just one specialty crop block grant program ($265K of which goes to indirect administrative costs) that supports school programs and marketing of specialty, some would say "designer," crops that appeal to a limited consumer base. Yes, there is a decline in the number of professional farmers and ranchers, however, it is not due to lack of interest so much as the lack of ability to make a viable living in the industry. Farming has never been a get-rich scheme. It has always been an occupation of people dedicated to the land and the lifestyle. Making ends meet is an ongoing struggle that has become, more and more, so restricted by government regulation that generational ranchers and farmers can no longer keep their heads above water, forcing them to sell off their land.

Projects like Zumwalt Prairie are a case in point. Nature Conservancy, which owns millions of square miles around the world, buying up arable land and fencing it off to production of crops and livestock, is mostly set aside for the production of research reports.

What purpose do these scientific studies serve? They provide non-producing jobs for scientists to generate thousands of pages of statistics that support the theories that provide rationale for legislation that supports the universities that do the studies. A circular scheme which purpose is: the institution of legislation restricting land use by the private sector.

The outcome is the reduction of crop and livestock production, providing less food for the general population, which in turn supports the theory that the world is overpopulated, in that there is no longer enough sustenance available to feed them. Another circular argument.

Yet where does the funding for the legislators and the researchers originate? The public trust, the people who work each day to grow crops, milk cows, build furniture, manufacture equipment, and on and on.

A major portion of funding provided by Oregon state agencies and federal agencies that support research such as how cattle affect grazing land, could easily be discontinued.

"In partnership with Oregon State University, we are studying the impact of livestock grazing on the habitat and wildlife by looking at a variety of grazing practices and intensities. The goal is to determine the most sustainable grazing practices to use, because this is a working landscape." It *was* a working landscape. Currently, the Conservancy runs about 450 head on 30,000 acres, a wholly inefficient usage of pasture which should support 160 head per 2000 acres. The idea was to protect the native bunchgrass, a naturally high protein content feed. However, in order to keep the bunchgrass healthy, grazing is important as an actual aid to propagation of the natural crop. Thus the inefficient grazing practice is actually diminishing the bunchgrass on the prairie.

Or look at the fencing to restrict elk and other animal access...
"ODFW biologist Vic Coggins, who works with the Conservancy on wildlife and habitat issues, points out several scattered aspen groves that have been fenced to keep elk, cattle and deer out so the trees can regenerate. Wildlife exclusion fences also protect an area of native grasses near Pine Creek to allow study of native plants."
http://www.dfw.state.or.us/conservationstrategy/news/2008/2008_se ptember.asp
Whereas ranchers and farmers are constrained from installing their

own fences and barriers to keep out government-protected predators, the very elk that the Nature Conservancy fences out (forcing them to the water on small private holdings and creating competition with their cattle) and the wolves that are devastating local ranchers' herds.

(Here's another kicker. A reliable source informed me that studies had been planned to set-up "predator trails" for wolves to follow in their travels across the expanse of the prairie. A university research project was in the planning stages - though it's unknown to me if it was ever fully implemented - to section off acres of the prairie to observe and possibly direct predator traffic across the endless fields.)

The conclusion is that the budgetary deficits facing government can be reduced dramatically by doing away with government grants that support private enterprise that, in turn, restrict production through sponsoring research that "proves" land use for crops and livestock is injurious to habitat. All the while instituting some of the same practices the stewards of the land have been using for generations.

The question becomes, what is productive and what is not? My sources tell me that generating report upon report to restrict land use is counterproductive. The state budget would tend to support their conclusion.

It would be far less expensive, and far more productive, to give researchers access to working farms and ranches on which to study the affects of cattle grazing, elk encroachment and predator activities than to expend millions upon millions, even billions of public funds to purchase good, fruitful agriculture operations and lock them away where no one benefits "except a few researchers and a slew of students trampling the fields with butterfly nets." The last image provided by an individual who once worked on a ranch that has since been consumed by the Nature Conservancy, and is now called the Zumwalt Prairie Preserve.

A. Dru Kristenev

Appendix B

Columns and links with information regarding claims for damages against government agencies:

September 8, 2015
EPA-fouled Animas River: How to sue gov't agencies and win using SCOTUS ruling

http://canadafreepress.com/article/epa-fouled-animas-river-how-to-sue-govt-agencies-and-win-using-scotus-rulin

After the August 5, 2015 Gold King Mine toxic waste spill into the Animas River and downstream watercourses that was caused by EPA incompetence (or intention, depending on the perspective), there was some misunderstanding about how claims for damages should be handled. Russell Begaye, president of the Navajo nation, was strong in cautioning members to hold off submitting Standard Form 95 that EPA employees were distributing on the reservation. The assumption was that claimants must sign the form supplying a final amount for restitution that cannot be amended, barring all possibility of pursuing legal remedy should damage accrue over time.

There are ways of dealing with the form that most of us wouldn't consider but is a necessary component to assure restitution for egregious damage which effects are long-lived. Our legal researcher, Toddy Littman, explained the process that, if followed, is the best avenue to receive full remedy.

Toddy explained it this way, beginning with the point that Begaye, like most politicians and even attorneys, "… doesn't understand the administrative process and is solely thinking of it in a civil rights law vein.

"Procedures carry with them a notice and opportunity component irrespective of the content of the instrument. This is why, as an example:

1) you file a lawsuit; 2) the other party fails to respond in a timely manner; 3) you go to court to get your default judgment. As you enter the courtroom, you're served with a response, even though late. The idea is you can't claim they didn't respond now in good conscience, and they'd have had it filed with the court so you can't get the judge to listen to you anyway. Or the lawyer for the other side shows up and then tries to serve you with their reply in open court as you stand to speak and say the words, "I am here for my default judgment." Or the attorney for the other side, and this happens often with bureaucrats, shows up with your envelope and claims, "Your Honor, I didn't receive notice of any such lawsuit. Sure I signed that postal delivery receipt but the envelope was empty," which is why you pay a little more for a proof of mailing where the postal clerk stamps it to indicate the envelope was not empty.

"This notice and opportunity component supersedes the content if your intention of use in pursuing your remedy is a legal strategy of notice and opportunity as the agency knew or should have known to reply, get an extension, grant a hearing, or deny your claim in a timely manner, which, thereof upon proof of their receipt of it, long before you filed a lawsuit, is notice and opportunity and their failure to respond in a timely manner (nihil dicit) is a waiver of sovereign immunity.

"If the case is about the specific content and pursuing a lawsuit for damages alone, some civil rights claim, not having read Begaye's comments, **the normal course gives concern that what is claimed on the SF-95 cannot be expanded upon.** In this situation with the river spill and EPA, the long-term effects are unknown. Thus, one would have to include environmental impact studies (which most people wouldn't have had completed within the week this spill has been going on) that are comprehensive enough to be inclusive of all potential future damages, which are the EPA's liability. He's well aware, I figure, that their [EPA's] attorney will come into court claiming limited liability if they try to amend the complaint to include later damages that are unknown at this time, and thereby those would be excluded from the lawsuit if they weren't mentioned in the SF-95.

"So there you have what I'd get into, **that the point of it is to be comprehensive, to include environmental impact studies as soon as possible,** and as many as correlate on a variety of results that I would cite with some expression as to the title or nature of your claim, such as, *"Claimant gives due notice that the nature of this claim is open-ended, while, however, any current denial would result in a complete agreement that those future injuries can be amended to any court action arising from such rejection, as this claim is to secure those rights for future claims by such rejection, (see attachments a-f environmental impact studies, and exhibit g compilation and correlation of likely to occur injuries that explain their entire and sole source is the original incident that is the basis for making a claim at all, and thereby rejection of this claim is rejection of those future environmental impacts, and any others that may occur no matter how obscure they may appear to be at this time)."* **Something to this effect (and that's just off the top of my head) and the reason is that by the rejection, or saying they can't accept the filing due to this clause/notation, they'd have rejected the claim, resulting in a right of suit for all that is included and even portions that aren't where it is mentioned in any manner in the studies attached.** You see what I am getting at?

"They probably haven't thought it out this far and, as they have accepted the national government's abuse of them for such a long time, they probably can't come to think making a rightful challenge will yield a positive result." (emphasis mine)

It's unfortunate that the people of this nation have been trained to immediately assume that any damage incurred by government actors, agents, bureaucrats or officials, appointed and elected, must be dealt with by first filing a lawsuit. What Toddy is trying to clarify is how exhausting the administrative process gives the claimant grant of right to sue in court. This is an important concept when agencies like the EPA and the IRS conduct their parody of the judicial system in their own administrative courts that, according to Sackett v. EPA, cannot render a final decision if the Administrative Process Act is properly applied.

There are thousands upon thousands of individuals who have suffered loss at the hands of government agencies, from Health and Human Services (Obamacare) to the United States Forest Service (forest and wildfire management). They have been beaten into believing that there is no recourse other than accepting whatever the behemoth administration dispenses.

We must learn how to use the administrative process to our advantage and the foregoing is a good start.

Note: Go to www.Changingwind.Org and use the search engine to look up more information on solutions to dealing with excessive government regulation. Also, check my Facebook page for a new reprint of Sackett v. EPA opens the door to relief published to our readers in March of 2012. It has links to Toddy's explanation of SF95 usage.

A. Dru Kristenev

http://tinyurl.com/SF95use
http://www.justice.gov/sites/default/files/civil/legacy/2011/11/01/SF-95.pdf
http://indiancountrytodaymedianetwork.com/2015/08/17/navajo-president-warns-against-signing-epa-claim-forms-mine-spill-damage-161408

September 29, 2016
Right to Farm - eating emotion
http://canadafreepress.com/article/right-to-farm-eating-emotion

Increasingly, city-dwellers seeking view lots or large acreage have been fleeing the metropolitan areas to build larger and even luxurious homes in rural America, often opposite agricultural operations. Once they'd invested in constructing homes and settled into their new digs, they were awakened to the realities of country living, including the sights, smells and sounds of working farms… and they didn't like it. The offshoot was a plethora of nuisance suits that shut down family businesses to create a "more pleasant" neighborhood for the metro ex-pats. As a result, all states of the union subsequently adopted laws to protect farms and ranches from encroaching exurbanites - the urban refugees relocating in the hinterlands.

What this exodus of city folk setting up housekeeping in the boon-docks created was a land war between food producers and food con-sumers. New arrivals wanted to enjoy the beauty of the country with-out interference from farm or ranch operations whose presence pre-ceded their arrival. Shortsightedness accompanied the transplant boom by restricting local farmers from, well, farming. The result of the pressures brought about closure and relocation of crops and live-stock, costing families their livelihoods and legacies as well as increasing the cost of food. In the end, a few exurbanites got their dream homes but they paid for it in a higher cost of living by closing farms or chasing them down the road.

In a stab at saving agriculture from the exurbanite invasion, right to farm legislation passed to halt the nuisance lawsuits but they didn't go far enough.

On the ballot in some nine states this election cycle are measures to extend the right to farm acts already on the books. As urban-centered environmentalists and animal rights organizations have interfered with regular farm practices over the years, attempting to impose their opinions of animal husbandry and crop management on practical operations, more farms and ranches have suffered bankruptcy and closure. Increased regulations from state and federal agencies (EPA, AQMD, WQMD, USDA and subsidiaries, etc.) have hamstrung the family, and corporate, farms and ranches, creating a need to rein in the agencies and constrain interfering advocacy groups.

Oklahomans' "Right to Farm" measure SQ777 would amend their constitution with this:

"To protect agriculture as a vital sector of Oklahoma's economy, which provides food, energy, health benefits, and security and is the foundation and stabilizing force of Oklahoma's economy, the right so citizens and lawful residents of Oklahoma to engage in farming and ranching practices shall be forever guaranteed in this state. The Legislature shall pass no law which abridges the right of citizens and lawful residents of Oklahoma to employ agricultural technology and livestock production and ranching practices without a compelling state interest.

Nothing in this section shall be construed to modify any provision of common law or statutes relating to trespass, eminent domain, dominance of mineral interests, easements, rights of way or any other property rights. Nothing in this section shall be construed to modify or affect any statute or ordinance enacted by the Legislature or any political subdivision prior to December 31, 2014."

Strange arguments have cropped up in opposition to these measures. One argument relates to the fact that three states' bills are similarly worded and, according to opponents, qualifies as evidence that the measures are being sponsored by corporate agribusiness. Animal rights groups promoting protection of feral hogs oppose the Oklahoma measure as allowing landowners the right to dispatch the problematic species that incur grave damage to their crops and holdings.

Mounting evidence of governmental interference with the natural business of farming and ranching around the country is rife in the media, and the courtrooms. Examples such as these - EPA fining a rancher $16 Million for building a stock pond, which penalty was finally reversed in court; Fish and Wildlife scheduling release of predatory wolves into the Heber-Overgaard ranch region of Arizona; and, in supposed violation of the Clean Water Act, a farmer being charged with illegally plowing his own fields, no less.

In Oregon, a non-native wolf species (Canadian Gray) has been unnaturally relocated in the eastern region of the state. Since 1999, the still protected marauders have been ravaging cattle, sheep, horses and even working dogs, costing ranchers into the millions of dollars worth of livestock. The decimation of current and future generations of breeding stock runs up the cost of beef, which PETA and other special interest groups hail as victory.

It looks like Oregon and Arizona could use the kind of expansion on the right to farm acts that Oklahoma, Missouri and Nebraska are voting on this year.

Clawing to defeat the measures are a coalition of out-of-state environmental organizations like the Humane Society and Sierra Club bent on forcing uneducated, impractical and unworkable stock and land management methods on experienced ranchers and farmers. In effect, this is already what government bureaucracies have been increasingly implementing for years and doing a fantastic job of making farming so inefficient that it becomes unsustainable or impossible. The expansion of federal land management by government usurping millions of acres in the form of national monuments has also diminished the availability of arable land.

Environmentalists' desired result is coming to fruition - the destruction of food production to the point that food is no longer affordable. Perhaps this is their answer to Scrooge's observation about how to lessen the "surplus population"…

Make sustenance so expensive they die of starvation.

A. Dru Kristenev

http://nationalaglawcenter.org/state-compilations/right-to-farm/

https://ballotpedia.org/Oklahoma_Right_to_Farm_Amendment,_State_Question_777_%282016%29

https://www.nolo.com/legal-encyclopedia/rural-neighbors-right-farm-29869.html

http://www.wnd.com/2016/05/wyoming-rancher-beats-epa-in-pond-fight/

http://www.mogollonrimnews.com/more-wolf-releases-planned-for-west-of-heber-overgaard/

http://www.freedomworks.org/content/federal-government-says-farmer-broke-law-plowing-his-land

http://nationalaglawcenter.org/wp-content/uploads/assets/rightto-farm/oregon.pdf

http://nationalaglawcenter.org/wp-content/uploads/assets/rightto-farm/arizona.pdf

http://canadafreepress.com/article/govt-could-swallow-your-back-yard-for-new-national-monuments

http://www.mcalesternews.com/news/local_news/ofb-pushes-right-to-farm----others-leery/article_04cd5adc-c856-543d-aaf4-f64e78044d2f.html

http://www.oklahomarighttofarm.com/

http://swoknews.com/business/cattlemen-support-right-farm-question

http://www.claremoreprogress.com/news/oklahoma-supreme-court-lets-stand-right-to-farm-initiative/article_a39d51de-5d8a-11e6-b3c2-c7cfb0ad8f6e.html

http://www.theadanews.com/news/local_news/other-states-have-issues-with-right-to-farm/article_f2afb490-2274-56f0-bdc3-5fb156b9eeb9.html

http://www.cato.org/blog/protectionism-crippling-atlantic-gulf-coast-ports?utm_source=dlvr.it&utm_medium=twitter

http://dailycaller.com/2016/07/18/california-dem-our-global-warming-plans-devastate-the-poor/

http://www.washingtonexaminer.com/epa-budget-stripped-to-save-coal-country/article/2596305

http://www.usatoday.com/story/news/politics/2015/06/10/house-sub-committee-cuts-epa-funding/71029768/

http://www.scotusblog.com/2016/06/opinion-analysis-narrow-loss-for-the-government-in-clean-water-act-finality-case/:

The landowners in this case sought immediate appeal of an Army Corps "jurisdictional determination" (JD) that wetlands on their property were subject to regulation under the Clean Water Act. The government disagreed, arguing that JDs are not final within the meaning of the Administrative Procedure Act. The Court sided with the landowners, concluding that JDs meet the requirements for finality. United States Army Corps of Engineers v. Hawkes Co

December 5, 2017
Reining in federal land ownership - a drop in the bucket
http://canadafreepress.com/article/reining-in-federal-land-owner-ship-a-drop-in-the-bucket

When the Grand Staircase-Escalante National Monument was designated under President Clinton's purview in 1996, it created real hardship for regional ranchers. New management rules locked up more than one and a half million acres, discontinuing grazing leases that were imperative to sustain cattle growers who'd been using the land responsibly for more than a century.

Part of the impetus for closing off natural resource development at the time was to halt access to one of the best sources of low sulfur coal, including from tribal populations, putting a stranglehold on arid land limited economies. Instituting the monument spelled financial disaster to Four Corners ranch industry as well as the Navajo that has tried to expand their coal industry. One of the reasons Clinton closed off the coal was a backroom deal made to bump up the price of the commodity being mined in Indonesia. It removed U.S. competition at the expense of Native America that, on the other hand, has been tagged to protest pro-growth projects like Dakota Access Pipeline and, now, truncating Bears Ears National Monument.

Related plans for state-of-the-art Desert Rock clean coal-fired power plant was later deep-sixed by environmental groups battling the Diné and partner, Sithe Global, invoking specious climate change arguments that the environmental impact statement finally rejected. Extreme environmentalists continue to use the Indians to further their agenda when convenient, but dump them if their goals diverge, such as improving the First People's living standards. Fair weather friends at best. Enemies of self-determination at worst.

Undermining (pun intended) the coal industry had begun long before

Obama took office, he only swore to finish it off by "bankrupting" it. The left has done such a good job that one of the most important employment opportunities on the Navajo reservation, generating power for the Southwest with coal-fired plants, is likely to be shutdown. The Navajo Generating Station that was lauded in the 1970s for building the Diné economy that has languished otherwise, is due to die because the new administration hasn't moved fast enough to remove industry-killing regulations.

On top of that, California, which would have benefited from more clean coal power plants, has cut off its nose to spite its face. How? By passing asinine legislation to refuse coal generated power in favor of *environmentally friendly* sources that has increased the cost of energy in that state, adding to their overburdened deficit of which Governor Brown and flunkies think the feds should bail them out. Just another reason for Moonbeam to call the tax cut bill "evil" because it removes the state and local tax write-offs, SALT, pressuring higher earners on whom the libs rely to carry their nanny state.

(As an aside, there's reason to ponder how involved was the Clinton Administration in allowing closed uranium mines on the reservation to remain untouched, continuing to pollute the environment, and then engineering the Uranium One transaction netting the Clinton Foundation $143 million.)

President Trump is moving in the right direction by returning public lands to be utilized by the public that owns it, but it's wholly inadequate. USDA via the Forest Service and the Department of the Interior (BLM, national parks and monuments) control millions of square miles that limit public access to the point that fires spread uncontrolled, thanks to another Clinton era disaster - the Roadless Act where fire roads have been steadily deconstructed.

The swell of federal land usurpation must be rolled back at the furious rate that it was instituted over the last 20 years. The West has been swallowed up by land trusts that sell to the government at a profit (Nature Conservancy being the main culprit) and the creation of national monuments, conservation easements, natural landscape registries, wildlife preserves, free-roaming protected species, fencing off wilderness to raise revenue, and the list goes on.

President Trump, don't stop here. Strip down the U.S. Forest Service, Fish and Wildlife, BLM, EPA, Department of the Interior, Department of Energy and any number of other overreaching federal bureaucracies. Put the land back in local hands that know best how to conserve it and its productivity.

Living in the West, hearing from landowners being forced off their own property by federal regulations, it has been a pet project to get the government out of the business of restricting private and public land use. Dismantling national monuments, which have appropriated productive land to purposely shut out food producers as well as limit recreational use under the guise of protecting it, is only the beginning salvo.

The real question is, from whom are the out-of-control administrative agencies protecting the land? Evidently, they're conserving it for posterity that won't be allowed to use it either.

BTW, Land Barons and Gold Baron are fact-filled novels that address these issues in depth. Upcoming researched tale, Unknown Predator, due to be released February 1, 2018, goes deep into the role land trusts and government-protected species play in impeding private property use.

A. Dru Kristenev

https://www.washingtontimes.com/news/2017/dec/3/president-trump-heads-to-utah-to-reduce-grand-stai/

http://www.washingtonexaminer.com/trump-announces-he-will-shrink-bears-ears-grand-staircase-monuments-in-utah/article/2642495

http://www.hcn.org/articles/the-life-and-death-of-desert-rock?b_start:int=3#body

https://www.pri.org/stories/2017-06-28/navajo-power-plant-likely-close-despite-trumps-promises-save-coal

http://www.eastbaytimes.com/2017/12/04/jerry-brown-tax-plan-gop-congress/

Appendix C

Oft-used acronyms within the text of **Unknown Predator** and appendices:

ODFW -   Oregon Department of Fish and Wildlife
USFWS -   U.S. Fish and Wildlife Services
USFS -   U.S. Forest Service
BLM -   Bureau of Land Management
EPA -   Environmental Protection Agency
ESA -   Endangered Species Act
AQMD -   Air Quality Management District
WQMD -   Water Quality Management District
USDA -   U.S. Department of Agriculture
SALT -   State and Local Taxes

ABOUT THE AUTHOR

Former newspaper publisher and editor, A. Dru Kristenev has more than three decades of experience in periodicals. Kristenev grew up in the publishing industry working every angle of a paper, from ad sales and production to writing and overseeing editorial content. The author carries a Bachelor of Arts degree, a Master of Science and a California Community Colleges Lifetime Teaching Credential and taught at the foremost colleges and universities in the Inland Northwest.

Since 2010, Kristenev has been on the road as an independent Christian missionary, crossing the United States more than ten times. She has also been a columnist for CanadaFreePress.com since 2014.

THE BARON SERIES

Four books in the series of stand-alone novels based on current, factual occurrences, the relationship of characters leads from one story to the next, weaving an ongoing tale of journalists running across criminally tainted philanthropy and politics. Caught by their own curiosity to uncover the truth, they are pulled deeper and deeper into the investigations, unexpectedly putting their lives at risk…

Land Barons - the first book in the Baron Series of romantic suspense novels that rely on solid research of environmentalist influence on American lifestyles, touching on the long reach of government regulation and media/corporate power. Anthea Keller is seeking a peaceful place to ply her trade as a PR agent. Instead, she finds herself in the center of a land scam, drawn in by Gary Mathers, an ex-cop who just can't reconcile the deadly misfortunes of local property owners forced to sell off assets. And who is waiting in the wings to snap up the firesale deals?

Gold Baron - the second work in the series. Fact meets fiction in the election process of the 2008 presidential campaign season, drawing on the reality driving the candidacies - who's influencing who and to what end with global markets and politics as the backdrop. Solana Greyfisher returns home to Idaho only to be snagged by a fascinating story that leads her to Toddy Littman, researcher extraordinaire. Together they dig through the morass of campaign funding paper trails only to attract the murderous ire of power brokers working the system to their own benefit.

Energy Barons - the third novel, whirls around political manipulation of the environmental movement causing economic upheaval in the West and endangering lives of the innocent. Ambitious Allie Maitland is caught by surprise while investigating what appears to be anything but an accident at the new power plant. Sawyer Aleman, former marine, wheedles his way into the FBI inquiry, under Allie's skin and into the role of guardian. Before they know it, the story rolls from Wyoming to Alaska and everyone involved is walking a perilous tightrope of greed, murder and mayhem.

BLOOD BARONS - the fourth novel in the Baron Series brings the tale full circle.

NYC: a metropolis of 8 million people; 500 disappear each year. Of those, three dead end case files lie open on Special Agent Roy Esteban's desk. Who are they? Why doesn't anyone know they're gone and why does no one care?

Lack of leads and an ASAC that wants the cases closed drives the FBI agent to take on an unorthodox partner in Researcher Debra Chorister. Together they track an unwholesome alliance between corporate science and government healthcare. And those three lone individuals? They're not the only ones who can't be found.

A. Dru Kristenev
ChangingWind Ministries
changingwind@earthlink.net

All the books are available online:
http://tinyurl.com/TheBaronSeries

Scripture Led Politics:
Mutual Exclusivity Be Damned

Wonder how Scripture relates to the political atmosphere in which we live?

Numerous legislative, judicial and regulatory decrees have altered life in America to a degree that our parents' generation would find it unrecognizable. To what end? Who benefits from the draconian coding that now cages the free thinker, particularly the faithful?

As government draws each new line in the sand, Author A. Dru Kristenev has taken a scriptural view of the cascading legal enactments, noting how they are fundamentally changing the American Dream. These commentaries open a deep discussion of how believers must tap their intellect and view the shifting political landscape in the historical light of the Bible, contemplating its significant lessons and their application.

••••••••••

Read all of A.Dru Kristenev's books available on Amazon.com...

THE BARON SERIES Political Suspense novels:

Land Barons
 Gold Baron
  Energy Barons
   BLOOD BARONS
and now: UNKNOWN PREDATOR

Non-fiction Books:

Scripture Led Politics: Mutual Exclusivity Be Damned

Pay Attention!! ...your life, family and nation depend on it

Made in the USA
San Bernardino, CA
21 June 2018